D0870247

DREAM SINGER

DREAM SINGER

++++

Frank O Smith

*To Julie,
who has fine
taste in friends.
This is a gift from
Paula Moraine.
Warm regards
F O Smith*

Artisan Island Press

Artisan Island Press is a registered trademark
of Artisan Island Press LLC.

Cover design and art by *Jurne*

Library of Congress Cataloguing-in-Publication Data
Smith, Frank O

ISBN: 978-0-9903266-0-1
LCCN: 2014912966

MANUFACTURED IN THE UNITED STATES OF AMERICA

First Edition
September 2014

DEDICATION

This book is dedicated
with love and gratitude to

Dale Stephenson

DREAM SINGER

I
The song
I walk here

Modoc Song

The Way

The wind started in the hollow of the night. It entered Elijah McCloud's dreams like a draft teasing at a closed door, stealing entrance as though it belonged. Out of the south, blowing up the narrow chute of the valley, it stirred the mixed conifers, the sound of the big trees in sway rising like a chorus of murmurs from the bottom of the sea. Beneath the headwalls of Bear Head and Red Crow Mountains, in the sculpted bowl of rock ground out under the heel of the last great glaciers, it blew with such insistence it finally roused Elijah, then wouldn't let him go back to sleep, to return fully to deep slumber.

He lay enveloped in the sound, agitated by the constant moaning of the tall trees, the big Engelmann spruce and western hemlock thick on the valley floor, the red cedar, whitebark pine, and fir all mixed together to the tree line. There was something about the wind, *this* wind, that was unnerving. Elijah lay burrowed like a feral creature in his makeshift earthen den beneath a mammoth old Douglas fir, driven to consider the prospects of the wind whether he cared to or dared to or not.

It wasn't cold enough yet to snow. And it had blown too hard and too long without the gathering patter of rain to suspect there was much moisture in it. Elijah didn't expect the real start of winter much before November, though it could come now, all of a sudden, he knew, with a swift shift of cold air out of Canada that could bring a big storm. An October storm could close the pass, leaving him no option but to hike down through the valley to get out—if leaving was the option he would exercise. But in the slow passage of summer, the urge to follow the old habit of leaving, heading south out of the mountains of Montana when the aspens and alder turned golden, had dissipated, evaporating with little notice. Elijah was usually gone from Glacier National Park by this time, on his way to the Feather River Canyon in the California Sierras. Deciding to stay on this year was not something he had fully considered as much as it had settled over him. He was too tired and worn out to keep up pretenses, if only for himself. Just past sixty, he had simply succumbed to the desire to sleep, felt compelled to it with a longing that was nearly an ache. Like a renegade old bear wanting nothing so much as to be left alone, he found that sleep was the only balm for the ache and regret that filled him, now that Emma was dead.

Two years now and the ache was only deeper, the regret undiminished. Elijah felt the coming of winter with deep anticipation, like the old grizzly with whom he shared the valley. He wondered if Ol' Icy Eye ever had any premonition of death. One eye a frozen, sightless orb, the grizzly must have long sensed the diminished parabola of its soulful orbit on the earth. Elijah felt a kindred spirit to the bear now that Emma was gone, as if the light of his world had been diminished by half—at least half, if not more. The memory of waking with tears in his eyes, knowing that Emma was dead, still haunted him with a freshness as if it were yesterday. Dead two years— three years in all since he'd last laid eyes on her.

This would be his last fall, his last winter. He was sure of it—determined, in fact. He doubted he'd live to see the new year. Like Ol' Icy Eye, soon after the first heavy snowfall, he intended to retreat into his den for the last, long night of sleep, never to see morning again.

The wind blew without cessation. Beyond the fact of its persistence, its meaning was obscure. Its unrelenting insistence annoyed Elijah more than its presence. Finally, long after the sun had come up, unable to ignore the howling blow any longer, Elijah threw back the covers, uncurling from the narrow cot he'd fashioned in his den under the old tree. He reached for his boots, his dark, knotted hand falling on them without bothering to look. Be nice to have one last stretch of Indian Summer days before the sharp drop in temperature due in late autumn. One could always be hopeful, he thought, running a rough paw over the whisper-thin tuft of white whiskers at his chin after pulling his boots on. He rose and ducked in one motion to pass beneath a long, serpentine twist of tree root that framed the vaulted interior of his den. He made his way through the small antechamber he'd cobbled from scavenged materials, grabbing his old dusty fedora and coat off the root hook where they always hung, and scrambled up the short incline to stand at the entrance of his hut, taking in full measure of the day.

The valley lay before him in one long view, held between twin swells of massive, brown-gray sedimentary upthrust. From peak to peak, the valley was only a mile wide, but ran like a giant trough carpeted in dense evergreen to the far horizon. The valley did not have a name. It was simply the deep groove carved by ice and time and the gradual emptying of an unnamed creek. In places the pale, exposed rock rose two thousand vertical feet and more in sheer fortress walls. Though the valley had escaped unnamed, the names of the peaks that rimmed it marked its desolate remoteness: Eagle Ribs, Brave Dog, Skeleton, Mount Despair. Up the long throat of the valley, directly in the face of Red Crow Mountain, poured the relentless rush of the wind. This wind had a name in Modoc, but Elijah could not recall it. Though he clung to the old ways as best he remembered, it was as if he lived in a world whose voice he no longer understood. It was wind with a voice, but no longer a language. Yet he sensed it sought to speak to him.

What? he wondered. *What?* It was a bad day for a Modoc when the world spoke but he couldn't hear it.

Elijah snugged his coat and hat against the wind and stared at the world with gray eyes, eyes startling to behold, pale yet dark, dark yet light, accentuated by the dark cast of his skin. He stared intently beyond Summit Peak, past Brave and Little Dog Mountains, the wind whistling in his ears like a harsh whisper. *What is it?* he wondered, his eyes sweeping the forest, the rise of rock wall, the scudding flood of clouds sweeping across the sky like froth atop a raging river. The valley floor was a pattern of shifting light and shadow as the billowy white clouds swirled beneath the mantle of blue heaven.

The edge of a dream, a discordant disturbance, snagged his mind. Elijah squatted and absently ran a stubby finger through the coarse talus at his feet. Dream, here? Now? Elijah hadn't dreamed in years. He let his hand circle, his finger trying to pick up the pattern of the dream that had been dislodged by the wind. Again and again his finger circled through the dirt. Nothing. It was there, but not there. It was maddening. He flattened his palm and rubbed the earth smooth. *Odd*, he thought as he straightened slowly, careful not to strain with the foolish, impulsive motion of youth. He squeezed the stiffness from his body. He was tired, bone tired. He had not slept well, caught between the pull of a shadow of a dream and the push of the wind.

Elijah let his eyes sweep over the periphery of his camp, there at the edge of the tree line in the bowl below Red Crow Mountain, taking idle inventory of the landscape. Nothing struck him as being disturbed or trig-

5

gered recall of the dream. He wondered whether one stopped dreaming as he aged, or merely ceased being able to remember. At moments like this, he was sure it was a *forgetting-to-remember,* as though the lake of dreams froze over the instant the dreamer emerged from it. Why was that? he wondered. Was it something in the dream itself, or simply the act of waking? It was a torment not to be able to remember. It had not always been so. But this time, this dream carried the echo of torment.

He shivered. *I must be crazy,* he thought as he turned and stared at the summit of Red Crow Peak behind him. It was awash momentarily in clouds. He pulled at his thin goatee again as if for balance. "Must be crazy," he muttered to himself as he began to pick his way along the edge of the talus slope, following an old animal trail from the edge of camp, up out of the tree line, out across the steep exposure of the mountain. Elijah hadn't spoken more than a dozen words to another human being in the five months he'd been in Montana. He had kept to himself to such an extent over the last few years, staying to the mountains of Montana in summer, then migrating to the mountains of California in winter, that he had become like an old grizzly when its range is continually reduced: it retreats deeper and deeper into the wild until one day, no one is sure whether the old beast even exists anymore.

It had been more than a month since he'd made the twenty-four-mile round-trip over Firebrand Pass to East Glacier for resupply. He was completely out of sugar and flour, canned goods and rice, and was down to his last ounce of coffee. He'd been living almost entirely on huckleberries the last two days. There had been a Park Service trail crew camped for a week at the small lake on the valley floor, replacing an old footbridge along the river, and he'd not thought it wise to steal down, even during the day when they were out, to take a batch of cutthroat trout from the lake. Five years at Glacier, he'd had only one encounter with the Park Service, after which he moved his camp deeper into the woods, far from any hiking trails. He didn't want to give them any reason to suspect that any form of wildlife not officially sanctioned as endangered had taken up residence in the park.

Without a dependable supplement of trout, he had counted on snaring any of the species of grouse that inhabited the park, especially the spruce grouse, the so-called "foolhen" for the fact that it seemed to have no wariness of humans. But something strange was happening. Although they were usually common, he'd not seen any grouse in several days, though all of his snares had been curiously disturbed. Elijah tried not to dwell on it, working his way around the sculpted edge of the large basin at the foot of Red Crow Mountain, moving toward the line of snares he'd put out under Mount Despair. His Native instinct still cautioned him to be respectful in pursuit of game. All the while, the wind whistled plaintively in his ear.

Still, he couldn't help but ponder it. It was odd, the snares being disturbed. They were elemental things, primitive, but ever effective in design. Made of a looped bit of line rigged from a limber sapling along an animal run, they were amply clever enough for the dimwitted foolhen. But over the past run of days, though all had been sprung, he hadn't caught a thing. It would take a blow stronger than the wind this morning to set them off, the way he rigged them. Yet he could not find any telltale sign of trespass. When he was a boy growing up on the Sprague River in southern Oregon, his uncle called such inexplicable events "spirit signs." It was not just an idle expression. Though Elijah was only half Modoc, his uncle was full Modoc and took such things as articles of faith. For that matter, so did Elijah.

He stopped abruptly and raised his eyes to the rim of sky that encircled him. The distinct caw of a crow pierced the moaning of the wind. He heard it again, and followed the sound to find the dark speck hanging in the sky like a piece of funeral cloth drifting down and away to the left, slipping behind a rocky headwall, disappearing from view. Such inelegant birds, crows: wings sculling laboriously as if their aerodynamics were not really suited to flying; more terrestrial than aviary. *Odd. Very odd,* he thought. He'd never heard the cry of crows here in the valley. Crows are social beasts, gathering primarily where there are people. There was an obstreperous flock in East Glacier, gathered around the big dumpsters kept full by caravans of tourists. *Odd,* he thought again, studying the track of sky where the black bird had carved its passage. Crow, here? Now? A nervous spasm tickled his spine. Again, a fragment of a dream teased his mind.

Long ago, as a boy on the cusp of manhood, Elijah had dreamed Crow. *Two Crows: one the shadow, the other the light.* Crow was auspicious, powerful, *but difficult, too,* his uncle told him. *Difficult. The way will be difficult.* Twinned crows were a sign of the gift of dream singing. Until Elijah, dream singing had not been witnessed or spoken of with credence since it had failed the ragtag band of Modoc resisting removal by US troops when Uncle was a boy. Elijah shook his head and smiled ruefully. He'd lived a life believing he had seen only the shadow, never the light. Difficult, yes. Difficult indeed.

On this morning, under the rush of wind that pushed and shoved like an impatient child, Elijah found the first, the second, and the third snares all triggered. All empty. Elijah cursed his luck, his hunger expanding like a noxious gas. The thought of the long walk over Firebrand Pass to East Glacier for groceries was not how he'd imagined his day. If he left now, it'd be dark before he made it back again. It was a good twelve miles each way with a two-thousand-foot hump to get through the Firebrand saddle. Oh, he'd made the journey in a day numerous times, but seldom on an empty stomach. When the fourth snare turned up empty, it was all he could do to contain his despair.

"Son of a dog," he cursed through clenched teeth, kneeling to finger the empty noose. "*Dirty* son of a dog." With meticulous care, he reset the snare and stood. He balled his fists and rubbed his kidney points in the small of his back, trying to ease the knots of tension that were building.

"It ain't too much to ask," he said to the wind as much as to himself. "All I want is *one*," he lamented, watching a mountain chickadee dart from a nearby branch into dense growth. Other than the crow, it was the first wildlife he'd seen that morning. The wind was keeping most creatures quiet and close to home.

Elijah turned and headed downslope, into the thick tangle of alder and seedling pines, toward his last trapping point along a small game trail that ran down to its junction with the creek where the creek settled into the valley bottom proper and began its winding course toward the small lake. Elijah pushed his way deeper into the brush, becoming enveloped in the profusion of growth that rose over his head. He picked his way carefully, following the drop of the land southward into the brush, into the wind, toward the river.

The sound of the river was slow rising to the ear, competing as it was with the steady blow of the wind. Elijah knew by feel he was close, but was agitated, disoriented by not being able to hear the river despite the wind. He stopped to check the direction of the cloud movement overhead just to be certain he was still heading south. He pushed ahead, wading through the dense understory, cursing the wind and the run of luck he was having. He broke out of the alder into a glade of ferns where at last the sound of the river rose to greet him. He waded through the ferns, working his way toward the faint game trail that paralleled the river. He was feeling soured on the whole prospect of the day when, coming around a short bend in the trail, he saw the plump, red-eyed spruce grouse standing docilely in the trail, a snare snugged tight around its neck.

Elijah stopped. He stared in surprise, barely able to believe his luck. The bird eyed him curiously but showed no agitation or nervousness. Elijah could almost taste the hot, succulent meat in his mouth. He was about to step forward to claim his catch when something caught his attention out of the corner of his eye. He paused, turned slowly, and sucked his breath. There, not fifty feet away, stood Ol' Icy Eye, a very large and wildly moody male grizzly, staring coldly right at him with his one good eye.

Elijah stood motionless for a long moment, letting the fact of the big bear register deeply within him. He tried not to reveal anything of the first flush of fright that passed through him. The Montana Blackfeet believed grizzly medicine was powerful—too powerful to be near for long. It could make you crazy. *Spirit with Claws,* they called it. The bear was close enough for Elijah to clearly make out the battle scars around its head from encounters with other solitary males.

Unless a mother with cubs, or a male with a fresh kill to defend, grizzlies prefer flight to fight in most encounters with humans. Ol' Icy Eye stared mutely, the light in the sighted eye not half as penetrating and disturbing as the dim icy orb that fixed Elijah with frozen sight. The big bear slowly began to swish its head side to side, making low growling noises. Elijah did not fail to notice its ears were pressed back, its neck fur raised, ready for action. For their size, bears have impressive, explosive speed: it would take little more than a couple of seconds for the bear to be upon him in a charge.

"O' Bear," Elijah cooed ever so gently, loud enough so the bear could hear him, but not feel challenged. Elijah pivoted slowly at the hips to turn his body at an angle to the bear, to show he was not seeking confrontation. "O' Bear, now," he whispered in a low but firm voice. He gazed into the middle distance of the forest, careful not to let his eyes wander back to the bear. "Hey, big grizz," he said slowly, trying to sound confident, unafraid, but nonthreatening at the same time.

From the trail in front of him, he heard the spruce grouse fuss at the snare that held it. Elijah strained to keep his attention focused. All hint of hunger had fled him. *Eat or be eaten,* an inner voice whispered.

Very funny, he thought, focusing to maintain his calm. The bear growled more loudly now, swinging his head vigorously from side to side. In these woods, the grizzly stood at the top of the food chain; man was just another item on the menu. The thought pumped a powerful kick of adrenaline, a dose he could almost taste in the back of his mouth. Elijah tentatively started to tense in order to lift a foot to take a step backward, conceding retreat. His mind raced in calculation of the odds in such encounters. Nine times out of ten, the bear flees. Nine times out of ten, if they charge, it's only to bluff. One in a hundred results in a mauling. Not bad odds, perhaps, until you're facing a bear. Elijah began ever so slowly to shift his weight to his forward foot, intending to lift the other to take a small step backward.

The bear exploded in a flash of motion and noise. Instinctually Elijah turned, drawn to the suddenness of the charge. He saw the heat in the iris of the big bear's lone good eye. The bear rushed like a rocket with unfathomable speed, ripping through the vegetation that only moments before had half shielded him. At the last instant, when Elijah knew that this was no bluff, he started to turn and curl inward into a ball.

He was knocked into the air from the bear's blow, sent flying to tumble and roll in a thick patch of ferns. Voluminous sound enveloped him, the stench and heat of bear breath searing the side of his face through the small exposed crook of his arm that wrapped his head. Elijah stifled the impulse to cry out, drawing tighter, tighter into a ball. The bear batted him like a toy, knocking him from side to side, his big claws ripping at his coat, shredding a sleeve. Elijah stayed curled but motionless, letting the bear have at him as it wanted. He felt the press of the bear's wet muzzle against his ear. An angry, hellish, bellicose sound pressed itself into his ear, driven like a rifle shot to the core of his soul. It was both a shock and a primitive marvel that such a sound was part of the living, conscious world. It seemed to grow and multiply in fathomless amplitude. At the highest pitch of the penetrating howl, Elijah was stunned to hear a whisper. Was it an inner voice, or that of the bear? *You heard the wind. You saw Crow. GO.* The whisper filled him with its power, lifted him, carried him a great distance high above the trees, to a great height, higher than the peaks that surrounded him. *GO!*

For several long moments Elijah floated in the sound. He remained motionless. Then, slowly, he began to realize that the roar behind the whisper had ceased. The bear had retreated.

Elijah lay still for an interminable time, as if gathering his spilled life energy up off the forest floor. Once provoked, bears often return for repeat maulings. In this moment, Elijah wanted desperately to live and lay deathly still so as not to tempt the old bear to return and attack again. Now and again he heard a rustling that pumped a fresh surge of adrenaline into his system. After several minutes, when he was sure that the bear was gone, Elijah lifted his head to peer through the smashed and matted vegetation all around him. The foolhen stood stoically where he'd first seen it, as if waiting docilely for the fate of its day.

Slowly, quietly, Elijah rolled onto his hands and knees and lifted his head to survey the woods. He listened intently. He was surprised now to hear only the wind. The constant rush of the wind in the trees was somehow reassuring. He pushed himself to standing, inspecting himself carefully, as though fearful he would find a gouged wound, a patch of flesh torn free. Other than the mangled coat sleeve and a deep claw mark under his jawline, he'd come through entirely intact. He surveyed the damaged forest floor, pulling a cloth out of his coat pocket to wipe the blood that flowed from the wound. He walked over and picked up his crumpled hat and straightened the brim, recreased the crown. He rose to his full height, tugging on the hemline of his coat as if to compose himself.

Elijah eyed the grouse. The grouse eyed him. He brushed his hands together, knocking the forest debris loose where it had been imprinted when he was trampled by the bear.

He eyed the grouse again, then let his gaze rise and sweep the forest in all directions before returning to the bird. "Did you *see* that?" Elijah whispered incredulously. "Had me all but skinned and in the pot."

He slowly scanned the forest once again, not wanting to trust the bear was gone for good. He shuffled slowly toward the bird and knelt down. The bird blinked, but otherwise showed no sign of fear. Elijah stared at the bird for several long moments. He leaned forward and gently cupped it in both hands as he carefully worked the snare loose. When he had the bird free, he released it. He leaned back on his haunches and considered it.

"I'm a lucky son of a dog," he said to the bird. "I mean *lucky!*" The grouse eyed him and took a tentative step of freedom. It ruffled its feathers, as though reasserting its dignity. It took another step, turned to consider the distant safety of the woods, then turned to eye Elijah again.

He gave it a knowing nod. "This your lucky day, too," he whispered hoarsely, shooing the bird with his hands. "Go." The bird took three or four quick steps away in fright, then stopped and turned to look at Elijah again.

"Go on. Hurry up. Before I change my mind," Elijah coaxed. The bird continued to stare at him. Elijah looked up into the tops of the trees overhead to watch the swaying wash of the wind. "No mistake. Time we both go," he said, studying the sky and the pattern of clouds. He rose and fit his hat to the top of his head.

He considered the bird again. "When the Spirit speaks, you *best* listen," he said. The bird cocked its head to one side, transfixed by his voice. "I'm stubborn, but I'm no damn fool. And if I were you, I'd get along, too, before I change my mind and cook your scrawny ass."

A shiver passed through Elijah and he looked nervously about, worried, perhaps, that he might have angered the spirit of the bear.

"Just kidding," he said with a meek smile.

Elijah turned slowly, scanning the forest, then started back along the way he'd come, pondering Ol' Icy Eye and the disturbing resonance of the night's dream that was caught like a cocklebur in his mind. The big trees swayed and moaned in the wind, and he found himself listening to the world in a way he hadn't in a long, long time.

He stopped abruptly, frozen. His eyes shifted side to side. He pivoted slowly, his gaze working to pierce the dense understory of ferns and alder. *What?* he wondered, pulled by a vague hesitancy.

"Getting jumpy," he mused, shaking himself as if to shed a cloak that had fallen over him. Then it hit him: the dream. The mist that had veiled it lifted. He felt the meaning more than saw it. The way would be difficult. Dark. Threatening. *But you won't be alone. Not alone.*

He eyed the darkest depths of the dense woods. *What the hell does that mean?* he wondered, turning in a full circle as though he expected an answer. A shiver washed through him.

"I'm going batty," he muttered, wishing to dismiss the whole morning's cast of taunting agitation.

A shiver washed through him again and he stopped dead in his tracks, taking measure of the moment at the core of his being. It was only then that he fully sensed that what was coming was, indeed, going to be difficult. This was what the dream was about, he realized, the dream he couldn't remember. This was what it had wanted to tell him. *The way will be difficult.*

Home . . . And Not Home

Elijah cursed the dawn's cold. Three days out of Montana, he was yet to cross the Columbia River on a path that carried him true south toward the sun. He shuffled noisily up a spur line on the edge of the Pasco, Washington, rail yard. The clamor of his belongings, his coffeepot and tinware, disturbed a flock of pigeons nesting in the beams of the trestle overhead. He stopped to watch them take flight in a wide sweep over the yard. They circled in the gray morning sky, over the top of silent boxcars, before settling again on the lee side of a yard shack near the old icehouse down near the middle of the yard.

Elijah put down his water jug and blew into cupped hands to warm his fingers. He pressed the fingers of his left hand against the wound on his jawline where Ol' Icy Eye had clawed him. It was slow in healing, and Elijah was worried it would become infected. If the puffy soreness didn't begin to subside, he knew he would have to find some bearberry root to make a poultice to draw out the poison.

The wind kicked up a pair of dust devils and rolled them down the center of the freight yard. He tried to read in the wind what truth there was to talk at the Pasco soup kitchen the night before that the yard was hot. Talk at the kitchen was abuzz with news of two bodies found in a boxcar the week before, their throats slit. It was always hard to know with tramp talk where truth ended and the yarn began. The wind this morning told only of the threat of rain.

He shifted the weight of his bedroll to his left shoulder to ease the dull pain in his right leg. His leg and hip were stiff with pain from sleeping in a weedy field adjacent to the tracks. From behind him to the east in the direction of Walla Walla and the lightening dawn came the low rumblings of a switch engine idling in the hump yard. He picked up his jug and stepped along, keeping close to the brush that grew in the ditch that paralleled the mainline. He heard the honking of fowl. He craned his neck to eye the long line of Canada geese high overhead. The string of birds looked like a dark stitch being drawn through dirty linen. His eyes followed them south, then fell to earth to search for an open car on the manifest going down the Columbia Gorge to Portland.

Elijah spied the lone boxcar with an open door at the same time he spotted movement in the shadow of the underpass at the far end of the yard. He stopped abruptly. He watched as two figures emerged from the underpass. It was clear that they, like he, held one thought in mind: making it to the open boxcar before the freight was called to leave the yard. Unlike Elijah, they were streamlined, without bedrolls, water jugs, or other accessories except that one appeared to be carrying a small backpack. He watched as they approached the black square of the open boxcar door. They paused, climbed up and in, and disappeared from sight.

Elijah scanned the length of train again. Not a single other boxcar was open. He lurched ahead. He left the mainline and crossed the first set of yard tracks, then the second. He made his way directly out across the open yard and approached the empty boxcar just as the air pressure blew through the brake lines, signaling the engineer was preparing to get under way. Elijah set his water jug up on the threshold of the open door and swung his bedroll in. He slipped his pack in one fluid movement, transferring it to the floor of the car. Clasping the lock bar, he swung himself up and into the dark container just as the train started to creak forward. He acknowledged his two traveling companions with a cursory nod, but got neither a wave nor a word in welcome in return. He stowed his gear at the end of the car opposite from them.

Best to sleep with one eye open, Elijah thought as he sat down on his bedroll. As the train picked up speed moving out of the yard, he settled back against the bulkhead. He sighed deeply as much from exhaustion as relief, soothed by the familiar rhythm of the rolling freight.

The train crossed the Columbia River just above the confluence with the Snake on the outskirts of town. The train gathered speed as it entered open country, quickening the cadence of rail joints beating beneath the wheels. It was a familiar rhythm, well drummed into Elijah's bones. There was a period of years where pretty much all he did was ride trains, up and down the West Coast, all through the intermountain West. The tempo and constant motion soothed a deep grievance for all he'd lost—his own damn doing, absolutely. Another stretch of years he sought to drown the ache with alcohol. He'd tamped down the impulse over time, but with Emma's death, he went cold turkey. Though he strangely felt her presence painfully close after she died, he wouldn't allow himself to smother it in drink. It was all he had left of her, and he didn't want to lose it or suffuse it in the vapors of alcohol. He'd come to terms with the fact that it was too late to make a difference in her life. Occasionally he slipped off the wagon, usually when he was passing through some town or city where he knew people from the old days. It was why he increasingly spent more time alone in the mountains. "Crossing the flats" could be treacherous. The "flats" were the low ground, out of the mountains, where people pooled into cities and towns. It was too easy to become untethered crossing the flats. When he needed a few dollars, he'd work awhile at a ranch mucking stalls or feeding livestock, but never far from the deepest hold of the mountains. He avoided settlements of any size. The mountains were the only thing that anchored him.

Elijah leisurely pulled his pack open and pawed through his belongings. His hand found what it was searching for. He extracted a large, bright orange that seemingly glowed in the semidarkness of the car. He raised the fruit to his nose and sniffed its succulent fragrance. It smelled of sunlight and the humming of bees. He peeled it slowly, deftly, enjoying the feel of the meaty hide as it came off under his fingers in one long, cool strand. He pulled it apart and separated a single wedge and popped it in his mouth. He bit down slowly, savoring the explosion of flavor.

The long freight rattled along at a good clip beside the Columbia toward the twin cities of Vancouver on the Washington side and Portland across the river in Oregon. Elijah finished the orange and rolled himself a cigarette. He struck a wooden match, touched the tip to the cigarette, and inhaled deeply. He hadn't decided yet whether he intended going all the way to Portland or only as far as Wishram where the tracks forked, one line turning to cross the steel trestle over the Columbia to the Oregon side, the other continuing westward through the Gorge. He smoked his cigarette and stared at the view out the open door. It was only a narrow, vertical slat of light in the darkness from the angle where he sat deep in the back of the car. Pewter sky, dull brown line of high desert, the churning face of the river. It would be a couple of hours before they left the arid high plains and entered the Gorge proper below Wishram. He smoked meditatively, lost in thought, the thin sliver of a view across the river to Oregon enough to generate a dark churning deep within him.

Oregon. Home. And not home.

—+—+—+—

Being Modoc, or partially so—enough to carry the burden of it—Elijah's heritage was that of displacement. Once, long ago, his people had simply called themselves The People. But *Modoc* now was communally thought of as only *less than*: less than whites, less than human, less than they once were. As a boy, he had been told by his uncle he possessed the power of dreaming, the ability to *see* what was to come. He was a *dream singer.* It was not something that was talked about openly, whites not wanting to hear anything of pride from a Modoc. But his uncle had never given up hope that one day it would be possible for the Modoc to be The People again. It was a destiny, Uncle told him, that Elijah was born to, to bring dream singing back to The People. *Don't ever forget. Ever,* Uncle constantly instructed him. *No matter what happens. No matter how difficult the way.*

Memory of that time came back to Elijah in glimpsing the Oregon side of the river. The vague disturbance of the shadow dream his last night below Red Crow Mountain also came back to him. He'd not forgotten, though God knows, he'd tried. The destiny, like the dream beneath the scuttling wind, had never provided him firm ground to stand on. Like the Modoc homeland that had been taken away. He shook his head: How can one hear what the world has to say—carried on the wind, in dreams, in the cry of birds and the roar of beasts—when the land of The People is stolen and silenced? Or worse, when you do not listen, or hear only what you want to hear?

As a young man, Elijah was graced with many gifts. The one that stood him in the best graces with white men was his gift with horses. His reputation was widely respected, even among whites who wouldn't credit a Modoc with being able to spit. Elijah was a wonder in the ring with a wild horse. He cued on nuance in the quickenings of animals that others could not detect. He moved and breathed a ballet of intention that nervous horses understood. He calmed them with a gaze and soft mutterings. He commanded them with the power of a raised hand, the fix of an eye. It was magical how he could bring a wild creature to halter, then bridle, then blanket and saddle. He joked it was his *medicine,* but gave it the respect it deserved. By the time he was twenty, his medicine was strong, ensuring him employment wherever he cared to work.

Elijah was handsome, his mixed heritage casting him with a curious blend of features even whites secretly noticed. Though not a big man, he carried the poise and stealth of a wild creature, proud like a stallion, self-possessed like a cat. Most striking of all were his eyes, a gray light radiating in his dark face. There was no mistaking he was not Modoc alone. Elsewhere he might have passed as a curiosity, but in eastern Oregon, in the rain shadow of the Cascades, there was no escaping the enmity whites still harbored for Modoc, gray eyes or not. Displaced by early settlers, forced off their homeland onto a reservation with the Klamath, neighbors and time-less enemies, Modoc history was etched in discord and blood. Even with time and the gift of working horses, Elijah could not escape the dark mark of history. The very fact that he was so clearly of two worlds made him an outlier among whites and Indians alike.

Though the golden day of horses had come and gone in the West by the time Elijah reached manhood, horses remained at the center of the myth of old families in eastern Oregon who had holdings the size of small kingdoms. One such realm belonged to Thomas English, a man who'd carried the confidence of a patriarch even before he had a family. English had emigrated as a young man from Pittsburgh, coming to Oregon just after the turn of the century to stake a homestead in Jefferson County. He'd grown his original stake—west of Smith Rocks on the Crooked River, north of what would prosper into the community of Bend—into a vast holding. Over time, shrewdly and patiently, he'd cobbled it together parcel by parcel, especially during the hard years following 1929. Antelope Creek Ranch was a mixture of timber and rangeland that stretched from the foothills of the Cascades well out into the dry high-desert sage country of the Columbia Plateau. Thomas English prided himself in his ability to discern quality in men as well as horses and selected Elijah as his chief wrangler when Elijah was not much older than he'd been when he first came west from Pittsburgh. Good horses were central to the ranch's cattle business. It was prime employment for any man, and doubly so for Elijah in that English did not carry the burden of history and memory of things Modoc.

It was a good time—actually the best of times in the life of Elijah, those first years on the ranch. Elijah had married his heart's true companion, Emma Roseleaf, a full-blood from a large family from down around Chiloquin. They had their first child, Toby, a son, the first spring they took up residence in the head wrangler's cabin on the English ranch. It was a time when Elijah had ambitions of one day owning his own land, raising his own horses. He did not imagine an empire like English had; he was not as naïve as that. But he was not afraid to envision a Modoc having land of his own, beholden to no one. He could look any white in the eye and know himself to be an equal. And those on the reservation who'd tormented him as a boy, he would know himself as a man despite their slurs.

A way to achieve that had come to him in a dream. Thomas English had won in a poker game a small place down below Klamath Falls, just across the border in California, a homestead with a derelict barn, a dusty place English had no real interest in. The other man had picked it up for next to nothing in a foreclosure sale in 1931, and felt no grief in losing it to four aces. But Merrill was near the heart of the ancient home ground of the Modoc, near Tule Lake and Lost River. Even though Elijah had known only Oregon, born to this century rather than the last, the pull of the past twitched inside him like a phantom limb, a thing cut from the body but still present in the mind, susceptible to aches and pains and spasms, seeking to be assuaged and soothed. This would become home to his family—a kind of repatriation, too, of the spirit of his people with their ancient homeland.

Elijah worked hard for Thomas English and made him money in the selecting and breeding of horses. The two had an amenable arrangement: Elijah agreed to forgo cash at sale for any mustangs he captured on his own time that still ran in wild herds in the high-desert scrubland of eastern Oregon. In return, in five years' time, the place near Merrill would become his. Of the forty or so horses he'd captured in the first four years, all had gone to English except for two, a handsome dappled gray stallion and a bay mare. The stallion, which Elijah called Smoke, and the mare were to be the seed for what he envisioned as a great line of animals.

English, for his part, admired his wrangler's pluck, caring not a wit that Captain Jack, a distant Modoc kinsman and leader of a renegade band, had been the one to shoot and kill a US Army officer under a white flag of truce in the closing days of the old West. English never broadcast his sentiments, but in truth he was a pacifist and thought the government's handling of the Native people a shameful legacy in American history. He treated Elijah with uncommon respect, which set the tone for everyone else on the ranch. Everyone, that was, except English's son and only heir, Marshall. Marshall was his father's only surviving child, one who'd never felt confident of his father's affections. He'd been raised by a housekeeper after his mother died in childbirth when he was twelve. The baby girl, Marshall's infant sister, survived for eleven days, then passed as well, leaving Thomas totally bereaved for months. Marshall was sent away to boarding schools and came home only for summers when his father was the busiest with matters of the ranch. He'd returned to the ranch for good after an undistinguished stint at the university in Eugene and a failed attempt at business in Portland to find Elijah comfortably settled in the nicest quarters on the ranch, outside the big house. Marshall took an immediate and instinctual disliking of Elijah. Elijah regarded Marshall with practiced deference and wariness, being smart enough to steer clear of him as much as possible. He knew of Marshall's reputation in the county, away from the ranch and his father, for intimidation and bullying Indians from the Warm Springs and Klamath Reservations. Marshall was never directly involved in violence, but he was always on the periphery of it. Staying clear of him didn't require much effort on Elijah's part, what with his long hours in the corral and devotion to Emma, who had recently learned she was pregnant again.

Elsa Garnett was Thomas English's sister's only daughter. Though he loved his sister, he detested her husband—Elsa's father. Frederick Garnett was a blue-blooded easterner from a long lineage of interwoven generations of first families of Philadelphia—and God help you should you ever forget it. In sharp contrast, English devoutly believed in the golden rule of the West: that a man's most inalienable right was freedom from his heritage, that he was at liberty to reinvent himself in whatever mold furnished him the fullest expression as a man. So long, that is, as it did not infringe on the rights of any other man.

Thomas English was never able to determine with any certainty what had happened that previous winter, on the eve of his niece's marriage. He had heard variations on two themes: that she had been left waiting at the church for the groom to show; and more darkly rumored, that she'd become involved with a cousin on her father's side of the family, a young man who, as it happened, was the best friend of the intended groom. English always suspected the worst, if only because his sister was completely beyond discussing it. He was delighted, however, when Elsa wired early that spring to ask if she could come and stay awhile at the ranch. Thomas English wired back a purposefully open-ended invitation, hoping to provide his niece the luxury of redefining herself free of her parents' privileged-class bearing.

Elsa Garnett was a striking presence. She was the kind of woman men can't help but notice, not for any intoxicating beauty, but for a remote, alluring ascetic that begged to be deciphered. Marshall English was clearly enamored, if not improbably smitten. Not unattractive, blessed with his father's blue eyes and his mother's sculpted cheekbones, he was nonetheless a pretentious ass. Though he hadn't ever cared to see his cousins—Elsa and her three brothers—when he'd been invited to visit back east, he couldn't see enough of her now that she was in residence on the ranch. Elsa, for her part, seemed unfazed if not altogether oblivious of his adoration.

Over the weeks leading up to her arrival, a kind of mythology grew up around her, fueled by tidbits garnered from conversations overheard in the big house by the housekeeper, maid, and kitchen staff. Elsa was a graduate of Swarthmore College, in Pennsylvania, founded by abolitionist Quakers. She was willful and independent, trumpeting equality of the sexes, often as a guise for doing whatever she damn well pleased. She was an affront to her mother's straitlaced Quakerism and an embarrassment to her father's sense of propriety as a respected banker. She'd had an affair with one of her professors and become pregnant, causing him to lose his job. She'd had to "go away" for a while until the fetus came to term, and then was forcefully separated from the baby at her parents' insistence. The fallout from her failed engagement was the final straw. Both her parents and Elsa looked to her extended trip west as an opportunity to start afresh. In her uncle's mind, he believed that all Elsa ever wanted was to be loved and accepted by her parents for who she was.

The day she arrived at the ranch, she created an immense stir. From the distance of the corral adjacent to the barn, Elijah could not fail to perceive the small drama her arrival was generating among the circle of family and servants gathered around her on the porch of the main house. Other ranch hands found a reason to ride past just at that moment, though the big yard had been silent and empty all morning. This was no ordinary creature, Elijah could tell; she remained composed and gracious, yet observant and aloof at the same time. She did not fail to take in anything in the surroundings. When she caught him eyeing the spectacle from the shadow of the barn, where he stood holding a young colt on halter, he felt a visceral transmission of energy between them. She held his eyes for a long moment, then turned smiling to one of the cooks who approached, bearing a cool glass of refreshment. Elijah knew she'd taken his measure in that moment, and he knew she knew he knew.

Elijah would look back years later and wonder if it all could have somehow been avoided. It was so much of who he was, who he'd become, it was difficult to know. Elijah was certain that life was made up of countless such moments, molded by happenstance, where the spark of life was deflected, caused to flow in a new direction that was both strange and unanticipated. Did one have any control at such junctures, or was man simply hapless in the flow? Even though he'd recognized the force of alteration at numerous other points in the past, he was always mystified by this one event. He always wondered if, perhaps, everything that followed—losing Emma, his children, himself—might have been averted if he simply had missed that first flashing of Elsa Garnett's eyes.

It began innocently enough. Elijah was in the corral as usual when Thomas and Marshall were preparing to take leave in Marshall's big new Buick for a ten-day fishing trip in the mountains. Elsa had been on the ranch nearly two months, and yet Elijah had managed to completely avoid her presence. As the two men loaded the car, she announced from the porch steps of the big house that she wished to go horseback riding. Fixed in their routine and schedule as men can be once their course is set, the pair, father and son, were impatient to leave. Marshall summoned Elijah, who was shoeing a horse, with a loud shout. Elijah finished driving the last nail before climbing the rails of the corral and crossing to the big house a hundred feet distant. He was aware of being observed keenly by the woman standing in the shadow of the porch, even though he avoided her gaze.

"Miss Garnett needs a horse to ride," Marshall said curtly. "Pick out one that rides well. And make sure it's one of the gentler ones."

"Yes sir," Elijah said simply. "Now? Or can it wait while I get the last shoe on Mercury?"

"I can do it myself," Elsa Garnett interjected confidently, "if you're busy."

"No ma'am, not at all. Now is fine, I guess. Ol' Mercury isn't going anywhere," Elijah said, still avoiding her eyes.

"Well, since you're not busy," Marshall said sarcastically, "I want you to ride with her so she doesn't get lost or hurt."

"That's unnecessary, Marshall," Elsa returned sharply, annoyed at her cousin's condescension. "I don't mean to be a nuisance to Mr. McCloud." Elijah couldn't help but turn his eyes to stare at her. He'd had no idea that she knew his name.

"Not a problem, ma'am," Elijah said, touching the brim of his broad-brimmed hat. "I'll be ready in about fifteen, twenty minutes." He turned and crossed the yard again to the corral.

They rode that day and every day that Thomas and Marshall English were away fishing. Though Elijah was accommodating, he maintained an increasing reserve at the same time he grew more intrigued by this strange woman from the East. A more startling pairing one could not imagine, and yet for the stark differences, there was also an odd sameness in the two. Both were content to ride long stints without speaking. Occasionally, Elsa would ask a question about something they encountered; occasionally, too, Elijah would point something out. As they explored the rim rock of the Crooked River Canyon to the northeast, and the enveloping forest of juniper and ponderosa at the flank of the Cascades to the west, both became inexorably drawn to silently question and consider exploration of something far more compelling and mysterious and dangerous.

On the fifth morning of Thomas and Marshall English's absence, as they headed out of the corral together, Elijah turned his horse to the northwest. It was a spontaneous, impulsive turning. There was no way of knowing at the time, however, that this singular turn would alter so much of what would soon follow. They rode with Mount Baker flanking them, rising majestically in the distant, dark svelte of the Cascades, still snowcapped in the hot languor between the Fourth of July and Labor Day.

They rode across the newly cut hay fields, riding almost abreast, Elijah slightly advanced, keeping Elsa out of his field of vision as they had become accustomed to riding together. They rode toward the ragged line of distant forest, dull under the glare of the midday sun. Beyond the first line of western juniper, a scraggily, humble evergreen, they entered the thickening of the forest as the mixture of trees increasingly included the tall, red-and-black scaled rise of stately ponderosa. They rode in silence, letting the horses move at their own pace. They rode into a nearly pure stand of ponderosas. Here and there small glades of wild grasses opened before them, lit with a splash of sunlight in sharp contrast to the dim filtered light of the forest. They startled a deer and two yearlings from their day bed at the edge of one clearing, and halted to watch them prance away with regal elegance. When the deer had dissolved completely into the forest, Elijah heeled his horse forward. Elsa followed.

At the edge of another open clearing in the trees, Elijah slowed, then halted. Without speaking, he dismounted. He turned for the first time to face Elsa as her mount drew up beside his horse. Elijah reached out and caught her reins. Elsa sat still, unmoving, staring down at him.

"Come," Elijah said simply. "I want to show you something." He lifted his eyes and they stared lingeringly at each other, neither turning away until finally, Elsa sat forward, swung her leg over, and dismounted. They left the horses standing untethered at the tree line as they walked out into the open glade.

The opening was more fully a meadow than a glade, perhaps five acres in all. The sun's direct exposure raised a rich mixture of scents, of pinesap and sage and dry flinty earth. The center of the clearing rose like distension from the bowels of the earth. It was slight, but unmistakable. As they moved toward the center, the ground became more uneven, rockier, with stony fissure-like wounds opening underfoot.

"Watch your step," Elijah cautioned. Bunch grass gave way to thickets of sage, and Elsa gathered her riding pants—more skirt than pants except for the inseam that divided the legs—to keep from catching on clawed branches of twisted sage. They walked single file, Elsa matching Elijah step for step.

The fissures grew into tortured, bowled depressions, yawning crevasses, and finally, a series of sunken caves. The spot was an ancient lava protrusion, a distant rent to the main thrust of activity that had aligned the peaked chain of summits forming the spine of the Cascades. Elijah stopped and stared into the largest cavern in the center of the clearing.

"Many, many years ago, this was a sacred place," Elijah said softly. "Still is," he said solemnly. He turned and the two looked at one another without barriers, without embarrassment. "Nobody comes here anymore. Nobody but me."

"Who came here—before?" Elsa asked quietly.

"The ones my people call the Ancient Ones. From long ago. It was back when the animals spoke a language we could still understand. Even still, the Ancient Ones knew that they were different. They were not like the animals."

"Who are your people?" Elsa asked directly.

"I am Modoc. But I am sure it was not Modoc who came here. This is not Modoc country. The Klamath live to the south. The Warm Springs to the north. The Modoc were made to live with the Klamath when we lost our land, but we once had caves like these. Ours were places of great power. Like these. I could feel it the first time I came here."

Elsa stepped closer to the edge of the opening. In the midday light, the slant of her shadow was thrown into the mouth of the cavern, framed in the oval ring of light on the floor of the cave. She stood and stared at the relief of her presence, trying to picture what Elijah spoke of. She looked up, letting her eyes sweep the surrounding landscape then circle slowly and fall on Elijah, to hold the gaze of his startling gray eyes.

"Why did you bring me here?" she asked in a soft yet direct voice with nothing to hide.

Elijah studied her. "It was not a decision," he answered. "I was led, much as you."

Elsa held his gaze for a long moment, then turned away. She spied a rocky bench of stone and stepped over to it to sit down. She closed her eyes and turned her face to the sun and drew a long, deep breath of dry air.

"I like it here," she said, her face still turned to the sunlight, her eyes closed. "I like it a lot." She opened her eyes and raised her hand to shield the glare as she peered at Elijah. "May I ask you a question?" she said.

"One can always ask," he replied, squatting, changing the angle to reduce the glare. He reached down and ran his dark hand over the earth, scooping up a small handful of the dusty, parched soil. He held it with one hand as he idly drew the index finger of his other hand through the mixture.

"Are you always so reticent with people?"

He looked to consider her. "Reticent?" he asked, not understanding the word.

"Reserved. Withholding."

Elijah smiled. "Reticent," he said thoughtfully, as if to absorb the halting sound of the word, imprinting its meaning. "A good word," he said finally, dropping his gaze. He continued to draw his finger through the dirt in his hand.

"And?" Elsa said after a long pause.

He smiled. He nodded. "Reticent. A good thing for an Indian."

"In the company of whites, you mean."

"Yes," he said evenly.

"In the company of a white *woman*," she added.

He stared at her. He drew a breath. "Yes. Reticent. A good thing."

"Are you reticent with your wife?"

Elijah narrowed his eyes and appraised her more intently, his eyes fixed on hers. He drew another breath and straightened, letting the dirt sift slowly through his fingers.

"Come," he commanded. He stepped forward and down into the opening of the cavern in front of them. He picked his way slowly, pausing to look back, making sure Elsa was coming. He extended his hand. She rose and stepped forward and took his hand. He held it firmly, providing balance, not tenderness. Step by step they worked their way down into the belly of the cavern. Even in the sunlight Elsa could feel the cool drop in temperature from the lingering shadow at the edges of the shaft. Elijah led her across the broken, rocky floor of the cavern, out of the sunlight, back into the shadows.

"Close your eyes," Elijah commanded.

Elsa looked at him questioningly. He let go of her hand. "Close your eyes," he said again, more playfully. Elsa took his measure, then closed her eyes. She drew in two nervous breaths, then sighed, then drew a full, deep breath of air. Elijah stood less than an arm's length away, admiring the exquisite mystery of this woman.

"Open your eyes now," he said softly after an incalculable time. He watched as her eyes fluttered open, her gaze adjusting to the dimness. He watched as her eyes roamed slowly over the surface of the cavern's dimly illuminated walls.

"*Oh my,*" she whispered breathlessly. She turned and looked at him with a penetrating gaze, then turned to study the walls again.

All about them, wherever there was a smooth surface, was a multitude of handprints. Handprints outlined and painted in muted patinas of earth colors. Dozens—scores—perhaps a hundred in all. Elsa stood and stared, taking them all in, speechless.

Elijah watched as she stepped forward as though propelled by a force not her own. He watched as she raised her hands and fitted them into a pair of prints on the wall. In the dim twilight, he saw a shudder pass across her shoulders and down her arms, into her hands. It was like she had discharged the spark of life, a part of herself, into the dark stone—that, or perhaps responded to a discharge from the stone that had imparted the binding power of timeless time, burning its memory into the core of who she was, who she had been.

She stood with her hands pressed to the wall for several long moments. "*Incredible,*" she whispered, her eyes closed, leaning into the imprint of hands that held her. Slowly, she let her hands separate from the rock face and let them fall back at her sides. She turned and caught Elijah studying her.

Elijah stepped past her, making his way to leave. The cavern seemed infused with a spirit he had never felt before, dark and electrifying at the same time. Unnerving. As if against the pull of an undertow, he began to ascend the crude staircase of tumbled stone, climbing up from the hold of the earth, reaching for the light.

Rising out of the dark, standing at the lip of the cave in the bright sunlight, he looked down, watching her as she started to ascend. Nervous, he turned and scanned the clearing. Something felt auspicious and threatening at once. Looking down again, he saw her start to stumble, reach to catch her balance, then stagger-step quickly to regain her footing. It was in that instant he saw the snake. The timber rattler struck with blinding speed before he could cry a warning.

Elijah sprang into the cave as Elsa lost her balance and began to fall. He caught her hand and pulled her to him, catching her in his embrace as he stumble-stepped down the broken stone staircase to the cavern floor. Once on steady legs, he gathered her up into his arms and turned to look for the snake. Like a vapor, it was gone. He inspected the whole face of the rock steps, and only when he was sure that it had retreated, he carried her out of the cave and laid her on the ground, her back against a large stone, the length of her washed in light.

"Are you okay?" he asked, leaning back to take in the full sight of her. Elsa's face was drained of color, except for a small scrape on her left cheek. "Where did he bite you?" he asked, trying to sound calm. He saw her glance vacantly at her leg, saw the small puncture marks in the dark pleating of her outfit, high up on her thigh. He took his knife and cut the material so he could inspect the wound. The twin punctures were small, precise. The raised ventings were stark, red beads against the pale flesh.

He studied the bite, then studied Elsa's face. A bit of color had returned to her cheeks. "You okay?" he asked again.

"Yes," she said soundlessly. He was surprised at her composure.

"We need to get back. But first I need to get the poison out." He expected her to protest, but she merely stared at him. "It might hurt. I need to make small cuts to help the bleeding." She continued to hold his gaze without emotion. "Look away," he commanded.

Elijah flicked the razor edge of his knife over the punctures, causing blood to rise and pool, then spill over the creamy flank of her thigh. He folded and put his knife away. He started to bend to the wounds, then paused, reluctant, realizing what he was about to do. He looked up. Elsa was studying him again.

Slowly, deliberately, maintaining his gaze on the steady light of her dark eyes, he lowered his mouth toward her wounds. At the last moment, he paused, unsure, then turned his eyes to the tender flesh of her thigh and pressed his mouth firmly over the flowering points of blood.

Hands

Elijah sat and smoked and surreptitiously observed his two traveling companions at the other end of the boxcar. They rode in silence, seeming to doze, heads slumped, arms wrapped around themselves for warmth. He wondered idly what their story was, for every tramp had a story to tell. Elijah doubted it would be one he hadn't heard before.

An hour out of Pasco, the taller of the two strangers rose and stumbled down the length of the rocking boxcar toward Elijah. Elijah knew from the way he walked, feet too close together, that he was a novice riding trains. He lurched and pitched like a drunk looking for a place to fall.

"Smoke?" the man yelled above the din. The stranger was young, barely more than a boy. His face was puffy from lack of sleep. Elijah studied it, drawn to the emptiness of the eyes. They caused him to remember again the look of Ol' Icy Eye before the charge. He unbuttoned his vest pocket and offered the fixings for a cigarette, a small bag of tobacco, and a pack of rolling papers. The kid stared incomprehensibly for a moment. His expression soured, turning into a full sneer. He regarded Elijah bitterly, as though he had been beaten in a deal. He turned abruptly without a word and stumbled his way back to the other end of the car. Elijah watched him go. He took the opportunity to roll himself another cigarette before returning the fixings to the safety of his pocket. He lit up and blew a light cloud of smoke into the middle distance that separated him from the others. *Best to sleep with both eyes open*, he thought.

At Wishram, the freight pulled down the mainline parallel to the rail yard and rolled slowly to a stop. Elijah rose and stretched and walked to the open door. Wishram was a small enclave of simple clapboard houses and a few modest businesses tucked hard between the high bluff of the Gorge and the railroad tracks. Its history was tied inextricably to the fortunes of the railroad; it had once been a bustling makeup yard for regrouping strings of freight cars shunted from one train to be reattached later to another. The yard was almost always empty anymore, the result of corporate re-alignments made in distant offices by men who knew nothing of trains but gross weight, costs, and margins. The atmosphere in Wishram was somber. The Beanery, the local eatery in the old depot, once the center of life at all hours, was now open only for lunch.

The shuttering of the makeup yard had had stark consequences for lo-cals and tramps alike. Where once a live-and-let-live attitude had prevailed, Elijah had heard stories of tramps being beaten and burned out of en-campments at the edge of town by hostile residents. Word had spread up and down the line to avoid Wishram. Most heeded the warning. Most, that was, except the Junkman. Junkman Willie, once a far-roaming tramp, had given up the desultory itinerary of the tramp's life to take up as the self-appointed caretaker of the local dump a mile downriver from the depot. He cultivated a reputation for being terminally unfriendly, keeping his own company and expecting all others to do likewise.

Elijah stood in the door of the boxcar inspecting the silent yard. There is no place quite as desolate as an empty rail yard. The broad, vacant space, the weave of steel rail, mesmerizing and hypnotic, invites the mind to con-template motion in stillness like the memories of a spent life. All those tracks leading somewhere and nowhere at once. Elijah pulled at the tuft of his thin goatee, ruminating. The thought of getting out here, waiting to catch another train turning south to run the trestle over the Columbia to the Ore-gon side, did not appeal to him. Traversing down the length of Oregon was always the hardest part of the journey for him, especially when the weather was dark. This train would carry him to Portland. He didn't know anyone there—at least no one he cared to share an evening with—but the city as an alternative offered far more than the despair of being waylaid in Wishram.

Elijah caught movement in the corner of his eye. The stranger he had offended earlier rose and approached him again. Elijah remained stolid but alert. The boy came over and stood beside him in the doorway for a long moment, scanning the emptiness of the yard. Neither spoke.

The boy jumped down all of a sudden and ran across several sets of tracks. Elijah watched as he disappeared around the back of a small outbuilding. He heard the shattering of glass. Elijah shook his head in disgust and turned and went back to his bedroll and sat down. He rolled and lit another cigarette, but took no pleasure in smoking. Whatever option there might have been of getting out here had just been expended. One nameless traveler was just as good as another when somebody else was looking to avenge a grievance.

The air pressure in the brake lines hissed with insistence as it came up with the engineer's preparation to get under way again. A single, plaintive note sounded from the lead locomotive, shattering the stillness of the morning. A shuddering wave rolled down the length of the train as the slack in the couplers was drawn out. *Might be able to sleep with just one eye open,* Elijah thought, studying the lone remaining rider in the far dark corner of the car. But as the train began to pick up speed, the other jumped up and ran to the open door. Elijah could see now that he was only a boy, perhaps twelve or thirteen. Although his clothes were smudged with grime, it was glaringly apparent that he was no seasoned traveler of the road. He wore an expensive leather jacket and a Giants baseball cap snug around his ears. Elijah could not put the image of the two traveling companions together. The boy stood in the open door, dancing nervously from foot to foot, looking for his companion. Elijah rose and edged toward the door, afraid the boy would get thrown and be hurt if the train took a sudden lurch.

The two stood side by side, Elijah and the boy. They stood watching the other come lumbering away from the shed with a toolbox in one hand and a lantern in the other. He crossed the first and second set of tracks. When it became apparent that he wasn't going to make the train with the burden of his theft, he dropped the tool chest, spilling wrenches and sockets in a clattering maze in the middle of the yard. He crossed a third and fourth set of tracks.

The train lurched forward. Elijah instinctively reached out and caught the youngster beside him by the arm, steadying him. The boy glanced quickly at Elijah, then back at his companion. Elijah released his hold once the boy had taken a grip on the frame of the boxcar door.

"Gimme a hand," the other boy yelled, sprinting hard to keep pace with the train. He raised his arm expectantly.

The boy stood motionless, frozen with fright.

"Damn it, Jackie, give me a hand."

The boy threw a panicked look at Elijah, then back at his friend. His companion let the lantern drop, the chimney glass shattering in a small explosion of sound all but swallowed by the rumble of the train.

"Jesus. Come on!" the boy screamed, waving his hand frantically.

The youth beside Elijah started to reach down, but Elijah caught him by the shoulder, stopping him. The older boy's eyes flashed to Elijah, incredulous at this unexpected affront. Elijah stared coldly in return, evaluating the options. He had a mind to be done with this stranger with the lifeless eyes. But what of the younger boy? What were they to each other? In this instant, there was no way of knowing. Elijah shook his head, then stepped forward, knelt in the door, and steadied himself. He reached down with one hand and gripped the outreached hand of the other. With one powerful snap of his arm, he jerked the boy upward, over the threshold of the boxcar, and onto his belly, bringing him tumbling into the car.

Elijah pulled his hand free of the clutching boy and stood. He eyed the younger boy for a moment. There was an expression in the boy's eyes that Elijah couldn't quite read: relief or resignation, he couldn't tell. Elijah turned and walked back to his end of the boxcar and sat down.

Best not to sleep at all, he thought as he began to calculate the hour and distance and anticipated time of arrival in Portland.

—+ + +—

On Antelope Creek Ranch in central Oregon, Elsa remained in a feverish state, bedridden and secluded over several days. A solemn silence emanated from the heart of the big house, spreading over the close quarters of the barn, corrals, and adjacent outbuilding, including Elijah's small cabin. Thomas and Marshall English were summoned and returned early from their fishing trip, but there was nothing to do but to fret as Elsa lay feverishly suspended between this world and some other. Emma, usually carefree and fluid, even though heavy with child at six months, seemed stiff and bound. Usually tolerant of noise in the house, she constantly shushed her rambunctious son, now nearly four and always underfoot. By day, Elijah went about his duties much as always but gave both Thomas and Marshall English wide berth for the suspicious accusations they seemed to hold in the cast of their eyes. Where, they'd demanded to know, had he taken her? How had he let this happen? Elijah answered only that they'd ridden west into the trees and had dismounted to rest. He feared some darker suspicion, that perhaps in her delirium, she spoke of the entangling desire she'd ignited in him.

At night, Elijah lay in the narrow bed of his cabin beside his pregnant wife, listening to her heavy breathing as she slept, his mind tormented by that desire and the struggle to smother it. Long into the night, when he finally slept, it rose unconstrained, fueling his dreams. Always, it was Elsa coming to him, her hair flowing in a dark halo that gave added light to her face. Again and again, she stood before him, their eyes locked in embrace. And then he would step forward in the dream. And awaken.

Dreaming of Elsa always sent disrupting tremors through Elijah the following day. He'd never known a woman like her, never imagined that they even existed. Her hold on him was like nothing he'd ever experienced before. He could make no sense of why dreams of her were so powerfully alluring. Surely it must be for some reason, but what? *Dreams are guides to the future,* his uncle always said. *But the way will be difficult.* Was there a lesson here?

When Elsa awoke the morning of the eighth day, her fever broken, Elijah was the first person she asked to see. Word spread quickly that she was beyond danger, even reaching Thomas and Marshall, who'd gone into Bend on business.

It was the first time Elijah had ever been summoned anywhere inside the big house other than to the kitchen. He delayed, sending the maid back without him, saying he had to check on something in the barn first. Inside the dark barn, he washed his face and hands in the stock trough, toweling himself with a blanket in the tack room. He pulled his hair back out of his eyes and tucked his shirt neatly into his pants.

The maid led Elijah in to see Elsa. Elijah felt a flood of relief at the mere sight of her, pale and wan, nestled amidst the spread of linens in the big four-poster bed. The maid stood silently near the door as Elijah stepped slowly toward the bed. He stopped respectfully a few feet removed, waiting for some entreaty from her.

"Please, would you get Mr. McCloud a cup of coffee," Elsa commanded the maid, her voice weak but her intent clear. The maid hesitated, pondering the impropriety of leaving Elsa alone with a man in her chamber, then curtsied nervously and left the room. Elsa's eyes turned to gaze at Elijah. She lifted her hand. He stared at the long slender fingers that looked like porcelain in the pale light of the room. The distance between the two of them was minimal, but the chasm of history was great. Elijah had almost never touched a white woman before. Had never desired to—until now. His hand came up slowly to take hers. At the touch of flesh, all shyness vanished. Elsa squeezed Elijah's dark fingers in hers, pulled his hand to her lips and kissed the hard knuckles with such supplication that it seemed to suck the air from the room. Elijah felt the force of life pound at his temples.

"You cannot imagine the dreams that have possessed me," she whispered in a rush of words. "Hands, hands, *your* hands, *everywhere* . . ."

Elijah was stung by the image of the words. Before he could give any thought to a reply, or whether to tell of his dreams of her, the sound of footsteps caused them both to instinctively retract from the embrace that was not an embrace. The maid with Elijah's cup of coffee was followed immediately by Thomas and Marshall English, hastily returned from Bend. Their twin expressions of relief at seeing Elsa awake and alert were blunted instantly in seeing Elijah standing beside the bed. Elijah stepped back as the two men rushed forward.

"My God, you're all right," Marshall gushed, grabbing Elsa's hand, nearly falling on the bed in his eagerness to reach her before his father had time to claim dominance in the room. Elsa smiled.

"Yes," she said. "I'm fine. Thanks to Mr. McCloud. Please, Sadie, Mr. McCloud's coffee," she commanded. The maid scurried nervously to extend the tray with the cup to Elijah, fearful at the same time to be seen by Mr. English as accomplice to the impropriety.

"Tell me how this happened," the elder English beseeched, eyeing Elijah quickly, his disapproval of Elijah's presence in his niece's bedchamber clear in his castigating glance.

"Quite simply, Uncle Thomas, I stepped where I should not have stepped. And thanks to Mr. McCloud, I'm here to tell you about it."

"Where? Where did it happen?" her uncle asked, his voice softening, but still suspicious. Elsa hesitated, turning to eye Elijah. Elijah did not turn to meet her gaze, but kept his eyes fixed on his employer. Elsa read Elijah's stoic stance precisely. She turned back to her uncle, feigning momentary confusion.

"To tell you the truth, I'm not sure. Somewhere to the west," she said. Thomas eyed his niece, then Elijah.

"Well, thank God you're all right," Thomas said. "We've all been so worried."

"If you'll excuse me, Miss Garnett," Elijah said, "I think I should be getting back to work. I'm glad you're feeling better."

"Thank you," she responded. "And thank you for coming as I asked. I'm so grateful to you. You'll never know." Thomas and Marshall looked at each other, then at Elijah.

Elijah nodded to the two men and stepped around the end of the bed and exited the room.

—┼─┼─┼—

Elijah continued to be tormented by dreams of Elsa. They were deeply troubling in their eroticism, but also for their mystery. In one particularly distressing sequence, she was led to him by a small, blond child, her hair loose in long tendrils. Elsa came forward, pressing herself hard against his body. He could feel the suppleness of her flesh, the beating of her heart in her breast where it was pressed against his. Fearful and enflamed with desire at once, he held fast to her, afraid to either yield or withdraw.

Are you the shadow? he asked. *Why are you here?*

I am the shadow and the light, she responded. *Not one. Or the other. But both.* The dream shook him, startling him awake. He bolted upright in bed, scanning the dark space as if in an unfamiliar place. Emma lay sleeping soundly beside him. He lay back slowly, staring up at the blackness of the ceiling. *Not one. Or the other. But both.* What could this mean? he wondered. The familiar echo of his dream from his quest for a vision when he was a boy becoming a man? Distressed as he was, he also felt possessed with the desire to possess. He sat up again and slipped silently from bed and wandered through the small cabin, looking in on the small, slumbering form of his son.

He went out on the small porch of the cabin to smoke a cigarette, to settle himself. His family slept peacefully. Yet he was wrought with agitation. In his heart, he desperately wanted to explore the dream. And not merely in sleep, but here in the realm of living, breathing flesh. *Not one. Or the other. But both.* He finished his cigarette and slipped soundlessly back into the bedroom to gather his pants and shirt from their peg on the wall.

Elijah crept as though stalking game across the divide of earth and history that separated him from the big house. In the light breeze eddying in the lee of the house, he could easily make out the fluted wash of curtains in the open door on the side porch, the double French doors leading to Elsa's room. He stood for a long moment, listening to the sound of the night and the beating of his heart.

Without causing so much as a single porch board to squeak, Elijah stealthily committed himself irreversibly to the dream. He crossed and stood in front of the flowing curtains, the last veil of caution in his path. He stepped forward, pushing through the thin material, into the room.

"Elsa?" he whispered, the question of his presence, his purpose, contained in the simplicity of her name.

"Yes," came the reply, as fully shaped as the query. "Yes," she uttered again, her compliance expressed fully in the simplicity of a single word.

Elijah crossed the room to find Elsa sitting up in the big bed, waiting as he had imagined it. He stopped a half pace from the bed and straightened, drawing a full breath, letting his eyes search the outline of her form.

"Come," she whispered. "Please," she encouraged, fearing his reticence might prevail. Elijah breathed deeply again, feeling the white heat propagating in his belly, swelling upward. "Yes," he breathed, unbuttoning his shirt, letting it fall away. He unbuckled his pants, letting them drop quietly to the floor. He moved forward on a long slow, soundless glide. He moved in, across the barrier of the edge of the bed, into the silken heat of Elsa's embrace. She slipped down, pulling him with her, enfolding him, surrendering to the enclosure of his arms. Boldly she ran her hand down the taut length of his chest and belly to find his hardness. There would be no more waiting. Not now that he was here with her, in her arms.

That night was recklessly replicated again and again over the next several nights. Every other night—sometimes a string of nights in succession—after Elijah was certain that Emma was asleep and his son deep in slumber until morning, he would steal from his bed in the small cabin to lie with Elsa in her room in the big house. Her touch reached a place in him that he hadn't known existed, terrifying but enflamed, a place of darkness and of light. She would place her hands on his flesh and light a fire that was all-consuming, that created no smoke and left no ash, so thoroughly did it burn. Elijah did not know whether it was something in him or inside of her that was so incendiary; perhaps it was a volatile concoction of base elements in the two of them. Whatever it was, it did not need language to verify, sanctify, or excuse. It was sustained by the compulsion to experience it. Again and again.

Though Elijah believed himself too smart to be careless, relying on some unvoiced, inbred, primitive instinct for survival, suspicion was inevitable. Emma asked him on more than one occasion where he had been when she awoke late at night, the discomfort of her pregnancy growing with each night's waxing of the moon. Tending to livestock, he lied: a young mare needed watching, a colt that was suddenly feverish. After many absences, she confronted him outright, catching his hand as he rose quietly, Elijah believing Emma was lost to sleep.

"Why do you do this?" she asked, her voice soft but firm.

Elijah was startled, but responded evenly. "Just checking the horses," he answered. "Go back to sleep." He was angry with himself for waking her, but angry with her, too, for waking. Emma, for her part, was less angry than frightened. She needed him to be steady now. Her own dreams had become disturbed in recent days, and she was fearful of the intimations they held for the baby on the way into the world.

"Why?" she implored in a tone that conveyed her vulnerability.

"*Shh*," he whispered softly. "Go back to sleep. I'll only be awhile," he said, wanting to convince himself as much as her. He hated himself for his deception, his betrayal, but the yearning was too powerful.

"I am fat but not blind," she whispered. "There is something bad in this, Elijah, and I worry for the baby."

"It's nothing," he said, leaning in, trying to reassure her with a kiss. She turned away, freezing him in motion and thought. He straightened and stared at the dark form on the bed.

"I'll be only a moment," he said, pulling on his pants, buttoning his shirt. "Now go to sleep." She remained silent, unmoving.

The very next day Marshall English confronted Elijah while he was shoveling out the stalls in the barn. Elijah read the rage in his eyes and knew to be careful, to not misjudge this man. He knew Marshall had never cared for him and would have run him off long ago, except for the regard the elder English held for his talent with horses.

"Keep away from her," Marshall commanded in a fierce whisper.

"How's that?" Elijah responded, straightening, wiping the sweat from his eyes. He wanted to appear neither solicitous nor acquiescent.

"I said stay away from her," the younger English said, his voice rising.

"Who?" Elijah feigned, knowing the game had been joined.

"You know who."

"Who?" he demanded, staring hard at the big man.

Neither man flinched before the other's gaze.

"Elsa," Marshall hissed through clenched teeth, his words conveying clearly his sense of possession, of entitlement.

Elijah stood staring, mute as stone.

"I'm warning you. Once. That's all you'll get. Stay away from her." Marshall turned on his heel and stomped out of the barn.

Elijah was so deeply drawn into the web of desire and deception that he could heed neither the premonition of his wife nor the warning of Marshall English. Again that night he stole stealthily into Elsa's chamber, the threat of exposure merely serving to enflame his desire further. He stayed most of the night, taking her again and again, dozing lightly between, only to be awoken and aroused to heightened frenzy. It was Elsa, finally, alarmed by the growing light of dawn, who drove him away.

Midday, Elijah was in the tack room repairing a bridle when a squalling wail sent shivers down his back. Unmistakably, it was the terror-stricken cry of a child: his child—Toby, his son. He dropped the bridle and dashed outside, fearful his son had been bitten by a snake—the only image to come to mind. Running hard, blind to everything except the sound, he followed it across the open ground between the barn and the big house, around the back of the shiny new Buick parked in the shade. Coming around the back of the car, he saw Marshall English towering over Toby's small form, his son's shirt grasped tightly by one hand as the Marshall let fly with the other, striking the boy repeatedly across the face.

Elijah dropped Marshall English with a doubled-fisted chop to the small of his back. He went down without knowing what had hit him, releasing his grasp of the boy as he fell. Elijah stared at the boy, fear etched in his tear-stained face. He saw the boy's muddy handprints patterned along the freshly washed fender of Marshall's car—multiple handprints, proof of the life in the child more than mischief.

Marshall groaned and started to roll over. Elijah kicked him with the toe of his boot, his leg striking with the lightning speed of a rattler. The man howled in pain. Elijah kicked him again. Then again. And again. The big man tried to slither out of reach, but the boot found its mark, always.

Another wail penetrated the mayhem, this one different, more high pitched, more shriek than cry. It barely registered in the blind fury that gripped Elijah. Then it was Elijah who was sent sprawling, knocked off balance by the labored charge of his wife, barefoot in smock dress, the terror in her eyes making her appear lethal in her intentions.

"Elijah?" she shrieked, rushing forward, shoving Elijah back onto the ground each time he tried to get up. "Are you mad!?"

Elijah finally stayed on the ground. He turned reflexively, hearing Marshall's moan from a deep, dark pit of pain. Enraged anew, he sprang at him again, pummeling his face with both fists. Marshall did nothing to defend himself.

Emma rose against Elijah again. She dove on him, knocking him from atop the prostrate, unconscious form. Their heads cracked together, stunning Elijah and nearly knocking Emma unconscious. She collapsed in a heap beside her husband.

The vulnerability of her plight brought Elijah to his senses. He looked at Marshall, unmoving in the dirt. He saw movement and looked up. He saw his son, back-crabbing down the length of the car, not wanting to draw attention to himself, wanting to flee, to run and hide and be done with the offense that had stirred such violence.

He saw, but did not acknowledge the presence of Elsa standing on the porch off her bedroom, one hand to her mouth as if to stifle a scream. Hearing Emma moan, Elijah turned to her lying dazed on the ground. He jumped to his feet, swept Emma up in his arms, and carried her across the big yard toward their cabin. He walked determinedly, resolutely, up the steps and into the small structure, shutting the door after him with the back sweep of a foot as he went in.

Emma was alert by the time Elijah put her down on their bed. She was ashen with fright and drained by the rush of emotion that had prompted her to attack her husband. The two stared at one another for a long moment. Neither spoke for what seemed an eternity. Finally, Elijah started to speak, but words failed him.

"You must leave," Emma said. "They will have called into town. Mr. English will be here soon. The sheriff, too. Go. Before they come."

Elijah stared at the distraught form of his wife laid out on the thin coverlet of the bed in their Spartan room. He stared at her, then around the room, out into the tiny kitchen where a pot of stew simmered on the woodstove. This was where they had made a life. In this small space. Where they had dared dream big dreams for a future forever together. And now? Only months from gaining title to the dry land below Klamath Falls. What now?

Elijah drew a deep breath and closed his eyes. He tried to sear the memory of this moment, the rising steam and the aroma of the kitchen, the smell of pine smoke and stew into his mind; he wanted to distill the quality of the sunlight through the window, striking the bare-board floor. *The way will be difficult. I am the shadow and the light.* At the echo of the thought, his eyes flashed open. He turned to gaze at his wife.

"I'm sorry," he whispered. He started to speak, but she cut him off.

"Go. *Now.* Just go."

He saw the tears brimming in her eyes. He wanted desperately to reach out, to hold her, but knew she spoke true. He must go.

Elijah turned and pulled his heavy coat from the peg on the wall. He gathered his saddlebags as well, always ready. He strode from the bedroom and pulled his big sheath knife from the plank shelf over the woodstove. He turned to the small wooden table, grabbed four big biscuits left over from breakfast, and stuffed them under the flap of the saddlebag. He went to the door of the bedroom again. He stared at Emma, the curve of her back, where she'd turned toward the wall. He saw the heave of her shoulders.

"I'll be back. I promise," he said.

Emma did not respond.

Elijah turned and fled the cabin. The house that was home, but not home. Not his own. Ever.

And he was gone.

Blade of Black

From the light in the sky, it was hard to tell what time it was when the train reached Vancouver, across the river from Portland. Though it had rained coming through the Columbia Gorge, it was merely heavily overcast now. On the outskirts of the Vancouver rail yard, Elijah threw down his pack and bedroll and jumped out of the slow-rolling boxcar. He gathered up his gear and took a beeline for the trees along the river.

Two men shared a log in front of a small fire in a clearing a hundred feet into the thicket. Though their backs were to him, Elijah recognized Leo the Lonesome right off. Though Leo had been slowed since losing an arm attempting to catch a train while drunk, it didn't impede him any tilting a bottle for a drink. Leo sat shoulder to shoulder with another man, patiently waiting his turn.

"Ho, now," Elijah cried out, announcing his entrance, coming up on the two from behind. The two men turned as one, nearly knocking each other over.

"Watch it, what the hell," Leo's partner complained, fearful of losing his grip on the bottle.

"Oh, watch it your ownself," Leo snapped back, snatching the wine away from his companion. He turned and eyed Elijah. "Well, lah-de-dah," Leo proclaimed. "Damned if it don't look like Elijah McCloud. And I heard you was dead."

"Dying. But not gone yet," Elijah joked, coming into the circle, setting his gear down, squatting to warm his hands in front of the fire.

"That's what I heard," Leo said, sitting back to eye his friend. "Bunch oī people said that. Burned up. Eaten by dogs. Something awful anyway."

"Eaten by dogs," Elijah said, laughing. "That'd be one way to go," he mused, remembering his encounter with Ol' Icy Eye.

"This here is Lucky George. Lucky George, Elijah," Leo said before tipping the bottle up again. "Lucky's a sorry ass, but he's okay." Leo handed the wine back to him. "Lucky, too. Found a twenty-dollar bill in the street this morning. Give Elijah a taste," he commanded, nudging his companion.

Lucky grimaced, eyeing Leo disdainfully.

"None for me," Elijah said.

Leo eyed him curiously. "Never knew you to turn down a lick of liquor."

Elijah shrugged. "You know what time it is?"

Leo fumbled in his coat pocket to retrieve a watch missing half its leather band. He held it to the light, squinting, raised it to his ear and shook it, eyed it again.

"Quarter past," Leo said, dropping it back into his pocket. He grabbed the bottle away from Lucky.

"Past what?" Elijah asked. He saw in Leo the worst of himself, once upon a time. "Past three," Leo said, taking another swallow. "If the damn thing's still running. It gets a little persnickety sometimes. But I don't mind. I don't keep up with time much anymore. Moves too damn fast."

A noise behind them caused the three to turn. The two other riders from the train came through the brush into the clearing. Elijah eyed them fully, taking keener measure. There was something about the pair that disturbed him, but he didn't know what. He caught the younger boy's gaze and held it briefly until the boy looked away. The boy hung back while his traveling partner moved forward toward the fire.

"Damn party," Leo said. "Care for a drink?"

"Oh, hell yes," the older of the two declared. He walked right up to Leo and held his hand out for the bottle. Leo handed it up to him.

"What the hell, Leo," Lucky cut in. "You're offering it around like it's yours. It's my damn bottle."

"This here's a gift horse—you tripping over that bill this morning," Leo said. "A man's supposed to share his good fortune. Otherwise, it'll dry up on you."

"My bottle's gonna go dry fast enough as it is," Lucky protested.

"Name's Leo," Leo the Lonesome said, extending his hand in greeting. The boy ignored Leo and tipped the bottle up again.

"You got a name?" Leo said, dropping his hand, his cheerfulness tempered by the boy's ingratitude.

"Luke."

Lucky took hold of the bottle to reclaim it.

"How about you?" Leo asked, turning to the smaller boy.

"My name is Jackie."

"This here is Lucky George. Luckiest sorry ass you ever met."

"I got a favor to ask," Elijah interjected.

"It don't cost nothing to ask," Leo said.

"You planning on being here awhile?"

"Only about fifteen, twenty years," Leo said, laughing.

"Mind watching my gear while I run across to Portland, see if I can make the Red Cross? Thought I'd trade some blood for a little cash. Hoping to catch out south at daylight. I'll never make it to the blood bank before they close, hauling all this crap."

"Run along," Leo said, waving Elijah on. "Have a good time. Don't stay out too late. I'll watch out for your stuff."

"Appreciate it. Just don't forget who it belongs to," Elijah said. "Any luck, I'll be back before dark."

Elijah touched the brim of his hat. He turned and started back the way he'd come. He eyed the boy as he passed him, but the boy avoided his gaze. There was something deeply troubling about this one, Elijah thought. Or maybe just troubled.

A blade of black on the ground caught his eye. Elijah stooped and lifted a wing feather of a crow and turned it slowly, eyeing it. He hadn't seen it on the way in, yet it was smack in the middle of the trail. He ran his fingers along the spine. He scanned the trees. *Two crows: one the shadow, the other the light.* A nervous tingling passed over his shoulders. He turned back to catch the younger boy eyeing him silently. The boy turned back to the fire. Elijah's breath caught, a bad feeling flushing through him. He inhaled deeply, calming himself. He stared at the feather again. *The way will be difficult.*

Elijah removed his hat and tucked the feather in its band. He refit the hat snugly on his head and started back out the trail toward the rail yard.

—+—+—+—

Bud Keaton sat in the cab of his truck absently chewing on an unlit cigar. He stared out the windshield in the fading light of late afternoon, idly watching two tramps feed a small fire on the periphery of the Union Pacific yard near Union Station in downtown Portland. Keaton was tired—exhausted, really. Since reassignment and relocation to Portland, he hadn't slept well. He was a creature of habit, a man of fixed routines, but there was little in his life since leaving the familiarity of Seattle that resembled routine anymore.

He hadn't expected any great favors in his last eighteen months until retirement, but he hadn't expected to be put on special assignment either. It was a bunch of bull crap, is what it was. Nobody really cared about a string of tramp murders on railroad property. Seven bodies had been found in all, including two just the week before in a boxcar on a siding north of Eugene. The fact that the last two had been college students on a lark—a very fatal one, as it proved—had moved the story from the back pages to headline news, especially with one of the boys being the son of a friend of a powerful Senator on the transportation committee. Though the murders were not on Union Pacific property, no other rail line cared to touch it. Keaton hadn't cared to stick his dick in it either, but it hadn't been his decision.

He was frustrated. There was little chance they could catch the perpetrator except by complete fluke or an odd turn of fate. The murders had taken place in five western states. He knew—and he knew his boss and his boss's boss knew—that appointing one special investigator was like pissing in the ocean—nothing more than a public relations ploy.

It exhausted him just to think about it. Watching the two tramps heat a can of beans on the small fire outside the boundary of the rail yard caused him grave annoyance. He'd like nothing better than to roust their butts for trespassing, but he knew they knew the lay of the land at least as well as he did. Probably better. If they were outside railroad property, he'd have to call a city patrolman to run them off, and he wasn't up to the bother.

A hostler engine pulling a short string of cars cleared the switch on the edge of the yard and pulled down past the little campfire. Keaton watched the slow movement of the train as it entered the yard. He saw a tramp jump down from an empty and start across open space toward an access road that led out of the yard. Keaton smiled. He laid his unlit cigar in the ashtray and started his truck. He pulled forward. The stupid sons a-bitches should know better, he told himself. This one was clearly within the boundary of the yard and warranted getting more than a firm reminder about respecting the property rights of others. Keaton came in at an angle, cutting off the quickest route of escape. He hit the tramp with his headlights even though it wasn't yet full twilight. He set the brake, grabbed his flashlight, and jumped out of the cab.

"Hold up there," Keaton called out as he strode quickly toward the man.

Elijah McCloud slowed his gait and stopped. "*Aw,* sweet Jesus," he seethed under his breath. *Not likely to make the Red Cross now,* he reasoned, catching the time on the big clock tower above the train station. It was twenty of five.

Keaton approached Elijah at an oblique angle. He stopped a full stride away and commanded Elijah to face him, putting the spot of his flashlight full in his eyes.

Keaton watched as the man turned slowly, his eyes squinting to break the glare. Keaton studied the face. A small smile lifted his scowl as well as his mood.

"Got some ID?" Keaton asked, continuing to keep his distance.

Elijah fished a pouch on a lanyard from inside his shirt and extracted a card and held it out. Keaton stepped forward, into the path of light, breaking the glare that blinded Elijah, and took the card.

"You running me in or what?" Elijah asked.

"I'll be asking the questions," Keaton said, inspecting the card. No mistaking it, though the photo didn't do justice to the hard, prideful gaze Elijah McCloud gave him.

"Get in the truck," Keaton said, continuing to finger the card. Elijah's shoulders slumped, dreading the prospect of a night in jail. He stepped forward as Keaton stepped back, allowing him to pass. Elijah started to climb up into the bed of the truck.

"In the cab," Keaton commanded.

Elijah stopped abruptly, not sure what to do. Bulls never asked tramps to ride in the cab.

"I said in the cab," Keaton said sternly.

Elijah walked around to the passenger door and opened it. "You sure about this?" Elijah said, hesitating. He waited, but Keaton said nothing, slipping in behind the wheel on the other side.

Elijah decided to pursue another tack.

"Ya know, you could just let me go. I'm just passing through. Wanting to get to the Red Cross to give blood before it closes. I'll be gone, out of town before morning."

"In the cab," Keaton commanded sternly again. It was clear Elijah wasn't going to be giving blood to the Red Cross anytime soon.

Elijah climbed into the truck and shut the door. Keaton wheeled the truck out of the yard and down a dark access road. He merged with rush hour traffic at the end of the street as they headed away from the yard and the railroad security offices. Keaton lifted a pack of Pall Malls from the dash and lit up. He offered one to Elijah, but Elijah refused.

"How you been, McCloud?" Keaton asked evenly, pulling up to a stoplight, preparing to turn right on Burnside and head away from the river. Keaton turned his head slowly and smiled, the two men eyeing each other. Elijah knew Keaton to be a tough, relentless railroad dick, a man without much of a sense of humor.

"What do you want, Keaton?" Elijah said, exasperated.

"How long's it been? Three years now?" Keaton said, blowing a cloud of smoke toward the light, easing forward as the signal changed. They rode in silence for several blocks. Elijah couldn't make any sense of where they were going. They weren't headed for the police station or the county sheriff's office.

"You running me in, fine," Elijah finally said. "Otherwise, why don't you do your good deed for the day and drop me off at the Red Cross?"

"You hear anything lately about these murders, dead tramps turning up like rats in a sewer?" Keaton said, ignoring Elijah's question.

Elijah stared at Keaton. "What? You think I did 'em?"

"No, no. Not at all. Isn't your style," Keaton said. "Just wondering what you heard, what you might know about 'em."

"Nothing," Elijah said. "I've been out of circulation."

"There's been a bunch," Keaton said, pulling up to another traffic light. "A whole slew of them. Some nut, I figure. Heard anything?"

"Like I said, I've been keeping pretty much to myself."

"Always did, didn't ya?"

"More so lately," Elijah said. Keaton accelerated up Burnside once they cleared the last of the business district, drove up into the hills, and took a left into a residential area. Elijah said nothing, then laughed sardonically.

"What's so funny?" Keaton said curiously.

"Kinda ironic, ain't it. Having to be concerned about the welfare of tramps."

"I'm not. Just doing my job."

"So what's this have to do with me?"

Keaton cruised a quiet street of grand, older homes, a mixture of architectural styles. Political campaign yard signs lined the street, most of them for the Ford/Dole ticket, with one lone green-and-white Carter/Mondale sign in front of the smallest house on the street. He entered Washington Park, pulled down past the tennis courts on the left, and wheeled up a narrow drive on the right. He stopped in front of a locked gate that led up to the Japanese Garden.

"That's odd. I thought they stayed open until six," Keaton said.

"Only in the spring," Elijah said.

"Yeah?" Keaton said incredulously, turning to stare at Elijah. "I hadn't figured you as a garden variety type."

"Nor I you," Elijah retorted.

"You been here, have you?"

"Long time ago," Elijah answered. He remembered the beauty and peacefulness of the Japanese Garden, not as a tourist, but traveling through on occasion, an itinerant worker needing a quiet spot in the big city where he could sleep the night without being molested by cops or other tramps looking for trouble. He'd found it quite by accident, but it had become something of a favorite place for him, quiet and deserted at night.

"Nice place. Peaceful," Keaton said. "I discovered it just this past weekend. Never been in a Japanese garden before. Really rather pleasant."

"What do you want with me?" Elijah said wearily.

"Cut yourself shaving, did ya?" Keaton asked, eyeing Elijah's jaw. Elijah touched it tenderly, and winced. It was still painful.

"Careless," Elijah said dismissively.

Keaton stared hard at Elijah. "I want to ask you a favor."

Elijah laughed again. "That'll be the day."

"It isn't too late to run your ass in for trespassing," Keaton said, smiling.

"Wouldn't be the first time."

Keaton crushed out his cigarette in the ashtray and lit up another.

"I figure I owe you one," Keaton said, blowing smoke into the tight cab. Elijah stared resolutely straight ahead.

"You don't owe me anything," Elijah said solemnly.

"Well, yeah, I figure I do. I'm lucky to be alive 'cuz of you. You hadn't come along when you did, breaking up that blanket party those three punks were giving me in Seattle five, six years back."

"This is rich," Elijah said, clearly amused by the bizarreness of the turn of events.

"I'm serious," Keaton said. "You didn't need to do what you did."

"Forget it."

"Well, maybe I will. But I want you to consider something." Keaton pulled a card from an organizer clipped to the overhead visor and handed it to Elijah. "You hear anything, see anything that would help put a stop to these murders, you call me."

Elijah studied the card: *Charles Keaton Jr.—Special Investigator—Union Pacific Railroad.*

"There's a toll-free number you can call anytime."

Elijah eyed the card: *1-800-RRLines.*

"Anybody who answers will know how to reach me."

Elijah flipped the card up on the dash. "Be kinda difficult. No phones, most places I go." He pulled the handle and opened the door. "That it? That all you wanted?" he asked, starting to get out.

Keaton reached across and caught him by the arm. "I'm serious. You hear anything, anything at all that would help—call me."

"Don't hold your breath," Elijah said, staring intently at Keaton, then at the hand that held him by the arm. Keaton let go his grip. Elijah slipped out the door, then closed it gently and stared again at Keaton.

"Hope you get your man, Keaton." Elijah touched his fingers to the rim of his hat and stepped back. "I do. I really do. Just can't see how I'd be much help to you." Elijah turned and sauntered down the drive, across the street, past the tennis courts toward the fall of land and bright lights of the city below.

"Shit," Elijah muttered, discouraged, hating the whole long prospect of crossing the flats again. He wished he'd stayed in Montana; he cursed Ol' Icy Eye. "Enough to make a man take to drinking," he mumbled, disappearing down into the trees.

The prospects for the evening weren't bright.

Stay or Go

The flood of the Columbia flowed out of the blackness of night, between the shimmering lights of Portland and Vancouver, then back into darkness again. It was the night of the new moon. Along the fold of the river, the air was damp and cold.

The flickering of the campfire in the thicket near the Vancouver yards pressed the night back to the edges of the understory of trees, its golden light reflected and magnified like a candle flame in a glass chimney. The dance of light and shadow drew the four figures close around the fire, drawn by the promise of security as much as warmth.

Jackie Logan sat Indian-style with legs crossed on the cushioning of an old tire, listening to Leo and Lucky George regale Luke with tales of life on the road. Jackie said nothing, barely hearing the drunken palaver, his chin resting wearily in his hands, his arms propped on his knees, eyes staring with a fixed gaze at the smoldering embers beneath the crackling sticks of wood.

"I was down to Barstow one time," Leo began. "There were two old boys got on the train, drunk as cougars. They had half a gallon between 'em. I was up in one end of a ratty old box and they settled down in the other. We pull out of Barstow heading for Vegas, highballing 'cross the desert.

"I was pretty well greased myself," Leo said, leaning forward to lift a burning stick from the fire to light a cigarette. "Otherwise, I'd have offered to help them boys finish it. After a little while, I nodded off. Then a while later, I hear this big ruckus and I wake up. These two old stewbums are carrying on like they was married to one another—who paid what for the bottle, who was gonna get the last drink." Leo laughed a thick, raspy guffaw, taking the bottle from Luke, upending it for a big swallow of the too-sweet muscatel. "Just like a drunk to look a gift horse in the mouth," he said, passing the bottle to Lucky George.

"Anyways, one of these ol' boys tells the other, it's his, by God, he paid for it, and he ain't sharing another drop. The other jumps up and yells, 'The hell you say,' and snatches it away from his partner and heads for the door. I guess he forgot where he was, 'cause he stepped right out the door into the sweet-ass black of night. The train just kept a-screaming across the Mojave. That other ol' boy, he don't even flinch. He just closes his eyes and lays down, mumbling to himself." Leo shakes his head.

"So what happened?" Luke asked, urging Leo on.

"Nothing," Leo said. "We both went to sleep. Woke up the next morning pulling into Vegas. I thought maybe this other fella wouldn't even remember what happened the night before. So I tell him, 'Your buddy jumped off the train last night.' And he looks at me real melancholy like and says, 'Yeah, I know. The sumbitch took my jug of wine with him, too.'"

Leo and Lucky George roared with laughter. Luke grinned drunkenly, waiting for Lucky George to take a turn at the bottle before passing it along to him. Jackie studied the three, wondering what was so funny. Lucky George raised the wine and tilted back to swallow, nearly falling backward off his perch on a crate before Leo caught him by the shirtfront and yanked him upright. Luke took the bottle and downed a big mouthful before passing it along to Leo.

"Goddamn, that's sweet," Luke said, shivering, his face puckered in revolt.

"And good, too," Lucky George added.

Jackie straightened and hugged himself for warmth. Even with the fire, the night's dampness pressed hard along his spine, deep into his bones. He watched Luke act the fool of good times, trying to remember what had attracted him to him when they first met that night in the Seattle bus station playing video games. Streetwise and confident, Luke had bragged that buses were for pussies; the way to travel was by freight train. It was simple, he said: "Nothing to it—you know how."

Hardly.

Luke managed to run through in a day and a half nearly all the money Jackie was going to use to buy a bus ticket to California to get home to his mom—and that was without even getting them out of the state of Washington.

"That reminds me," Lucky George chimed in, getting up to totter off to where the trees folded with the night to relieve himself. "Old buddy of mine." He stood, fighting for balance. "Crazy son of a gun," he muttered back over his shoulder. He stood staggering back and forth for a bit, then zipped himself up and turned and came stumbling back toward the fire. Jackie noticed the whole front of his pants was stained dark where he'd pissed himself. He collapsed, relieved of the effort, atop the crate he'd been sitting on. He stared blankly into the fire.

"You was saying," Leo said, prompting Lucky George to continue with his tale.

"Saying what?" Lucky George said.

"That's what I want to know."

"Whatta ya mean, 'that's what I want to know'? That's what *I* want to know."

"Goddamn, man, you was saying something about some old crazy-ass sumbitch buddy of yours."

"Who's that?"

"*Aw*, Christ. Just shut up then, will ya. You can't tell a story. You a sorry-ass excuse for a tramp."

"I am too a damn tramp. I may be a fuckup, but tramping's in my blood."

"Hell, you ain't rode no train in a year of Sundays."

"The hell you say."

"Getting where you can't tell a good tramp from a sorry-ass bum anymore, trash that's riding now."

"You can say that again," Lucky George said agreeably. Leo stared at his friend, shaking his head in disgust.

"Just be quiet," Leo said, lifting the bottle to take a swallow.

"I gotta right to talk," Lucky George complained peevishly. "It's a free country."

Leo took another swallow and let Luke take it out of his hand. Jackie watched as Leo slipped his coat off and peeled a shirtsleeve up the stump of his arm, exposing the flipper-like nub of forearm extending just below the elbow. Jackie sat mesmerized by the sight of it, fighting the urge to lean forward and inspect it more closely. It was chilling and engrossing at once. He watched as Leo took a packet of cigarette rolling papers out of his shirt pocket, deftly worked a sheet free, and re-deposited the pack in his pocket. Leo raised the stump to his lips and licked the cleft at his elbow with his tongue. He creased a fold in the paper with one hand and then pressed it into the crook of his arm, sticking it on the saliva. He fumbled out a pouch of tobacco and shook a narrow line of cut leaf into the fold. He pulled the drawstrings with his teeth to close the bag. With only one hand, he dexterously rolled the paper into a tight cylinder and ran his tongue along the seam to seal it. As he raised it to his lips, he looked up and caught Jackie staring at him. He fixed the boy with an odd grin, causing Jackie to look down.

"Didn't used to be so damn dangerous riding trains," Leo said, rolling his sleeve down, slipping his coat back on. He grabbed a smoldering stick at the edge of the fire and brought it up to light his home-rolled. He blew a cloud of smoke into the column of superheated air rising above the fire. He eyed Luke with disdain.

"Know what I mean?" he said. Luke ignored him, taking the bottle as it was passed from Lucky George, upending it for another swallow. Leo turned his eyes on Jackie again and smiled slyly, causing a shiver to run along Jackie's shoulders. Jackie looked away, nervously scanning the edge of the glade.

Fatigue weighed heavy on him. He was deeply chilled. He wanted nothing so much as to close his eyes and sleep, with the dim hope that when he awoke, the bad dream of the last few days, the past several months, would be over. Nothing but bad memories seemed to bookend his life. His mother and the memory of his brother, Terry, dead a year, was all that seemed to remain in the frame of Sacramento. His father, busy with work and distracted by a series of relationships, mostly with much younger women, framed the reality of his time in Seattle. That and Stardancer. Katherine Lemay was the most recent in a line of women his father had dated, but Jackie almost liked her, for she owned a place on the Snoqualmie River east of the city. That and a stable of quarter horses. Stardancer was a chestnut mare, sleek of line and gentle of spirit. She was Katherine's favorite, though Jackie always got to ride her when the three went riding. Jackie had never meant to hurt the big beautiful mare. It had been an accident. A stupid accident.

Jackie shuttered his mind to the memory of it. He let his head drop. He failed to hear Lucky George stumbling over toward him. Jackie jerked upright with fright as Lucky George dropped a tattered old blanket around his shoulders.

Lucky George recoiled, stumbling backward, barely managing to remain upright.

"What are you doing?" Jackie complained, slinging the blanket free of his shoulders.

"Thought you'd 'preciate a blanket, keep you warm."

Jackie stared at the blanket, then at Lucky George.

"It's gonna be cold," Lucky George said. "Real cold. It don't bother me none, but you better wrap up. There's a mattress on yonder," he said, pointing back over Jackie's shoulder. "You might oughta try to get yo'self some sleep." He waved his hand as if bidding the boy farewell. "Go on now. Get some sleep." Lucky George turned and stumbled back to his crate and sat down.

Jackie sat mute, staring at the three in front of the fire. Slowly, he reached out and pulled the blanket up over his shoulders, pulling it tight around him. He shivered against the cold. He closed his eyes and nodded off immediately, his head dropping, causing him to jerk upright again. He looked at the three, his eyes closed, then opened again. He rose slowly and wandered back in the direction that Lucky George had pointed.

+++

Jackie woke as though drugged, as though pulled through a thick wad of wool by a thread of sound that begged to be heard. The sound rose in power to compel attention, causing Jackie's eyes to flutter. He lifted his head from the press of the old mattress. Sound exploded in a rush like a gunshot. Jackie bounced up into a crouch, confused by the dim light, the unfamiliarity of the place, the agony of the cry that filled the night. His gaze fixed on the glow of the fire. In the weak light, he saw movement, the dark form of a man—two men, one standing over another.

The frozen scene erupted in a blur of motion and sound, another wail of terror filling the night. Jackie caught a flash like quicksilver as the one standing plunged forward. The one on the ground crabbed backward, kicking and waving an armless sleeve in pitiful defense. Jackie saw another flash, heard another scream.

The one on the ground, Jackie realized, was Leo. He saw a long-bladed knife slice into the empty sleeve of Leo's coat. Leo kicked backward as the knife ripped free. It rose and fell again, up and down, up and down. Jackie stumbled backward in shock, compelled to flee, but captured by the sight of the slaughter. Leo tried to roll away, to get out from under his attacker, but the blade descended again, disappearing deeply into his back.

Jackie's breath caught as the attacker quickly caught Leo by the hair, drawing the knife under his chin. Jackie staggered weak-kneed, feeling faint, lost his balance, and went down into a pile of old cans.

The dark figure pivoted.

"W-w-what the f---f-fuck?" he muttered, fixing Jackie with a cold stare. He straightened slowly, stepping over the limp body toward Jackie.

"W-w-who the f-f-fuck . . . ?" the man growled.

Jackie shrieked. He pirouetted and fled, diving headlong directly into the dense growth of brush in front of him.

Branches tore at him, roots tripped him, yet Jackie drove through the growth with a fury fueled by terror. He broke free out the other side. He sprinted forward, fleeing the sight and sound of horror his only thought.

A light mist shrouded the periphery of the rail yard, the dim silhouette of dark warehouses shimmering like a mirage. He glanced back over his shoulder. The attacker broke out of the thicket, stumbling wildly, nearly falling, then straightening, coming dead on after him.

Jackie powered his legs, digging for every ounce of energy he could muster. *"Please,"* he pleaded to no one.

He reached the first warehouse, glanced back, and then dashed onward. He reached the second, scrambling up on the long loading dock. He tried a door; it was locked. He turned and saw the intruder lumbering toward him with an awkward gait, as though he were injured, crippled, or deformed. Jackie saw the swing of arm, the glimmering of steel. He jumped off the loading dock and raced on to the next warehouse. He scrambled up a set of rickety steps onto the loading dock and tried the door. It rattled loosely in its jamb. He shouldered it frantically once, twice, and on the third impact, felt it give way, scraping roughly across the splintered floor, opening just enough to let him slip inside.

The interior of the huge frame building was eerily lit from the glare of the rail yard security lights, the light falling through dirt-smudged windows high in the walls near the ceiling. Jackie dashed across the floor through a maze of wooden crates, his footsteps echoing loudly inside the cavernous space. He ducked into a narrow aisle between two rows of crates stacked four high as he heard the harsh scrape of the door again. He crouched and squeezed into a tight recess between a tower of crates and an old workbench. He bit his lips until he tasted blood, trying to silence his panting. His heart pounded in his ears. He pressed himself back inch by inch, flattening himself against the back wall. He pulled his knees up, hugging them to his chest, wanting to dissolve in the darkness that enveloped him.

Who is that? He didn't dare contemplate an answer.

Softly, the sound of shuffling feet came to Jackie's ears. He tried to stanch his breathing, but being winded it was all but impossible. The footsteps came closer, then stopped. Silence was all about him.

A minute passed. Then two. Then the sound of footsteps again. Jackie felt the calf muscle in his left leg start to cramp. He tried to ignore it, but the seizure intensified. He kicked out reflexively, forced to uncurl his leg. He winced from the pain.

A dark silhouette came into view at the front of the narrow aisle. Jackie almost gasped with fright. The form moved, passed from sight. Jackie's eyes closed. He sighed a quiet exhalation of relief. He felt a fresh stab of fear and opened his eyes. He stared directly at the dark form, standing at the end of the aisle again, unmoving.

Though Jackie could not see the face, the man saw him; he was sure of it. The man took a step forward and Jackie screamed impulsively, uncurling, scrambling blindly on hands and knees out of his hiding place, into the aisle, then through a tight, narrow crevice between wooden crates, pain exploding in his leg where the man rushed forward, kicking madly at him as he slithered away. Jackie came into the next aisle and jumped up. Instinctually, he leaned hard against the stack of crates, sending them tumbling. He heard the man cry out as the wooden boxes crashed down on him.

Hide or run?

Jackie duck-waddled through a short opening in another wall of crates. There was no time to think, no time to plan. He moved on pure instinct, raw reflex. He was like an animal being hunted, seeking escape.

The attacker roared, enraged, filling the dim warehouse with sound, flinging boxes, stammering madly. Jackie convulsed with terror. *Escape, escape,* his mind commanded.

He peeked around the edge of a box. He saw nothing. He rose to a half crouch, lifting his head to steal a quick look across the top of the scattered crates. The man stood stolidly like a statue staring back at him, barely more than three feet away.

The man swung his arm. There was a flash of quicksilver. Jackie screamed and fell back before the whoosh of air, the knife missing him by inches. The man's hand struck a pillar on the wild swing, the knife clattering to the floor. Jackie jumped up and dashed across the open floor toward the door. He heard the man cursing, stammering, kicking crates, searching for the blade.

Jackie was out the door. He leapt off the side of the elevated landing. He came down off balance, twisting an ankle. Pain exploded up the length of his leg as he crumpled. He tried to get up and run, but the pain was too great. His eye caught sight of a small opening in the slat facing of the loading dock. He scrambled over and worked his way into the dark, cramped space. He heard the rush of footsteps overhead.

"F-f-fuck!" the man roared.

Out of the night came the far-off wail of a siren. It grew louder, increasing rapidly. It was joined by another.

"Little b-b-b-bastard."

Jackie heard the scurry of footsteps back along the loading dock, down the stairs, crunching through gravel. The sound faded quickly.

Jackie sat hugging his knees, rubbing the center of pain in his ankle. Was he gone? Where? The sirens were very close now. He drew a big breath, letting it out as quietly as possible. He looked around the small space he was in. It was filled with the strong odor of decay, of something long dead. The smell didn't bother him as much as it reassured him. At least he was still alive.

The sirens, very close, snapped silent. Jackie remained still, listening to the night sounds. He thought he heard voices. He waited, hoping for their arrival. He waited for what seemed hours. Again and again, he saw in his mind's eye the flash of steel and heard Leo's scream. He wondered what had happened to Lucky George, to Luke. Had one of them managed to get away? A wave of grief and fear and exhaustion washed over him, pulling him down like a giant undertow. He buried his face in his hands and wept.

—+++—

Jackie awoke suddenly with a start, surprised he'd fallen asleep. He ached with stiffness from sitting so long in one constricted position. He saw now gray light filtering through the wooden slats that faced the front of the loading dock. He thought he heard someone singing. Had he dreamed it? Then he heard it again. Wincing from the pain, he uncurled and stretched his legs. He drew himself up on his hands and knees and crawled quietly to peer through the opening in the facing of the loading dock.

Elijah McCloud came along the rail spur, humming and muttering and mumbling bits of some song as he ambled in front of the row of warehouses toward the jungle.

"Says the bum to the son, Oh, won't you come, to the Big Rock . . .

Candy . . . ?"

The singing stopped abruptly. "Whoa, now," Elijah mumbled. He was barely twenty feet away. He stood motionless, staring down past where Jackie was hiding, down toward the far end of the warehouses. He was still unsteady from a night of drinking with a couple of Burnside Street stewbums he'd run into.

At the trailhead leading into the trees to the hobo camp, three police cars and two ambulances stood parked, their emergency lights flashing. Jackie studied them, then turned and looked up the siding toward Elijah again. Elijah stood rubbing his face with his hands, massaging his temples as if adjusting his focus. His hands dropped away. He stood staring for a long time. Jacked turned and inspected the assemblage of vehicles again. There were no medical or uniformed officers in sight. He turned his attention back to Elijah, startled to see him retreating the way he'd come.

Jackie crawled hurriedly out from under the loading dock. He stood, assessing Elijah's ambling gait as he moved away, then turned to consider the throng of vehicles. He was dumbfounded that Elijah would just leave, having no worry or curiosity for what might have happened to his friend.

Stay or go? The horror of this place chilled him. Without hesitation, he turned and began trailing after the old man, hanging back in the dim shadows, not wanting Elijah to turn unexpectedly and see him following along behind. Jackie couldn't face the prospect that the old man would send him away. Wherever he was going, it was the only direction Jackie felt safe to consider. He didn't know why, but there was something about the dark-faced stranger that reassured him. For the time being, it was enough . . . it was enough.

In truth, it was all there was.

World Through a Window Frame

Elijah spurred the big dappled gray hard, north to the Crooked River, away from the Antelope Creek Ranch. He didn't allow Smoke to slow until they dropped into the river cut's shadow. In that part of Oregon it was near impossible for a man's travels on open ground not to be observed, even at a great distance, the land was so flat and unrelieved. Elijah couldn't breathe easy until reaching the river. Nobody in the county had greater knowledge of Oregon's high upland plateau; Elijah knew every declivity, waterhole, and hideout for thirty miles around. More critically, he thought like a wild mustang long wise to the wiles of staying free. He was banking on the fact that Thomas English or anyone else wanting to track him would consider that, giving good pause even if they knew which way he'd headed out. Elijah worked his way down the rocky slope to the river. He turned Smoke west, following the river a mile to take refuge in a spot that provided the greatest concealment with the quickest escape if anyone came along before darkness. Day was his enemy; night his friend. The hawk and the owl shared the same landscape, but each to his own, one by day, the other by night. Elijah had to think like the owl now to see his way through.

After dark, Elijah mounted again and climbed out of the deep crease of the Crooked River. He headed straight for the dark smudge on the moonless horizon he knew to be the rise of the Cascades. Like a deer being hunted, Elijah knew safety lay in moving to higher ground as quickly as possible. Before anyone decided he'd probably headed for the mountains, traces of his trail would be lost to the wandering of cattle on the open range. He rode steadily at canter, stroking Smoke's neck every so often in encouragement. By dawn, they were into the trees, well up a fork of a tributary of the Deschutes River. He unsaddled the big gray horse and hobbled him to graze. Ordinarily, he would leave him loose, but with cougars about in the mountains, he feared Smoke might run off if spooked. He needed Smoke now more than ever. He'd take his chances with a mountain lion. He had the Colt in his saddlebag if it came to making a stand.

Elijah kicked together a bed of pine needles and lay down in a stand of big trees along the stream's edge. Tired as he was, he was unable to sleep. He lay staring up through boughs of the giant trees at the distant stars beyond, bewildered by the wild turn of events. In less than a day, his world had been turned over, remaking his universe anew. Everything was different. Everything.

Dawn came. He knew he needed to sleep, to be clear headed, yet he couldn't escape the images of the day before: Marshall thrashing his son; Emma unconscious, splayed on the ground; the look of terror in his son's eyes. As the heat of day built, he finally slipped beneath the weight of his exhaustion and worry into a fitful sleep.

He awoke edgy in late afternoon, alert to the quiet of the forest, hesitant to trust his earlier assessment that he was safe here up a draw, along a quiet stream. He saddled up and rode higher, out of the foothills, into the mountains. But still he couldn't shake feeling vulnerable. He rode until near dark, until the twilight obscured the hard angles and edges to the world sufficiently to cause him to feel safe again. It was a bitter irony that night brought him safety, as it had also been his ruin.

Being Modoc, especially of mixed heritage, was a great distillery of irony. He would never be mistaken for white, but he had always been regarded with some suspicion and even animosity by other Modoc. He'd never held any truly friendly feelings for whites, other than for Thomas English, who accepted him as he was and respected him for his skill with horses. He'd certainly never felt any passion for them—until Elsa Garnett. It angered him deeply to be relegated to a clan-less class—neither white nor fully Modoc. He never was given the benefit of the doubt on the first count, and always paid full toll on the latter. Was that why Elsa had held such a powerful allure for him: a white woman who saw past his shaded heritage? But why would he risk everything he cherished—Emma, Toby, his desire for his own place—to seek what had been stirred by strange and disturbing dreams? He thought about what his uncle had said when dream singing was revealed to him as a boy: *the way will be difficult.* He'd never imagined that dreams could be menacingly self-deluding. Was that what his dreams of Elsa had been? Or were they fueled by some dark strain of vengeance for being a mixed blood keeper of The People's gift that was not meant for him to possess?

As the moon progressed night by night in its new phase, Elijah began to accommodate the fact that his life was irreparably altered. Already toughened in mind and body, he grew leaner and harder, dropping in weight as he rekindled the resourcefulness required to forage directly from the land. His good fortune in the beginning was that his saddlebags were provisioned out of habit with the essential comforts necessary to take to hardship with ease, with sugar and coffee and flour. The sugar and coffee went quickly. This heightened his sense of hunger, and though he saw small game he could take with the Colt pistol, he couldn't risk it. He put the line and hooks he found in a wrap of cloth in the bottom of his saddlebags to good use, and began to strip his lariat to create long, slender strands for making snares. These he had to chew, bit by bit, to make limber, but it helped fill his day. His adaptation to the wild kept his mind from being fully possessed with recriminations and concern for Emma, for lingering flashes of desire for Elsa that he seemed unable to control.

Just after the full moon, when moonrise moved on toward midnight, Elijah decided it was safe—at least safe enough—that he could risk returning to see Emma. He had moved down out of the mountains to the glade at the bottom of the foothills that held the volcanic caves, the cave of hands, having grown more comfortable with the idea that any search for him mustered early would have run its course by now. This camp put him only an hour's hard ride from the ranch, making it possible to go and return the same night.

He tied the big gray horse in a stand of cottonwoods along a small stream that cut through the ranch, a half mile distant from the big house. Keeping the big barn and corrals and Emma's cabin between him and the big house, he crossed the open ground to approach the ranch compound proper. He knew by the pale wash on the clothesline, shimmering in the light breath of night breeze, that Emma and his son still remained on the ranch. He had expected as much, knowing that the senior English had always felt fondly toward Emma and would judge her blameless for what had happened. Elijah came up on the cabin, stepped up on the narrow porch, and pushed silently through the door into the kitchen. He crept soundlessly through the familiar space, first into his son's room to stand over him and gaze longingly at the sleeping outline of the boy. Then he turned and passed into where

Emma slept. It was all he could do to keep from falling on her in the flood of grief and desire he felt in glimpsing her plump form under the thin cover. She had always slept hot, capable of going without a blanket most of the summer. Though the night was warm, she lay covered, a primal instinct, he thought, to protect herself and the unborn child.

He stood for the longest time simply gazing at her, one hand clapped to his mouth, appearing as though he held it there to censure the impulse to speak. He became lost to the lull of peace in being in her presence again, forgetting time and circumstance. The short whimpering cry of his son tossing in his sleep caused Emma to move in mirrored fashion, moaning and tossing with agitation. Elijah tensed. He let the silence settle again before moving. He eased himself into the hard wooden chair in the corner of the room and sat leaning forward, his elbows on his knees, head in the cradle of his hands, staring at her. Just the silhouette of her form was a feast to his eyes.

An hour passed. Two, maybe three. Finally, when he felt he could no longer risk remaining, he rose and went to the kitchen. He stood looking out the window over the drain board as he'd done countless times before, his eyes now watching the slow slap of wash on the line, the night breeze stirring more strongly here in the last stretch of darkness before dawn. How simple a thing, he thought, seeing the world through the frame of a window in the place you call home. So simple that its simplicity masks just how precious a thing it is. An act of belonging, of unquestioned trust in a refuge from the tumult of the world. Elijah dropped his gaze, his heart freighted with remorse. He spied the dipper in the water pail on the end of the drain board. He lifted it carefully and took a long drink like a man savoring the sweetest elixir. He drank from the dipper to the last drop, then returned it soundlessly to the pail and turned to go, catching sight of a bowl of apples in the dim light at the center of the table. It calmed him to see the apples, knowing that they were a gift from Thomas English, a continuance of his generosity of spirit. Whenever he received a shipment of apples from cold storage up in Wenatchee, he distributed them freely among all the people on the ranch. As casually as if arising early to get a start on a long day's work, Elijah reached and plucked an apple from the bowl and put it in his coat pocket, then turned and let himself out the door.

Elijah could not bring himself to return the next night, but couldn't keep himself away the night following. Again he tied Smoke in the stand of cottonwoods and walked in from there. He eased into the cabin and entered his son's room first. He bent and brushed a shock of dark hair off his forehead, then turned and went into Emma's room and stood over her for a long moment. He eased back and sat down in the hard chair in the corner. It was too risky to have her know of his presence—more for her sake than his own. He sat and listened to her fluted, labored breathing, a breath for two, he thought, here on the edge of the seventh month. As before, he merely sat and watched her sleep, then rose and slipped out as quietly as he'd come, lifting an apple again from the bowl on the small kitchen table.

He returned the next night as well, moving silently through the cabin, the touch of each chair back, each counter, each door frame charged with the tantalizing shock of felicity, first into his son's room to take in the sight of the boy in his bed, then turning to enter Emma's room again. He stepped close and began to bend to gain a glimpse of her face, an image of delectable power. He jumped back suddenly, forced away as she rose explosively from the bed, exclaiming his name in a sharp whisper, moving with the grace of an antelope despite her carriage.

"*Elijah, Elijah, Elijah,*" she exclaimed, pressing him to the wall, her lips fluttering like a tormented butterfly over his cheeks, his nose, smothering his eyes, seizing upon his mouth hungrily.

"Shh, shh!" Elijah admonished, excited and frightened at once. Finally there was no need for words, for any sounds, as they drank longingly of each other's kisses.

"*Oh Emma . . . Emma,*" Elijah moaned, holding tight to her, unable to find the shape of any word other than her name. Now it was her turn to admonish him, clasping a hand over his mouth, his breath hot on the flesh of her palm.

"You'll wake Toby. Come to bed. Come. Lie with me, hold me," she said urgently, dragging him with her as she retreated. He caught her weight as her knees met the edge of the bed, letting her down gently. He lifted her legs and swept them into bed in one motion, her arms still wrapped around his neck. The old mattress touched the length of his body like loving hands as his own hands worked the sculpture of her body.

"You came, you came," Emma whispered breathlessly. "I knew you would return."

Elijah pulled back where he could take clear focus of her face even though it was masked in dusky twilight.

"How did you know? I was so careful," he said incredulously.

"The apples," she said, moving in to smother his face with kisses again.

Her fingers began to unbutton his shirt, helping him shirk out of it, then his pants. He was already hard when her hand slipped down the smooth slide of his taut belly, taking his hardening flesh in her hand, sending a shock through his body. He tried to protest as she turned under the weight of her own body, working her nightgown up in the same motion, pressing her back against him.

"No," he protested, his voice edged with desire and concern.

"*Yes*," she said in a tone that was more commanding than his. "*Please.*" The request was laced with vulnerability; he could not refuse. He surrendered with the ease of falling rain. They moved together, their rhythm rippling one to the other, wave upon wave. As her passion peaked, Emma could not help but cry out sharply, swept up as she was in her hunger for him. Elijah tensed for an instant, fearful of such unrestrained exaltation, then surrendered, drawn on by the rush of his own desire, thrusting quickly, a cry emptying from his center like a crack of tension released deep in the earth.

They lay in the heat of their lovemaking without speaking. The weariness of his exile was set aside, commanded to the edge of the room like a nervous dog, disobedient and threatening, yet ignored. They lay curled together unmoving until their breathing fell into syncopation. Elijah began to run his hands over the swollen smoothness of Emma's big belly, amazed at how much larger it had become in his absence. The slow rhythm of hands circling, circling, lulled her. It comforted Elijah, too; at last he was close enough to her not to worry. His hands continued their fluid glide until finally the last vestige of tension seeped away. He dozed.

"What? What is it?" he said, startling awake. Emma was crying.

"Emma, what?" he lamented.

"I . . . didn't," Emma began haltingly, fighting to speak through her sobbing. "I . . . didn't," she began again.

"Shh," Elijah whispered. "Shh."

"I didn't think . . . you wanted me," she cried.

He pressed forward, against her, burying his face in the nest of her hair. He started to speak, to find the words for his shame, when suddenly a sound startled them both rigid.

"Mamma?" a meek voice beseeched. Emma turned and rose on one elbow, laboring but agile, too.

"Toby," she said to her son, *their* son, who was standing at the door of their room.

"Poppa?" the boy said, his voice timid, unsure. Elijah started to rise to turn to find his son, but was knocked flat by the force of Toby's mad rush to envelop him.

"I'm sorry, Poppa. I'm sorry," the boy cried, his grief as shattering a force as his mother's.

"*No. No,*" Elijah scolded softly, confused.

"It was my fault, Poppa. I'm sorry. It was all my fault." He lay across his father's chest, consumed by grief and the burden of responsibility.

It took Elijah and Emma nearly an hour to calm him, to still his crying, to quiet the tension locked in his small body, to bring him back from reflexive spasms, the trailing edge of the storm of tears. Elijah was patient with his son, taking the time it took, like gentling a colt, aware also all the while of the growing lateness of the hour. Finally it was left to Emma to broach the issue.

"No!" Toby demanded. "Don't leave."

"Toby, he must," Emma insisted.

Elijah pulled his son fiercely to him. After a long moment, he spoke the only words that came to him, words he'd said countless times while hiding off in the mountains.

"I'm sorry, Toby. It's not your fault. I'm sorry."

Emma gently, slowly, but steadily, unwrapped Toby's arms from around his father's neck.

"Why are you leaving?" Toby repeated again and again, the departure and absence of his father an impending, unfathomable truth. Elijah could say nothing that provided an acceptable answer to the riddle of the boy's question.

Dressed finally, the night sky beginning to gray, Elijah knelt and gathered his son in his arms and insisted firmly in the tone fathers use to express the finality of the inexplicable.

"This must be our secret," Elijah said, leaning back to hold his son by the shoulders at arm's length, where they could take measure of each other, man to man. "*No one,*" Elijah said emphatically. "You must not tell anyone. This is our secret. The three of us. If you must tell, speak of it only to your mother. No one else. Do you understand?" There was no mistaking the unwavering command in Elijah's voice. The boy nodded solemnly.

"When are you coming back?" Toby asked.

Elijah looked up at Emma for guidance, uncertain what he should say.

"Not long," Emma said. "Not long. But you can't tell anyone. Keeping the secret will make it possible for your father to come back."

The boy turned his head to look at his mother, then turned back to his father. The boy collapsed against him again, grasping him with surprising ferocity.

"You promise to come back?" the boy asked. "You promise?" Elijah squeezed his son, his eyes shut against the burden of words.

"I promise," Elijah said, his voice faltering. "I promise," he repeated with conviction. He released his son and rose. "I promise," he said one last time, leaning in to kiss Emma goodbye. He bent to kiss the top of his son's head. Toby stepped back and offered his small hand instead, like he'd seen grown men do. "I promise, Poppa. I promise not to tell."

— + + + —

Elijah returned again later the next night and left earlier, exchanging promises with his son again, but saying this time it would be a while before he could return. The moon was fattening, bringing more light for a longer stretch of the night. It was too dangerous, Elijah explained, to risk traveling long distances across open ground. His son pleaded with Elijah to take him with him.

"Who would be here to take care of your mother?" he said.

"Miss Garnett," the boy answered without hesitation. The mention of Elsa's name in Emma's company, a topic they had implicitly agreed not to broach, struck Elijah like a kick in the stomach. His eyes darted to the dark silhouette of his wife sitting in the middle of their bed.

"She has been . . . ," Emma began, then paused. "Helpful," she said. "Little things," she went on, reading Elijah's confusion by his silence. "For Toby. And for me."

"She brings us good food," Toby offered excitedly.

"Leftovers, really," Emma said. It was painful enough merely to talk of her, but this admission, of taking food from her, seemed to hold an admission of her culpability to the whole sorrowful episode. "To be sure we don't . . . go without," Emma added as if needing to excuse her acquiescence in accepting it.

Elijah drew a deep breath, a hand coming up to pinch the bridge of his nose in weary contemplation. The pain he'd caused—was causing—was inexcusable. What was there to say?

"No one," Elijah said emphatically, turning to the boy. "You must tell . . .

no one." He was unable to utter Elsa's name.

"No one," Emma said reassuringly. "We won't tell anyone, will we, Toby?" The boy hesitated, then nodded.

"Emma," Elijah said sadly, a question and a plea at once.

"Go," she said. "Go. And when the moon grows shy, come back again. Don't worry. The secret is ours. Just the three of us."

—+ + +—

It was less than a week before Elijah returned again, unable to wait out the dimming of the moon that would help hide him. He came and lay with Emma for a long while, moved by the magic of feeling new life coming to term inside her. After they had sated their desire in the space only two can hold, Elijah woke his son to a jubilant reunion.

"I knew you'd come back," Toby screeched. "I knew it. You promised."

"You promised," Elijah said, carrying him into the bedroom to join him and Emma on their bed. Emma had prepared a small feast in anticipation: deer jerky she'd cured herself, bread she'd made, and apples. Elijah ate hungrily, wanting to savor the nutrient of love laid before him while wanting it to last at the same time.

Elijah returned the next two nights. Each time, Emma had prepared another bundle of food and supplies for him to take away. The second night, she gave him a new wool shirt she'd bought in Bend.

"How . . . ," he began before faltering.

"Mr. English gives me money." Elijah eyed her curiously. Emma explained that the senior English had begun to give her a small stipend to get through her pregnancy, telling her it was not a gift, but a loan, to quiet her protest. After the baby came and she was up and about again, she would work as one of the housekeepers in the big house. Elijah could barely bring himself to take the shirt, but Emma, anticipating this, remained firm, knowing he couldn't refuse her. As he took the shirt from her hands, she realized she had a power she'd never had before. The responsibility for the well-being of the household, a responsibility that she had not sought but had had thrust upon her, gave her a sense of power that she knew she would never likely surrender. It was a refraction of a facet of who she always was, a quality Elijah had not ever seen before but was not surprised by.

Elijah bade them goodbye and slipped away, into the night. Though alert, he had become comfortable with the routine of his nighttime comings and goings. He carried the bundle of foodstuffs and the shirt under one arm as he crossed the distance to the barn. He came around the corner of the barn about to start out across the big field that separated him from the stand of trees where he'd tied Smoke when a flickering of movement in the shadow of the barn caught his eye. He spun defensively, crouching, his free hand sweeping behind him to seize the handle of the knife he carried in its sheath tucked in the small of his back.

"Elijah," a woman's voice called from the darkness. The sound of his name, crossing the lips of the person he feared most, caused him to freeze, his knife half drawn.

"Elijah," Elsa said again as she stepped from the dark shadow of the big barn, her pale face framed by her raven hair, her form muted by the long drapery of the black cape she was wrapped in against the coolness of the hour. In that half second of paramount confusion, Elijah was filled with a flood of thoughts and images too great to sort, an avalanche of impulses. His hand trembled on the handle of his knife.

"I've been so worried," Elsa said, coming forward, closing the distance between them, stopping only when there was the space of but one more step separating them. The wave of her presence rolled over him, the aroma of her exotic eroticism filling him, dulling his alarm.

She moved to close the final step.

"Don't," Elijah commanded, his fingers uncurling from the handle of the knife, his hand coming around in front of him, rising, palm flat to her, blunt in its command.

"Elijah," she said, making his name sound like the soft brush of wind in pine boughs. "You have no idea. The agony."

"I do," he said, the image of Emma and Toby weeping in their grief flooding his mind.

Misreading his intent and meaning—either that or disregarding the warning in his voice—Elsa slowly raised her hand, the mirror of his, and pressed it flush against his palm. The heat of her was searing, like a discharge of lightning. Elijah's hand recoiled reflexively.

"Elijah. What is it?" Elsa said, not understanding. The image of a word he had only recently learned ignited in his mind, jolting him, causing him to take a half step back. It was contrary to everything that surged through him at the moment, charged by the first time he'd ever laid eyes on this woman. *Reticent. Are you always so reticent?*

"Elijah," she said, part question, part plea.

"Please," Elijah countered. "I can't." He could feel the fix of her eyes on his. "I can't. It's too . . . dangerous." They stood with their hands still raised, shadow images of one another. "I can't," Elijah said imploringly. He sensed more than saw her gather her energy like a cat about to move with lethal intensity.

"I *can't*," he said coldly. He took a deep breath. The gulf was too great now to bridge. He stepped back farther. He pivoted suddenly and began to walk away, glancing back every few steps, sure that she would not let him go unmarked. He gathered speed, began to trot, then run. The night was both his enemy and his friend. It was a choice. It was a choice only he could choose.

Elijah stayed away the next night and the night after that. He delayed again the next night, and then again, knowing the anguish he was causing Emma, causing Toby. It couldn't be helped. That Elsa had been in the shadows anticipating his passage unnerved him. How did she know? How? Elijah felt betrayed by Toby, and felt shamed for even the thought of blaming his son. But blame was not even the question. It was much bigger, more imponderable, and recognizing it for what it was terrified him.

How was it possible he still desired this woman?

It couldn't go on. He had to do something. The fourth night he saddled up and rode straightaway to the ranch, tying Smoke to a corral post, making certain this trip was brief.

Emma clung to him, not wanting to hear what Elijah had come to say. He could not come back. Not for a long while, he said. "It is too dangerous."

"When the moon is shy again?" a pleading more than a question, her words ragged with the emotion of loss.

"No," Elijah said coldly. "I can't say when."

"Elijah," she wailed into his chest, fighting to stifle her cries, to remain quiet, not to wake the boy.

"Emma, shh," Elijah whispered, his hands stroking her face and neck to reassure her. "I'll come back. I promise. But not soon."

Emma pulled her face away, her eyes wide with discomfort. "What about Toby? What about your promise to him?" she said accusingly. "He won't understand."

There it was again, the threat of betrayal, that of the son by the father.

"You must tell him it can't be helped. He'll understand," Elijah said.

Emma said nothing, her gaze a stinging rebuttal.

"Soon," Elijah said, offering her a wisp of hope—but one with no foundation. "I promise." He took her face in both his hands and kissed her tenderly.

Emma said nothing more, only looked at Elijah, into the eyes of the only man she knew she'd ever love. He was her life.

"Tell Toby I love him. To be brave. Strong. That I'll be back." Elijah let his hands slide free of Emma's face, drop to his side. It was time to go. He stared at her, her gaze unwavering, her resolve set. He saw her true, a woman of great strength. Of great heart. He closed his eyes, not wanting to witness his own turning away. He turned slowly without saying another word and walked out of the room, out of the cabin, out into the night.

In a Fix

Junkman Willie's place overlooked the desolation of the dump and the clean broad sweep of the Columbia River. Depending on the line of sight and the way the wind blew, it could be viewed as unimaginably squalid—or idyllic. Willie shared the dump's prodigious gifts with a peripatetic flock of seagulls, a garrison of rats, and a squad of fat raccoons that waddled lazily amidst the rubbish with keen noses for eatables and sharp ears for Avenger, Willie's dog, a creature of primitive breeding. Willie didn't care one way or another about the raccoons, but he loathed rats. He hated rats almost as much as people.

Willie and Avenger were absent from the dump when Elijah and Jackie arrived, fresh off the train out of Vancouver. Jackie had climbed in the same boxcar as Elijah at the last moment, just as the freight was preparing to leave the yard. Elijah was too surprised to make sense of the boy's appearance straightaway, but once they were under way, with the long ride ahead of them, he extracted the whole horror-filled story of the night's events. "What happened? Where's your friend? Did he do something to Leo and Lucky?" Elijah had insisted. The boy could barely give voice to what he'd witnessed. The story left Elijah deeply distressed. It wasn't enough that he had had to forfeit all his gear, but he had to accommodate the unshakeable feeling that this all was foreordained. He felt more than anything else a resonant echo from his disturbed sleep the last night in Montana: *you won't be alone.* The two barely said a word to each other after the story was told, riding in silence the greater part of the journey up the Gorge.

Elijah set about busying himself, rummaging through an old battered kitchen cupboard Willie kept adjacent to his fire ring, set squat upon the ground. He was deeply absorbed in the silence of his own ruminations. He found a pot of leftover stew that looked adequate for taking the edge off hunger. He built up a small fire and set the pot to heat. He sat on a wooden box and stared into the fire. A mad man with a penchant for cutting tramps was no idle conjecture anymore.

"Come help yourself to something," Elijah called when the stew was steaming. "Ol' Willie never was much of a cook, but this will fill a hole where you won't complain."

Jackie came over and sat on a short stool and took the bowl Elijah handed him.

"This Willie," Jackie said. "He a friend of yours?"

"You might could say that."

"He won't mind you messing with his stuff? Eating his food?" Jackie asked nervously, toying with his spoon, hesitant to eat.

"I suppose he might. But I doubt he'll harm us," Elijah said, ingesting a big spoonful of the dark concoction.

Jackie sighed deeply, lifting a small taste to his mouth. It was surprisingly delicious. He spooned it with growing relish. The two ate in silence, cleaning the pot to the bottom.

—+—+—+—

Elijah lay stretched out asleep on a bit of ratty canvas on the ground in front of the discarded milk truck Willie called home. Jackie sat watching the sun being swallowed by the Gorge, the remnants of its light cutting streaks of low-lying clouds into ribbons of gold and amber. He was so lost in its bright colors and the darkness of his thoughts that he didn't notice Willie coming up the path from the river until the dog barked. It made him jump as though shot. He spun toward the sound. Even at a distance, Jackie could tell this was no ordinary dog. It was huge, with a wooly coat like some prehistoric beast. Though he couldn't see the eyes in the dark face, he could feel them. They stirred a buzz of electricity along his spine.

"Elijah," Jackie said nervously, standing. "Elijah, you better wake up. Someone's coming."

Elijah lifted his head and looked off in the direction Jackie stood staring.

He pushed himself up on one elbow, rubbing the sleep from his face with his other hand.

"We'll see soon enough how welcome we are. Willie's nothing if not direct." Elijah rose stiffly and raised an arm and called out. "Ho, now."

Willie left the dirt path where it curved back toward the dump and advanced directly up the knoll toward them. He strode forward, stooped beneath a black bag slung over one shoulder. He wore dirty dungarees and an old sweatshirt with "Oregon State" emblazoned in block letters across the front. He kept his head cocked at an odd angle to look up at them. Avenger moved out ahead of him, coming steadily forward, a low but audible growl rolling up from the depths of his breeding.

"Don't make any sudden moves," Elijah said. "Avenger is gonna have to check us out, get the okay from Willie first."

"Friends here," Elijah called out, waving his hand slowly.

"Friends?" Willie barked back. "Ain't got no friends. No use for 'em. They're like fleas. Always working to get close, causing no end in irritation." He climbed the knoll, coming along behind his dog. Avenger slowed as if stalking them, each paw placed deliberately in front of the other. Fifty paces out Willie let the bag slip off his shoulder. He swung it along at his side as he approached. He stopped and straightened where he could take them in fully.

"Friends? Ha!" he said derisively. "Friends in need."

"There any other kind?" Elijah said.

Avenger closed the distance toward them. Willie raised the bag again and started up the last stretch that separated them. As the dog narrowed the distance, his growl took on ominous tones, like the threat of approaching thunder. The closer the dog came, the more slowly he moved.

"They smell bad—I know, boy," Willie said, speaking to the dog. "But they're okay. Go on now. It's okay."

The dog paused to look back at Willie. "Go on, it's okay," Willie repeated. The dog turned to stare at the two standing at the top of the rise. He moved in, still cautious, one deliberate foot at a time. He approached Jackie first. He sniffed him top to bottom, blowing hot breath up into Jackie's face. Satisfied, he moved past the boy to Elijah, repeating his inspection. Jackie noticed a faint quivering in the tip of the dog's tail, barely discernible, but present nonetheless. Slowly, the quivering intensified, breaking into a full sweeping wag as Elijah reached out slowly to rub him behind the ear.

"Hey there," Elijah said, stroking the dog more vigorously. "Remember me, do you?"

"How could he forget," Willie said, coming into camp, dropping his sack on the ground. "You smelled bad the last time you was here, and you ain't had a bath since."

"You're as pleasant as ever," Elijah said, eyeing his old friend.

Willie saw the empty stew pot on the fire and the two dirty bowls sitting on top of the cupboard. He slowly shook his head, whether in amazement or disgust, Jackie couldn't be sure.

"And you," Willie said, turning to the boy. "You must be Jackie."

Jackie blinked hard and turned and quickly eyed Elijah, then turned and stared at Willie, his mouth open, neither breath nor sound passing his lips.

"The two of you come from Vancouver, did ya?" Willie said, stepping between Elijah and Jackie to unlock the big padlock that secured the double doors on the back of the truck.

"News travels fast," Elijah said.

Willie turned and stared hard at Elijah, then at the boy. "Bad news always does. Looks like you're in a fix this time, my friend. No doubt about it."

+ + +

Lucky George, as it happened, had been unbelievably lucky yet again. According to the news story Willie had caught on the little black-and-white TV belonging to the man to whom he redeemed empty bottles and cans, Lucky George was the only one to survive the savage attack on transients near the Vancouver yards. Apparently he'd wandered off to relieve himself before the attacker arrived, but stumbled and fell in the darkness, where he remained the rest of the night. The telecast was replete with footage from the scene. Though not an official suspect, Lucky George was being held for questioning.

The report told how Leo Cartwright and another victim, a white teenage male, had both been stabbed numerous times. The story linked the murders with those of a series of transient deaths throughout the West. Cartwright had nearly been beheaded. Authorities were eager to find and question a youth known as "Jackie" who'd been traveling with one of the victims. There was also an alert for another transient: Elijah McCloud.

"Guess I ought to keep an eye on you fellas," Willie said, laying a small length of wood on the fire, stoking it to give them a little light and a hint of warmth against the cooling flow of air through the Gorge.

"Very funny," Elijah protested. He lay propped on one elbow in front of the fire.

"Well, you can't never be too sure," Willie said. "They say if you lay down with dogs, you gonna get up with fleas." He paused. "Then again, maybe you won't get up at all, you lay down with the wrong dog."

"It ain't funny. Willie, you know me. I go out of my way to leave people be."

"Yeah. I know," Willie conceded earnestly. Then he smiled broadly. "Just the same, can't never be too sure."

Elijah fixed Willie with a withering look. "Damn it to hell. It ain't *even* funny," he cursed.

Jackie sat cross-legged on a scrap of old carpet next to the big dog, Avenger, who had stretched out with his belly to the fire. Jackie rubbed the dog's head absently as he stared into the glowing coals. He pondered the imponderable of the last twenty-four hours. After spilling his tale to Elijah, he'd maintained an almost stoic silence, responding in flat, simple sentences to any queries put to him.

"Sorry, Elijah," Willie offered finally, throwing another stick on the fire, sending a shower of hot sparks skyward to dissolve quickly beneath the dazzle of stars. "I guess I don't get the opportunity to josh much anymore." He stoked the fire again, setting a good little blaze burning. Nobody spoke for a long time.

"Strange how things work out," Elijah said absently. His attention was sidetracked at that instant by the blazing streak of a shooting star roaring across the gulf of sky to the east.

"How's that?" Willie asked.

"What's that?" Elijah said.

"You were saying . . . strange how things work out."

Elijah shot a look at the boy, who gazed into the fire. Elijah let his head fall back again where he could look up into the vast whirl of night sky.

"I wasn't planning on leaving Glacier this year."

"You were gonna winter through?" Willie asked doubtfully.

"Something like that," Elijah said. "Now, here I am . . ." He left the thought hanging in the space between them.

"Better than being in Vancouver last night," Willie joked.

"You gotta wonder," Elijah complained. He rolled over onto his stomach and pushed himself slowly to standing, gathering up the blankets Willie had given him.

"Think I'll turn in," he said, rolling the blankets into a bundle under one arm. "See you all in the morning."

Jackie looked up and eyed Elijah curiously. This stranger, both giving and gruff, was a complete mystery to him. He watched Elijah pause to stare out at the flow of the river, then turn and walk back toward the rising summit of the ridge behind them, dissolving slowly into the shadows of the night.

—+—+—+—

The Southern Pacific hotshot carrying US mail to Salt Lake City rumbled through darkness, its piercing eye of light sweeping at the blackness like a giant scythe. The manifest to carry mail gave it priority on the line. The light swept steadily, side to side, the horn blaring its mournful warning at every grade crossing as the train roared along at seventy miles an hour through the bottom of the Columbia Gorge, rocketing eastward past The Dalles, on toward Pendleton, La Grande, and Baker under the cover of night.

The train carried a crew of three, a string of 148 silver containers stuffed with mail, and an odd mix of empty freight cars being shuttled down the line. Three-quarters of the way down the length of the train in a dented, dirty old Burlington Northern boxcar, curled on a pile of broken-down cardboard boxes, rode an unaccounted bit of extra freight: a lone stowaway, a freeloading tramp. He lay still, as if sleeping. But this was no ordinary tramp, and sleep was far from his mind.

Head resting on a curled arm, the old fedora he'd scavenged carefully laid aside, he lay rocked by the rhythm of the train, lost in his own dark thoughts, arguing with voices that spoke only to him.

Wrong. It was wrong. All wrong.

No, the voice came back to him. *It wasn't wrong. It was you. You fucked it up.*

But the boy. He knows. Nobody was to know.

You didn't listen. When you don't listen, you fuck up.

The form rolled over to face the wall. *Leave me be.* He closed his eyes and let the steady jostling of the train carry him to a thoughtless place, where time and sensation dissolved into a dimness where nothing could reach him.

East of The Dalles, where the train blew past the trestle that crossed over the Columbia from Wishram, a twitch convulsed his body, bringing him back to consciousness.

What? he wondered. *What?*

Close. So close, came the voice.

To what?

He sat up abruptly. His eyes scanned the darkness of the empty boxcar. *Near? Where?*

Very near.

The man rose and went to the open door. The moonless night was awash in starlight, the cold blade of the Columbia flat and dull and wide. He saw the twinkling of lights tucked in the blackness at the base of the dark rise that rose from the river on the opposite shore. This would be Wishram, beneath the headland bluffs at the eastern end of the Gorge, he knew. From here on, the train would be in the high-rolling, arid plateau of eastern Oregon.

Where, he wondered. *Where?*

No voice answered, leaving him to ponder.

A Sense of Trespass

Elijah awoke with first light. He lay snug in his blankets, letting the dawn brighten, watching the dimming of the stars as the darkness in the deepest part of the sky drained slowly away. It had been a night of strange, convoluted dreaming; he was sure of it. Tracings in memory were only thin shards, however, more feelings than images, floating quietly in an eddy of time. This was the worst of the gift of dreaming, to be disturbed by the echo but unable to clearly hear the voice. Elijah pressed the bridge of his nose, trying to coax, to squeeze an image up from the deep into clear focus. Memory of the last morning in Montana filled his mind, the howling of the wind, the roar of Ol' Icy Eye in his ear. A weak smile came to his face. Bear was powerful dream medicine, and he guessed if you couldn't catch the dream and hold it, Bear was likely to show up in this world and scream it in your ear. But what was it Bear wanted to tell him? Go? That hardly seemed significant. And why had the perplexity of dreaming returned, creaky and obscure as it was, now after so many years of lying fallow? He massaged his eyelids, the rough calluses of his weathered fingers probing gently as though feeling for a crevice, a pocket, a recess that would yield a surrendering of dreams. Brief glimpses flashed like fish: a cut of silver light, then gone.

Elijah's eyes popped open like bubbles bursting the surface of a lake. An uncontrollable shiver washed over him, a shiver of fright, of *knowing*. He rose up on one elbow, his eyes searching the dim landscape. It was light enough to distinguish shadow from form, but not clear detail. A thin band of angry gray light pushed back the lid of night along the horizon to the east, the giant cracking of an eye. Elijah sat up and then stilled himself, alert to all senses. He became aware of faint bird sounds, swallows near the base of rock cliff where water seeped from the earth. They were up early, like Elijah. *What?* Elijah wondered of a premonition that seized him. *What?*

He shook his head, sat up. He inspected the space around his blankets as if looking for a sign. Something in the flash of memory from sleep had distressed him, alerted him in the way animals sense trespass in their territory. It was as if something had passed and had left its scent in the echo of dream, something odious and malicious, like a wolverine. Elijah rolled from his blankets and stood. The feeling clung to him like a foul odor. Elijah believed that every animal had its place in the circle of life, but he'd never cared much for wolverine. Pound for pound, wolverine was fiercer than bear; it was a beast not to be trusted. He'd never known wolverine to inhabit anyplace but high country. But here at the mouth of the Gorge, his unease felt like a feral trespass.

Elijah slipped his boots on, fitted his hat, and padded quietly around the periphery of Willie's camp. Nothing seemed out of place, disturbed. Avenger lay motionless next to Willie's jumble of bedding, but followed Elijah's movement with his eyes. He watched as Elijah headed out toward a small promontory overlooking the river.

Elijah squatted and studied the dawn. He rolled a cigarette and stuck it in his mouth without lighting it. He pondered the sense of being on the edge of things, as though approaching a long-sought vista overlooking how things are. Elijah had no feel for the interior landscape he was traversing, though he felt more alive now than he had in months. Through the summer encamped beneath the headwall of Red Crow Mountain, he had had a strange feeling now and again, not of dreaming, but of being dreamed. Since the night of the big wind, all had changed, though he didn't know exactly how. There was an increasing hum that was not quite dream, but almost. It was a disturbing state of mind, alarming: he'd experienced it before, always as a precursor to a critical juncture. There was no rushing it, he knew; it would manifest in its own time.

Elijah rose and lit his cigarette. The light in the east was sharpening. It would be sunrise soon. Without ambition but feeling drawn, Elijah wandered down to roam the piles of trash in the dump. He idly eyed the mounds of refuse, toeing a pile here, cigarette dangling from the corner of his mouth, smoke lifting, causing him to squint; stooping there, flicking away some obscuring piece of refuse to get a better look at something that had caught his eye. A tin plate, dented but otherwise salvageable. He straightened and tucked it under his arm and moved on. He stopped and stooped again: a good length of nylon rope. He coiled and tied it and cast it up under his arm next to the plate. It's amazing what people throw away, he thought, making it possible for others to find utility in their sparse survival. The corner of a tattered photograph called his eye, and he bent and extracted it, wiping the soot and grit from its face on the side of his pant leg. He lifted it for closer inspection. A young woman with dark hair sitting at a picnic table with two children. The woman and the photograph were dated by the way she wore her hair coiled in imitation of a 1950s Hollywood star. The children, a boy of about ten and a girl about eight, sat at a remove from the woman, but close to each other. Brother and sister, Elijah guessed, though not children of the woman. He wondered what had happened to her, how her life had gone. And what of the children? Grown now. Probably had children of their own. The picture was strangely haunting. He didn't know what to do with it. He didn't want to keep it, but it felt disrespectful to simply toss it away. He tucked it gently into the chest pocket of his jacket and carefully snapped the closure. It was a gesture not of thoughtfulness but of expediency. Out of sight, out of mind.

+ + +

Standing in front of Willie and the boy, Elijah upended a tattered but serviceable burlap bag scoured from the dump and poured its contents on the ground. The pile spilled in a clattering torrent of small treasures. Elijah knelt and raked his fingers through them, spreading them for inspection. He leaned back on his haunches and smiled.

In addition to the tin plate and length of yellow nylon rope, there were two leather belts; three candles; a large sheet of clear plastic; four disposable lighters; a Clorox bottle with a metal cap—perfect for carrying drinking water; a pair of denim work pants—long in the leg but the proper fit in the waist; a pot and skillet that both needed scrubbing; a cup and fork and two spoons; a hand towel; and two bars of Ivory soap still in their wrappers. Willie eyed the collection of goods like a bemused shopkeeper. He bent and picked up the fork and eyed it closely. It was good silver, an heirloom piece with the craftsman's stamp "Oneida" on its shank.

"Damn," Willie offered, his eyes sparkling with delight. "Don't imagine this ever found its way to a beanie weenie." He turned it reverently, as though taking in the facets of a finely jeweled stone.

"Run out of grub, I could always hawk it," Elijah said, impressed at his good fortune.

"People's amazing," Willie said, picking up the soap in its wrapper. "One time I found two dozen dress shirts, all neatly folded, starched, still in plastic from the cleaners. Somebody just grew tired of 'em, I guess. Wrong color. Wrong style. Wrong husband. Who knows. You'd think they'd at least take 'em to Goodwill." Willie dropped the soap, shaking his head in amazement. "You'd be surprised. You truly would. What people toss out. As if it all just grows on trees. I've found stuff that ain't even got a name. But it must have been worth something. Somewhere . . . to somebody."

"Bet you never found any money," Jackie challenged.

"Money? Are you kidding?" Willie snorted. "I found twelve hundred dollars once. Found two hundred fifty another time. Money's nothing. I mean, jewelry, watches, rings, false teeth, an artificial leg. A doctors' bag full of expensive stuff. Guns, swords, an old iron helmet, what you see them Spanish explorers wearing. I think I still got that thing around here somewhere," Willie said, pondering on it. "Might have traded it, though. Fella in town that runs the bar. He's good for a drink, sometimes a bottle in trade. I've given him more worthless crap than you can imagine. Don't know what he does with it."

"Probably packs it away in the back of some old milk truck up on blocks behind the bar," Elijah said, gathering up the goods and putting them back in the burlap bag. "Hope you don't mind me siphoning off a little of your booty, Willie."

"Hell, help yourself. Not that I ain't particular. Don't let just anybody wander in here. But you and me? We go back a ways. You ain't never held back all the time I've knowed you. Never held back from anyone, by God. And that's the truth."

Elijah put everything back in the sack except the ceramic mug he'd rescued. He poured water from a jug near the fire. He scooped up a small handful of dirt and dropped it in, scouring the cup with the muddy mixture. He rinsed it thoroughly, then filled it with coffee from Willie's blackened pot. He sat back and took a slow sip, delighted with his morning's effort.

Jackie stared in astonishment. "I'm not believing you just did that. That's like, *totally gross.*"

Elijah smiled, took another sip, savoring his first cup of coffee of the day.

—+—+—+—

Jackie spent the morning close to camp. Neither Elijah nor Willie paid him much attention. They were both silent, content to pass the time in each other's company without conversation. Didn't invite or welcome any conversation from Jackie, either. The boy didn't know quite what to make of it, wondering perhaps if he had somehow caused offense. He'd been solicitous at first, wanting to be useful, but then stayed quiet and out of the way, just watching. Toward midday, he began pestering Willie again, asking if there was anything he could do to "help out."

Willie snapped cantankerously at him. "Take a stroll, why don't ya. I'd be grateful for it." Elijah lifted his eyes to measure the boy's reaction. He watched the boy turn and march toward the edge of the bluff on the trail down to the river. Elijah wondered what the boy's story was. Though his clothes were filthy from riding freight trains, they were nearly new. The leather jacket he wore must have cost somebody a piece of change. The Giants cap he wore wasn't a cheap Japanese knockoff. It was wool felt, fitted and well made. He watched Jackie disappear over the lip of the bluff, then leaned in and poured himself another cup of coffee.

Jackie came down through the cut to the mainline. He stood in the middle of the tracks, pondering what lay to the east, then west, then straight out across the Columbia. From the height of land of Willie's camp, the river appeared flat and tranquil, but down close at eye level, it moved along with visible force, dipping and spilling and rising and cresting like a living thing. Its motion was hypnotic. Without thought, he turned toward the west and began walking. He fell naturally into a striding pattern that matched the lay of railroad ties.

He walked. And he kept walking, mindlessly, eyes locked on the ground in front of him, watching the blur of ties underfoot.

After a while he stopped, looked up, shocked, not knowing where he was. He scanned the track ahead. He turned and scanned the distance he had come. He saw nothing remotely familiar. He had no idea how far he'd walked.

Panic shot through him. He turned and started running back up the tracks the way he'd come. Rounding the first big bend, he saw the trestle crossing the river at Wishram. He stopped abruptly, doubling over to catch his breath. He licked his lips, lifted his head, and looked around. He felt oddly embarrassed, as though being observed.

"Fuck you," he muttered disconsolately, an oath of condemnation of the whole world in general. He started off again, falling into a swagger, as though challenging anyone with a contrary opinion.

—+—+—+—

Elijah and Willie both lay in the narrow shade of the milk truck under the stillness of high noon, dozing in the dry, languid heat. Avenger raised his head, his ears cocked forward, all his senses keen when the boy came clomping noisily up the path. Avenger's ears twitched; his nose quivered, lifted to pick up stray scents and premonitions of trespass. Recognizing Jackie, he dropped his muzzle back into the cradle of his forelegs and sighed, the alert tension in his body ebbing in one fluid breath.

Jackie came up and circled the fire ring. He toed the ashes, cast a sidelong look at the two men stretched out on their blankets. They were dead to the world, or well practiced in the art of playing possum. He scanned the confines of the camp, aimlessly looking for something to catch and hold his interest. He stepped over to a metal milk crate and sat down noisily. He picked up a piece of pine kindling from a broken crate, and fished his pocketknife out of his pants and began idly whittling. The tender wood peeled off in quick curls. He began to whistle softly. As his whittling grew more animated, his whistling rose in volume, too, until he was peeling long strips of wood that crackled and popped free under the vigor of his knife, whistling cheerily as he worked. Willie rolled over to see what the disturbance was, grimaced, and rolled back over, shifting fitfully on the ground, grunting his displeasure. Jackie stopped whittling, his whistling silenced like that of a kettle lifted suddenly from a fire.

The cry of a locomotive floated up through the stillness of the day. Jackie cocked his head to fix its direction. It came again, from the east. He stood and ambled over to the height of land where the bluff fell away toward the river. In the distance, beyond Wishram, he spotted the string of green-and-white Burlington Northern locomotives pulling a long freight on its slow approach to the yard. The lead end disappeared beneath the lip of the bluff, but the length of it came on, car by car in a slow processional. Jackie heard the short note on the locomotive horn and began running along the top of the bluff, out through dry brush and weeds, drawn by the arrival of the train.

Jackie stopped on a short promontory overlooking the little settlement of Wishram. He leaned against a rock in the shade of an overhang, his attention fixed on the train in the center of the yard. He watched as a brakeman on the ground directed a dance of motion, signaling the engineer to pull forward then back, uncoupling and shunting a string of cars, then hooking up again with the rest of the train. The brakeman walked with casual non-chalance back to the stairs on the lead locomotive and swung up, confident in the economy of effort he made. The engineer blew a departing note on the horn and pulled forward, gathering speed as the train pulled down beneath the bluff where Jackie stood, heading out on its appointed schedule.

The Wishram yard stood silent again. The arrival and subsequent departure of the train seemed to deepen the stillness. From above, the yard appeared flat, dimensionless. The spirit of the scene filled Jackie with despair.

It seemed like ages ago he'd turned thirteen, though it was less than two months. He'd once looked forward to it with such eagerness, he thought it would never happen. Now it didn't seem to matter. Life seemed measured in the drift of epochs: life before—and after—Terry's death; before and after his parents' divorce. They were less drifts than cataclysms, like earthquakes rendering sudden, catastrophic change.

Terry had been three years older than Jackie. He was not merely his older brother, but his *big* brother. Jackie looked up to him, and Terry looked out for him, tolerating if not welcoming him to hang out with him and his friends. Terry was bright but bored by school. His freshman year in high school, he'd started running with a group that was often in trouble for truancy or loitering or some nuisance that upset others. He was grounded several times for coming home drunk or high. First it was alcohol. Then pot. Then pills. Terry's interest in school, already wavering, plummeted.

The relationship between Terry and his dad had never been easy, but with his escalating delinquency, tension between them erupted into volatile clashes. In an exchange of bitter accusation and counter-insult the previous fall, Jackie's father had struck blindly with rage, backhanding Terry across the face. More surprising, Terry gave back as good as he got. It took Jackie's mother and Jackie both physically interceding to break them apart. Jackie's mother was furious with both of them, but appalled by her husband's behavior. The breach rent the passive accommodation between Jackie's parents. Within six weeks, the two had separated. Attempts at reconciliation ended always where dissolution had begun, in rancorous disputes over how to discipline Terry. Jackie's father felt vindicated when Terry took his Saab 900 from in front of his apartment and totaled it while driving drunk. His righteous indignation was only briefly savored. A week later, Terry's body was found in a cheap boardinghouse on the Flats of Oakland. He'd died of an overdose of cocaine and alcohol and pills.

Three months later his parents' divorce was finalized. In six months, his father moved to Seattle. In seven months, one week before the end of the school term, Jackie's mother broke it to Jackie: "it was best," she and his father had decided, that Jackie go and live with his dad. Best for whom? Jackie demanded. Nothing his mother could say assuaged his feelings of being abandoned in the obliterating wreckage of the family. Things just happened: no plan, no consideration, no place of refuge. Jackie surrendered like a prisoner against his will, swearing an oath of silence and hatred of both his parents.

If Terry's death sucked the oxygen from Jackie's life, it served only as prelude of what was to follow. Just about when Jackie thought life couldn't get much worse, it surprised him. It did.

Katherine Lemay was disarmingly gracious and down to earth for someone as beautiful and privileged as she was. Her father had been a prominent Seattle attorney. She'd gone to the best private schools, from Lakeside Day School in Seattle to Stanford University. At graduation from Stanford, her father gave her a piece of land on the Snoqualmie River east of the city, and built her a house that looked up the valley with fabulous views of the distant Cascade Range. She worked in a small firm as a foreign investment adviser to companies seeking joint ventures in Asia-Pacific markets. And she indulged her love of horses. What she saw in his father, Jackie never could fathom. But she was a vast improvement over the first two women his father had introduced him to that summer. And she endeared herself to Jackie in extending an open invitation to come out to the valley to ride whenever he wanted.

Stardancer, a beautiful chestnut mare Katherine affectionately called Star, was a gentle, good-natured three-year-old with long legs and a full chest. Star was gentle and playful and endlessly curious whenever Jackie entered the paddock. Star would approach and sniff him top to bottom, looking for the apple Katherine had given him to bring as an offering of friendship the first time they met. Jackie had never been around animals before. But the two took easily to each other.

Jackie started looking forward to accompanying his father to the ranch those weekends when he didn't have to work, when Katherine wasn't traveling. Star had been mated with an Arabian quarter horse toward the end of summer. Katherine had Jackie riding a roan gelding since Star's pregnancy had been confirmed, though Jackie still spent most of his time in a small pasture with Stardancer, brushing and currying her, stroking her haunches and neck, talking quietly, sharing intimacies and commentaries on the fate of being a lonely, displaced thirteen-year-old.

Early-October, Ed Logan, Jackie's dad, and Jackie went out to Katherine's for the weekend. Jackie much preferred the open space of the Snoqualmie River Valley to Queen Anne Hill, one of the older, more posh Seattle neighborhoods, where his father lived. Late the first afternoon, when Katherine came down to the stable to ask Jackie if he wanted to ride into the city to Pike Place Fish Market on the Seattle waterfront to shop for dinner, Jackie declined. His father wandered in and tried to insist on his going, but Katherine pleaded his case, and the two left without him, leaving him to be alone in the stables with Stardancer.

The urge to ride Star rose up and nagged at him from the moment Katherine's silver BMW slid out of the drive onto Snoqualmie Valley Road. It would be a good two hours before they returned. Jackie knew he couldn't take her out of the enclosed paddock, that he couldn't run her hard, but a little walkabout seemed sufficiently restrained. What harm could there be in that? The exercise would do her good.

"You're up to it, aren't you, girl," he cooed. "If you didn't want to, I wouldn't do it. What do you say?"

Star raised her head and shook her mane. She stomped her foot.

"Thatta girl," Jackie whispered, stroking her withers. "That's a good girl."

Jackie crawled through the barbed wire and went down to the tack room to get a bridle. With so little time and her being pregnant besides, he figured he wouldn't bother with a saddle. He'd ridden her bareback once before, and loved the sensation of the powerfully muscled creature beneath him.

"Just a short ride," he said, slipping the bridle on. Alive with nervous energy, he guided her over to a wooden corral fence where he could climb up and slip onto her back. Gently, he prodded her forward with his heels, gripping the reins in one hand, a hunk of mane in the other.

For all her latent power, Star ambled like an aging swayback. Jackie sat high atop her, swept up by the simple joy of being aback her again. With little prodding, Star broke into a lazy trot, circling the small pasture.

On the fifth pass along the fence line that ran up to River Road, Jackie prompted Star to canter. Just as he heeled his shoes into her belly, the big horse passed a patch of thistle, jumping a jackrabbit that darted almost directly underfoot. The sudden movement spooked Star, causing her to jump sideways, then explode into a furious run. Jackie was nearly dismounted. He dropped the reins and caught her mane with both hands, gripping her sides fiercely with his legs.

Star was given over completely to fear. She ran hard, straight toward the road. Too late, the horse spied the barbed-wire fencing and tried to turn, pressing forward with a sweeping, lashing, twisting motion that sent Jackie over her neck, over the wire fence, into the weeds at the side of the road.

For a long moment, Jackie lay where he'd landed, struggling for breath. He stared at a wisp of white cloud overhead, fearful he was dying, the wind knocked out of him. He gasped finally, and rolled onto his side and lifted his head. That was when he saw Stardancer limping slowly, moving away from him inside the fence line.

"You all right?" a man demanded, appearing as if out of nowhere, kneeling beside him in the weeds. The man was older, deeply tanned, with wrinkled creases etching his face. "Jesus but you took a terrible fall. You okay?"

Jackie struggled but couldn't speak. The man helped him up.

"You all right? You break anything?"

"I don't think so," Jackie responded weakly.

"Well, you're one lucky cowboy. Looks like you fared a whole lot better than Miss Lemay's mare."

Jackie stared at the man, then followed the man's gaze. Stardancer had turned toward them and was standing motionless. Her eyes were glazed, wild with fear, her breath coming in ragged bursts. Her chest was torn open, with deep lacerations that streamed slick, wet blood that coated her chest, right shoulder, and forelegs.

"Oh shit," Jackie cried.

The man grabbed him to keep him from scrambling through the fence. "I wouldn't go in there, son. No telling what that horse'll do."

"We gotta help her," Jackie wailed, struggling to get free.

"Hold on now. She's pretty tore up. We better have Miss Lemay get a vet up here fast."

Jackie turned and stared at the man as if seeing him for the first time. Miss Lemay—Katherine. His father. He turned and eyed Star again. "Oh God," Jackie moaned pitifully. "I didn't mean to. I swear," he said pleadingly, turning to the man again.

—+ +—

Jackie sat in the back of a King's County Sheriff's car at the side of the road. He was numb with guilt and remorse. Besides two sheriff's cars, there was a fire truck and an emergency rescue unit. Someone had put a bucket of water inside the fence, hoping to entice Star to approach. She remained where she stood, motionless, unmoving, breathing hard, bleeding heavily from her wounds.

"The vet better get here pretty quick," someone said. "Or we'll be putting that animal down for sure."

Jackie's eyes closed leadenly. He imagined the shock and horror that would seize Katherine and his father when they drove up, seeing the cluster of vehicles, catching sight of Star.

"Boy said she's pregnant," the old man said.

"What the hell? What was he doing riding her?" a deputy muttered angrily.

"Here's the vet now," the old man said. "Hope it ain't too late."

The knot of people at the fence line moved down toward where the vet parked his truck. Jackie stared vacantly. He felt on the verge of exploding.

"That horse needs a shot, all right," one of the men said, "but not from anything the doc's got in his bag. She oughta be put down."

Time seemed to stop. Jackie squeezed his eyes tightly as though trying to obliterate the truth of what he'd done. Without thinking, he opened his eyes as he slid across the backseat of the patrol car and fumbled for the door handle. He let himself out. The group of men stood fifty feet distant, gathered around the vet, talking in an overlay of voices, fingers pointing at the horse standing in the middle of the corral. Like a hunted fugitive, Jackie darted quickly across the road, into the trees that grew where the land began to climb out of the valley. He scrambled through the brush, his legs churning. He had no idea where he was going.

Away. Away. Simply *away.*

FRANK O SMITH

California Man

The distant wail of another freight broke Jackie's reverie atop the bluff above the Columbia at Junkman Willie's. He scanned the run of track to the east, the direction from which the first train had come. Nothing. As he started to turn to look west into the Gorge, he saw the train crawling slowly through the ironwork of the trestle. It was a Burlington Northern freight up from the south, snaking its way across the Columbia. Jackie raised a hand to shield the sun's glare. A steady breeze midchannel dappled the face of the river, fracturing it into a million facets of light. The train was a rumbling dark form against the harsh brilliance. It broached the landing and began an eastward curve toward the Wishram yard.

It pulled down deep into the yard, and then once again, a brakeman and engineer executed a well-practiced dance: uncoupling, shunting cars, recoupling again. The shunted string included six boxcars, three hoppers, two tankers, and a crummy. The brakeman swung up on the ladder of the lead locomotive as the train began to slink heavily out of the yard, the lightening of its load imperceptible in the sluggish gathering of speed, heading eastbound out into the dry, upland rolling plains toward Pasco.

Jackie wound his way down the face of the bluff, picking his way by a circuitous trail that brought him along the edge of the tiny hamlet. He wandered down a deserted side street past a half dozen small clapboard houses, obviously lived in, judging by the clutter of scattered toys and bikes and old tires, yet mute and still. The heavy smell of diesel fuel and old oil saturated the dry, heated air as he passed from the shade of the tree-lined street into the open glare of the deserted yard. He paused, cautious about entering. He eyed the object of his curiosity: the battered old caboose, what he'd learned train people called a crummy. He crossed the first set of tracks, entering the workings of the yard proper on a beeline for the caboose.

He climbed the steps to the rear platform of the squat little structure and turned the door handle. Surprised to find it unlocked, he glanced nervously over his shoulder, then quickly slipped inside.

For all his expectations, the interior was Spartan, stripped to essentials. It was barely more than a box. In one corner stood a potbellied stove. A water cooler was secured to a length of wall. The only partitioned space was a bathroom no bigger than a closet with a toilet that emptied directly onto the gravel roadbed beneath the train.

"*Nasty,*" Jackie exclaimed, peering down through the straight drop, seeing gravel and ties below. *No wonder they call it a crummy,* he thought in disgust.

Jackie's attention was drawn to the ladder that ascended the sidewall to the small turret midsection. He walked over and paused, listening closely again. Assured he was alone, he climbed the ladder to the observation cupola. He flounced down onto one of the long, leather-cushioned bench seats.

It felt grand, noble even, imagining himself riding high, casting a seasoned eye on a world displayed as if on a stage. He drew a deep breath and settled back into the cushions. His eyes fluttered heavily. His breath rose and fell. It felt luxurious to be comfortably seated, the languid heat of the day lulling his senses. He sighed. His eyelids narrowed into slits, then closed. He let his head drop toward, slipping sideways where one shoulder came to rest against the turret window. He wiggled down to curl on the bench seat. He slept.

Jackie lay oblivious to the frenetic droning of two black wasps that rose to tap a maddening cadence on the window glass over his head as if trying to escape; oblivious too, to the crunch of footfall on gravel outside, beyond the enclosure of the caboose.

The sound of boots clunking up the steps to the rear platform caused him to stir. He squirmed to find a more comfortable position. The door to the caboose sprang open and slammed shut, startling Jackie awake. He bolted upright, saw the wasps in the same instant, and nearly gasped out loud. Footsteps echoed in the vacuous interior of the crummy. He pushed himself hard to the back of the cushion, pulling his legs in, squeezing himself into an imagined invisible space. The pungent bite of cigar smoke filled the air.

Jackie heard the faint rhythmic splash of a fine spray of water. The sound abruptly stopped. Jackie's face contorted, picturing the scene, the stream of yellow urine raining down through the tight hole in the small enclosure at the far end of the car, puddling briefly in the gravel, then disappearing. Echoing footfalls again. The smell of cigar smoke grew stronger, seemingly increasing the annoyance of the wasps at the window. One wasp backed away from the glass and hovered over Jackie's head like a menacing gunship, rotating first one way, then another. It ascended, then suddenly dropped as if sensing an invader, turning to face Jackie directly, threatening attack. Jackie gasped and swatted nervously to drive it away.

"Who's that?" a gruff voice commanded.

Jackie froze.

Footsteps drew up at the bottom of the cupola. "Who the *hell's* up there?" the voice demanded. Jackie squirmed madly, trying to retreat from the more pressing threat of the wasp. He cried out, swatting wildly at the wasp.

"Jesus," the man exclaimed. "What the hell are you doing up there?" The man seemed as startled as Jackie by the unexpected turn of events. Jackie still sought to remain out of sight.

"Come on now. Come down out of there," the man said impatiently. "I'm not kidding. Get on down."

Jackie leaned forward to gaze into the puffy face of a balding, middle-aged man, his face reddening as he chomped furiously on the stub of a cigar.

"My God. You ain't nothing but a boy," the man exclaimed. The two stared at each other in disbelief.

"Come on, come on," the man said, waving an arm in a rotary manner as though winding Jackie in. "Get on down here. Now!"

Jackie eyed the wasps that had collected in the far corner of the turret.

"Damn it, boy, I ain't got all day. I said *get down.*"

"Okay, okay," Jackie said peevishly. "Jesus. I'm not doing anything," he complained, sliding forward to turn and start down the ladder.

"You ain't done nothing, why you look so damn guilty?" the man asked, backing away to make space for Jackie as he descended.

"I didn't do nothing," Jackie retorted defensively.

"Then what are you doing in here?" the man said, eyeing Jackie fully as he turned to face him.

"What are *you* doing in here?" Jackie replied defiantly.

"Don't sass me, boy. You could be in a heap of trouble. This here's railroad property."

"Yeah?" Jackie said testily. "This *your* railroad?"

"Watch your mouth, boy. I'm forty-two years with the Burlington Northern. I might be retired, but I still keep an eye out on the yard. And you're trespassing."

"I'm not doing nothing wrong."

"Maybe. Maybe not. But you sure ain't supposed to be playing inside this here crummy." The man rolled the cigar from one side of his mouth to the other, then back again, considering Jackie.

"Why ain't you in school?" he said finally, cocking his head as if puzzling an imponderable. "You ain't from around here," he stammered, offering a complete summation of his assessment of the situation.

Jackie stood mute.

"Answer me, boy. Where you from?"

"I'm visiting."

"Who you visiting?" the big man said, cocking his head in the other direction.

"My aunt?"

"What's her name?"

"Shirley."

"Shirley what?"

"Aunt Shirley."

The man stared fiercely at Jackie. "Say, you that boy from down in Vancouver?" He chewed on the stem of his cigar. "Mixed up in them killings?" The man pulled the cigar from his mouth, pulling himself erect, puffing himself large with all the authority of forty-two years with the railroad.

Jackie feigned confusion at the association, stalling for time. He considered his options. He was in a fix and he knew it. He thought better of trying to bluff his way out of this one. He bolted for the door.

"Hey!" the man shouted.

Jackie was out the door and jumped clean of the steps in a dash for freedom. He came down wrong and bent the ankle he'd hurt before. He yelped and went down, rolling into the fall to lessen the weight on his ankle. He saw the man come out on the landing at the end of the crummy and stare at him, then start down the steps to the ground. Jackie clamored up and began hobbling away as fast as his legs would carry him.

"You come back here, you little shit. I'm warning you," the fat man yelled after him. "You're in a heap of trouble. Don't go making it worse. Come back now. You hear?!"

—|—|—|—

"Shit," Bud Keaton roared. "Why the hell wasn't I notified—*immediately*!?"

The two deputy sheriffs eyed each other and then turned to Rowland Tidwell, who stood with his hands stuffed in his coat pockets, rolling an unlit cigar from one side of his mouth to the other. Rowland had been the one who'd encountered the boy and notified the sheriff's department, and because of it, considered himself something of a celebrity in the only drama to come to Wishram since the Beanery closed.

"Look at it this way," one of the deputies finally offered, a bit defensive. "You could consider it lucky you were called. We never know what's going on with the railroad since you all pulled outta here."

Keaton went rigid, his jaw muscles popping like they were doing push-ups. He stared the man down, forcing him to look away.

"We've been in touch with every sheriff's department whose jurisdiction touches these tracks. You knew—or should have known. *Jesus*," he spat. "What's it take to get a break on this?" He snapped a glance at his wrist-watch. It was twenty minutes to eleven. It had taken him slightly over an hour to make the hundred-mile drive from Portland. The boy had been seen around four. Four and a half hours for someone to think of making a phone call. "The damn kid could've *walked* to California by now," Keaton steamed.

"I really rather doubt that," the other deputy said earnestly.

Keaton sucked his breath to hold back the impulse to abuse the man. "I was being *facetious*," he whispered harshly. He spun and walked in a tight circle, nursing a slow simmering rage. "Anybody see where he went?"

"I got a bad leg," Tidwell, the heavyset man, offered. "I seen him run off into them houses back there," he said, pointing toward the middle of the village. "Didn't see after that. But it was him all right. As soon as I guessed it, he was gone. I mean, *pronto*."

"Any *idea* where he went? Anybody in the vicinity who might take him in? Any jungles nearby?" Keaton rambled, fishing for anything to go on.

The two deputies conferred with one another with a glance, shaking their heads.

"Yeah. Well, there might be," Tidwell suggested. "I don't know for certain, you understand. But possibly."

"Possibly *what*?" Keaton pleaded vehemently.

"There's an old fella lives downriver. Down at the dump. Tramps call him Junkman Willie. But I don't know," Tidwell said, reconsidering. "He's not much for company."

"Anybody bother to check?" Keaton asked, the irritation rising in his tone again.

"No sir," the younger of the two deputies offered timidly.

"Would you *mind* checking?"

"Like I say," Tidwell interjected with self-importance, "the old man don't take to strangers. I wouldn't think you'd find the boy there."

"I didn't ask for an opinion or a personality assessment. I just want it checked out," Keaton said. "If you *don't mind.*"

"Not a problem," the younger deputy said eagerly, glad to have something constructive to do. He turned and marched crisply over to one of the two Klickitat County Sheriff patrol cars. He removed his cowboy hat and settled in behind the wheel. He gunned the motor, whipping the car in a reverse circle, then powered gravel and a cloud of dust to all but obscure his retreat.

Keaton shook his head in utter amazement. *Four goddamn hours,* he thought. No telling where the boy was. Elijah neither, for that matter. But if his hunch was right, they were probably together. Or *had been* together. It was hard to imagine Elijah being slowed down for long with a greenhorn.

—+++—

"That's odd," Willie said, tossing another stick of wood on the fire. "Don't usually get anybody nosing around this hour." He studied the height of land above them where a pair of headlights bounced along, coming down the dirt road from the summit toward the dump.

"Looks like they finally put two and two together," Elijah said. "I knew they would, *goddamn it.*" He avoided looking at the boy, who avoided looking at him.

"Stopping for the gate," Willie said. "If you're thinking of getting, this would be a good time. He'll be here in another two, three minutes, once he figures out how that chain works."

"Ah, *shoeshine,*" Elijah spat, taking a last swallow of coffee and tossing what little remained into the fire. It hissed and smoked in the bright coals. He spun around and began gathering up his things. He rolled and cinched his new bedroll with the two leather belts he'd scavenged from the dump.

He eyed Jackie surreptitiously as Jackie tied up the blankets Willie had given him. It distressed Elijah having the unwelcome burden of a traveling partner, especially one so young. But he didn't see any real alternative. He couldn't just *leave* the boy, not after what he'd been through. Elijah checked the cap on his water jug to be sure it was tight and threw it into the burlap sack with the rest of his gear and stood up. He pulled his hat down tight on his head.

"Thanks for the hospitality, Willie. Wish I could stay and chat, but you know how it is. The road calls." Elijah swung the sling of nylon rope attached to his bedroll over his shoulder and picked up the burlap bag. Willie rose to see him off, pulling a nearly full pack of Pall Malls from his coat pocket.

"Here. A little going-away present," he said, extending the pack to Elijah.

"Thank you kindly," Elijah said. "That's mighty white of you."

Jackie was up with his bedroll tied—more or less—with a section of the rope Elijah had salvaged from the dump that morning. He walked over and rubbed Avenger's head. "Bye, big fella," Jackie said sadly. "You take care of yourself. And Willie, too."

Willie laughed to break the tension created by the sudden departure. "Whoever that is in that car better have some good reason for coming in here. Otherwise, Avenger will be caring for me real quick."

Elijah turned without a word and started off down the slope toward the river, away from the fire and the company of his old friend. Jackie's eyes brimmed with tears. He bent and hugged Avenger. He straightened, gave Willie a quick glance, then stared after Elijah fading into blackness.

"You take care of yourself. You be careful," Willie said softly. "You keep by Elijah and you'll do fine."

Jackie stopped and turned back. He tried to speak, but no words came.

"Get along, now," Willie said more firmly. "Git while you can."

Jackie drew a deep breath and turned from the light of the fire. Elijah had dissolved into the night. Jackie stiffened, then started off in Elijah's track at a half trot, raw with the pull to stay, propelled by the desperate need to go.

—┼┼┼—

The night was cold and damp. Elijah sat unmoving in the tall weeds at the edge of the Wishram yard, an unlit Pall Mall caught between his lips. He sat and stared silently, his attention riveted on the occasional movement of a truck or a sheriff's patrol car, the brief opening of a car door illuminating the occupants inside, on shadowy forms patrolling the periphery, consulting in whispers before slipping into darkness again.

Jackie lay slumped in a heap along the top of his bedroll, dozing fitfully. For this, Elijah was grateful. They'd been lying in wait for what seemed half the night. Sleep at least silenced the boy's incessant questioning.

Keaton was a tenacious bastard, Elijah thought, watching the dark outline of the Chevy truck parked in the middle of the yard. He'd recognized Keaton earlier when he'd gotten out of the truck to take a call on the radio in one of the patrol cars. Smart, too, in a way that couldn't be calculated. Elijah had begun to suspect that Keaton was playing the hunch that he and the boy were together, waiting, no doubt, to catch the next train out. They were, Elijah knew, playing the old game of cat and mouse in the rail yard. It always amused Elijah, the lengths to which bulls would go to catch a tramp riding on one of their trains. The existence of old-time tramps was job security for railroad dicks. Without them, bulls were damn near as useless as coal tenders on diesel locomotives. And old-time tramps weren't likely to cave your brains in either. They respected tradition as much as an old railroad man.

Elijah had won Keaton's begrudging respect one dark night several years before in a yard in Everett, Washington. Elijah never did learn how Keaton had let three young punks offloading a freight car of tires get a drop on him. Keaton always packed a .38 Smith and Wesson. Three against one were rough odds, though, and the three were deep into inflicting serious pain on Keaton when Elijah happened along. Elijah was only looking for a ride east across the Cascades to Wenatchee, and normally was quite content to mind his own business. But he didn't like the odds, even with a bull at the receiving end of things. A two-by-four across the shoulders put the drop on two of the punks, but the third had quick reflexes, and hightailed it before Elijah could wind up again. Bleeding profusely from a series of cuts, Keaton was up and after the departing thief and just mad enough to run him down. Elijah should have known better and taken the opportunity to quietly make an exit. Keaton dragged his captive back and summarily arrested all four trespassers—Elijah included—and had them all hauled off to jail. Though he paid Elijah's bail in the morning, once he'd cooled down enough to realize Elijah had saved his life, Elijah had long harbored insult at being handcuffed to one of the young lowlifes. Elijah had to smile, remembering it. Keaton was probably still pissed that he had jumped bail on him before going to court on simple trespass.

Out of the east came the faint cry of a locomotive horn signaling the approach of a train.

"Son of a bitch better hurry up," Elijah muttered.

"Who?" Jackie asked, lifting his head sleepily.

"Damn California Man." Elijah's voice sounded both more spirited and tense at once.

"Who?" Jackie asked again, as though he'd missed something.

"California Man," Elijah said, turning, his white teeth flashing in his dark face, his grin about the only thing Jackie could distinguish in the darkness.

"He a friend of yours?" Jackie asked, still struggling to make sense of Elijah's delight.

"Oh yeah," Elijah said, chuckling. "You could say that."

The cry of the locomotive came again. "Son of a bitch is moving, too. Ought to be," Elijah said, studying the night sky. "Running about as late as I've ever seen it come through here."

Jackie pushed himself into a half-sitting position. "A train?" he said incredulously. "It's a train?"

"What'd you expect? An airplane?"

Elijah's attention was fixed on the two deputies climbing out of one of the patrol cars. Both approached the Chevy pickup. Their breath was clearly visible in the cold air, backlit by a security light forty feet distant. Keaton got out of his truck to stand with them.

The roving beam of the lead locomotive's headlight spun through the dark air like the beacon of a lighthouse. The engineer pulled the freight deep into the yard, well past the trio standing in silhouette. It ground to a slow, rolling halt not forty yards from where Elijah and Jackie lay in hiding. Jackie reached down and slipped the sling on his bedroll over his shoulders.

"Easy does it," Elijah whispered, pushing Jackie lower into the weeds. "All things in due time." His voice was barely audible above the heavy drumming of the big electro-diesel engines that powered the train. "Easy," he said, lowering his own head, shielding his eyes from catching and reflecting the glare of the light with the brim of his hat.

The engineer throttled down the engines and snapped off the big headlight, casting Elijah and Jackie into deep darkness. Elijah cocked his head to watch Keaton climb back into his truck and pull down alongside the head engine of the train. Keaton got out and climbed the ladder to the locomotive cab.

Elijah and Jackie studied the train with nearly a full, unobstructed view down its left flank. Three or four minutes passed. Finally, they spotted the jostle of two flashlight beams coming up the length of the train. As two dark figures approached the head of the train, Elijah could make out that it was a deputy sheriff walking the train with the brakeman. When they reached the lead locomotive, they too climbed the ladder to the cab.

"Must be getting kinda crowded in there," Elijah said, chuckling softly.

"What are they doing?" Jackie asked.

"Who knows. But they better hurry up about it, or we're in deep trouble."

"Why?" Jackie asked nervously.

"Another half hour, we're gonna be about as plain as the day that's fast coming up behind those hills," Elijah said, nodding toward the distant horizon. Jackie noticed for the first time the weak strain of dawn pushing at the lid of night.

A sudden, mounting roar from the engines sent sparks spewing into the dark sky like the effluence of a volcano. The rumbling made the ground tremble. Elijah and Jackie instinctively crouched tighter. The deputy, the brakeman, and Keaton exited the locomotive cab single file and climbed down the ladder. Elijah reached over and pushed Jackie's head deeper into the weave of weeds in front of them, followed almost immediately with the brilliant illumination of the big headlight. A lone blast of the horn split the air, causing Jackie to jerk as if shot.

"Don't spook now," Elijah whispered hoarsely. "Another minute now and we're on to California."

Jackie reset the cap Elijah had knocked sideways when he pushed him down into the weeds, fitting the bill where it shielded his eyes but so he could still peer out from under it to watch the lower portion as the train began to move.

The huge, hulking outline of the locomotive began to creep forward, pulling itself to life as if a rousted beast. Elijah's hand on Jackie's shoulder squeezed firmly, holding the boy steady. Jackie fought the rising fear that the beast inside the train could sense them as it came prowling forward. The noise intensified, increasing the vibration running through the earth. Elijah's hand held firm. Jackie squeezed his eyes tightly closed.

The ground shook as the noise became deafening. Then, all of an instant, Elijah clapped Jackie twice on the shoulder. Jackie lifted his head and saw Elijah easing into a standing crouch, slipping his bedroll over his shoulder. The lead locomotive had pulled past, darkness closing over them once again.

"Come on, come on," Elijah shouted excitedly, grabbing up his burlap bag and his bedroll. He waded through the thistle to the rise of the roadbed.

Jackie was up in an instant, following Elijah's lead. Elijah lumbered up out of the thicket onto the edge of the graveled right-of-way, ascending toward the train like a laden ox straining at a plow. The train built speed. The second locomotive in the string rolled alongside of them, the roar and rumble of the engines all-consuming. Jackie followed Elijah instinctively, knowing he must run but not knowing why.

As the third locomotive came abreast of Elijah, he reached out, grabbed the handrail with his lead hand, and with a sudden surge of power, swung inward and up, landing on the first step. He pitched his burlap sack and his bedroll to the top of the ladder, scrambling up a step, then turned to face Jackie. The train jerked forward, accelerating.

Jackie ran hard, barely keeping even with the train. He reached for the railing, frantic with fright, afraid of being left behind. Elijah caught his hand.

"Now," Elijah shouted. Jackie leaped. Elijah pulled. The boy magically soared free of the pull of Earth. He landed squarely on the bottom step of the ladder.

The two stared at each other, both grinning madly. "We got the Man," Elijah bellowed against the roar of the engines. "The Man gonna carry us home."

*"The White Chief brought me here.
I feel ashamed for my people because they
are poor. I feel like a man in a strange country
without a father."*

—Captain Jack
Modoc Clan Chief
upon arrival at the Klamath Reservation

Dark Talisman

Oregon: The subtle seduction of the sound pulled like a dark tide in Elijah.

The train rolled across the trestle as he settled into the engineer's seat in the third locomotive. He was relieved to be under way again, yet disturbed, too, by a small tick of agitation, not quite pain, that gnawed at him.

The train snaked away from the Columbia into the canyon of the Deschutes River. It rose out of the river mist into the pale light of dawn. The engines lumbered in the growing dawn light, then rounded a shoulder of land, gliding back into dim shadow thrown by the far rim of the canyon. In the shadows, the air was still heavy with cold. Elijah stared down into the fold of the canyon where dark twilight yet ruled. This was the *edge time* when creatures of the night walked side by side with those waiting to take full dominion of the day. Raccoon might still be out while deer would be nursing its night hunger, starting to feed on tender grass that grew sweet and green along the river. Owl dominated the hunt still, lord of the air with soundless wings, moonlight its only enemy. Within the hour, owl, too, would surrender and retreat, giving back the lordship of the sky to the red-tailed hawk, keen eyed and lethal.

These things Elijah knew. He knew them at his core as though inbred. *Oregon: home—and not home.*

─┼─┼─┼─

Elijah had savored time alone as a boy. Even after marrying Emma, there were times he simply had to take leave with little more than a bedroll and his horse, content with whatever came, fair weather or foul. But being forced out, fleeing like a thief after his bloody confrontation with Marshall English, that was another thing. He chafed at the burden of his isolation. And of this guilt, his betrayal and abandonment of Emma and Toby. Other than Uncle, and for a time, his grandmother before she died, he had never had family. He never spent time with cousins who lived on the reservation north of Klamath Lake; they were older and made sport teasing him for his pale eyes. They taunted him that he was not truly Modoc. Living removed up the Sprague River from the main part of the reservation, he grew up sharing his life with the young roan gelding Uncle brought home one day when he was eight. Uncle was the one who taught him the value of patience in training a horse to bridle and saddle, prompting him to be watchful to glean the secrets that he first had to learn from the horse. Elijah became a good student, soon going far afield in the rocky, rambling rangeland surrounding his uncle's place when his horse was ready to ride, spending whole days away before he was ten.

But life hiding out—being hunted—was something else entirely. It was not time alone; it was lonely time. As a boy, he'd made the choice to make something other of his loneliness and had come to find solace in solitude. But he'd made a different choice now, a selfish one that had brought loneliness back into his life. He had desired something and had let his emotions lead him. It was a violation on so many levels, including his most basic rule in working with horses: one could not afford to be governed by emotions when bringing a wild thing to halter. Greater still, he'd violated what had been entrusted to him through the vision he'd received as a boy. He'd let his emotions become untethered and had stumbled over his own wildness. And for what? To know the heat of a dream while fully awake? He'd selfishly risked all for so little. And now he was alone, with neither dreams of this world nor those of sleep to comfort him.

Antelope Creek Ranch was only ten miles away the way the crow flies, but it might as well have been a distant planet. Thought of his old life, held in the small familiar circumference of waking up to the new day and then lying down beside Emma again at night—memory of it tormented him. He missed her with an ache as though part of him had been cut away. Indeed it had. Memory as a prison was unbearable; so too the lacerating question *why*?

Elsa Garnett was attractive, there was no denying that. But Elijah had never given more than cursory notice to other women, and never to a white woman. It wasn't that he didn't have an eye for beauty. But it was more an aesthetic, like his love of strong lines in a horse. With Elsa, it had been something other than simple beauty: it had been an intoxicating, alchemical mix that had loosened his tether.

In his camp far west of the ranch, Elijah kept busy in an effort to keep his mind from grinding the woe of his folly to bitter flour. On one of his early nocturnal forays to the ranch, he'd collected three traps from the barn. He began to supplement the snares he used for catching *tika ka*, what Modoc call quail, with rabbit and muskrat. He stripped willow sapling to make frames for curing furs. *Waste nothing*, Uncle had taught him, not time or money or what the earth gives you. Scraping and stretching the furs was one of the few activities in which Elijah could lose himself for its power to conjure a world when he'd been comforted by the silent presence of his uncle. The old man had been father and mother and patient teacher all in one. Weaving and tying the sinews to the frame, Elijah could almost sense again the guiding touch of Uncle's coarse hands, revealing secrets of how that long-ago time could be rekindled in something as simple as the cinching of a rawhide knot.

For diversion, Elijah began to take Smoke on long rides into the high mountains on late afternoons. He rode bareback, something he hadn't done since he was a boy. The feel of the horse beneath him, the supple motion of the big animal's movement, was exalting, one of the true pleasures to be found in his day. For stretches of time he would lie forward, pressing his chest to the horse's withers, his arms absently stroking its neck, letting Smoke proceed as he willed. Sometimes Smoke would pass into a piece of sunlight falling through the trees, lighting a patch of wild grass, and he would stop to graze. Elijah lay unmoving, breathing in unison with the horse, the sun warming both of them. Smoke would eventually become sated, his curiosity piqued by something in the wind, a sound that Elijah might have missed but would now attune to, keying on the flick and set of the horse's ears: the faint creaking of a blowdown caught and held in the boughs of another tree, or the almost imperceptible weeping of a trifle of water from a rock face.

On occasion they ran across sign of mountain lion. The scent always brought agitation, a snort and rippled flexing of muscles in the big horse as it sidestepped to a primitive fear. Sign of bear, however, always seemed to amuse Smoke; he would sniff the fruity fermentation of scat, then toss his head, shaking it from side to side as if tickled. One afternoon as they meandered their way back toward the lava caves, Elijah managed to catch the flash of a bobcat dissolving in a tangle of alder at stream's edge. It was there—or almost there—then gone, a ghost of movement. As Smoke sauntered on, Elijah pondered the similarity of his life now with that of lynx: secretive, fleeting, ever cautious. As they approached their camp, the whinny of a horse in the trees down below brought Smoke and Elijah up short. In an instant, Elijah was on the ground, his arm wrapped around Smoke's muzzle commanding silence.

Elijah moved where he could see down through the trees and could glimpse a riderless chestnut standing in the middle of the clearing. From the markings, the white blaze and stockings, he recognized it as one from the string at Antelope Creek Ranch. Elijah cursed himself for not having the saddlebags with the Colt. Cautiously, he advanced, easing Smoke forward beside him. More than his knife in its scabbard, which he always carried, Smoke was his only true defense. There wasn't a horse on the ranch that could outrun him.

The glade appeared to be empty, unnerving Elijah even more. He scanned the forest, worried someone was lying in ambush. He moved forward soundlessly. His darkest thought was that Marshall English had finally somehow managed to hunt him down, seeking closure to their feud.

Elijah caught sight of a slight disturbance in the earth, a flickering of darkness. He strained to see, his brow furrowing deeply as he squinted intently to focus better. Had it been his imagination?

No, there it was again: a head rising from the cavern of a hundred hands. Dark hair, jet black, gathered in a braid. Elsa.

Elsa stepped up and out of the cave into the full light of sun, an arm coming up to screen her eyes as she searched the meadow and periphery of forest. Instinctually, Elijah ducked in behind the line of trees. He couldn't help but see the after-image of the lynx dissolving in the alder. He turned quickly to check on Smoke. The horse remained a few steps back as he'd left him. He bobbed his head and blinked, as if curious to know what was up. Elijah brought his hand to his face, pressing its edge to his lips, cautioning Smoke to be silent. Smoke bobbed his head again, then dropped it to nibble at the thin grass at his feet.

Elsa wore black riding pants and a brilliantly white shirt, with a startling shock of scarlet tied at her throat. She gathered the reins of her horse and stepped slowly around the cave, moving to inspect the hoops of fur curing in the sun. Elsa knelt and ran her hand over the velvety touch of rabbit.

She looked up, scanning the tree line again, forcing Elijah to shift back out of view. When he looked again, she had her hands raised, untying the scarf from her neck. She pulled it free, bent slowly, and laced it through the topmost part of the rabbit frame.

She straightened. She turned to the horse and lifted a canteen from the saddle horn and uncapped it and took a long drink. She spilled a bit into the palm of her hand and quickly brought it up to her neck, bathing it with the water. She capped the canteen, strung it over the saddle horn again, and mounted. For the longest time, she just sat as if listening, waiting for the forest to divulge its mystery. Finally, she reined her horse and headed it back toward the far side of the glade, turning in the saddle twice before the horse entered the trees and disappeared.

Elijah was shaking. He'd never imagined she could find her way here again. She was more observant than she'd let on, he realized. More alluring, like the lynx, but more dangerous, too, like the cougar. His senses were afire, his mind calculating a hundred different possibilities of what might have happened had she found him.

He had misjudged her. He had seen only what he had wanted to see, a small fraction of who she was, what she was capable of. When he was absolutely sure she was gone, he rose and moved down into the meadow, crossing to the furs in their frames. He bent and pulled the scarf free. He rolled the soft material under his fingers, surprised at how luxurious it was. He lifted it slowly, holding it under his nose. He closed his eyes and drew deeply of her exotic, erotic aroma. A smoldering heat ignited deep within. *Dangerous.* She was much more dangerous than he'd imagined.

That night, the torment of dreams began again. In the morning he awoke exhausted, as if he hadn't slept at all. Unable to muster any clear memory of images from his dreams, he was, nonetheless, haunted. She was a ghost shadow like the lynx—there and not there.

On the fifth night, he slept soundly. He awoke rested, grateful. He spent the morning being lazy in camp, going down to the creek for a soak in a small pool. That afternoon he rode more keenly alert, senses tuned to the breeze, to the nuance of sounds, to the touch of sunlight and shadow. He and Smoke traveled through the deepening forest to come out high on a rocky overlook. The whole of the distant eastern plain lay before them. The summer haze, however, obscured what he'd come to see: a view of the ranch. They returned midafternoon and Elijah made a day bed for himself on the shadow side of the meadow and lay down to nap. He left Smoke to free graze in the meadow.

He awoke to Smoke's snorting hot breath in his face. He fumbled up out of a deep sleep to stare into the horse's dark eyes.

"What?" he said, irritated. Smoke bobbed his head and shook his mane. Elijah sat up abruptly, his eyes sweeping the glade. He saw movement in the trees. He stood, his heart pounding. A horse and rider. They came forward, weaving their way slowly through the trees. When they emerged on the far side of the meadow, Elijah's worst fears were confirmed. It was Elsa, again on the chestnut mare. She rode slowly straight across the meadow to stand in front of him. Neither spoke for the longest time.

"It's good to see you," she said, smiling. Elijah simply stood and stared. "How are you?"

Elijah shrugged. "Okay." He watched as Elsa rose briefly in the stirrups to swing a leg over as she dismounted. She turned and stood before him, looking intently at him, then cocked her head slightly, first to one side and then the other as if evaluating which offered the sharper focus.

"I'm glad," she finally said. "I've been worried about you."

Elijah said nothing. He focused on his breathing to calm himself. He was aware of Smoke breathing at the nape of his neck. He turned and looked into the eyes of his horse. Smoke looked back, unwavering, his eyes meeting Elijah's fully. Elijah reached up and ran his hand lightly over the horse's muzzle. The feel of the horse, his hot breath under his hand, grounded him firmly. He turned to face Elsa again.

"You seem comfortable riding," he said.

"I've quite taken to it. I ride every day. Uncle Thomas says I'm a natural."

Elijah nodded. "How is he? Mr. English?"

"Fine. You know him," Elsa said with a laugh. "Nothing seems to faze him."

Elijah pursed his lips and squinted to sharpen his focus. "Yes. I know," he said finally. "I don't doubt that he is fine," he said, thinking of his kindness to Emma.

"Have you had lunch?" Elsa asked, stepping back to her saddlebags to unbuckle the flap.

"Of course," Elijah said matter-of-factly. In truth, he'd eaten only lightly when he first got up.

Elsa turned to eye him as she reached into the bag. "Well, I hope you have room for a bit more. A snack perhaps," she said, pulling a bundle from the bag, slipping the canteen from the saddle horn. "Sorry I don't have any tea."

"Never cared for tea."

"Your dining room?" she asked with mock formality.

Elijah didn't catch her meaning at first, then smiled. He turned to inspect the glade. "Over here," he offered, pointing toward a large flat table rock just into the trees.

"Should I tie my horse?" Elsa asked.

Elijah considered it. The mare was one of the sweetest in English's herd. Elijah had brought it to saddle himself three years before. It was the daughter of a skittish dame, one that Elijah had had to "retrain" after Marshall had tried to break it. He stepped forward and lifted his hand for the chestnut to smell. She extended her neck and sniffed, then nibbled his palm with her lips.

"Good girl," Elijah said, moving closer, stroking her along the jaw. He patted her face and turned toward Elsa. "She'll be fine. Smoke will watch after her," he said, moving past Elsa, giving Smoke a pat on the rump. "Be a good boy," he said under his breath, to himself as much as to his horse.

He came up on the flat rock and stepped back, letting Elsa choose where to sit. She put the bundle of food and canteen down and sat. Elijah sat opposite, the bundle between them. Elsa brushed a loose strand of hair out of her face, tucking it behind an ear. He watched as she unfolded the blue-and-white-checked kitchen towel, spreading it like a tablecloth in the narrow space between them, her hand brushing his thigh lightly in the process. She had brought apples, a hunk of sourdough bread, a slab of cheese, and several strips of deer jerky. Elsa gestured for him to help himself. He hesitated, then reached for an apple, it being the handiest. Elsa selected a small piece of jerky. Elijah took a bite of apple as he looked out upon the meadow, wanting to avoid seeing her bring it to her lips. He chewed on the tart apple, staring at nothing in particular.

"It seems I forgot to bring a knife," Elsa said. "For the bread and the cheese. Do you have one?" she asked, selecting another small strip of jerky. Elijah turned to consider her, watched as she pulled loose a strand of the dark meat and raised it. Their eyes met. She smiled briefly as she put the jerky in her mouth, then used her hand to politely shield her lips as she chewed. Elijah reached back and unsheathed the knife in his waistband and brought it forward. He raised his eyebrows, his hands wavering over the bread, an unspoken question. Elsa chewed quickly and swallowed.

"Yes please," she said quietly, her Philadelphia breeding showing. Elijah cut deftly, slicing three pieces, then put the knife down between them, handle turned toward Elsa. He picked up a piece of bread and tore off a corner and popped it in his mouth. Elsa unwrapped the cheesecloth and, picking up Elijah's knife, pressed the edge into the firm white flesh. She glanced up quickly, catching Elijah watching her. She sliced off several slivers, then laid the knife down, the handle turned back to Elijah.

"You should try the cheese," Elsa said, laying a piece on a portion of bread she'd taken. "It's quite delightful."

Elijah fingered a piece and ate it plain. He swallowed almost without tasting it.

"You've been very kind to my family," he said, meeting Elsa's gaze without reserve. "You and your uncle."

"It's nothing really," she said, shaking her head as she prepared another bite of cheese and bread.

"No," Elijah corrected her, causing her to look up again to meet his gaze. "I appreciate what you've done. You didn't have to."

Elsa straightened and drew a breath as if to take in the full enjoyment of the day: a nice outing on horseback, a small picnic in the forest. She looked out into the meadow meditatively. Neither spoke for a long while.

"Emma is a very proud woman," she said finally, not bothering to address Elijah directly. "Not unlike you," she added, turning to eye him. "I'm glad there is something I can offer."

Elijah was discomfited by Elsa commenting on the nature of his wife. It felt like a keen betrayal, almost greater than his violation of her trust, her faith in him.

"I'm not sorry," Elsa said, speaking plainly, the meaning of her words clear. "Not for what we did."

Elijah could not bring himself to look at her. "I am," he said finally. "It was . . . unwise," he said.

"To be human?" she said, her accent on the last word making the sound of it plain and mysterious at once.

"To be . . . selfish," he said, remembering many years ago what his uncle had told him about misusing his gift of *dream singing*. He turned toward her, meeting the challenge of her eyes. Elsa smiled as if mocking Elijah's discomfort. He looked at her quizzically.

"To be selfish is to be human," she said softly.

Elijah reached down and selected the biggest strip of jerky and bit into it, ripping off a section with his teeth. It was all in the open now.

"Your cousin. How is your cousin?" he asked.

She snorted a soft exhalation. "Fool," she said bitterly. "It was reprehensible, inexcusable, what he did to Toby."

"Yes," Elijah said. "It was. But perhaps understandable. At least from his point of view."

"Can we not talk of that?" Elsa said curtly. "I detest the man."

Elijah turned at the stinging vehemence of her words.

"I detest him," she repeated as if to underscore the depth of her feeling. "There was no reason, he had no right . . . to concern himself," she said. She reached out impulsively and placed a hand on Elijah's leg, an emphatic gesture of communion, the two of them against Marshall, the others, the world. Elijah did not move. He could not move. The heat of her hand on his leg flushed through him. When the silence that blossomed between them grew unbearable, Elsa straightened, withdrawing her hand slowly. Elijah realized he'd stopped breathing. He took a deep breath.

"Emma," he stammered nervously. "Is she okay? The baby?"

Elsa composed herself. "She's fine. The baby, too. She thinks it will come any time now. Perhaps with the full moon, she says," she added with a light laugh as if it were the most foolish notion in the world. "She's fine, really," she said, misreading Elijah's questioning look as worry.

"I like her very much," Elsa said. "I can see why you like her. She's very strong. And pretty. And a good mother." To say she liked Emma was disingenuous. True, she begrudgingly admired her, and did, in fact, think she was a good mother. But she was jealous of her, not for being married to Elijah, but for having such a hold on his heart's true affections. In Elsa's world, it was not enough that a man desired her; what she craved was his devotion.

Elijah could barely take Elsa's words of praise for Emma. They bit at his eyes like the sharp sting of smoke.

He rose to break the spell. "I have something for you," he said, reaching into his pocket and extracting the bright silk scarf. He handed it to her, his arm outstretched as though fending her off. Elsa looked at the scarf and smiled.

"I wondered where I had lost that," she said, taking it, letting her fingers run over his ever so slightly. She brought it up close, pressing it under her nose for just an instant. She straightened and looped it around her throat and tied it loosely. "It's one of my favorites. It's a lovely color, don't you think?"

"It's a long ride back," he said. "You probably should be starting. They'll worry if you're not back before sundown."

"I probably should. Would you ride with me a ways?" she said, standing. "Just to keep me company," she added, taking a slight step toward him. Elijah did not respond. They stared at each other, her desire for him plain in her eyes.

"A ways," he said finally, turning to go to the horses. He began saddling Smoke with keen efficiency. Elsa came down to stand by her horse to watch. He bridled him quickly, not lingering like he normally did, causing Smoke to toss his head in complaint.

"Stop," he commanded sharply, forcing the crownpiece over his ears. Smoke started to backstep, to pull away, but Elijah caught the rein ring and tugged hard, bringing his head down. He buckled the strap, then paused, looking into the horse's eyes. The horse stood unflinchingly, staring back, his ears pressed back flat, causing Elijah to suffer a flash of remorse. He raised his hand and stroked Smoke's muzzle. "Sorry," he said softly, causing the horse's ears to stand upright again. The horse dropped his head, nudging Elijah several times in the chest as if to say all was forgiven. Elijah reached down and picked up his saddlebags and cinched them to the back of the saddle. If there was need to run, he could leave everything without regret but the Colt. Elijah set his foot in the stirrup and mounted smoothly, bending to rub the sleekness of the big animal's neck affectionately. "Good boy," he said, causing Smoke's ears to pivot around to the sound of his voice.

"Would you hold these, please?" Elsa asked, handing up her reins. Elijah looked questioningly at her.

"I need to get my things," she said, gesturing with a slight toss of her head back in the direction of the flat rock. Elijah followed her gesture and saw that she hadn't bothered to bring her canteen or the residue of their picnic. He watched her start back for them, then turned and sat forward, looking up at the sky to measure the lateness of the day, concerned Elsa might be missed soon.

Elsa returned and stood beside him, taking a quick swallow from the canteen before offering it up to him. He shook his head, declining. She capped it and hung it from the saddle horn, then took the reins and mounted her horse.

"I left the bread and cheese and things for you," she said, giving her horse a slight kick, starting out ahead of him.

110

Elijah turned and looked back at the bundle on the flat rock. It was tied up neatly in the scarlet silk scarf. A shiver passed through him. He *saw* exactly what Elsa was wanting to do: she wasn't going to let go, she was working to draw him back and bind him to her. The scarf was a dark talisman warning him to beware.

—+—+—+—

Elijah devoted himself the next few days to the routine he had settled into at the lava caves. He tended his traps, fished, and gathered berries in the morning. In the afternoons, he took Smoke for a leisurely ride, all the while keeping an eye out for some spot that might offer better shelter against the winter. At night sitting in front of his small campfire feeding it twigs and small sticks, tending it only enough to keep it burning, more for company than for warmth or light, he watched the moon move toward first quarter. He studied it each successive night as it began to fatten, worrying about Emma and the baby and what was to come. Fall was already beginning to show in the hint of color in some of the trees. He tried to imagine how it might be for all of them, living out the winter here. Like The People once did long ago. It was a fantasy, he knew. The old ways were dependent not on the resourcefulness of one man, but the collective of families that made up a band. The band was the smallest unit of survival. All life revolved around preserving its integrity: eating, sleeping, gathering, hunting—even dreaming. Dreaming was about the fate of the group, never the individual. It was one of the truths Uncle had instilled deeply in him. There was no sense in one, the lone individual, for one could not exist without the group. Even one family was not enough in the before-time. Thought of it made Elijah feel lonelier than ever.

With the crescent moon high overhead at sundown. He made the ride to Antelope Creek Ranch and tied Smoke in the cottonwoods and walked in from there. There was no other choice, he'd decided. He'd go north, somewhere up into Washington, Idaho maybe, somewhere far enough away where he would feel safe to bring his family without the risk of the ranch intruding on them like a shadow. The Yakimas had a reservation in southern Washington, the Blackfeet in southern Idaho. He would go to live not with them, but near them. Find a job on a ranch somewhere. Start over.

It was what he had to do now, he decided. Leave. Now more than ever. Elsa was gaining presence in his thoughts, those thoughts stirring the old torment. *You don't know. The agony,* came the echo of her voice. It had begun to haunt him by day as well as by night. *Reticent. Are you always so reticent?*

When he got to the corral, he hesitated, standing where he could view both the cabin where Emma and Toby slept and the big house beyond. Elijah's bay mare, the one he'd brought to saddle for Emma, found him at the fence line and greeted him with the extension of her neck across the top rail in an attempt to nuzzle him. He reached up and scratched her between the ears, then hugged her neck to him, burying his face in her mane. The animal nodded her head as if caressing him.

He patted the bay and stepped to the end of the corral. He considered the cabin. Emma must be very big now, he thought. His gaze turned to the big house. He wondered if the glass doors out onto the porch would be open. In expectation? Temptation? His eyes swept back to the cabin. He wondered what Toby thought of him now. Was his father a man to be trusted, a man of his word? The bay came down the fence line and stretched her neck over the railing and snorted softly.

"Shh," Elijah whispered, stroking her face. He moved off toward the cabin.

Emma was beside herself with joy at seeing Elijah again. She made him crawl into her bed, hold her, feel her belly. Her joy was short-lived, ended by his telling her he would leave soon to go north to find work, to save enough to send for them.

"How can you leave, Elijah?" Emma whispered desperately. "I will need you. The baby will need you. And Toby. Toby misses you so much."

"Shh," Elijah whispered in reply. "There will be a way. Somehow, there will be a way."

"How can you be sure? How can I be sure I'll ever see you again?"

"I have seen it," he said.

"Where?" she demanded.

"In a dream."

"Tell me," Emma said hoarsely, turning awkwardly to face him, her breath hot on his face. "Tell me what you saw." Her voice was eager, rising with excitement. Elijah did not talk casually about dreaming, Emma knew.

"Shh." Elijah stroked her face, attempting to gentle her like a skittish colt. "Shh," he cautioned, thinking better of following this tack, stabbed by the pain of his deceit.

"Tell me. Tell me what you saw."

"It is not clear yet, Emma. But I know that things will work out. You must be patient."

"Be patient?" she said sharply. "Be patient! How can I be patient? This baby cannot be patient, Elijah. It has its own mind how things will be. It needs a father. I need a husband."

Elijah stroked her face, drawing a deep breath, feeling trapped by the lie but knowing he had to offer something more. He began to weave a story about dreaming of an earthquake, a terrible earthquake that was frightening to all the creatures. No one knew what was going to happen, whether they would live, whether things would be the same, how it would end. But the shaking, he said, was a good thing. It caused everyone to look into their hearts and measure the truth of how they lived in the world, how they treated others. Some resisted what they saw, they were so frightened, but others grew calm even as the tremblings grew. Those who were afraid began to shake and then shatter. But those who opened the door to what they saw in their hearts, to the strength of their beliefs, they began to collect together, gentling the earth.

"Like a horse that is frightened but grows calm under the touch of a soothing hand," he said. Elijah's hands played over Emma's body with the lightness of a soft breeze. He held her and felt her start to quiet, her agitation dissipating slowly. They lay in each other's arms for a long time, the swelling of new life between them, cradled by their bodies, saying nothing, their breathing falling into fluid syncopation.

It was a lie, what he told her, but only because it was a dream that had not occurred yet. It was a dream he knew that Emma needed to hear, a dream that he wanted to believe in. He lay in Emma's embrace, focusing his mind on the image of the earth growing still, shutting out all else but the image and presence of Emma. In that moment, it was enough simply to believe. Elijah began to grow peaceful himself, envisioning the dream.

He awoke with a start, bringing Emma up out of sleep as well.

"What? What is it?" she asked.

Elijah was out of bed, at the window looking at the pattern of stars.

"It's late. I need to go," he said.

"Oh, Elijah," Emma said, suddenly frightened again.

Elijah reached out and touched her face, sat down again on the bed and stroked her. "It's okay, Emma. It's going to be okay."

Emma reached up and pressed her hand over his, pressing it more firmly against her cheek.

"Tell Toby I'll see him soon. I promise . . . ," the word out of his mouth before he could catch it.

113

"Can't you tell him yourself?" she lamented, her words coming to Elijah's ear like an accusation. "Before you go? He's missed you so."

"There's no time," he said. "Already the sky is lightening. The next time I come, I'll tell him myself."

"When? Tomorrow?" she asked eagerly.

"Not tomorrow," he said. "Before I go. Before I leave."

He bent and took Emma in his arms, the immediacy of new life large in his mind. "Don't worry," he said, releasing her. He rose from the bed.

"Be careful," Emma said as Elijah slipped from the bedroom into the darkness of the kitchen. "For the baby," she whispered softly to herself as she heard him go out the door.

+ + +

All the next day, Elijah was distraught over the story he'd told Emma. He could picture all of it in his imagination up to the point in the story where the door to his heart was to open, to release the wellspring of faith that was to pool together into a communal hand that could gentle the earth. It was at this point that thought of Elsa always appeared.

Elsa had entered the story of a dream he'd invented. He found himself fingering the soft, silky fabric of Elsa's scarf in his pocket. It was madness, he knew. He kept seeing her in the image of the dream, her dark hair splayed across the whiteness of her pillow like a dark halo, accentuating the paleness of her features. By sundown, he was in a state of full agitation. He found himself saddling Smoke again, preparing to make the night ride to Antelope Creek Ranch.

Elijah rode directly to the barn again and tied Smoke to the back side of the corral. It was a risk, but a risk he'd decided he was willing to take. It would ensure he didn't stay long.

The cabin and the big house were both dark. Elijah could almost feel the heat of Emma's breath in deep sleep as he crossed in front of the cabin and proceeded across the open yard to the big house. He mounted the porch and crossed the short distance to the doors to Elsa's bedroom. He was surprised to find them closed, but grateful when he tested the latch and found them unlocked. He hesitated, turning to scan the yard, his eye lingering on the dim outline of the cabin at a distance, then pressed the latch and slowly pulled the door ajar, only enough to ease inside. Elijah drew a breath, his back to the door panel as he closed it soundlessly, hidden still by the drape of the lace curtain. He stood listening to the silence of the house. He parted the long curtain and waited for his eyes to adjust to the near darkness of the room. He could hear Elsa's shallow breathing, the short cycle of breath in sleep. He could feel the hard beating of his heart in his chest; he could hear it at his temples just behind his eyes. The room smelled of Elsa, a faint touch of soap and perfume mingled with the singular odor that was hers alone. He stood without moving, his hand still on the handle of the door as if to steady himself, waiting for his heart to quiet. It struck him as being loud enough to wake the whole world.

Elijah stepped soundlessly across the floor to stand at the foot of Elsa's bed. He could see the vague outline of her body beneath the comforter, her dark hair on the pillows. For a moment, the sight of her rose up and overwhelmed him, forcing a hand up to grasp one of the tall corner posts of the bed to steady himself. He waited to regain control of the shaking of the earth beneath his feet, then stepped around to the side of the bed. She moaned in her sleep, spasming lightly, nothing more than a twitch, the response to some turning in a dream, causing Elijah to bite back his breath, frozen in terror, fearful she was about to awake. He waited for her to settle again before taking a breath, her scent arousing the tormenter within. He watched as his hand rose, reached out, extended toward her as if reaching to touch her, bring her awake to announce his presence and the flush of his desire. He stiffened. He backed away from the bed, feeling the bedroom wall come up behind him, both hands falling to his sides. Slowly, he slid down the wall into a crouch, one hand coming up to massage the muscles in his cheeks and jaw and lips, taut with tension.

He rose. He moved forward, toward the bed. He reached into his pocket, then raised his hand over her. His fingers opened slowly. A dark gathering slipped free, floated down onto her shoulder, then slid onto the comforter. Elijah watched as Elsa's arm came free of the cover, her hand settling over the red silk scarf he'd dropped.

Elijah's heart was racing. He started to turn, to cross to the doors again when he heard movement overhead. Was he imagining it? He fought the impulse to bolt in escape. Before he could calculate what to do, he heard footfalls coming down the stairs. His eyes went wide as if to absorb as much light and clarity as possible from the darkness. He heard the sound of feet in the hall coming down toward Elsa's room. He could see the soft light of a lantern seeping under the crack in the door. Elijah moved instinctually, stepping back behind the edge of a large stand-up bureau in the corner of the room. The door opened.

Elijah pressed himself into the narrow shadow cast by the bureau. The light beams from the lantern wavered and danced on the walls of the room. Then they shifted, drawing out different shadows as the angle of the light changed. Elijah heard the dull clunk of the lantern being set down, the ambient light on the walls steadying. A large shadow passed over the wall, then he heard the movement of a body settling heavily onto the bed.

"Elsa?" A man's voice. "Elsa," more insistently, the tone a cross between desire and complaint, urgency and suppression. It was Marshall English.

Elijah's mind flooded with images; confusion, rage, terror. Marshall English?

"Elsa," the younger English coaxed more loudly. There was a rustling of covers.

"What?" she said sleepily. She rose slowly, then gasped. "Marshall! Are you crazy?"

"I couldn't sleep," he said plaintively.

"What?" Elsa said again, her tone a mixture of incredulity and outrage.

"I couldn't sleep," he said again, more assertively. "I thought maybe you'd be up. I just wanted to talk."

"This is crazy," Elsa said, disgust in her voice.

"Since you're up . . ."

"Get out. Out! Get out of my room!"

"Why," he said angrily. There was the sound of movement.

"Don't," Elsa's voice cut harshly. "Don't," she commanded. Elijah tensed.

"Why?" Marshall English demanded seductively. "It was fine with you before."

"I was drunk."

"You wanted it more than I did."

There was more scuffling.

"Don't," Elsa said. "You're hurting me."

"Once more," he demanded. "Just once more."

"Don't," Elsa shrieked, her cry cut off, muffled.

Elijah stepped forward. Marshall lay bent over Elsa, pressing her into the pillows, his mouth fumbling for hers, one hand groping crudely deep beneath the covers.

"Marshall!" Elijah said sharply.

Marshall jerked, rolling away, turning at the report of his name, catching sight of Elijah at the end of the room, slipping off the edge of the bed, landing clumsily on the floor.

For a moment, no one said anything, Elsa and Marshall both staring at the shadowy figure of Elijah.

"You son of a bitch," Marshall said in a hoarse whisper, disbelief writ large in his expression. He stared at Elijah, then turned to stare at Elsa. "You whore. You fucking whore," he said, scrambling to find his footing as he filled with rage. Elijah crossed the distance between them in three quick steps and planted the face of his boot in the middle of Marshall's chest, sending the man crashing into the nightstand, knocking the lantern to the floor where it shattered, bursting into flame. Marshall screamed, flailing in a pool of flames. Elsa shrieked. Elijah turned and ripped the blankets off the bed and threw them on the flames. The room, filled with light one moment, went black.

"Elijah," Elsa called out, shocked, confused.

"What is it?" came a shout from upstairs. The sound of footfalls pounding overhead.

Elijah turned and raced to the doors.

"Elijah," Elsa called again, desperation in her voice.

Elijah sprinted across the big yard toward the barn. He could hear shouting, the banging of doors. He crossed directly through the corral, scattering horses, slipping through the railings on the far side of the big pen. He untied Smoke, agitated and dance stepping.

"Whoa now, whoa," Elijah commanded, trying to slip his boot into the stirrup. The horses in the corral were dashing about, a whirl of motion, crashing into one another, whinnying loudly. Smoke jerked sideways, and Elijah's boot came free. Smoke was beginning to move away. Elijah reached up and grabbed the saddle horn with both hands and pulled forcefully, swinging up in one motion, reaching down and gathering the reins as Smoke broke into a run. Elijah dug his heels hard against the horse's flanks. They broke out of the shadow of the barn on a dead heading due west, the shortest distance to the foothills.

"There," a voice shouted. Elijah glanced quickly in the direction of the big house. There were two, three dim silhouettes in the yard. He leaned forward, pressing himself across the pommel, his body stretched along the outstretched neck of the horse.

"Go, Smoke," he commanded, challenging the horse to go faster.

He heard the sharp whistle of a slug passing nearby, then another, then the two reports of gunfire finally reaching them. He kicked the horse harshly, again and again.

"*Go!*" he shouted. "Run."

Smoke's hooves drove madly, his mane flagging wildly with each stride. Elijah reached down with one hand and stroked the horse's neck in a series of short, coarse motions. "Thatta boy," he called. "Good boy. Go."

He stared out across the flat blackness. He began to believe that they would make it. He gave rein to the horse, letting him run.

Elijah felt the powerful body of the big dappled gray shudder, start to stumble. Instinctively, Elijah straightened.

"Come on, boy," he shouted, the report of rifle fire reaching them again. Then the horse shuddered violently. He lost his footing, the big head dropping suddenly.

From the yard in front of the ranch house, there was enough light by the fattening moon to see the flashing silhouette of horse and rider going down, dissolving into the inky blackness near the earth. There arose a horrible cry, rising, rising, filling the night with sound. The sound was unmistakable: the burst of agony of an animal giving up its last breath. Then all was still.

Seeing a Man About a Horse

The train wound slowly up the western cleft of the Deschutes River Canyon, the locomotives laboring like slaves under the yoke of the eight-thousand-ton train. The engines' deep drumming sounded like distant thunder, a storm without end. An inky veil of diesel smoke curled from the engines like a dark scarf whipped in the breeze. As the train ascended, the light of sunrise brightened until finally, forty minutes out of Wishram, the train broke above the lingering shadow of night thrown by the distant canyon rim. The sun warmed the ancient, red rim rocks, the scent of high desert in the air.

The California Man pulled onto a siding and stopped near the small community of South Junction, a collection of a few modest houses nestled in a broadening of the canyon, almost a plateau. A herd of whiteface cattle grazed languidly in a lush, irrigated pasture. For a moment they stood transfixed by the sudden halt of the train, staring wide-eyed and curious, but totally unafraid. As soon as the train ground to a stop, Elijah was out of his seat and out the door of the helper locomotive cab, gear in hand, making his way along the catwalk to the ladder at the rear of the deck.

"Where you going?" Jackie yelled, sticking his head out of the cab, watching Elijah disappear down the ladder.

Elijah didn't bother to slow up. "Come on," he yelled as he hit the ground. He turned and started quickly back along the length of the train.

"Damn, we just got on," Jackie complained to no effect. He turned abruptly to gather up his things. "Wait-hurry-up, hurry-up-wait," he whined under his breath. He bolted from the cab in pursuit of Elijah, who

119

was already fifty yards down the line. "Wait up, will ya," he called, shuffling along as fast as he could, his bedroll slapping him on the butt. "What's the damn rush?"

Elijah continued down the train until he came to a battered, old Great Northern boxcar. He slipped his fingers into the narrow crack in the door and worked it open. He threw his gear up and swung himself up and inside in one fluid motion. Jackie rushed forward at an awkward trot. When he reached the boxcar, he unslung his bedroll and turned to pitch it up, halting in midswing, startled by the sudden appearance of two strangers who emerged out of the shadows of the car's interior to stand near Elijah.

"Hope you don't mind a little company this morning," Elijah said to the strangers, smiling, then reached down to offer Jackie a hand. "You coming or not," Elijah teased, his mood greatly enlivened from the previous two days, pleased to have outfoxed the posse at Wishram and heartened to be on the move again. "Come on. Gimme your hand."

Jackie eyed the two men. Both were middle aged: one tall, one short. The taller of the two looked downright stylish for a tramp, dressed in dusty, hand-tooled cowboy boots, clean blue jeans, and a crisp denim jacket. The other stood in sharp contrast, looking road weary and haggard, draped in a drab woolen overcoat several sizes too big, with three days' white stubble on his face. The cowboy stared at the boy with piercing blue eyes, his jaw set as if ready to bark an order. The mousy one eyed the boy suspiciously with red, watery eyes, chewing nervously on the corner of his lip. Jackie considered first one, then the other. He noticed the taller of the two, the one in denim and cowboy boots, held a rolled cigarette in a heavily bandaged hand, only his fingertips showing.

"Suit yourself," Elijah said, turning from the open door, moving his things back out of the way. Jackie hesitated a moment longer, considering his options. Being that there really weren't any, he stepped forward, swinging his bedroll up onto the boxcar floor. Elijah came back and offered his hand again, clasping Jackie's, lifting him easily with a powerful snap of his arm.

Despite its ragged exterior appearance, the interior of the old boxcar was clean, with a solid wood floor, much preferred for comfort over steel plating on a long ride. Jackie spied the nest of men's belongings in the far corner. Jackie nervously sidestepped the little man in the overcoat, who shuffled past to the edge of the door to glance quickly, first up the track in one direction, then back in the other. The man put his shoulder to the lip of the door and started to heave it forward, to close it again.

"Whoa now," Elijah protested, putting a hand up to shove the door open again. The little man jumped back as if struck by a jolt of electricity. He twitched nervously inside the huge coat, eyes blinking frantically.

"We don't want to close out the sunlight," Elijah said. "It's gonna be a beautiful day." The little man squinted out the door as if in deep assessment, then at Elijah. He scurried to the door again and leaned out carefully, looking up the track one way, then down the other.

"Nobody saw you, did they?" he asked, stepping back. Fearful of looking Elijah full in the eye, he stared at the placid landscape as if studying the whiteface cattle ruminating quietly in the pasture near the track.

"Well, I don't know," Elijah offered, amused. "I didn't see nobody, but I guess that don't mean that nobody saw me."

"You didn't see that mess of railroad dicks? Back in Wishram?"

"Oh yeah," Elijah said agreeably. "I did. I did. They were the ones that put me on the train."

The little man's eyes swiveled to lock on Elijah.

"You're kidding?" he stammered.

"In a manner of speaking," Elijah said. "Wasn't like they gave me a written invitation."

"There was a *mess* of them," the little man said. "I mean, they was like ants crawling over a rotten persimmon."

Elijah chuckled. "They were. You're exactly right." He took out the pack of Pall Malls that Willie had given him for a going-away present. He shook one up and put it between his lips. He shook up two more and offered them to the strangers.

"Obliged," the cowboy said, flipping his home-rolled out the door. "Where you fellas headed?" he asked, cracking a lighter and lighting up, then extending his hand with the flame for Elijah. Elijah leaned forward, eyeing the flame, the bandaged hand, and then the deep blue eyes of the man in front of him. He inhaled and then blew a cloud of smoke into the dank cool air inside the boxcar.

"South," he answered simply. "You?"

"Same," the man replied, snapping the lighter closed without offering a light to his buddy. In that one gesture, Elijah saw the whole simple truth of their partnership: a simple matter of happenstance, finding the same empty boxcar somewhere up the line. Riding trains was powerfully lonesome, where even a dullard was welcome company. Elijah was grateful himself for a little company this morning.

"Coming from Wenatchee," the cowboy said. "Picking. What there was to pick this year." He coughed, hawked, and spit out the open door. "I worked three weeks in three different orchards, and in every damn one they said I was working too rough, bruising the fruit. *Sheeezzz* . . . ," he complained. "Wasn't nothing to bruise. Pitiful crop. Just pitiful. You had to pick fast or go broke trying."

"I heard that," Elijah said, blowing a cloud of smoke in the air. "Late frost pinched the blossoms."

"You pick?"

"Did. Don't no more."

"What's your get-by?" the cowboy said.

"Get-by?" Elijah said.

"What do you do to get by?"

"Don't need much. Trap some. Pan a little gold."

"Keep you in spending money?" the man asked, surprised at the idea of it.

"Don't spend much. Don't have much I need."

"Must be nice," the cowboy said, turning away, walking back to his pile of belongings in the far corner. He rummaged up a glass bottle and uncorked it and drank. He came back to the open door and handed it to the little man in the overcoat, who took a quick pull and handed it back. The cowboy held the bottle out to Elijah. Elijah eyed it.

"Something tells me that ain't water," Elijah said slowly.

"Hell no," the cowboy said. "Fish fuck in water. This here is *antifreeze*. I know an ol' bootlegger in Pasco."

Elijah took the bottle and swirled it, eyeing the contents, debating. It was what he most hated about "crossing the flats," the insult to the senses that always seemed to justify the temptation. This trip was stacking up to be a real load of insult, what with being wanted for questioning about something he knew nothing about. He wished he'd stayed in Glacier. Elijah lifted the bottle to his lips and took a long pull.

"*Aaaggh*," Elijah roared, staggering backward a half step as if punched, his eyes watering, his face turning crimson. He coughed hard, shaking his head. He straightened, handing the bottle back.

"Damn, but that has a kick," he said hoarsely. "Tastes like battery acid."

"Wouldn't know," the cowboy said, tipping the bottle up, taking a swallow. "I ain't never drunk battery acid. But this ol' fella's liquor is quicker than anything I've ever had," he said, passing the bottle to the mousy one in the overcoat.

"Name's Jethro," the cowboy said. "But everybody calls me Blue Jay."

Elijah nodded acknowledgment. "Elijah. This here is Jackie-boy," he said, turning to the boy. Jackie avoided both men's gaze.

"Little Eddie here," Blue Jay said, introducing his traveling companion. "Met in a bar in Yakima playing pool. Don't look like much, but he can shoot the balls off a mosquito. We're heading down around Oroville, pick olives. Hear there's a pretty good crop this year."

The wail of a train whistle on the wind drew everyone to the open door. The approaching northbound was still out of sight, but its blaring horn floated full in the confines of the canyon. Elijah leaned out the door for a better look. He saw the green Burlington Northern locomotives break around the bend up ahead. It was a hotshot hauling mail and came roaring down on them, blowing past, sucking and pushing air, rattling the old Great Northern boxcar as though they were in a gale. The doorway was a blur of light and shadow as the van train thundered past. Just when it seemed it would never end, the red crummy shot past and there before them were the stolid whiteface cattle, standing like statues except for an occasional swishing of a tail. A single whistle note broke the silence, followed by pressure blowing up through the brake lines. The California Man creaked forward, building momentum slowly, under way southbound once again.

The train climbed out of the narrowing river canyon, rolling onto the high plateau of fields and rangeland of eastern Oregon. To the west lay the dark, jagged line of the Cascades. A haying crew was at work in the middle distance, putting up tumbled round bales for the winter. By this point, the three tramps had nearly finished the last of the liquor, Elijah and Blue Jay carrying on now like old friends in the open doorway, smoking Elijah's tailor-mades, drinking the cowboy's gin, their conversation all but lost to the roar of the rolling freight train. Jackie sat in the far corner of the boxcar, struggling to stay alert in the company of strangers against the pull of exhaustion of the long night's wait in Wishram. He wasn't concerned about Little Eddie, who'd settled into reclusion amongst his belongings in the opposite corner, but Jackie watched Blue Jay warily as he consorted with Elijah in the open door.

As the contents of the bottle were drained away, Jackie noticed that Elijah began to circle unsteadily on his feet more, his boots shuffling in search of equilibrium. Jackie studied the stranger with the bandaged hand. There was something about him that was unsettling, but Jackie didn't know what. He seemed somehow too friendly, which made him suspicious. What if he suddenly pulled a knife on Elijah? Or simply bumped him hard, causing him to lose his balance, tumbling out the open door? *It wouldn't take much,* Jackie thought, annoyed. *Then what?* he worried.

The cowboy took a swallow from the bottle and passed it to Elijah. There was only a finger or two of liquor left. Elijah took a quick swig, leaving one last swallow in the bottle. He lifted it and flipped it away, out the open door. It hung for an instant in the air beside the train, then was swept from sight by the rush of wind.

"What the hell," Blue Jay complained, leaning forward to watch it tumble in the weeds at the side of the tracks. He straightened and gave Elijah a shove. "You *son of a bitch!*"

Elijah staggered back a half step and smiled. He raised a hand, waving his companion into silence. "Leave something for the next man," Elijah yelled over the din of the rattling train.

The cowboy stared speechlessly, first at Elijah, then out the door again, back down the train.

"Up to just a second ago," he said bitterly, "*I* was the next man. Now I got shit."

"Not to worry," Elijah said. "We'll be stopping in a little bit. Next one's on me." He stood and rocked on his feet, smiling dumbly, staring out at the flat weave of alfalfa fields and pasture and the far distant outline of the Cascades. There was no mood a little liquor couldn't levitate, even the conflicted feelings about being in Oregon again.

In five minutes' time, the train began to slow under the steady grind of steel brakes.

"What'd I tell ya," Elijah said, grinning. A pair of grain silos filled the view out the open door. Jackie got up to make inspection. A meadowlark sat on a nearby fence post, twilling melodiously as if celebrating the arrival of the train.

"Where the hell are we?" Little Eddie asked, stumbling to the door.

"Oregon," Elijah said. "A good place to be from."

"I know we're in Oregon," Eddie said peevishly. "Where in Oregon?"

Elijah smiled, amused at how easily Little Eddie got rattled.

"Madras," he said simply.

"Madras," Eddie repeated, his brow furrowed in deep folds as if pondering an abstract fact. He peered out the door, his head bobbing rhythmically, then turned and stumbled back toward his corner of the boxcar.

Elijah eased himself down to the threshold of the door and slipped free, tumbling in a heap in the weeds at the side of the track. Jackie jumped up and raced to the door.

"What are you doing?" Jackie asked anxiously, watching Elijah pick himself up and brush the stickers from his hands.

Elijah straightened, composed himself, then crossed down through the weeds to the fence line that ran parallel to a county road. "Going to see a man about a horse," he called over his shoulder.

"A what?" Jackie yelled back, incredulous, taking Elijah at his word. "But what about the train?"

"Tell 'em to wait," Elijah called back. He crossed through the barbed-wire fence, getting hooked for a moment, then managing to come free.

"*Elijah!*" Jackie yelled plaintively.

Elijah stopped and turned to eye the boy.

"Just tell 'em to hold their damn horses. Won't take but a minute."

Jackie stood and watched as Elijah wandered down the road. The cowboy stared at Elijah, then the boy, then back at Elijah again.

"You and the half-breed been together long?" the one called Blue Jay asked casually. Jackie stared straight ahead, offended by the cowboy's pejorative reference to Elijah. At the moment, however, he felt in no mood to defend Elijah.

"He some sort of kin of yours?" the cowboy asked.

Jackie turned and eyed the stranger. He felt like saying something rude, but hesitated, feeling newly vulnerable with Elijah gone.

"How'd you two come to travel together?" the cowboy persisted.

Jackie stared hard at the man. "You got some reason to know?" he asked flatly, not taking his eyes off him. If the man even twitched a finger at him, he was out the door.

"No offense," the cowboy said, laughing, raising his hands in mock surrender. "Just curious. Just looks kinda funny, I guess. Hooked up with some ol' man."

Just then the slack in the couplers popped and the train jerked forward, throwing the two off balance. Jackie stumbled against the stranger, the man clasping him. Jackie backpedaled madly to escape his grasp.

"I guess the ol' man ain't gonna make it," the cowboy said. He seemed to be amused by Jackie's plight. Jackie dashed to where his and Elijah's things were stowed and, gathering them up by the armful, ran back to the door and threw them out. He repeated the maneuver again, getting the last of their belongings to carry to the open door, where he threw them out also.

He sat down and hopped free of the train.

The train rolled forward a couple of boxcar lengths, then stopped. It reversed direction, backing down a sidetrack in front of the silos. Jackie saw now that the train had been broken in two, leaving the tail end on the mainline, permitting the head end to ease onto the siding to hook onto a string of waiting grain cars. Secured, the head end rolled forward again, dragging the grain cars out onto the mainline, where the train reversed and backed down to recouple the whole length together once again. The Great Northern boxcar car now stood four car lengths or so farther up the track from where it had started out. The cowboy stood eyeing Jackie, laughing easily.

Jackie turned his back on him and stared down the road. He was startled to see Elijah coming along, sauntering as if out for a Sunday stroll. He seemed to be singing to himself, cradling a paper bag in one arm. He came up the road and stopped opposite where Jackie stood. Elijah stared at the boy, at the train, and the blue sky overheard.

"What a great day to be alive," he said, smiling joyously. He crossed through the weeds, managed his way through the barbed-wire fence, and came up on the roadbed beside Jackie.

"You going somewhere?" Elijah asked, staring curiously at all their belongings scattered along the track.

Jackie fumed silently. He snatched up his own bedroll and turned and marched up the track in the direction of the open boxcar. Elijah made a puzzled face, bent to pick up his bedroll and bundle and water jug, careful not to drop the paper bag, then straightened and started up the track after the boy. Just then, the pressure hissed in the brake lines. The engineer sounded a long plaintive blast on the horn, and the train creaked forward. Elijah and the boy began to waddle along faster to come abreast of the open boxcar. The boy threw his gear up, then caught the edge of the door and, looping a leg up and in, rolled up onto the boxcar floor.

"Whoa now," Elijah said, handing the bottle up to Blue Jay, dropping his bedroll in the process. He laid his bundle in, trotted back to retrieve his bedroll, then scrambled forward, coming up alongside the rolling Great Northern boxcar again.

"Goddamn ya," he roared, throwing his bedroll up. He jumped to grab the lock bar, struggling to get a leg up. He let go a string of profanities. He kept kicking a leg like he was getting onto a horse, but the sag of his pants restricted his range of motion. The train began to pick up speed.

"Dirty son of a dog," he cried. "I say *whoa*." He swung again and got his foot in the door. He hung straddling the door frame, half in, half out, as the train began to gather momentum. He looked up at Jackie and grinned. He inched his boot heel in, got a knee up, then pulled and rolled up onto the floor of the car. He lay there panting, smiling up at Blue Jay and the boy.

Elijah rolled and pushed himself to standing. He took the bottle from the cowboy and uncapped it. It was a bottle of Night Train Express, a cheap ruby wine favored among hoboes for its high octane and low price. Little Eddie roused himself and came over to join the party in front of the door. Jackie picked up his bedroll and stomped back to his corner of the car. The California Man gathered speed quickly. Jackie threw his bedroll down and dropped on top of it. Now and again, he stole furtive glances at the three standing in the sunshine, wishing maybe, with luck, the train would lurch and send all three ass-over-elbows out the open door.

The three men worked on the bottle steadily, until at last Elijah capped it off with a mouthful remaining, and pitched it into the wind. For a brief instant, it hung suspended, then fell away, a token of generosity to the next man with a thirst and nothing to quench it.

Blue Jay and Little Eddie drifted away to their corner of the boxcar. Elijah stood unsteadily, clinging to the side of the door, framed in the light, staring at the countryside as it rolled by. He stood at the door all the rest of the afternoon, lost to his own private reverie.

As the train rolled out across the trestle over the deep chasm of the Crooked River Gorge, Elijah leaned far out the door to stare directly into the yawning maul of the trench. The dark thread of river held in shadow nearly two hundred feet below was lined down both sides with luscious green growth. Elijah felt a warm updraft of air brush his cheek, bringing the sweet smell of the river to his nose. He smiled, imagining the caress of an unseen hand, tempting and reassuring at once. Elijah stared at the soft curving of the river, a random bit of trivia floating into mind. He'd heard or read somewhere an odd bit of news about a woman, a young mother, who'd come to the gorge with her two small children. Despondent over some turn of fate now forgotten, she'd flung first one, then the other child into the pit. Then, while picnickers at the rim rock park watched in mute horror, she climbed up onto the railing of the bridge and opened her arms to embrace the abyss. She leaned forward and fell, her dark hair and pale dress splayed by the wind. Elijah remembered that someone in a retelling said she must have been unbalanced. He'd thought first they were trying to make a joke: unbalanced, falling from the bridge. But then he realized they meant mentally. Elijah understood the notion of that, the weight of that. More truly, he thought, she'd simply lost her way. Mukaluk—The People— would have said she'd lost touch with her Dream. She no longer had a dream singer to show her the way.

The ground rose up at Elijah in a rush as the train cleared the trestle and the gorge disappeared from sight. Elijah fell back from the open door as if propelled, unnerved by sudden vertigo. Above the howl of the wind he heard the engineer's horn crying warning as the train approached the first grade crossing after the gorge.

Elijah stooped slowly and let himself collapse in the middle of the floor. He lay back and closed his eyes. "No more dreams," he muttered forlornly to no one. "No more dreams now. Just sleep."

No Littering

The Three Sisters sat like white-robed guardians above the low skyline of Bend, Oregon. Even in mid-October before the first winter snowfall, the jagged peaks in the Cascade Range to the northwest of town were snow mantled. Yet in town, the evening was pleasant. The night sky was clear, and though it would be crisp by morning, there was a soft ambience to the twilight settling into night.

The streets of Bend hummed with the ritual of end of day. A steady flow of traffic streamed through the Greenwood and Franklin Avenue underpasses, twin viaducts that benchmarked the Bend rail yard, such as it was. As yards go, the Bend yard was small, almost inconsequential, except for its busy maintenance shop.

Jackie sat in the open door of an idle Santa Fe boxcar on a siding, absently swinging his legs and listening to Elijah's drunken snoring reverberate inside the car. The first thing Elijah had seen to upon their arrival in Bend was laying hands on a jug of wine and ingesting the lion's share of it as commodiously as possible. Elijah had managed to go from sour to soused to unconscious like a light going out, timed perfectly with the sun dropping behind the mountains to the west. Being witness to the slide toward oblivion had depressed Jackie. There was something inexplicably sad in Elijah's sodden withdrawal from the world.

The shifting melody of tires on asphalt as traffic flowed back and forth through the twin tunnels under the rail yard provided an almost lyrical counterpoint to Jackie's mood. Music, rock music mostly, rose on the crescendoing roar of cars powered by heavy feet. Jackie couldn't remember whether it was Tuesday or Friday, Sunday or Wednesday. The past several days had been mostly a blur punctuated with terror, loneliness, and regret. He couldn't make sense of how it had come to this, listening to an old man sleep off a drunk in a boxcar in a strange town.

Jackie's mood was blue, but he was also bored. And hungry. Every time his hunger spiked his consciousness, he became angry all over again with Luke. Running into him in the Seattle Greyhound bus terminal on Stewart Street had been just more bad luck heaped upon the misery of the incident with Stardancer. Luke was slick. He managed to work his way from getting Jackie to pay for video games to buying dinner, to having Jackie follow him aboard a slow rolling freight train working its way through the city. It was easy to make it all Luke's fault, but the idea of him bleeding his life away in the Vancouver yard turned Jackie's anger inward. The recriminations were eloquently simple: *stupid. That's the lamest excuse I've ever heard. Nobody's responsible here but you.* The voice in his head intoned its abuse in the familiar pitch of his father.

Jackie pushed forward and slipped free of the boxcar, landing on the ground. There was nothing he could do about anything that had already happened: the death of his brother, his parents' divorce, hooking up with Luke, or the night in the Vancouver yards. Nothing. Not a damn thing would change any of it. But his hunger, he reasoned, was another thing. He didn't have a clue how to address it, but it was a compelling impulse, and sitting in a boxcar all night certainly wasn't going to alleviate the pains of an empty stomach. He turned and peered back inside the boxcar where Elijah lay sleeping. It wasn't like Elijah was likely to go anywhere, he thought. Jackie turned and appraised the small frame houses that lined the street parallel to the tracks. He tucked his shirt into his pants and squared his cap on his head. If he had learned anything of value from Luke, it was that where there was a will, there was wile to fill it.

Jackie crossed Division Street and started down a quiet narrow side street framed by modest clapboard homes. In the darkness, his foot skimmed an old bottle, sending it clattering down the walk. A chorus of howling dogs rose from behind pulled curtains, beyond dark wooden fences. Jackie pulled his leather coat tight and stepped along quickly through the shadows.

He was drawn like a moth toward the glow of lights on Bond and Wall Streets, the heart of old downtown Bend. He crossed Bond and continued on to Wall. But for all the glow of burning lights, downtown was nearly deserted. A lone pedestrian strolled under the soft streetlights that filtered through hardwoods growing in planters along both sides of the street. Jackie's eye was drawn to the rise of bright neon of the Tower Theatre marquee. He crossed Wall and walked down to stand in front of the theater to read the playbill. *Rocky* was playing, one of his favorite movies. The idea of a dark cozy theater, a big bag of popcorn and a Coke made him yearn for his old life. Thought of Luke arose to dispel the idea of it. Jackie seethed in thinking of him, spending all his money. *That's just stupid,* the voice in his head railed. Jackie turned away from the welcoming glow of the theater.

He wandered up the street and turned, spotting the lights of the Greyhound station a block over. Next to the bus station, a neon sign out over the sidewalk flashed the word *Grill* in cool blue letters. He crossed the street and ambled down to cruise slowly past the windows of the restaurant.

Two men sat drinking coffee at the counter, talking to a dark-haired man in a white T-shirt and cook's apron behind the counter. A dark-faced woman with a small child sat at one table, the woman eating soup, the child munching stoically on the saltines. Jackie walked past the entrance to the restaurant and pushed through the swinging doors into the bus terminal.

The air was stale and tight. A row of wooden benches filled the narrow waiting room. Cigarette butts and candy wrappers littered the black-and-white-checked linoleum floor. An old man in coveralls with a cardboard box tied with twine sat on a bench closest to the door leading to the boarding zone. Jackie walked back to the ticket counter. The man behind the counter was busy filling out the day's receipt log.

"You have any buses that go to California?" Jackie asked.

"Six every day," the man answered without bothering to look up.

"How much?"

The man stopped and looked out over the rims of his glasses, studying Jackie with a peevish squint. "Depends," he said. "How far you going?"

"Sacramento," Jackie said.

"Thirty-seven fifty," he answered brusquely before dropping his gaze to the ledger in front of him.

"When's the next one leave?"

"Eleven thirteen. After that, ain't another one till tomorrow. The eight o'five."

Jackie studied the bald spot on the top of the man's head. Dander scaled in long disgusting flakes on the bare pate, making Jackie's scalp crawl. The man raised his eyes to peer again at Jackie over the rims of his glasses.

"You interested—or just wondering out loud?" the man asked, irritated.

"Oh yeah," Jackie answered enthusiastically. He thought the man a complete idiot and took pleasure that his presence was annoying.

"Which?"

"Which what?" Jackie said, acting stupid.

"Interested. Or just being a nuisance?" the man retorted.

"Oh yeah," Jackie said, smiling, taking a step backward. "Yup. I sure am."

The ticket agent straightened to focus through the black frames of his glasses.

"You read?" he said, his annoyance growing.

"Oh yeah," Jackie said again, nodding his head for dramatic inflection. "Oh yes. Yes, I can," he said, continuing to back away from the counter. He kept his gaze locked on the reddening face of the agent.

"Well, can you read *that?*" the man said, pointing a crooked finger up at a sign on the wall. A *No Loitering* notice was posted in big black letters.

"Well. Yeah. Of course," Jackie said slowly, hesitantly, stopping to stare studiously.

"What's it say?" the man asked, his anger causing his voice to squeak.

"It says no . . . *littering,*" Jackie replied, a mock smile lighting his face.

The man's face flushed bright red. "You mocking me?" he sputtered.

Jackie couldn't help it. "Oh yeah," he said, an authentic, big grin burning through the phony smile.

"You want me to call the cops?" the man said, pounding the counter.

"*Ooh yeah,*" Jackie sang, turning on one heel and slowly, dramatically stepping off the distance to the door. "Me and the law. We're tight." He held his left hand up over his shoulder where the man could see it. The first two fingers were crossed, intertwined. "Like *that,*" he said, pushing the door open with his right hand, making his exit.

"And don't come back," the ticket agent yelled as the door slammed shut.

"You can count on it," Jackie said defiantly, folding down his index finger, giving the man the finger. He dropped his hand and jammed it in the pocket of his jacket, hunching his shoulders against the loneliness of the night. He stood motionless in front of the bus station, looking up and down the street. He was the only pedestrian in sight.

"Bend," he muttered, mimicking Elijah's drunken complaint. "A good little town. A good town to be from."

Jackie turned and entered the diner next to the bus station. The two men and the cook were still collected at one end of the counter; the woman with her soup and the child with her saltines, still silently engaged. Jackie noticed now, however, that there were three boys in the far corner, two watching the third play a video game. They were all about his age—the taller one at the video controls maybe a little older, the other two perhaps a little younger. They were darkly complexioned, like Elijah, with thick, black hair. Jackie couldn't tell whether they were Chicano or Indian. They were deeply engrossed in the flash of light and action on the video screen. Jackie approached them from behind, peering over their shoulders to see how the game was progressing. They were playing Death Comet, a game Jackie was greatly skilled in. Jackie stood silently watching the boy play. The boy ran up a total of 750,000 points before finally being obliterated by a hail of space trash.

"Not bad," Jackie said.

The three boys turned as one to eye Jackie, their smiles fading into stony stares.

"Whatta ya mean, *not bad?*" the leader of the group demanded, elbowing through the other two to confront Jackie directly.

Jackie shrugged. "Not bad," he repeated, trying to sound nonchalant. "I used to play. I was pretty good."

"Shit," the boy seethed. "That was *fucking* incredible."

"Hey," the cook in the T-shirt yelled, straightening menacingly behind the counter. "What'd I tell you kids about that kinda language? Take it out on the street."

"Kiss my ass," one of the smaller boys said under his breath, pushing past Jackie, rocking him sideways. The other two followed his lead out the door. Jackie stared at the three men at the counter, then fell in behind the three boys.

The oldest boy pulled a pack of Marlboros out of his back pants pocket and handed one to each of his friends. "You smoke?" he said, nodding at Jackie. Jackie shrugged and nodded back, taking the cigarette offered. They all lit up on a Zippo lighter one of the younger boys carried. The leader turned and started strolling down the street. The other two followed dutifully behind. Jackie took a puff on his cigarette, shuddering at the thick taste, stifled a cough, then turned and started to follow along behind the others. Maybe they'd offer him something to eat, maybe make him a sandwich or something. Anything.

"How come you're following us?" the biggest boy challenged, turning back to confront Jackie. "You some kinda fucking faggot?" He cuffed Jackie hard on the side of the head with the butt of his palm.

"What the hell?" Jackie protested, stepping back, drawing himself to his full height. The two were about evenly matched. "It's a fucking free country."

"Not if you're a faggot," the boy said. "Where you from?"

Jackie stared at the boy for a long moment. "California," he said evenly. "Yeah?"

"Yeah," Jackie said defiantly.

The boy smiled. "What are you doing here?"

"Passing through," Jackie answered. He didn't like the tenor of things. He took a long slow breath. He eyed the other two boys. In a fair fight with any one of them, he could give as good as he got, he figured, though probably taking the worst of it from the bigger boy. But three against one—there wasn't a chance. If Terry were here, he'd even the balance, if not the score. Jackie could always count on his older brother to look out for him. A dizzying flash of anger surged through him: Terry was dead; his father was an asshole. And his mother? He couldn't bring himself to hazard an opinion.

The leader crowded forward, fueled by the confidence of superior numbers. Fortunately he suffered the overconfidence of bullies, expecting Jackie to stand defenseless. In that instant, Jackie was in no frame of mind to suffer abuses. The big kid didn't notice Jackie dropping his cigarette, nor the punch that sprang up as if out of nowhere.

The boy fell back, stumbling, losing his balance, going down on his butt in the middle of the sidewalk. His hands covered his face, his head down; he was moaning loudly. The other two boys stared wild-eyed, backing out of the range of a second stealth attack.

"What the fuck! What did you do that for?" the boy said in a muffled voice, his hands trying to stop the flow of blood. "You broke my fucking nose." He stared up at Jackie in disbelief.

Jackie stood with his fists cocked in front of him, surprised by the sudden turn of events. "I didn't break your damn nose," he said, part apology, part defiance.

"Hey, man," one of the smaller boys cautioned, backing up farther. "He's Golden Gloves or something. Be careful."

The other boy backed off. The leader sitting on the sidewalk pulled his hands away from his face and stared at them, covered in blood. He looked up at Jackie. "You bastard," he cursed softly.

Jackie's hands danced threateningly. He shuffled his feet slightly, imagining himself Rocky, the undervalued underdog finally triumphant.

The boy on the ground crabbed backward. He scrambled to his feet, careful to keep his distance. "Fuck you, asshole," he said, trying to regain some semblance of dignity. Jackie feigned threat, pushing the limit. The three backed up yet another step, then turned and started putting distance between themselves and Jackie. Jackie watched them disappear down the street, feeling a mixture of triumph and despair.

"Assholes," he whispered, mocking their false bravado. He stuffed his hands in his coat pockets and hunched his shoulders the way Stallone did in *Rocky*. He was momentarily buoyed. He started sauntering down the street like Rocky stalking the dark streets of Philly. His hunger roiled up to consume his attention again. His mood deflated like a sad balloon. He assessed the situation. He was no closer now—perhaps further away, even—to getting something to eat than he had been an hour ago. His mood sank lower still. *Food.* It was all he could think about. Getting some was the only thing that would lift his spirits.

Jackie came to the end of the block and noticed for the first time the distant glow of night-lights beyond the rail yard. He was drawn to them, hope rising with each step, like eagerness at the approach of Christmas.

State Highway 97 was awash in the glow of the modern pageantry of strip development. The main north-south corridor on the eastern side of the Cascades, running more or less parallel to the tracks between Madras and K-Falls, looked as if it had siphoned off all of the commerce in old Bend, what with its car dealerships and shopping centers and franchise restaurants and motels. The beckoning lights of Pizza Hut, Burger King, and Denny's made Jackie feel almost at home.

He walked up the street, drawn inexplicably to Denny's. He rounded the ivy plantings in front and pushed through the main entrance to suck in the rich panoply of odors, a heady mix of steaks and burgers and fries. His eyes feasted on the display of pies sitting in the glass case behind the counter. He stared dumbly, then caught himself and moved quickly toward the bathrooms at the back of the restaurant.

He pushed through the door to the men's room and inspected himself in the mirror. He was shocked by what he saw. His face was deeply tanned, lined with weary exhaustion and dirt. He removed his cap. His hair was a nest of tangles, dull and dusty and greasy looking. He curled his lips back to expose dark grit pasted to his teeth.

He stripped off his jacket, sweater, shirt, and T-shirt, the offensiveness of odors increasing with each layer that was peeled. He sniffed his T-shirt, recoiled, and balled it up and flung it into the trash can. He lathered his hands with soap and began washing his face, neck, and ears; his chest and arms. Soapy water splashed everywhere. He bent and soaked his hair, then soaped his hands again and scrubbed the lather into his scalp. The soap burned his neglected scalp as badly as it did his eyes. He rinsed and dried himself with paper towels, wiped down the counter, and tossed the paper wad in the trash on top of his T-shirt. He slipped on his shirt and combed his hair with fingers as best he could, and refitted the cap on his head. He smiled at the improved image, noticed the grit on his teeth, and rubbed them clean with the tip of a finger.

No question he looked well traveled, though now much improved. He folded his sweater and jacket into a tight bundle and put it under one arm and pulled the door open.

Jackie slipped into the first vacant booth, one littered with dirty plates. He spotted a four-dollar tip amidst the clutter. He scanned the dining room, then quickly palmed the bills, sliding them off the table into his lap. He folded them quickly and pressed them into his pants pocket. A waitress appeared at his left as if out of nowhere, gathering up the dirty plates like a card dealer picking up tricks. Table bare, no tip, she straightened, her arms laden with platters. She cocked one hip and smacked her gum loudly. Jackie turned to eye her. She was middle-aged, thin, with hair pulled back in a clip at the back of her head. She wore red rouge powdered high on her cheeks, accenting the thinness of her face. Jackie noticed she had nice teeth. Her name tag declared "Shirl," and from the look of her, she was no-nonsense when it came to trouble. Jackie smiled angelically under Shirl's withering gaze. She narrowed her eyes and gave him a mock smile.

"The booths are for parties of two or more," she said coolly.

"Ah . . . there's two of us," Jackie stammered. "My dad's coming. He's fixing something with the car. Told me to come ahead and order for him."

Shirl rolled her gum slowly in her mouth, set her jaw, and pivoted smoothly on one heel. She was grace in action hauling dirty dishes to the kitchen.

Jackie sighed. "My *dad?*" he whispered to himself, pulling a menu from the rack at the end of the table, amazed with his inventiveness. "Wonder what ol' Pops wants for dinner," he said, poring over the glossy pictured food spreads. "I know he's hungry. Should order for the both of us."

Shirl returned with two glasses of water and two sets of silver, set them down with a fluid economy of motion, and started back toward the waitress station.

"I'm ready to order," Jackie called out impatiently. He could barely contain his eagerness, so close now to food.

Shirl stopped, whirled, and eyed him with a frosty gaze, letting him know exactly who it was who'd stiffed her for the tip. "Hold your ponies, sonny. I got other customers to attend to," she said.

Jackie watched her go around and freshen everyone's coffee. He watched as she brought out two orders the cook had put up, lingering to chat up the customers, letting him stew in his nervousness. Shirl finally returned with order pad in hand. Jackie ordered two double cheeseburgers with fries, a vanilla shake, and a cup of coffee, "for my dad." He wanted to order two pieces of pie, but couldn't bring himself to do it for fear of being too obvious. Shirl dutifully took his order, circling the dot of her *i*'s, and twirled about and was gone. Jackie was flushed with so much agitation, he was sweating. He sipped the ice water Shirl had brought to steady his nerves.

He studied a teenage couple in a booth on the far side of the dining room. They were about the same age his brother had been. Terry wouldn't have liked them much; or maybe he might have: he was pretty accepting of others—but he wouldn't have hung out with them. The boy was a block of stone: cropped reddish hair, round face, no neck from too many hours under a barbell, all nicely packaged in a varsity letterman's jacket with a chest of medals. The girl was cute: long blond hair flipped up at the end, pretty face, sparkling smile. She wore a thin blue ribbon in her hair. She eyed No-Neck with devotion as he talked. Jackie didn't get it: why were girls always attracted to No-Neck dimwits?

Shirl brought the milk shake and placed it in front of him. "Your dad coming? You want me to bring the coffee now?" she asked drily.

"Yeah," Jackie stammered, his face feeling hot. "I mean no."

"Yeah, you want the coffee now, or no, he's not coming?" Shirl asked, skewing her jaw to one side, puzzling through what was going on here.

"Yeah, he's coming, but no, why don't you wait to bring the coffee. He likes his coffee real hot."

"What's the problem?" she asked, softening slightly, still suspicious, but curious, too.

"Just some car trouble," Jackie said, looking down into the top of his milk shake.

"Want I should call a tow truck?"

"Ah, no," Jackie said nervously. "It's nothing serious, not like that. Just . . . a little trouble. Happens a lot. My dad knows how to fix it." Jackie watched tiny air bubbles rise to the surface of his milk shake, then burst. "But my mom," he said forlornly. "She just died."

"Well, I'm real sorry to hear that," Shirl said kindly, a sucker for sap, deciding her suspicions had been ungrounded, feeling guilty for having doubts.

"Thanks."

"Say, your burgers will be up in a minute. You want me to hold them under a heat lamp till your dad comes in?"

"Ah, no," Jackie said. "He just waved a minute ago. He'll be along in just a sec. You can bring them both when they're ready."

"Whatever you say." She turned and walked away.

Jackie struggled not to fidget. He hadn't a clue how he was going to wiggle out of this one. The four bucks he'd palmed wasn't about to cover the check. A little sympathy had seemed to open a door of possibility, but he suspected once his dad didn't show, the story of the death of his mother would leak water like a sieve. He watched her pull two platters off the setup shelf and turn toward him. *The last supper,* Jackie thought. *Might as well enjoy.*

Shirl set the platters down. "Sure you don't want me to hold this one in the warmer till your dad comes in?"

"No, no," Jackie said. "He should be along any second."

"Anything else for you right now?"

"Nope," Jackie said, staring fixedly at the steaming burger and mound of French fries in front of him.

Shirl departed, leaving him to his feast. Jackie snatched the burger off his plate and jammed it to his face. He tore a bite free, closed his eyes, and chewed vigorously. He swallowed and took another bite, then another. *Oh my God,* he thought. *This is so good.* He put the burger down and uncapped the ketchup bottle and poured a big puddle of it next to his fries. He doused two fries in the red sauce and stuffed them in his mouth. He'd never known that ketchup and fries could taste so good. He slathered up two more and popped them in his mouth, too. *Oh my God.*

Jackie was halfway through his burger when he saw a uniformed sheriff's deputy walk through the front door and take a seat at the counter. He froze in midbite. He saw the deputy unobtrusively scan the late-night crowd. Jackie looked out the window as the deputy's gaze ran past him. "Holy shit," he whispered under his breath, staring at his reflection in the dark windowpane. He felt a flash of panic. He drew a deep breath and turned his gaze slowly back toward the counter. He caught Shirl and the deputy unpuckering from a light kiss. Jackie's mouth fell open.

"I *ain't* believing this," he said, turning to stare out the window again, feeling like he was transmitting radio signals of distress any fool could pick up on.

"What'll it be, sweetie," Shirl asked.

"The usual," the deputy said.

"You need to do like the doctor says and lighten up on the fat," she said sternly.

"Listen, Shirl. I'm hungry. I gotta pull a double. You wanna hassle your customers, I'll go down the street to get me something to eat," the deputy said in mock frustration, starting to rise out of his seat.

"Like hell you will," she said, pushing him back down. "I'm just trying to look out for you."

"I appreciate it. But right now, I've got ten minutes to eat, and I'd appreciate a little speedier service, if you don't mind."

"Pushy, pushy," she said, turning to fill a cup with coffee for him. "I bet you're real rough on people who give you trouble," she teased, handing him the cup.

"Not usually. But tonight, look out. I hate working doubles."

"Ah baby," she cooed lovingly, patting his arm. Shirl wrote out an order ticket and passed it to the cook. She picked up a pot of coffee and began her rounds to freshen everyone's cup again.

"How's that burger, sonny?" she asked Jackie as she stopped at his table.

"It's really good," he said, grateful to be telling the truth for once.

"You want me to take the other one back to keep it warm? Seems it's taking your dad a long time to fix your car."

"No, you can leave it," Jackie said, picking up his burger to take another bite, filling his mouth to discourage any more conversation. As she stood there, the deputy came up on her from behind and goosed her lightly.

Shirl shrieked, jerking upright and spinning around. "Don't, Henry," she protested in a hushed voice. "I'm working." The deputy smiled, looked at Jackie, and winked. He patted her gently on the butt as he slid past on his way to the men's room. Shirl went back to the cash register as No-Neck and the blonde slipped out of their booth.

Now is the time, Jackie thought: *Deputy Henry's taking a whiz, and Shirl's busy with No-Neck.* Jackie reached across the table and pulled the second dinner platter toward him. He slid the burger off the plate and into his lap. He grabbed a handful of napkins out of the dispenser, knocking over the pepper shaker. Jackie glanced toward the register and saw Shirl making change.

He quickly wrapped the burger in napkins, then the fries. He slipped the two paper bundles into a fold of his jacket and tied the sleeves together to make a tight little packet he could carry easily.

Jackie slid across the vinyl cushion and stood as Shirl closed the cash register. He hesitated, pausing next to his table while No-Neck held the door for his girlfriend. The two exited into the night. When Shirl turned and went back to pick up the deputy's order, Jackie made his move for the door.

"Hey, you okay?" Shirl asked, catching movement in the corner of her eye and turning to Jackie as he put his hand on the door. Jackie shoved his way into the entry foyer, then through the second door without bothering to turn back.

"Hey," Shirl barked. "You little bastard. Henry, that kid . . ." The door closed and cut her off in midsentence. Jackie turned away from the main thoroughfare, sprinting across the dimly lit parking lot. He dashed past No-Neck, who was holding a car door for his girlfriend.

Jackie heard someone shout. "Grab that kid!" He glanced back quickly. The deputy was on the run. Jackie accelerated. He tucked his jacket up under his arm like a football. He pumped his legs. He thrilled at the terror of it, imagining for an instant he was sprinting toward the goal line. He imagined the blaze of stadium lights, the roar of the crowd. And then he saw the cyclone fence ahead, an unbroken line thwarting his advance. He glanced left and right. He was boxed in.

Jackie feigned left, then right, the thought of imaginary tacklers replaced now by the reality of someone on his heels in close pursuit. He looked back again. No-Neck was closing in. Jackie kicked with the last bit of reserve he had. He uncurled the bundled jacket and tossed a looper over the top of the cyclone fence. He sprang at the face of the tall fence and clawed his way toward the top.

The fence shook with No-Neck's impact, and Jackie felt a sweeping clutch of hand grab for his leg. He locked his fingers into the fence and kicked, trying to free his foot. The third shake broke the hold, and he started to climb again. As he pulled himself up to the top, he glanced down at the jock, surprised at the agility with which the big guy could move. Jackie raised a foot and aimed carefully. The bottom of his shoe caught the boy square on the shoulder, tearing free his grip on the fence. The last thing Jackie saw before going over the top was the jock with the chest of medals all a-jingle crashing down on top of the deputy. Jackie vaulted down the other side of the fence into a pile of sand and, snatching up his jacket, sprinted off into the darkness.

Guardians of Dream Time

Emma visited Elijah in prison only a dozen times the whole eight and half years he was there. It wasn't such a great distance across the mountains, but travel cost money she didn't have. It was nearly six months before she could afford to come and see him the first time. She had been reluctant to leave the baby, and wouldn't accept her sister's offer to come and stay with the children until baby Marna could sleep fully through the night. Even then, Emma might not have agreed to her sister's insistence had she not received a visit one afternoon from Elsa Garnett. Elsa brought by a basket of fruit marking the first time they had encountered each other alone since the night Elijah's horse was shot out from under him and he was arrested. Emma greeted her with cold but polite reserve, but it was everything she could do to refrain from lashing out at this woman, the seed of such cruel pain and loss. Elsa was solicitous but not fawning—in truth, more curious to know whether Emma had heard from Elijah than concerned for his family.

"You're lucky," Elsa said, speaking boldly finally, causing Emma to catch her breath. "Despite what you may think of me, I am not ashamed of what happened. I'm not ashamed for loving him. I wanted him to choose me," she said almost bitterly. Seeing Emma's flush of shock, misreading it, she smiled. "Is that so hard to believe? That I wanted him to choose me?" She paused. Emma said nothing.

"But he didn't," Elsa said. "The last night he came"—she paused, staring hard at Emma, as though trying to discern what Emma offered that she did not—"it wasn't to see me. It was to be *done* with me."

Her admission was a shock and a revelation to Emma. Emma believed

Elijah had gone to be with Elsa the night of the trouble, that it was just one more betrayal of her love for him. That night's incident, her false belief of his intentions, had been the cruelest betrayal of all. But now she knew without reservation or doubt that what Elsa said was the truth. That was what Elijah had been trying to tell her when he said he had to go away, to leave with Emma yet pregnant with Marna, that it was too dangerous to stay. She had begged him to stay, then felt doubly betrayed upon hearing he'd been in Elsa's bedroom. It was true he had betrayed her before, but not again, not that last night. She accepted the truth of it, and it was then that she decided she had to make the journey to Eugene to see her husband.

In the 100 months Elijah passed inside the fortress walls of the prison, he spent nearly half of them in solitary confinement. The first stay, coming the second month after being admitted, lasted ninety days. It was the longest ninety days of his life. Locked in a cube of hard angles and unrelieved harshness, he slipped into a silent dementia where it was all he could do to endure. He clung to a frayed refrain, a prayer for strength, repeating it endlessly: *I am Modoc, I am Modoc, I am Modoc.* He came to feel he knew what Captain Jack had gone through in those dark days in the winter of 1873, holed up in caves in the Lava Beds, surrounded by men in uniforms with guns demanding his ragged band surrender, the soldiers willing to starve them to death if they did not. They lived on the sun-bleached bones of dead animals scavenged at night. During the worst of it for Elijah in his cell, when he felt about to lose his grasp, he was strangely comforted by the sense—a delusion, an hallucination, a waking dream, he couldn't tell which and didn't care—that Captain Jack was there with him, keeping vigil against the threat of consuming darkness. Captain Jack did finally surrender the Lava Beds, but not to blind darkness. He and a handful of compatriots gave their lives on the gallows so the others—mostly women and children and the aged—could live. Most were removed to Oklahoma; some were forced to resettle with the Klamath, their mortal enemies to the north.

After the first trip to solitary, Elijah gathered increasing strength from his ability to endure isolation, and even came to prefer it to living with the noise and mayhem in the general population. More than the quiet was the privacy it afforded—privacy such as it was. Elijah created mental games to occupy his mind and fill the time, mostly games of the imagination: picturing in vivid detail the features of horses he'd favored, envisioning long rides into the open high desert of eastern Oregon or up into the Cascades. One horse he never rode in these sojourns of the mind was Smoke, and one place he never visited was the meadow with the cave of hands. They were off-limits. But most of the rest of the world that he had known and the horses that he had loved lay before him, waiting for him. Still, there were some things he could not touch, no matter how much he desired them. He couldn't touch the earth with his hands, drink in the sky with his eyes, or inhale the heat and aroma of Emma.

The last eighteen months of his sentence were the hardest, for he was forced to accommodate the rules and whims of guards and other inmates. He was required to live clean, without incident, without any violations that warranted a trip to solitary. He had to silently suffer all offenses, show no indignation, seek no retribution. He had to make himself small, smaller still, becoming also invisible. Indeed, he grew diminished.

Elijah did his job scrubbing pots in the kitchen, and marched the long Red Line, a strip painted on the floor that ran throughout the prison. He was required always, like all prisoners, to be within one step of the line when out of his cell. Nights were the hardest. At night when he slept and dreamed, it was of Emma and Toby and little Marna. He could keep thought of them at bay during the day, but he was defenseless at night. He was always caught between welcoming them, savoring their presence, and the insufferable ordeal of waking to find them but a dream.

When Elijah was released from prison, he was a different man. He was diminished, as though his time of confinement had shrunken him. It had taken every bit of resolve to endure the last months in the general population on the cellblock. The constant noise, the clattering of tin cups on bars in protest and defiance, the yelling, the verbal jousting, and the petty insults were impossible to tune out. Having to live in lockstep with a swarm of men who were little better at coping than he was kept him on the edge, teetering between *light* and *darkness*. Each man's demons were his own, but the hell they all awoke to each day was universal.

The first night Elijah was home after being released, he arose and left Emma sleeping in the small room she'd taken in her sister's house, and went out in the backyard with a quilt and lay down under the stars. During the years he gave to the state of Oregon for assaulting Marshall English, he hadn't been able to look up at the night sky, to gauge the time, sense the season, feel the simple joy of the breeze cooling his flesh. Here he felt he could again touch the stars and the stars could touch him. Stars were the guardians of *dreamtime*, and he hoped that they would welcome his finding a new dream so he would know the way forward. But he would discover he could no longer dream, and came to fear he might not ever dream again. Why should he think otherwise? He had abused the gift that had been entrusted to him.

Emma awoke later that first night of freedom, frantic with fear that he'd gone off somewhere again, rekindling her old nightmare. She went in search of him, driven by the dread of abandonment she'd felt years before at Antelope Creek Ranch. After that, every night for two weeks they bedded down together outside under the stars, Elijah holding her, stricken by her grief, consoling her again and again when she was taken by night terrors. Finally, reluctantly, he agreed to move back inside only when the children demanded they be permitted to join them outside under the stars as well. Even then, Emma would often awake to find Elijah gone. Though it always generated a flutter of apprehension, she became accommodating, understanding his restless need to be out, knowing that it was not a wish to abandon them but rather a deep need he seemed unable to sate.

It was made no easier by the fact that Elijah was virtually silent about his experience being locked away. Emma left it to him to decide what to share, hoping in time he could let it out, and in letting it out, let it go. But he did not speak of it, did not share, could not escape its hold.

His readjustment was aggravated by Toby's growing remoteness. Twelve, almost thirteen, Toby became increasingly defiant of both his parents, angry at the abrupt insertion of his father in his life and his mother welcoming it. There was a chasm neither he nor his father could or would attempt to cross. In contrast, Elijah found Marna's company easiest of all to take in. She'd never known her father and was joyous to have him back in the family. Now nearly nine, she was a blend of both her parents: she had the strength of heart of her mother, and the reflective mind and love of nature of her father. Elijah and Marna took long walks together in the hills, often uttering little more than a dozen words the whole time they were out. Still, Elijah would share things, point her attention with a nod, a pause, a stopping to listen to a sound or to follow the flight of birds. Their relationship deepened while Elijah's relationship with Toby hollowed out.

Emma's tolerance for Elijah's need for solitude slowly expanded. She was happy just to have him back. She kept hoping he would take a job working with horses, thinking it was the one thing that could heal his wound. She encouraged him, but he had no interest. When she persisted, he became sullen, then angry. Without his saying so, she knew it was the penitence he carried for causing the death of Smoke. Emma couldn't help but wonder at times whether he had loved that horse more than he loved her.

The routine of their lives, such as it was, was upended toward the end of the second year he was home when Elijah was arrested for assault. He claimed it was self-defense, that he'd been provoked. The pulp wood hauler he had recently hired out to had cheated him of wages, he said. Words were exchanged, then insults, finally blows. The only witness to the incident, the man who'd hired the pulp wooder to clear his land, said he wasn't sure who threw the first punch. Everyone in the county, however, knew the pulp wooder to be a liar and a cheat. Still, it was Elijah who was charged. He was the one, after all, with a prison record.

Elijah spent eight months of a two-year sentence in the county jail. When he was released, he was home only a few short weeks before he announced he had found work in Yuba County, down over the border in California. He was supposed to be gone only two weeks at a time, but ended up being gone three and four months at a stretch. It was hard on Emma and Marna, but despite the friction between the two when they were together, it was Toby who seemed to take it the hardest of all. He began to skip school and was caught stealing. It was never anything of value: a broken chain saw, two bald tires, a chest of rusted tools. In exasperation, with Elijah absent, Emma finally arranged for Toby to go live with her brother in Bend.

Elijah subsequently took a job in Klamath Falls in the stockyards near the rail line. He was saving money to bring Emma and Marna from Chiloquin to live with him there when he was charged with assault and battery again. He used the money he had saved to bail himself out of jail, and then simply disappeared. Emma and Marna didn't hear from him for four months. He returned unexpectedly one evening after dark, only to disappear again two days later. He was back two months later, stayed a week, then was gone yet once more, despite the charges against him having been withdrawn.

It was a year before they heard from him this time. From this point on he was never home for more than a few weeks. They never seemed to know where he went, gleaning only traces from postmarks when he sent money. There was little mention of how he was or what he was doing. He was just gone. The pattern was set.

Though it grieved her deeply, Emma understood it even more clearly than Elijah did. Elijah had always been a proud man. It was one of the things that attracted her to him. Being so, he was never able to forgive himself for how he'd squandered their dreams and their unity as a family. He loved Emma dearly, and adored both Toby and Marna, but he could never again find his footing as the man of the house. He was shamed by his self-ishness. Toby's open bitterness toward him was like a public lashing—one that Elijah felt he deserved.

Elijah showed up unexpectedly, completely out of the blue, when Emma turned fourty-seven. Marna was married and living in Sacramento by then, and Toby and his family had come down, bringing Emma with them to Marna's for a special celebration. Marna was the one to spy Elijah sitting on a bench in the park across the street. She was surprised that he knew where she lived. She went out and coaxed him to come in. Emma welcomed him, but Toby never said a word to his father.

By then, Elijah had forged a life living in Montana half the year, the other half in northern California. He panned a little gold, worked the fall fruit harvests, and helped to bale hay when he needed a little cash. On rare occasions he would stop to see Emma on his passage between Montana and California. The very last time he dropped free of a train on his way south to the Feather River Canyon, Emma was not in good health and Elijah stayed two weeks, tending to odd jobs on the little place where she lived, laying in firewood for the winter before moving on.

Through all the years, not a word was spoken between Elijah and Emma of the fate of Elsa Garnett and Marshall English. Emma knew but never spoke of the fact that the two of them were killed in a freak car accident while Marshall was driving Elsa to the airport to return to Philadelphia. The car went off into a big gulley on a straight stretch of road. There were no skid marks; there was nothing to mark where or why it had happened.

For his part, Elijah never truly understood his entanglement with Elsa, why he would risk so much in exchange for so little. He accepted it as part of the mystery of his life, of the talisman of *two crows, one the shadow, one the light*. It was, ultimately, a part of *the way being difficult*, he felt. Over the years he'd given up the notion of ever dream singing again. What was the point? If he dreamed, he didn't seek to remember or glean the dream's meaning. Until one night in Glacier.

Elijah was living in Glacier when he awoke abruptly, shaken deeply by a *knowing*: Emma was dead. It had come to him in a dream. The prospect of her death was something he'd never considered, even though she was in de-clining health; he'd always believed he'd die first. He rose straightaway and used his knife to cut his hair and marked his face in mourning with pinesap and ash. He was a fright to see, though there was no one to see him. Even Ol' Icy Eye seemed to keep his distance. Elijah fought the impulse to simply take his life, to end it all. But he resisted, compelled to mourn for her for a full year, as was the custom of The People.

He had been preparing to stay on at Glacier through the winter when he encountered the old grizzly in a thicket of ferns, the wind howling in the trees overhead. He'd had a premonition of it, but was so out of practice that he hadn't been able to read the fainting glimmering of the dream that had come to him in the night. The wind had tried to tell him. Crow had tried. Finally, there was nothing left but Ol' Icy Eye to confront him.

Go! the bear had roared. For what purpose, to what end, there was no inkling. Elijah was seized again by a *knowing*: it was simply a matter of an unfolding yet to be. For some reason, he didn't dismiss it, didn't question it. Bear was keeper of the *dreamtime*. Bear had appeared not in spirit, but in the flesh. It was enough to penetrate the prison of forgetting he'd sought solace in. *The way will be difficult. But you won't be alone.*

This, finally, was the dream—or part of the dream—Elijah had always longed for. Not to be alone, even if the way was difficult.

Two Inches of Type

Bud Keaton sat in the small, windowless office, his temporary quarters in the Portland train station, staring at the clock on the wall. It was nearly half past nine, though there was no way of knowing inside the tight airless room whether it was day or night. Keaton thought of the switchman he'd run into in the men's room when he'd come in that morning. The man wore a cap with a patch saying something about feeling like a mushroom— *kept in the dark and fed shit*. That was pretty much how he felt. Keaton had been trying to reach his boss in Seattle for three days. When he'd finally connected with Hank Claxton an hour earlier, he had been directly put on hold for another call. Claxton came back momentarily to say that he'd be a while, and promised to call back in ten minutes. Ten minutes had grown into almost forty-five.

Keaton had worked security for the Union Pacific for twenty-eight years. He'd relished his job at first, viewing the world simply as a place divided between good guys and bad. He was one of the good guys, and anybody trespassing on railroad property by definition was thrown into the lot with the bad. He'd knocked heads and kicked ass, had worked in four different rail yards around the Northwest, but had grown weary, finally, tiring of all the bullshit that came down from the top. He had eighteen months to retirement. He had once looked forward to it with pleasure, but that was before his wife, Beverly, died of a rare kidney disease. He took six months' medical leave to be with her to the end, grieving all the while over the promises he'd made and now would not keep, of all they'd planned to do together when he retired.

For the past eight months he'd worked "special assignment." Each detail lasted from several weeks to a few months. Because he was a "cowboy," roaming from yard to yard, he was disconnected from the real pipeline of what was going on in the company. He'd come to think that his bosses had taken him on as a charity case, keeping him busy to get him through to retirement. It angered him: his heart might not be in it, but by God, he was a professional and couldn't stomach ending his career as a slacker. He had badgered them relentlessly to give him something real, something important to do. It had deeply galled him, however, that management had selected him to handle the detail investigating the random killing of tramps. *Detail my ass.* He was it; he had no associates, no clerical support, and no one to count on to cover for him. It was proof enough in his mind that they really didn't give a rat's ass about dead bodies turning up on freight trains or railroad property across the Northwest—except that it generated bad press.

Keaton had come to care about the mounting body count in direct proportion to the lack of interest of his superiors. It was now nine, with the last two in the Vancouver yard. Except for the two college students, a real random occurrence, all the others had been of a group that had caused Keaton no end of grievance over the years. Keaton didn't understand it exactly: whether it was the fraud of concern on the part of his superiors or whether he'd come to value all human life as precious in watching his wife die. He'd started making waves rather than suppressing them. He was quoted in the press that the string of deaths was something the local and state authorities should show more interest in, perhaps even bringing in the FBI. With that one, Hank Claxton called and reamed him hard, commanding Keaton to cool the public commentary. Keaton had used the incident to extract the promise of more assistance, and had been promised he'd get it. So much for promises. He was little more than a mushroom, kept in the dark while being fed a load of crap.

His irritation mounting, Keaton picked up the phone and dialed Claxton's line again. He was surprised when Claxton answered the call directly.

"Sorry, Bud. Haven't forgotten ya," Claxton said. "It's been hellish around here this morning. How's things in Portland?"

"You want the truth, Hank, or bullshit?"

Claxton laughed good-naturedly. "You're a card, Bud. Of course I want the truth."

"Where the hell is the help you promised me? It's been nearly a month. I haven't seen squat."

"Easy, Bud. These things take time. This isn't the only iron we've got in the fire."

"When, Hank? I can't be in eight places at once. We get a break, get a lead, then it evaporates because I can't follow all trails at once. I don't want any bullshit. All I want to know is *when*?"

"Soon, Keaton. Soon."

There was a long silence on the line.

"You know, Hank," Keaton said, doodling absently on the desk pad in front of him. The rough outline of a mushroom emerged beneath the point of his pen. "I'm beginning to feel like a mushroom on this project. Know what I mean?"

Another pause. "Excuse me?" Claxton stammered.

"You know, kept in the dark and fed shit."

"No reason to get nasty now," Claxton said sternly. "I'm working on it. But like I said, this is just one of the problems on my plate. You gotta understand."

Neither spoke. Keaton sighed bitterly.

"Keep up the good work, Bud. And remember, don't go overboard with the press."

"You have a nice day, too," Keaton said, slamming down the phone.

Keaton tore free the top sheet on the desk pad and crumpled it furiously. He fired it across the room.

He felt a sudden tightening in his chest. He closed his eyes, took a deep breath, and leaned back in his chair, trying to relax. He took several deep breaths, drawing the air in through his nose, blowing it out through his mouth. It was something his daughter had told him would help let go of tension. He finally opened his eyes, leaned forward, and extracted a Pall Mall from the pack on his desk. He lit it and exhaled a cloud of smoke. He picked up the phone and dialed his daughter's number in Seattle.

"Hey, darling," Keaton said when his daughter answered the phone.

"Hi, Daddy. Where are you?"

"Same old same old."

"I was hoping you were back."

"Me too, baby. Me too. If wishes had wings, I would be."

"They get you any help yet?"

Keaton closed his eyes, inhaling a long pull on his cigarette. He blew a noisy stream of air toward the ceiling. "Soon. They say soon, now."

"You're going easy on those cigarettes, aren't you, Daddy?"

Keaton smiled. The battle with his daughter over his smoking had been lifelong since she was a little girl. "Oh yeah," he said, chuckling. "You know me."

"Precisely," his daughter said, irritated.

"How *you* doing?" Keaton asked.

"Oh, just wonderful. I was in the bathroom when you called. Losing my breakfast."

"Bad?"

"Nah. I like throwing up."

"You know what I mean," Keaton said irritably. "Where's Dan?"

"Gone. As usual. Won't be back until next Thursday."

Keaton took another drag on his cigarette. He'd never really liked his son-in-law. Keaton thought he thought more about his career as a consultant in a big firm than staying home with his pregnant wife and young son. Keaton tried to keep his opinion to himself, as he knew that his daughter harbored childhood resentments that would call this a case of the pot calling the kettle black. Keaton had argued then that it was his *job*, that he couldn't help being gone so much. It had never evoked any sympathy from his daughter, and now, it didn't evoke much in his own mind either. He'd missed a lot of her growing up, of being part of a home and a family, a fact made all too poignant with the loss of his wife.

"How's William?" Keaton asked, his heart softening, thinking of his only grandchild.

"He's outside. Playing with some neighbor boys. You know William. If there's a mess to get into, he wants to be first."

"How's that cut on his head?" William had zigged when he should have zagged in a game of tag, and had tripped and tumbled against a picnic table at a park. It'd taken fifteen stitches to close the gash over his right eye. Fortunately the only thing he'd lost was a gush of blood and a couple of days of romp time with his buddies. It could have easily been much worse.

"What? *That little scratch?* That's what he told me this morning, when I told him to be careful."

"You doing all right?" Keaton asked again with a tone that implied he expected a serious, truthful answer.

"Yes, Daddy. And *you?*" The tone mirrored his own. His daughter had become much more solicitous of his feelings after the death of her mother, whom she knew was her father's confidante and closest friend.

"Oh yeah," he said, trying to sound light and jovial.

"Daddy?" his daughter admonished.

"No, seriously. A little trouble sleeping, maybe. But that's always true when I'm not in my own bed. But, yeah. I'm fine."

"You eating right?"

"Listen. I'm fine. Okay?"

"Okay," she said with exaggerated exasperation. "Just don't come bellyaching to me," she teased. "I gotta go," she said urgently. "I feel another urge to hurl."

"You put that so elegantly."

"Bye, Daddy. Call again. Soon, okay?"

"Love ya, baby."

"Me too."

Keaton rose and paced the room, consuming the space in two strides. Rather than release the head of steam stoked by his conversation with Claxton, his pacing served only to stoke it, causing him to feel like a boiler about to blow. He pivoted, grabbed his jacket, and strode from the room like a man on a mission.

He was down the stairs, out of the building, and halfway to his truck before any consideration for where he might be going. He halted abruptly. He stared at his truck, parked in a narrow slot between a dumpster and a power transformer. His gaze rose to the hard blue, cloudless sky that stretched away to the east, out over the weave of track in the Portland yard. It was a glorious, late October day. Perfect for bird hunting. Bud Keaton exhaled a big breath of air, puffing his cheeks. He fingered the truck keys in his pocket, eyed the hulking silent shape of the white GMC, and turned about-face and started walking. What he needed was a good breakfast. The little diner down the street from the Mark Spencer Hotel had the best coffee in town. Their eggs and sausage weren't bad either. The walk would do him good.

He bought a newspaper from a rack outside the diner and pushed through the glass door to take a booth along the back wall. He scanned the soiled menu as though looking for evidence of a crime. Nothing particularly appealed to him. He ordered eggs over easy, sausage, hash browns, and a biscuit with little enthusiasm, and picked up the newspaper to check the headlines. With less than three weeks to the election, Carter's strength in the polls was growing; Americans could expect no drop in oil prices anytime soon, and there was another major study out on the dangers of cholesterol. Keaton looked up, caught the attention of his waitress. He changed his order. Hot oatmeal, dry toast, and orange juice. It appealed to him about as much as the first order. He opened the paper and began ingesting the news with vigor.

He read the sports section, the business section, and the obituaries. Keaton wasn't morbid as much as he was curious. In a state paper like the *Oregonian,* the common citizen was lucky to get two inches of micro-type when they died. That was all a life was worth—if that—it seemed. Keaton found no pleasure in searching for the odd fact, the bizarre accomplishment among the honorably mentioned. He folded the paper and started to put it aside when a headline he'd overlooked caught his eye. "Serial Killer Marks More Railroad Deaths." God, how he hated news reporters. Never let the facts stand in the way of a good story. They weren't "railroad deaths"; they were merely deaths on railroad property.

Listen to me, he thought. *I sound like Hank Claxton. Minimize the truth to the point of extinction.* He snapped the paper up and read the article.

"Railroad authorities have no leads on the identity of the killer of two transients this week in the Burlington Northern rail yard in Vancouver, but suspect it might be the work of a serial killer.

"'We're considering that possibility,' said Special Agent Bud Keaton.

"Authorities are seeking information on the whereabouts of two individuals who might have witnessed Wednesday night's killings in the hobo jungle adjacent to the rail yard. Rumors that they fled to Wishram, perhaps east into Idaho, or south into Oregon were not confirmed. Local authorities are serving an ancillary role to the investigation spearheaded by Keaton of the BN."

Spearheaded? Ancillary? My Christ, Keaton thought, slamming the paper down. *Sounds like a damn army out there combing the wilds.* As for the dead? Barely a mention, and no mention of their names at that.

Keaton fumbled for his wallet as he rose from the booth. He dropped a five on the table to pay for his breakfast, turned, and walked out without bothering to wait to eat.

The Worst Lie

Elijah drifted in sleep like a rain cloud in a gray sky, caught in oscillating suspension between two worlds: one of air and light, the other of ever-deepening darkness. A nerve on the surface of consciousness, far removed, twitched, and he floated upward on a sleep thermal, up into a higher strato-sphere, into the realm of dream.

In the dream, he sat alone on a high, rocky hill in the shadow of a gnarled dwarf pine, the full intensity of the noon sun bleaching the earth of its color, making everything appear flat and washed out. He sat before a desolate landscape devoid of all life. He was content to sit and watch, to be the observing one, captivated by the shimmering heat waves that distorted the far horizon, making it impossible to tell where one realm ended and the other began.

A dark speck rose and spiraled like an ash up out of the simmering desert. It ascended from the southeast, followed in time by another that rose out of the southwest. As these twin specks rose higher, escaping distortion of heat waves, Elijah could make out finally that they were crows, a pair of crows. Though rising from separate origins, they rose as if sent on the same trajec-tory, destined to merge with the sun. Just as they were to converge, he heard one caw—*saw* more than heard. Then saw the other answer back. And then they were lost in the blazing white hole in the sky that held the sun.

Elijah-of-the-dream was blinded by the glare. In the dream, he smiled, for Elijah-of-the-dream knew that he was already asleep. He closed his eyes. Everything went black. He felt a cold spasm pass over him like a shadow darker than night, and in the dream, he forced his eyes open, alert to some unseen danger.

At a great distance, tunneling toward him through the wavering heat waves, he saw a single solitary figure approaching. The figure was coming up from the south. His journey was indeterminate in terms of how far away he was or how long it would take for him to arrive. Elijah-the-observing-one knew he had an immense space of time to consider who this was, why he was coming, what his purpose was. Out of the south, the place of innocence.

He had the distinct feeling that he knew this person, but could not fix who he was or why he was here now. Rather than a being of innocence, there was a disquieting sense to this one. The figure crossed the empty, bleached landscape to stand at the base of the hill. He stopped and stood as if waiting to be beckoned forward. Elijah-of-the-dream sat up straighter, waiting. The figure wore a large hat with a wide brim that hid his face in shadow. He lifted his gaze as if to focus on Elijah and then slowly began to climb the hill, one step after another, coming straight on toward Elijah.

Halfway up, Elijah thought he recognized the features of the man's face obscured mostly by shadow. *Uncle?* Could it be? But how? The figure came on slowly, slowly, but would not lift his gaze fully now to look at him.

Elijah waited silently, sensing that he must not bid encouragement of any kind to the one who approached. He sensed a growing disharmony deep within, an agitation, a riling of discordant feelings. The figure seemed to be taking forever. As he neared, almost to the point of arrival, he—for it was clear it was an old man very much like Uncle, but not quite—veered slightly to the right. Then he turned abruptly to the left, drawing closer, but moving obliquely, obviously shielding something he held in his right hand, hidden in the fold of his cloak. Elijah's disquiet caused a choking sensation. He wished the One-from-the-distance would speak.

Panic, then terror flared like a flame. What was it the One-from-the-distance carried?

Uncle? he cried, part greeting, part alarm. There was no response. And then Elijah-of-the-dream heard a voice whisper, as though someone was standing right beside him: *Careful. Careful. One is the shadow. The other is . . .*

"Caw-caw, caw-caw."

Elijah awoke abruptly and sat up as if torn from sleep by a hooked claw. Just as abruptly, pain ricocheted through his skull, hammering him flat gain.

"Son of a *dog*," he groaned, breathing in short gasps, massaging his head feebly with one hand. He lay still, catching his breath, the image of the

155

turning form and the sound of the voice whispering caution dissolving into the world of day. There was no explanation for the way he felt at this moment other than being poisoned. It was an old feeling—not one he'd known for a long time, but still familiar.

He was hung over, dreadfully so.

He opened his eyes slowly, letting the dark of the boxcar fill him. *Where am I?* It hurt to think.

Nothing came. He hadn't a clue. The thought of being untethered, loose in the world, unnerved him. He focused as though bearing down to lift a great stone.

In a rail yard . . . But where?

. . . Bend.

Elijah eased up and let go of his forced concentration. "A good little town," he muttered, rubbing his head, ". . . to be from."

Elijah raised himself slowly to rest on one elbow, careful not to move too quickly. He scanned the dim interior of the car. He stared at the lump of covers in the corner opposite. He scratched his gray chin whiskers and fumbled for the makings for a cigarette. He found the crumpled pack of Pall Malls Willie had given him. He ripped the top off to find one last flattened smoke. He extracted it and put it between his teeth and sucked a deep breath for strength. Drawing courage, he slowly extricated himself from his blankets, rising, turning to kneel. He studied the dark form beside him as he patted himself down for a light. He found a disposable lighter in one of his pockets and lit up. He was seized immediately with a paroxysm of coughing. The vigorous hacking brought a stir to the body in the blankets beside him. Jackie rolled over, his eyes puffy with sleep.

"You okay?" Jackie asked. He watched as Elijah tried to catch his breath.

"Elijah?" Jackie said, worried when the coughing persisted. Finally, Elijah expelled a huge volume of air, roaring like a wounded bear. He lifted his head and stared at Jackie, tears streaming down his cheeks.

"Okay," Elijah managed breathlessly. He took a slow, cautious breath and, finding himself in control at last, straightened again, pressing against the wall of the car for stability. Once erect, he drew another drag, managing to inhale without coughing.

"Son of a dog," he growled, steadying himself with one hand on the wall.

"You okay?" Jackie asked again.

"Just slow getting started. But okay, you betcha. Hand me my hat, would ya," Elijah asked, reaching, pointing with one hand, the other hand secure against the wall for balance. He didn't dare bend over and try to retrieve it on his own, afraid the top of his head would fall off. He took it when Jackie offered it up and fitted it snuggly like a lid to help keep things together.

"I gotta take care of a couple of things," Elijah said, turning to stumble slowly toward the open door.

Jackie sat upright with alarm. "Where you going *now?*" he demanded. "See another damn man about a horse?"

"No horse. No more horses," Elijah said imploringly. "Gotta take care of a couple of things. Be gone a while. Look after my stuff." Elijah eased himself down into a sitting position at the open door, wincing from stiffness. "Too damn old," he mumbled. He launched himself free, his hat falling to the ground as he struggled for balance, pain exploding like a bomb in his head. He stooped slowly to get his hat and rose on unsteady legs, fitting the hat to his head again.

"Where you going?" Jackie asked, coming to the boxcar door, his voice edged with frustration.

"I already told ya," Elijah said, starting off on unsteady feet. "Watch our stuff, boy. You hear?"

Jackie stood in his stocking feet, shivering in the chill morning air, watching Elijah make his way down the track through the center of the small rail yard in the middle of Bend. Elijah crossed Division Street and passed into the neighborhood of small houses. In a moment, he was gone from sight.

"God *damn you*," Jackie cursed bitterly under his breath as he padded quickly to the corner of the car and the warmth of his blankets.

+ + +

Elijah made the rounds of back-alley dumpsters and trash bins to attend to the first order of business—finding something to eat. As he wandered the deserted side streets of slumbering Bend, echoes from the night's dream kept rising, resonating in his mind.

As the fog of alcohol began to thin, Elijah found himself repeatedly drawn to the disembodied voice that had whispered to him right at the end of the dream. He was perplexed that he'd dreamed, that dreaming seemed to be returning. He hadn't dreamed in years. Gradually, as though still held in the dream, he became aware that each time he heard the echo of his uncle's voice—or what he thought was his uncle's voice—it was mirrored by the plaintive cry of crows somewhere in the distance. In the dream . . .

He drew up short, staring blankly. "Not *in* the dream," he exclaimed. The voice of Crow had come from this world, not the *other,* piercing the dream. He stood listening to the sounds of the world, the building hum of morning traffic. On the wind, mixing with the sound of his own labored breath, was the cry of a crow again.

"Caw-caw. Caw-caw." *Careful. Careful.*

Elijah closed his eyes and tried to fix again on the image of the solitary one in the dream, coming nearer, nearer, turning toward him. There was something deeply disturbing about the image.

"Caw-caw. Caw-caw."

Elijah opened his eyes and watched a pair of crows pass through the sky overhead. They flapped their dark, heavy wings, propelling their inky black bodies through the morning light.

Then it struck him like a hammer blow. "It wasn't *my* dream," he whispered, a chill passing through him. It was knowledge he had without thought or consideration, a simple *knowing.* Somehow, he had slipped into the dream of another—either that or someone had slipped into his dream. It was uncommon, but it had happened to him before. He remembered vividly a time in prison where it had carried foreboding, a warning: *careful, careful.* He hadn't heeded it, for he did not understand the power of the *knowing* that it embodied. Only days later, a grudge harbored by another inmate brought an attack that resulted in Elijah being put in solitary confinement for 120 days. A living death.

"*Who?*" Elijah pondered, turning slowly, his eyes scanning his surroundings as though he'd detected the presence of someone watching him. "*Why?*" he wondered. He hadn't done anything to anyone. He began a slow shuffle forward again, every now and then casting a backward glance over his shoulder to see if someone was following him. The feeling was inescapable.

The day grew warm as morning progressed into afternoon. Elijah found his way by a slow circuitous route across town, drawn like a rolling stone to where the Deschutes River slowed to a listless meandering through Drake and Columbia Parks, two beauty spots that were groomed and tended by the city for the pleasure of local residents. Elijah found an out-of-the-way place up under a bridge where he could bathe, such as it was, with little risk of being seen. Refreshed and sobered—at least *sobering*—he wandered southward along the west side of the river to a patch of sunny grass that called to him. He soaked his underwear and socks as discretely as possible and hung them out of sight in a holly bush to dry. He peeled and ate the last of the overripe bananas he'd salvaged from a dumpster and stretched out in the sun at the edge of a hedge for a nap.

Elijah awoke and sat up, confused for a moment about where he was. He stared out at the languid river, a large white swan scissoring the surface of the still water with the wake of its passage. The swan shimmered in the bright sunlight, dramatically framed by the deep shadow of the far bank. *Light* and *dark*, supple twining.

He stared at the swan and its reflection as it glided through the water. Elijah slowly shuttered his eyes, enjoying the lingering mind's image of the swan. In the silence a soft voice came to him: *The worst lie is the lie you tell yourself.* The voice was truly that of his uncle speaking to him from the past.

Elijah opened his eyes and looked around, then gazed intently at the swan. He was beginning to feel a little spooked by all the odd occurrences percolating up from below. The swan glided effortlessly, first one way and then another, as it zigzagged back across the water toward him.

—|—|—|—

Late afternoon found Elijah himself upstream on the opposite side of the river, sitting at a picnic table observing the end of shift at the big Cascade Products mill. The mill sat on the original site where it had been built after the First World War, helping to fuel the economy of central Oregon and Bend's rise to prominence. Though the economy had diversified since, timber products were still central to the prosperity of the city and the region. When Elijah was a young man, Indians weren't allowed to work in the mill, except for the dirtiest, meanest, most dangerous jobs. With government regulations now, equal opportunity was better. His son worked as a foreman on one of the big board-sizing lines. Elijah couldn't remember when he'd last spoken with his son, but it had been many months, and it hadn't been pleasant, he remembered. Toby had never forgiven him for his absence as a father, the desultory life Elijah had lived, dropping in to stay a while, then disappearing again. Not that Elijah blamed him.

Elijah studied a group of workers coming out of one of the big, cavernous buildings. They crossed the parking lot toward a row of cars. Even at 100 yards, he could easily pick out his son in the crowd. It wasn't merely the dark complexion, but the way he walked. Almost defiant. His son was unmistakably holding court with his fellow workers. He gestured with both arms and the group erupted in laughter.

Elijah watched as his son split off, walking to a dark green Chevy Blazer. He heard the sound of the engine turning over, being revved to life. He stared at the Blazer, its windshield filled with late-afternoon glare. The others departed, a farewell honking of horns. Though Elijah couldn't see for the glare, he had the distinct feeling he was being observed. He wondered what his son must be thinking, what he might do. Simply drive away, he figured. Leave the past well enough alone.

Elijah heard the engine die and saw the truck door open. His son stepped into the sunlight. He wore dark sunglasses now that shielded his eyes and gave him an edge of menace. He stood motionless for several moments. Then, with determination he strode forward toward Elijah.

Toby McCloud came down into the grove of pines, approaching his father directly. Elijah straightened a bit, giving himself a little more room in his chest for breath. Under the hard gaze of his son's piercing stare, even though he couldn't see it, Elijah felt lightheaded, as though there was not enough air to breathe.

"Hey," Elijah said quietly, a small smile pulling at the corners of his mouth.

His son approached to within a stride's distance, then stopped. "What are you doing here?" Toby asked in a tight voice.

"In Bend?"

"Here. *Right* here." His son's posture remained straight as a lodgepole pine.

"Passing through."

His son stood without speaking, his stance like a hawk perched on its killing stand.

"Don't come here," his son said bitterly.

Elijah stared without changing expression. "How's Connie? The children?" he asked.

Toby said nothing.

Elijah smiled. "You still don't like me much," he said, more an article of fact than question.

"You still aren't much of a father," his son responded. Toby let his head turn slightly, permitting his gaze to drift out over the river. Elijah studied the slow rise and fall of his son's chest, the ebb and flow of his breathing. It was even and steady, though everything else about him was locked in tautness as though ready to spring.

"I was sorry to hear about your mother," Elijah said quietly.

Toby McCloud's jaw flexed spasmodically. He said nothing.

"I'm sorry I couldn't . . ."

"Why did you come here?" his son demanded.

Elijah shrugged. "Passing through," he said.

"Always just *passing through*. Well, next time, don't stop."

Elijah could not hold his son's gaze and looked away. He noticed the dark outline of several crows in the spire of a big Douglas fir across the river. "I wanted to see you," he said quietly. "Wanted to make sure you were okay."

His son laughed darkly. "It's a little late." He shifted on one foot. "Mom's dead. Your welcoming committee is gone. You're not welcome here."

Elijah felt sorrow, such shame, under the withering fury of his son. He wanted to say something of the regret he felt, but he couldn't find the words. He looked at his son, and despite the fury, saw that this moment was a gift, a most precious gift. He had meant to stay in Glacier to see winter come. He had never imagined this moment was possible. And yet, here they were.

He caught movement in his field of vision and looked up to see his son step quickly toward him, raising a hand. Elijah thought his son was going to strike him. His son's hand came up and Elijah steeled himself to the assault, but Toby jammed something in his jacket pocket instead, then backed away. Elijah looked down, trying to square what happened with the expectation he had had. He eyed a crumpled bill pressed in his pocket. He raised his gaze to study his son. Toby's face was frozen in a mask of condemnation.

"Don't pity yourself in thinking I never gave you anything. But next time you pass through, just keep going. Think of me as dead. It's how I think of you."

His son turned and marched rapidly back across the lot toward his Blazer. Elijah watched as he climbed in, started the truck, and drove away. He stared down at his jacket pocket. He extracted a bill, something else coming free with it, pinched between his thumb and fingers. The bill was a twenty. He turned the other piece of paper over to see what it was. It was a photograph. The one of the woman and the two small children seated at a picnic table. The one he'd reclaimed at Junkman Willie's dump. He had forgotten that he'd saved it; remembered again his indecision, not being able to discard it but not wanting to keep it either. He recalled thinking how it was clear that the woman and the two children were not related. But what? he wondered again. They were destined to be together in that moment, captured frozen as they sat at a picnic table in some long-ago time. Her role in their lives was a mystery. Like the role he'd had in the lives of his own children. A mystery. Shame filled. Sorrowful. A moment long ago, now gone forever.

+ + +

Jackie could tell even in the dim light of twilight that Elijah was drunk again. Jackie stood at the edge of the rail siding, absently throwing rocks at old bottles and jars lying in the weeds behind the St. Vincent de Paul warehouse. He was faint with worry, wondering after Elijah, where he'd gone, if anything had happened to him, if he was ever coming back again. He'd been giving Elijah another ten minutes for the last two hours, since well before sundown. With the dark settling heavy around him, putting a shadowed face on everything, Jackie's mind had begun to work overtime, conjuring injury and worse: *abandonment.* He watched as Elijah stumble-stepped slowly toward him, humming a drunken ditty. Jackie bent over, picked up a rock from the roadbed, and fired it at an assortment of surplus windows leaning against the warehouse. Glass shattered loudly, sounding like the exploding of stars.

"*Whoa!* Whoa now," Elijah protested, alarmed at the sudden noise. He stood several paces off, staring at Jackie, then at the windows, trying to decipher the connection between the two. Jackie bent and retrieved another stone, and fired it with deft accuracy at the windows.

"Whoa now, damn it!" Elijah commanded gruffly. Jackie bent and retrieved yet another rock. Just as he was cocking his arm to throw, Elijah cuffed him on the ear with a wild swing of his arm. Jackie sprang away in surprise, recoiling his arm, turning to take aim at Elijah.

"What the hell?" Elijah said, standing as erect as he could manage. He held a brown bag in one hand.

"What the hell yourself," Jackie seethed angrily. "What'd you do that for?" His throwing arm remained poised, trembling with tension.

"You want to bring the coppers down on us, spend the night in jail?"

"Wouldn't bother me," Jackie said defiantly.

"Well, it would me. And I ain't gonna be a part of it." Elijah pushed past Jackie, heading toward the boxcar where they'd encamped the night before.

"Where have you been?" Jackie demanded.

"Been around," Elijah said cryptically. "What's it to you?"

"I've been waiting for you all day. I thought something happened to you."

"Something always happens, whether you intend it or not," Elijah answered, laying his bag up on the floor of the boxcar, managing with some difficulty to climb in after it. He rose from his hands and knees, brushed himself off, and disappeared into the murky darkness of the car's interior. Jackie scrambled in after him.

"I've been waiting here all day," Jackie continued. "Think I had a good time, waiting for you?"

Elijah sat down on his blankets and removed his hat. He looked up to study the dark silhouette of the boy.

"Brought you something to eat," Elijah said pleasantly, wanting to be done with the annoyance of the boy's ill temper. Make yourself a sandwich," he said, gesturing toward the brown bag. He scratched his chin whiskers, opened the bag, and peered inside. In the gloom of the car, there was no way to distinguish its contents. He reached in and found what he was seeking. He extracted the nearly empty bottle of port, uncorked it, and took a long pull from the mouth of the bottle. He put the bottle between his legs and leaned back against the bulkhead. "Helluva day," he muttered to himself. He lifted the bottle and took another swallow.

"You want a sandwich?" he said, lifting his gaze to focus on the dark outline of the boy again.

"I ain't hungry."

Elijah laughed. "Never knew a child that wasn't hungry."

"I'm no damn *child*!" Jackie said, his voice quivering with rage.

Elijah shrugged and took another swallow. A long silence lapsed between them.

"Don't you *care*?" Jackie finally said, his voice barely a whisper, hoarse with emotion.

"'Bout what?" Elijah said blandly.

"I thought you were dead."

"I am," Elijah said sullenly. "And you ain't the first today to tell me that." Elijah turned the bottle up and drained it in two swallows.

"You don't even care, do you?" Jackie said. "About anyone but yourself."

"That's right," Elijah agreed angrily. "You don't like it, you're free to leave. Anytime. Just head out. I ain't stopping you. I ain't some babysitter you gotta ask permission of."

Jackie's arm coiled instinctively. He let fly the rock that was still in his hand. Elijah reacted, hunching his shoulders, without clearly seeing what was coming, one hand coming up clumsily to shield his face. The rock ricocheted off the bulkhead of the boxcar about six inches right of his head.

"You little shit," Elijah protested, sobered by the vibration of steel ringing in his ear. "You're a fucking pain in the ass, you know that?"

"And you're a fucking drunk," Jackie spat back. "Indian, my ass," he said, shaking with rage and grief and hurt. "I've seen real Indians, and they don't look nothing like you."

Jackie turned and ran. He leaped in one long, fluid arc through the pale frame of light of the open door. He was gone.

Elijah sat in the dimness, pondering what had just happened. He couldn't make sense of it.

"Oh yeah," Elijah said finally, chuckling, dismissing the encounter. "You been all around. Seen cowboys. Indians. Seen it all, I bet. And you're right. I am a drunk. But I'll tell you one thing for certain: I ain't no fucking babysitter. Not now. Not ever."

Terror Unchecked

Luther Gon squatted beneath a stubby oak, studying the camp at the edge of the Wishram dump. Patience was a virtue, was it not? It's what his stepfather always told him—may his soul rot in hell. To any request Gon had made as a boy, exceedingly so after his mother died, the old man rebuked him with the commandment to be patient, whether he was asking to go to the bathroom or to be let out of the coal bin where he was locked in the cellar when he was, as his stepfather would righteously profess, "filled with the devil." The vile man had it ass-backward, for Gon knew him to be the one filled with the devil, despite having once been a Pentecostal preacher. Gon had learned he could wait for anything; indeed, he had the patience of Job. Yes, of Job, but not Job's simple-minded love-of-God patience. What a fool, Job, Gon thought. God's love and mercy was nowhere evident in the world. The darkness of the world that Gon had known as a boy had made him a true believer in only the Old Testament gospel of "an eye for an eye."

Patience in this case, however, had not yielded what Gon wanted, and he was growing restless. The one they called Junkman had come and gone, and come and gone, but there was no sign of the boy and the other called Elijah. The night in Vancouver had gone about as badly as things go, what with missing one drunk in the weeds, then the boy, and now this other, this Elijah. How had he missed him, too? It was hell to pay with the voice in his head. So careless. Sloppy careless. *And you call yourself the righteous avenger?*

The two tramps in Baker, Nevada, where Gon had jumped free of the express freight out of Portland, had been wrong. They said the paper suspected they were in Wishram, but Gon was sure now they weren't. Might

165

have been, but no longer. Lucky just the same for the two in Baker. Gon didn't have time for them. And the angry voice was insistent. *It's the boy you want. The boy. He's the threat.* Maybe so, but he wasn't going to leave until the one with the dog got what was coming to him.

The dog was the problem. Good size and mean, by the look of him. Gon had feared at one point the dog had scented him. People thought dogs were stupid beasts, but Gon knew better. Dogs were smart, and patient, too. Gon didn't like dogs, as he had never met a dog that liked him. He despised them, really, but he respected them for their patience. Gon knew he could learn a trick or two from studying dogs.

He untied the burlap bag beside him and deftly felt through the contents. He extracted the roll of salami and a crumpled loaf of white bread. He cut four slices of meat, packed them between two pieces of bread, and devoured it in a series of savage bites. He started to make another sandwich. He stared at the meat and smiled. He reached into the bag again and searched carefully in the folds of an old shirt for the small tin box. He removed it slowly, held it gently, and opened the lid. He studied the small silver devices lying in their bed of cotton wadding. He removed one of the silver buttons and fingered it gingerly. Other than the flares he'd rummaged from the railroad shed outside Baker, the tin of blasting caps was the only other thing he'd bothered to take. Like the flares, they were small, easy to hide and carry away. *How clever,* the voice whispered. *How very clever of you.*

Gon replaced the cap in its protective pocket and laid the box down at his feet. He sliced off a large section of salami from the roll. *This will be good,* he thought. He made a small slit in the length of it with the point of his knife, then carefully inserted one of the blasting caps. *Yes, yes,* the voice cooed softly. *Very clever.*

Gon lifted his gaze to study the expanse of the dump. The old man was building up the fire, for dinner, no doubt. It was already sundown and suddenly beginning to grow dark. Another half hour, there would be little remnant of light left. *Soon now,* the voice whispered. *Soon.*

Evil is less a matter of inbred nature than the infliction of terror unchecked. The voice in Gon's head was not a provocateur of evil, but a protector against the torment rained upon him as a boy. He'd come to love the voice only he could hear because it was on his side. The only one. And it never shamed him for his inability to speak without stuttering when mad. Luther had been born of a woman who held narcissism the highest form of love. She never knew which partner had seeded her with child, and was glad at his birth only because there was one man willing to give him his name. A gift of legitimacy, she always told Luther. Something she'd never had. But legitimacy was a gift Luther could have done without. When his mother ended up with her throat slashed by a drunken bar patron grown tired of her cockteasing ways, Luther became tethered unmercifully to the Reverend Gon. Such a fitting name, for the man was gone most of the time—God knows where. When he left, he locked Luther in the coal bin in the old house at the side of the rail yard. To imagine the state of mind of a child so detained is to envision the darkest pit of hell. Caged like an animal, starving, frightened, stammering pitiful cries for help. And then, for a period of months, borrowing a trick reserved for Job, came the old rummy-eyed wino bum who'd heard his cries and found his way through the brush at the back of the house. *The Bum*, as Luther came to think of him. The memory of *that* tormentor burned bitter in the heart of Luther Gon. Caged like a dog, teased and prodded, spat and pissed on through the barred, broken window that lit the coal bin, Luther clung to the only hope that was powerful enough to sustain a hold on wanting to live. *You wait, you bastard. You wait.* His faith became the sustaining belief that the Bum would be forever somewhere in the world. Gon became a student of trains, preoccupied with studying rolling strings of boxcars, keeping an eye sharp for anyone who might carry the plague of the tormentor. *You wait, you bastard. You wait.*

Luther waited now, whittling in silence on the stout sapling he'd cut. The long knife pared the green wood stroke by stroke, taking the end down to a fine spear point. As he worked, the voice began to whisper to him like the rustling of wind. Softly, it made the most perfect sound. The voice never stuttered. With the soothing presence of the voice, Luther never again felt the terror of the dark cage of memory that was his childhood. The insult of it, and the shame, was assuaged with anger. *You wait, you bastard. You wait.*

Luther rose and turned to the gnarled dwarf oak he'd selected. He lifted his burlap bag and tied it on a branch high up, out of the way. Carefully, he fixed the baited slab of salami to the end of his spear. He turned back toward the dump to eye the glow of the old man's fire. He studied the dim shadows. Then he whistled low and long.

He could see the silhouette of the big dog's head, backlit by the fire, rise and turn in his direction. He whistled again, causing the dog to push himself steadily to his feet. Luther whistled a third time now and saw the dog take a tentative step, heard the old bum mutter something to the dog, a lilting inflection, a question.

Luther smiled. He turned and climbed silently into the tree, to settle in the low perch he'd selected. *Soon*, the voice bade him. *Soon enough the old man will find out what is waiting. You wait. You bastard.*

Luther's eyes attentively followed the slow movement of the dog as it came through the dry weeds toward the thicket of trees. As the dog grew closer, Luther teased it once or twice with a soft moan, raising a primitive, rumbling growl in the throat of his prey. He knew the dog knew he was there. He knew the dog loathed his presence. He knew the dog was alert but overconfident, here on the periphery of its domain.

Avenger crept forward cautiously, a fire heating his eyes. Slowly, steadily, he moved within twenty feet of the tree.

Luther watched as the big dog lifted its nose, taking a scented reading to assess the danger. The dog's growl intensified, then died. The dog stepped forward a half step. Then another, and another, then halted abruptly a full body's length back of the meat dangling in front of him on the tip of the sharp spear.

Luther could feel the hot gaze of the big animal, could detect its lethal prejudice. He held the shaft steady, every muscle tautly controlled to prevent a false movement. He watched as the big dog stretched his neck, his muzzle inching closer to the meat. He stepped forward again, retracting his head, than extending it forward again. The growl rose up and faded away as he pressed his nose to the bait. They remained like that, dog and man, frozen in trance, assessing each other for several long moments.

The dog's lips curled back in quivering threat, exposing its teeth. His jaw opened slowly, his neck extending. He caught the corner of the bait with his big canines and tugged tentatively. Luther felt the pull run up the shaft, through his hand, up his arm to his brain. The dog pulled again, causing an involuntary shiver to spasm across Luther's shoulders. The third tug brought separation, and the meat dropped almost soundlessly in the grass beneath the tree. Luther watched as the dog bent its head, its eyes still fixed on the silhouette in the tree, then sniff the temptation at its feet. The head dipped, the jaws bit down.

A flash and roar, a yelp and snarl, a staggering motion. Luther launched from the tree, the spear point true, pinning the big dog to the ground. With suddenness so swift the dog barely suffered, Luther ran the blade of his knife through the dog's heart. The dog spasmed once and lay still.

Luther's focus shifted immediately to the dimming light of the old man's fire. He saw the outline of the one they called Junkman, standing, peering into the darkness.

"Here, boy," Junkman Willie called. "Avenger, come." Worry and agitation was distinct in his voice.

"Come! Avenger, come!"

Luther crouched in the darkness, one knee still pressing on the mass of the dog. He permitted himself a small smile.

Wait, the voice whispered. *Just you wait.*

Such a Big Name

Elijah stirred and woke suddenly at first light, and rose and went to the door of the old Santa Fe boxcar on the sidetrack in the Bend yard. The night had brought a sharp drop in temperature, and the cold stabbed through his threadbare socks, his breath rising in steamy white plumes in front of his face. He shuffled from one foot to the other, hugging himself for warmth.

What was it he had heard? A sound like an iron bar prying a stone from its earth wallow. It had entered his sleep and dislodged him from a dream, only now he couldn't remember it or determine whether the sound was from this world or the *other*. He shivered. The day was silent and still except for a faint, almost imperceptible hum. Elijah cocked an ear. It came from the west and south: the hum of wood mills on the river. Yet this was not what had wakened him. He turned and glanced back through the dim light of the boxcar. His blankets. And the boy's—empty.

The boy!

Elijah heard the *whuff* of wings and turned to follow what looked like the dark shadow of a crow—no, two crows—pass the open door, beating a line south down the center of the rail yard. He blinked; they were gone. Elijah was left with the feeling that perhaps they had not, in fact, even been there. Had they only been imagined, or *glimpsed* like a fractured image refracted as it passed from one dimension to another?

Two crows. South. The boy. The boy. The thought was loud and resonant in his mind.

Elijah padded back to their sleeping corner and slipped his boots on. He jammed his hat hard on his head and bent to roll the blankets, both his and the boy's. There was a freight due, he knew, just after sunrise. Heading south. That was where the boy had gone. He could feel it. South. The boy was *gone*. South.

—+—+—+—

The freight was a step-on, slowing to a slow roll to permit an exchange of crew like changing partners at a dance, the music never stopping. Seeing nothing open in the first half of the train, Elijah caught the tail of a grain hopper rather than risking there might not be another place to ride. Hunkered down against the cold above the clattering wheels, riding a narrow plate of decking, heading south toward Klamath Falls.

Grain hoppers were the worst place to ride, except maybe gondolas, where wind whipped dust and debris unmercifully. Only partially shielded from the wind that sucked down the length of the train, Elijah buttoned his jacket to the throat and stuffed his hands deep into his pockets, letting the hypnotic beat of the track carry him into a suspended state of imagination. Elijah's thoughts floated like jetsam, windblown and beaten, snagged in momentary eddies, then sent swirling again. The misery of the ride was penance for the neglect, the suffering he'd caused the boy. It was not easy being a boy coming to manhood, not now, not ever, Elijah thought. And it was an egregious offense for grown men to purposefully thwart the journey. He had been party to that, however unwittingly, with his own son. There was little he could do about that now. But that didn't mean the opportunity was universally lost. Not this time. Not yet anyway.

As the miles rolled under him, the clatter of the tracks loud in his ears, the image of his own journey, long ago, began to sift like flour out of memory. Time began to flow as in a dream, with flashing images followed by blank spaces, then images again, piling up one after the other. A waking dream took form, forged a focus, and Elijah surrendered to it, experiencing the sense of being lost within it, of being led to a precipice and told to jump. Was the command an inner voice or that of a tormentor? It wasn't like there was really any difference, for what did it matter? It was there. It was there.

—+—+—+—

Growing up Modoc in Modoc County, Oregon, was not easy. Being prideful and Modoc made it immeasurably more difficult still. Elijah's unbridled pride was a worry to his uncle, though he also took strength and found hope in it, as well.

Uncle was all the father Elijah had ever had, and Elijah was the son Uncle had always wanted. Uncle was Elijah's grandmother's older brother. It was she who first took Elijah in when he was a baby. Ruby, her youngest daughter, had run off at fifteen, she so hated life on the reservation. Distraught, Ruby's mother moved up the Sprague River to live with her brother. Two years later, when Ruby called from Salt Lake City with word she had had a baby, Elijah's grandmother boarded a train in Klamath Falls to go fetch her. A week later she returned without her daughter, a tiny, squalling infant in her arms. She never explained to anyone where her daughter was, or why the baby had come with such a big name. And when she died in 1922, it was her brother who took the boy and raised him. The boy was prideful even as a seven-year-old. But the old man was never ashamed of the boy, or the fact that he was proud to be Modoc.

Elijah and his uncle lived in a remote corner of the reservation, beyond the main tribal settlement. By special agreement with the local school district, Elijah was permitted to attend class with the children of the white families in the area surrounding Beatty rather than at the consolidated reservation school near the Agency. Elijah spoke Modoc in his uncle's home, though when his grandmother was alive, she forbade it. She'd grown up with a deep fear of God and of speaking in her native tongue instilled in her by the reservation missionaries on the Quapaw Agency in Oklahoma. It was against the wishes of God and also the law, and one could be hanged for it like a thief or murderer. But in the mind of Uncle—who knew about being defiant—the greater fear was that without the gift of his native language, the boy would be denied what little was left of the Modoc world and of the way of seeing and being in it. In Modoc, the word for a thing is not simply expressive, but embodies the essence of the thing itself. The word *his-wac-qas*, the word for "man," for example, carried the power of man himself. How can one speak to and be respectful in the presence of *his-wac-qas* unless one can convey the truth held in its name?

In Modoc, there is no word for *bathroom*. It is not a poverty of language, but rather an alien concept. In his uncle's cabin on the Sprague River, there was no bathroom. In Modoc, the essence of the urge is *last-ka*. Elijah was twelve, on the eve of becoming a man, when he raised his hand in Miss Mondragon's class at the white school to be excused to relieve himself. Miss Mondragon was a tall, thin, whippet-looking woman of high voice, pale skin, and insufferably thin patience. She had lessons to instruct and material to cover, and the needs of a dark-skinned, imprudent charge that had been forced upon her was of little importance to her.

If Elijah was anything, he was persistent. Finally, when he believed Miss Mondragon's refusal to acknowledge him had exceeded an acceptable level, he rose and left the room, leaving his teacher and fellow students in stunned silence.

In full fury, Miss Mondragon stormed from the room and down the hall to collar the boy in the bathroom, her outrage exceeding her prudery. When she demanded an explanation for such insolence, all Elijah could offer was the Modoc word *last-ka*. The utterance inflamed her sense of outrage. She slapped him repeatedly about the face and head.

"*Last-ka, last-ka, last-ka,*" Elijah intoned shrilly, as if calling on the power of the word to abrogate the crisis. Jerked on tiptoe by the pinched clamp on his neck, he could not help but lose focus on the matter at hand. Looking down finally, he saw the dark streak where he had urinated down the front of his teacher's dress. He froze—and by his stillness drew her attention to his insult. Her fury was redoubled, and blows fell harder yet about his ears.

Late the following night, Elijah and his uncle were just about to enter the *spo-klis,* the sweat lodge, behind the cow barn behind Uncle's cabin when a deputy sheriff stopped by to call his uncle aside to relay a message from the reservation superintendent. He was to bring his nephew and call at the Agency offices after Colonel Jason returned from church the following morning. Colonel Hiram Jason was a man of strict Christian principle and stern bearing and attended his duties as superintendent of the Klamath Agency in the same manner he practiced his faith. Elijah's uncle returned to the sweat lodge somber and subdued to conduct the boy's purification ceremony on the eve of Elijah's first vision quest. He tried to reassure the boy there was nothing to fear.

They started early, before dawn, to cover the twenty miles by wagon to the Agency. Neither spoke, but the old man knew Elijah was in turmoil by the way he fidgeted on the seat beside him. This day was to have begun a great event in the life of the boy, the beginning of his first day of his first quest for power as a man. It was a beautiful day, late autumn, the aspen and birches in quivering yellow splendor, the song of the river beside the road mixing softly with the steady clop of the horses' hooves. Now and again as they rode along, the old man reached out to lay a hand on the boy's leg. The boy sat rigid, ramrod straight, tense with determination and fear. In the old man's heart hung a heavy sadness, dreading what might come.

Colonel Jason was awaiting their arrival, annoyed that he'd arrived at the office barracks before them. He rose from the chair on the porch and stared coldly at the old man, then the boy. The old man passed the wagon reins to the boy and patted his leg again, not so much as a word passing between them, and rose to climb down from the buckboard. He came around in front of the team and ascended the steps to the office. He rose to his full height standing before the Colonel. The Colonel turned abruptly, dismissively, and walked into the building, Uncle following behind.

Elijah sat without moving for several minutes. He stared straight ahead, watching the rhythmic swish of the horses' tails as they swept the buzzing irritation of flies from their hindquarters. Finally, unable to contain himself, Elijah jumped down and tied the team to the hitching post. He scurried quickly along the side of the building to squat beneath the open window of the superintendent's office.

"We're beyond excuses now," the Colonel said harshly. "His insolence simply cannot go unpunished. My God, man"—his voice rose to a roar— "the boy pissed all over the woman's dress. You *must* leave him. With me. Until this matter is resolved."

Elijah shuddered at the thought. There was no leaving to be done, certainly not here, not on this day. He waited to hear what his uncle would say, but Uncle said nothing. The only sound was of the scrape of chairs.

Elijah jumped up and ran. He dashed down the length of the building, past the team tethered to the post, past the flagpole at the center of the open ground in front of the barracks, into the trees beyond. He ran as if possessed, the branches of the pines slashing and whipping at his face, his arms, his legs. A dread exploded through him. He stopped abruptly and looked back. What of Uncle? He stood considering it. No matter. He turned and ran. What would come would come. After this journey, he would face it not as a boy, but as a man. He could not hesitate, could not look back. The only way was forward.

. . . after the Indians are all dead, no doubt we will have some very human and Christian plans advanced by which they may be made a prosperous and contented people.

Life Amongst the Modocs
Joaquin Miller

No-Man's Land

Klamath Falls sat tucked beneath a cleft of land below Upper Klamath Lake, at the headwaters of the Klamath River. For all the water, there was a windblown feel to the town. The founding fathers situated it such that it stares southward into the empty, arid basin known as the Modoc Plateau. It was as if the first settlers felt compelled to brace their backs against the arm of land holding back Upper Klamath Lake, ever vigilant to the threat of the irrepressible Modoc, whose homeland lay in that inhospitable region to the south. It was only after Captain Jack and his compatriots were hanged at Fort Klamath in October 1873 that community building was undertaken in earnest.

Settlement and the raising of a community were greatly aided by the vast reclamation project to drain Tule Lake, begun on the eve of the First World War. Besides the wealth of timber in the mountains, prosperity lay in claiming the fertile ancient lake bottom to grow potatoes and alfalfa, to open up pastures for the free range of cattle. In the bottom of Tule Lake— the mother and the center of the Modoc world—the white settlers saw an opportunity to build a new Eden.

Elijah pressed himself against the bulkhead of the grain hopper as the Burlington Northern freight slow-crawled its way under the Main Street viaduct, entering the Southern Pacific yard on the south side of town. Elijah passed within spitting distance of two switchmen standing beside the track. They laughed easily in idle conversation. Elijah remained motionless so as not to draw attention to himself.

The freight rolled down past the Amtrak station, into the weltering weave of rails in the makeup yard. Long strands of idle freight trains in various stages of decomposition and assemblage filled the rows of track. After it crossed under the Lakeview Highway viaduct on the western edge of town, Elijah felt it safe finally to uncoil himself from his perch, to glance up and down the track to make sure it was clear. He grimaced from the stiffness that had settled in during the long ride from Bend. *Getting too old, too damn old,* he thought as he pitched first his, then the boy's bedroll to the ground. He swung out on the ladder, his gunnysack slung on a strap over his shoulder, and dropped free of the train.

The crummy pulled past him, and he raised an eye to meet the stare of the conductor standing on the back platform. The man gave him a hard look. Elijah let his eyes drop to the rocky roadbed underfoot. He trailed along in the wake of the train, following it out of K-Falls. The track ran along an earthen dike built through the marsh of an old lake, long since tamed. Once, long ago as a boy, Elijah had sprinted along this same causeway, fleeing a knot of older, angry white boys in hot pursuit. At the last moment, about to be overtaken, Elijah plunged down the bank into the tules, thrashed madly, and disappeared into the swampy, reedy mass. Rocks whizzed through the reeds, whistling with murderous intent. Not yet having learned to swim, Elijah was more fearful of the boys than of drowning and splashed and thrashed deeper into the thick growth, into ever-deeper water. Just as he lost touch with the mucky substrata and went under, his foot struck a rise of earth that was solid under his weight. He scrambled forward, pulling his way with fistfuls of tules, making it up onto a small island, a haven providing safety, completely encircled by reeds. It was not much bigger than a boxcar, but it was high and dry, and had appeared as if by magic just when he most needed it. Over the years, he alone came here—no one else. He never shared it with anyone, and in his mind it was No-Man's Land—nobody's but his.

Or so he thought. As he approached the hidden catwalk he'd long ago constructed out from the bank into the tules, he noticed that the dead willow he kept there to screen the entrance was not in place as it should be. He stepped forward silently, crossing down the embankment, starting out on the rickety catwalk, pausing to listen.

Unmistakably, he heard voices. It sounded like a woman's thin, false laugh. Elijah reset the willow behind him and eased along the catwalk toward his camp.

Two tramps sat on iron milk crates in front of a small fire in the middle of the cramped clearing, their backs to him. Elijah crept to the edge of the island, then halted to observe them. To his amazement, the two strangers were black. It wasn't that blacks didn't ride the rails, just that they were few and far between. The two sat tending the fire, brewing up an aromatic pot of stew. One was a woman. The other was none other than the Reverend Hobo—or simply Revbo, as he was known widely on the road.

"You fool," the man said, swatting his companion's hand. "Stop poking your dirty paws into the pot."

The woman laughed again.

"Ho now," Elijah called out, declaring his presence.

The woman jumped and shrieked and whirled around, her hand rising to cover her mouth as if to prevent an evil spirit from diving in. She was plump like a dumpling but had a pretty face. She wore well-worn dungarees and a blue flannel shirt with a man's white T-shirt underneath. A small mongrel pup bounced and barked at her feet, as surprised as the woman at Elijah's appearance. The woman bent and scooped him up and cradled him against the pillow of her breasts. The other tramp turned slowly on his crate to eye Elijah. A slow, haughty smile came to his dark lips. He laughed a deep baritone laugh.

"Well, I'll be damned," he exclaimed slowly with dramatic flourish, as though laying eyes on the devil himself. "If it ain't the prophet Elijah. Come out of the wilderness, have ya, to decry false gods? Lord-a mercy." His head rocked rhythmically side to side as he stared at Elijah and emitted a long rumble of laughter.

"Sorry to scare you, ma'am," Elijah said, touching the brim of his hat in apology. "But I didn't think you'd be one to scare easy."

The woman stared wide-eyed at Elijah, then at her man, then at Elijah again.

"You traveling and consorting with the likes of the Reverend here," Elijah added.

The woman cocked her head and studied Elijah through tightly slit eyelids. She turned again to study her man and gave him the same hard appraising look.

"It's been a *long* while, ain't it," Revbo said. "*Yessiree.* Longer than Moses in the wilderness." The black man placed his big hands on the knees of his pants and slowly pushed himself to standing, chuckling as he rose and rose. He was big, six foot six, and blacker than a charred forest.

"How's the flock, Reverend?" Elijah said, stepping forward, unslinging the bedrolls and his burlap bag, letting them drop to the ground.

"Will somebody tell this child what's going on," the woman said, an edge of irritation mixed with relief. She held her puppy cradled in one hand and stroked it with the other. The dog worked madly to bite at her dark, fat fingers.

Revbo ignored her. "Come, join us," he said, waving Elijah over.

"Ma'am," Elijah said, stepping forward, touching a finger to the brim of his hat again. "I'm an old friend of Revbo here. Rode a few trains with him one place or another." Elijah gestured for the woman to sit, and retrieved an old tar bucket, upturned it, and sat down in front of the fire beside her.

Revbo chuckled, taking out the makings for a cigarette. "Met in the joint the first time, I believe," he said, cutting an eye at the woman, then Elijah as he pulled the sack of tobacco open with his teeth. "Used to think you was snobby."

Elijah smiled. "How long you know about this place?" he asked casually, changing the subject. Revbo licked the seal on the paper and stuck the finely crafted cigarette between his lips. He extended the tobacco and papers to Elijah. Elijah nodded, taking them up, pulling a paper loose to roll a smoke for himself.

"Three . . . four years maybe. Bet you never knowed that. Thought you was the only one who knew about this little hideaway," Revbo said, picking a loose strand of tobacco delicately from his mouth, his face alight with a devilish grin.

"How do you put up with him, ma'am?" Elijah said, rolling his smoke compactly.

"Ain't easy," she said, eyeing Elijah, then Revbo. "Ain't you got no manners?" she said curtly to Revbo.

"What?" Revbo demanded, staring sternly at her.

"Aren't you gonna introduce me?"

"Oh hell, Sarah . . . Sarah, this is Elijah, by Christ. Elijah, Sarah. Ornery as a snake—and twice as wicked," he said, laughing.

"You hush," she protested, punching him in the arm.

"Pleasure to meet you," Elijah said, ignoring the private innuendos between the two.

Revbo reached into his coat pocket and pulled out a half-empty pint of Jim Beam. He uncapped it and took a pull, then offered it to Elijah. Elijah waved it away. "Thank you, no."

"What? When you ever refuse a free nip? You feeling okay?"

"Feeling fine. Just don't much feel like drinking."

"Damn," Revbo said, taking another snort. "Now I seen everything."

The pup finally spilled free of Sarah's embrace, falling to the ground, collecting himself to scamper over to Elijah. Elijah reached down and stroked his head. It was nothing but a mongrel, part shepherd it looked, but more than a few other strains mixed in for good measure. He turned his snout up to grab at one of Elijah's fingers with his little needle teeth.

"You a feisty little son of a dog," Elijah said, roughing up the pup's fur. "Kinda like ol' Revbo here."

"Ain't hardly," Sarah snapped. "This here pup is sweet." They both laughed, causing Revbo to scowl hard at Sarah.

"So you homesteading here, or passing through?" Elijah asked, still curious how Revbo had come to find No-Man's Land.

"Passing through. Out of Wenatchee. Caught a hotshot out of Pasco and would have been laying up in the sun in California right now, except Sarah done forgot to pick up the water jug when we caught out."

"Oh Lordy, don't start on that again," Sarah protested.

Elijah studied Revbo studying Sarah. Revbo's jaw worked like a muscle without a mind, tensing, flexing, grinding molar on molar. Elijah wondered whether Revbo was going to make something of this or let it drop. Revbo had never been known to forget or forgive a slight.

"How about yourself?" Revbo finally said, turning his attention back to the bottle, taking another swallow, then capping it and putting it away.

"South. Going south."

"Sure was sorry to hear about ol' Willie," Revbo said idly.

"Willie? How's that?" Elijah said cautiously.

"Ol' Junkman. You didn't hear?"

"Hear what?"

Revbo turned and eyed Elijah. "Somebody done cut his throat. His'n and that dog of his, too."

Elijah felt like someone had sucker punched him. He stared at Revbo incredulously. "*Ah, man,*" he moaned, shaking his head, rubbing his forehead with the rough of his palm. "Tell me it ain't so."

"Yup. Him and his dog both," Revbo said, shaking his head sorrowfully. "Only way I figure it, had to be somebody that knew him. That dog would never let no stranger get by him."

"I was with Willie two, three days back now," Elijah said, staring evenly at Revbo.

"Now tell me, why anybody want to go and kill a poor ol' dog?" Sarah complained mournfully.

"This weren't no ordinary damn dog," Revbo said, returning Elijah's stare.

"Still don't make no sense," Sarah said bitterly.

"You seen a boy?" Elijah interjected. "Mop of dark hair. Wears a cap. Leather jacket."

"Matter of fact," Revbo said, his eyes widening with curiosity. "Just this morning." Revbo's face softened, his suspicion of Elijah dissolving. No way Elijah would do another tramp like what happened to Willie.

"Where was this?" Elijah asked, his interest keen.

"He played with my puppy," Sarah said. "Sweet little thing. I felt so sorry for him. He seemed so lonesome. Kinda lost like. You know him?"

"I've got to find him," Elijah said, standing, pacing with agitation. "I got to find him before it's too late."

—+++—

The fan in Bud Keaton's office agitated the gray cigarette smoke that hung in the air like a storm cloud. A stack of train schedules was scattered across his desk. Keaton had consumed two packs of unfiltered Camels while studying over the time schedules before giving up in frustration. He simply couldn't *see* a pattern to how a man as sly as Elijah McCloud might disappear from sight. It was as likely that he was long gone as holding up somewhere. He could just as easily be in Canada as down the street. The man was a shadow, a ghost. You didn't live by your wits for as long as he had, staying out of the way of railroad bulls and yardmasters, without a touch of the spectral about you.

The phone jangled, causing Keaton to twitch in his seat. He snatched up the phone and barked into the receiver.

"Bud Keaton?"

"Who wants to know?"

"You have a call being patched through from an eight-hundred number. Somebody said it was important."

"This is Keaton."

"Keaton? That you?"

"Who's this?"

"Elijah. McCloud."

"Where the hell are you?"

184

"This is my call, Keaton. I talk. You listen."

"What's up?" Keaton said eagerly.

"You said if I ever knew anything—about the killings . . ."

"Yeah, go on."

"The boy's in danger."

"Where are you?"

"Just listen, would ya."

"God, man, get to the point."

"Who's the last on the list that's been killed?" Elijah asked.

"Some bum named Junkman."

"*Ah shit,*" Elijah said.

"You were there, weren't you."

"I didn't kill him."

"I know that, *damn it.* Elijah, tell me where you are."

"I'm in the dark."

"What?" Keaton said, incredulous. "Don't toy with me, man."

"Just shut up a minute. I'm telling you, the boy is in trouble."

"How do you mean?" Keaton asked.

"He's the only one who knows what the killer looks like. He saw the killings in Vancouver. Now the killer seems to be tailing him. God knows how. But it clearly seems that that is what he's doing."

"Where's the boy?"

"I don't know."

"Christ, man. I thought he was with you."

"He was."

"Was . . . ? What happened?"

"Took off."

"Where? You gotta give me *something* to go on."

"Hell, man, your damn railroad ain't *that* big. Just get busy and find this killer before he finds the boy."

"Jesus, McCloud. This damn railroad is a whole lot bigger than one man can cover, and you know it."

"Just do your job. You look where the sun shines. I'll look everywhere else."

The line went dead.

"McCloud, *damn you!*" Keaton roared, rising out of his chair. "McCloud!?" he screamed into the handset. "*God*damn you," he bellowed, slamming the phone down, scattering train schedules off his desk onto the floor. "Goddamn son of a bitch. I find you, your ass is *mine.*"

Imprisoned, Among the Dead

Elijah's body convulsed sharply, shattering the dream, bringing him abruptly into the world. He bolted upright in his blankets. He scanned the tight enclosure shielded by the profusion of tules encircling the small camp. Just first light, perhaps an hour before dawn. He could make out the dark silhouettes of Revbo and Sarah bundled in their blankets twelve, fifteen feet distant. A cloak of ground fog covered the camp like a thick lid on a pot, resting delicately on the tips of the thin reeds. There was not so much as a breath of breeze stirring the air. Elijah scanned the encampment, peering hard into the twilight at the head of the gangway through the marsh. Nothing. He lay down again, pulling his blankets around him, trying to find again the outgoing tide of sleep. His mind tripped once more on the sound of the words that had triggered him from sleep: *imprisoned, among the dead.*

Elijah sat up again. He stared into the dim, depthless fog. *The boy.* A chill passed through him, causing an involuntary shiver. The boy, among the dead?

Elijah fumbled out of the tangle of his blankets. He found his hat and stove it hard atop his head, then slipped his boots on. He was up and in his jacket almost without thought for what he was doing.

"Damn it all," he stammered. He patted himself to be sure he had makings for a smoke. In his noisy fumblings he woke the pup, who yelped and consequently woke Sarah. Sarah raised her woolly head to see to the commotion.

"The *boy!*" Elijah whispered hoarsely. "I'm worried about the boy." Sarah nodded knowingly, her face puffy with sleep. "I'll be gone a while,"

Elijah said, stepping closer to be sure she understood him. Sarah rubbed a sleepy eye with her fist, nodding again. "If you head on before I get back, leave my gear. Just be sure to put the willow back at the head of the trail." Elijah touched his fingers to the brim of his hat and turned away quickly. He disappeared in the wash of fog, leaving Sarah to wonder if he'd ever been there at all.

The fog cast a surreal glow to the advent of day. Elijah kicked along the causeway toward K-Falls, moving at a quick clip, trying not to think dark thoughts, feeling yet like he walked in a dream. He had no idea where he was going. The voice was a glimmering of muted sound, thin at the edges, deep at the center, like the sound of a bottom-feeder at night when enticed into the shallows. He hoped he wasn't too late. The sound seemed to reverberate in the air, a humming, penetrating, piercing sound that was felt as much as it was heard. Elijah wasn't used to dreaming. Try as he might, he could not catch the thread of dream that had cast the sound, the filament of memory severed, leaving it to float free, untraceable.

The blind leading the blind, he thought darkly. The fog shrouded everything in hints and whispers of their form. Knowing without seeing, Elijah moved through the landscape as if guided by a sixth sense. He knew that to the north, directly ahead, rose the prominent swell of Hogback Mountain, sculpting the skyline. *North: place of wisdom.* In his mind's eye he could see it distinctly, for the far side of Hogback Mountain was where he'd lived with Uncle. He'd come now to be on the periphery of home.

Elijah prowled along the gray linear form of freight cars silenced in the Southern Pacific yard at the edge of town. He rousted a couple of bums sleeping it off under a warehouse loading dock at rail side. He disturbed a brood of pigeons, startling them to flight with his passing.

Imprisoned, among the dead.

It was barely a whisper. Elijah stopped and cocked his head and strained to hear. He pirouetted slowly as though trying to adjust a receiver for clearer reception. To the east the light of day was growing. The morning mist seemed to part for a moment, then shifted on an unfelt current of air, closing again. Elijah turned fully to face the east. *East: place of fire and light.*

He took a step to the east, testing the feel of it in his body. He could not be sure. He walked toward the point of the rising sun. He stopped and strained to hear again. He spun and faced west. He focused a hard stare on the rise of land above downtown Klamath Falls, clear now in the shifting, lifting mantle of fog. *Among the dead: of course,* he thought.

"The cemetery," he whispered. *West, the place of dream.* He pictured the rise of earth that held downtown, a curl of water flowing around the summit, the canal that flowed out of Upper Klamath Lake, wrapping itself like a serpent around the foot of Linkville Cemetery.

Elijah hurried along upper Main Street, through the weathered warehouse district that straddled the upper end of the railroad yard. He followed Main into the heart of downtown, then turned to make the hill to the cemetery.

Linkville Cemetery was bathed in soft light and long shadows, the sun just then cresting the hills to the east with its first rays. Elijah entered under the red stone arch gateway and paused, letting his eyes roam over the scattering of headstones and monuments. The place was serene in the glistening of dew that covered the grass. The elms and maples planted long ago stood edged with the color of autumn, the dark cedars mute and tall like old sentries. The place unnerved him.

"*Imprisoned?*" he muttered. "*Imprisoned?*" He sighed and started forward, shaking his head, feeling foolish and alert at once.

Elijah moved as though stalking game, his eyes scanning back and forth, his ears tuned to the light morning breeze and the sound it made in the thinning leaves of the autumn-touched trees. The faint aroma of mown grass—not freshly cut, but recent—rose to rouse the nose with the subtlety of a garden broth gone cold.

Fermenting like yeast, Elijah felt the play of dreaming shift in and out of consciousness. The night in Wishram at Junkman Willie's came back to him, the sense of violation on waking, the image of wolverine, foul and malicious. This was similar, but different. As he worked his way up through the headstones, climbing the hill toward the back of the cemetery, he found himself repeatedly looking back over his shoulder to see if anyone was following him.

Imprisoned, among the dead. Was the boy already dead, or merely imprisoned? Elijah walked along the narrow lane at the back of the cemetery. From the peak of the hill, he had a view like a soaring bird, how the land fell away to the west and south and east. He slowly scanned the vista. His eyes roamed over objects near and far. He caught a glimpse of blue where the canal looped to curve around the football field at the high school below. His focus shortened. He found himself staring at a headstone, a squat, sun-bleached stone, a family marker. His attention sharpened: *Folsom.* Elijah had heard other tramps talk of Folsom Prison in California. *Among the dead.*

Imprisoned, among the dead.

Elijah left the lane and walked down under the trees to the Folsom family plot. It lay at the very edge of the cemetery, where the ground began to fall away steeply to the east. A stone retaining wall enclosed the burying ground. Elijah stepped to the edge of the wall and peered over. There, atop a huge mound of cut grass, curled in a canvas tarp, lay the boy, dead to the world, snoring lightly.

"Son of a dog," Elijah muttered, shaking his head. He stood staring down at the boy for the longest time, watching the gentle rise and fall of his breathing. A sparkle of reflected sunlight caught his eye, and his gaze drifted twenty feet farther on to take in the small motorbike, thrown down on its side, the headlight shattered, one mirror dangling from the handlebars, catching and throwing a bright blade of sunlight.

"What the . . . ?" Elijah whispered, fumbling to put the image of the boy with the wreck of the bike. He noticed now small friction burns on the boy's knuckles.

"Serves him right," he said, stooping, placing a hand on the retaining wall to vault down into the mound of cut grass.

"Hey," Elijah said, shaking the boy gently. "Time to rise and shine." Elijah straightened and scanned back over the cemetery, still cautious, still disturbed by the sense of threatening violation that hung in the air.

"Jackie, come on. Plenty of time to lie around cemeteries later. We got to get moving."

Jackie stirred and rolled over.

"Come on," Elijah said impatiently, irritation edging over the relief, his gaze roving over the silent headstones in the direction he'd come.

Jackie opened an eye and focused wearily on Elijah. He blinked as though trying to clear his vision, or perhaps merely to make the apparition disappear. The image of Elijah grew more focused, startling Jackie fully conscious.

"What are you doing here?" Jackie stammered, sitting upright.

"Same thing as you. Trying to lay low." Elijah swept the cemetery yet again with a cautionary glance around.

"I don't need you," Jackie said curtly, still hurt from the other night.

"Looks of the motorbike—whatever you call it—you can find your way to trouble, no problem."

"I borrowed it," Jackie said defensively.

"You *stole* it," Elijah said adamantly, pulling out the fixings to make a cigarette.

"And you steal rides from the railroad," Jackie said, rubbing the last of the sleep from his eyes.

"Maybe. But I don't go and wreck the damn train in the process."

Jackie turned and eyed the motorbike.

"Nice," Elijah said facetiously, striking a match to light his cigarette.

"Why don't you just leave me alone?" Jackie said, kicking the canvas tarp back, brushing grass clippings from his clothes. "I can take care of myself."

"That's debatable," Elijah said, eyeing the boy not unkindly.

"You aren't the boss of me, you know," Jackie said bitterly. "I can do what I want."

"Yeah. You can," Elijah said evenly.

"So why are you following me?" Jackie said, his words filled with loathing.

"I ain't trying to boss you, Jackie. What needs to be looked out for is bigger than the both of us," Elijah said slowly. He inhaled on his cigarette, expelled a stream of smoke as he peered at the boy, who was studying him hard.

"Look, if it'll make you feel better, I'm sorry," Elijah said, exasperated. "Whatever I said, whatever I did back in Bend that pissed you off, I'm sorry. It was just drunk talk. And I'm sorry for that. For the drinking. It's not something I'm proud of."

Jackie stared at Elijah with an appraising look. "Why are you so interested in me all of a sudden?" he asked suspiciously.

Neither spoke for a long minute.

"Listen," Elijah said. "I'm not here to hassle you. I'm here because I believe you—we—are in something of a pickle."

"Whatta you mean?" Jackie questioned.

Elijah drew down on his smoke and inhaled deeply. "Willie. The dog, Avenger," he said, raising his eyebrows. "They're dead. Both of 'em."

The boy stared unflinchingly at Elijah. He blinked once, twice, three times. "Dead?" he said flatly.

"Dead," Elijah answered.

"When? How do you know?"

"Ran into an ol' traveling partner of mine. He heard it on the road. News travels fast."

"How?" Jackie said, fearing the worst.

"Same as the others," Elijah said softly. "Happened the day after we left

190

him, apparently."

The boy's eyes closed over, his head dropped. His body shuddered involuntarily. "*Oh Jesus,*" he moaned, shaking his head.

"Come on," Elijah said, extending a hand to the boy. Jackie raised his head and stared at Elijah. He reached up and took Elijah's hand as Elijah shifted his weight, flexing his arm, pulling the boy to his feet. Elijah took one last pull on his cigarette, then dropped it at the base of the retaining wall and crushed it under his boot.

"What are we gonna do?" the boy asked tentatively, both for the *we* and the *do* of his question.

"I don't know. But I'm working on it," Elijah said. "For right now, let's just get the hell out of this graveyard."

Rich as Thieves

Through the afternoon, the wind shifted steadily from the north toward the west and would eventually, Elijah reckoned, swing all the way into the southwest, thumping the thermometer pretty hard, maybe even bring a dusting of snow. Elijah kept a small fire going throughout the day, as much for the good cheer of it as to pass the time, tending to the flame. He'd made a run earlier in the day and spent nearly the last of the money his son had given him on bread, beans, hot dogs, and coffee. He'd also stumbled across an old apple tree full of ripe fruit and topped off the sack the store had bagged his purchase in. Sarah and the boy had finished all of the hot dogs and most of the beans and bread without seeming to dent their hunger. The boy lay sleeping, curled up in his blankets now; Sarah and the pup were napping on her bedroll. Elijah smoked and drank coffee and tended the fire, studying the wind and the clouds and the scent of the breeze, trying to fix the odds on which would arrive first: the storm brewing somewhere beyond the mountains to the west, or the California Man out of Pasco, through K-Falls, due sometime after dark. Each degree of swing in the wind toward the southwest moved the wager in favor of the storm coming first.

Revbo was off somewhere; no one knew where. He and Sarah had bickered over the pup most of the morning. Mad as he was when he left, Elijah knew he'd be back, for he'd left his gear rolled and ready to travel at the edge of camp.

Elijah stood and stretched and rubbed his face vigorously with the coarse palms of his dark hands. He had not slept well the night before. He turned and eyed the boy sleeping soundly in his bedroll. *Why?* Elijah wondered.

192

Why this boy? Why me? Why now?

Elijah could not say, for he did not know. But he knew it was important. And that it was important to pay attention. The old feeling of *knowing*, a feeling that had been rich and true when he was a young man, was coming back to him.

The wind now carried the pungent, thick smell of the stock pens near the BN rail yard, having shifted around another several degrees to the south. The sky was milking up, leaching the brilliance from the blue, smoking over the sharpness of the late-afternoon light. Another hour, the sun would drop below the horizon, chilling the air further. Snow or no snow, it would be a cold one tonight. A good night to be somewhere in out of the weather.

An odd sound at cross currents with the wind struck Elijah's ear, almost imperceptible, but there. He turned and listened intently. There it was again. The crunch of footfall on gravel. Elijah turned and took stock of the camp. The boy was still sleeping. Sarah and the pup still nestled dreamily together. Elijah heard heavy footsteps now coming along the gangway through the tules toward camp. It was Revbo.

"Heigh-ho, Tonto, my man," Revbo sang out gleefully, seeing Elijah sliding into view. Elijah could tell by the glaze in his eyes that Revbo had been drinking. Revbo grinned wildly, brushed past Elijah, and strutted to the fire. He reached down and picked up the last handful of kindling and threw it in the fire to brighten the blaze.

"*Goddamn*," he swore, fishing a pint flask from his coat pocket and uncapping it, rolling his head back to take a swallow. He capped it quickly and put it away, smiling devilishly at Elijah. Sarah stared daggers at him, but he avoided her gaze, warming himself in front of the fire. Sarah turned and eyed Elijah, looking for some assessment or reassurance, but Elijah only arched his eyebrows. He stepped over to stand near Revbo by the fire.

"One of these days I'm gonna wake up and wish I'd been born rich," Elijah said, raising his hands and rubbing them over the fire's rising heat.

"Shit, man! *Every day* is one of them days," Revbo said.

"Some more than others," Elijah said, laughing and looking out at the clouds thickening in the west.

"Rich or not, you get wet up just the same," Revbo said, uncapping the bottle to take another nip. He swallowed hard and offered the bottle to Elijah. Elijah waved it away.

Jackie had awoken and untangled himself from his blankets and was slipping his shoes on, drawn by the light and promise of warmth by the fire.

"Rich," Revbo said derisively, taking another swallow before capping the bottle and putting it back in his pocket. "You *was* rich, you son of a bitch. Didn't have the sense to hang on to it."

Revbo turned and eyed the boy, smiling a smile that was impossible to read. "The whole bunch of you," Revbo went on, waving his hand at Elijah. "All of y'all Modoc. Rich as *thieves*."

Elijah ignored him, studying the boy shivering in the cooling air.

"Come on and help me gather up some more firewood," Elijah said to the boy. "Check out the rail yard, see what we can find out about the California Man."

The boy shrugged, struggling to his feet.

"Rich as thieves," Revbo said again, chuckling to himself. "Shame. Just a damn shame, I tell ya. If'n it had been *me*, now, I'd have been set for life."

"Some of us are just smarter than others, I guess," Elijah said. "We'll be back in a little bit," he said directly to Sarah, arching an eyebrow as if to ask whether she was okay with their leaving her.

"I'll be all right," Sarah responded, waving them along. "Me'n my guard dog."

"Who you calling a damn *guard dog*?" Revbo asked, straightening as if slapped.

"Oh hush," Sarah said, half turning away from him. "I was talking about the pup."

"Yeah," Revbo said, stirring the fire with the toe of his boot. "We gotta talk about that damn dog. And you better listen, too."

"Oh, hush your liquor talk," Sarah said under her breath, lying down again, pulling the covers up over her and the pup.

"What's that?" Revbo said menacingly.

"I didn't say anything to you," Sarah said defensively. "I was talking to the pup."

"Yes sir, you better listen," Revbo said absently, settling on a milk crate to contemplate the fire.

—+++—

"What did he mean about you being rich?" Jackie asked, traipsing after Elijah as the two of them headed down the causeway in the direction of the stock pens and the BN yard. Elijah pretended he didn't hear and kept walking, his hands jammed into the depths of his old coat.

"You rich?" Jackie asked, trotting up alongside Elijah so there could be no mistaking that he heard him.

"Oh yeah," Elijah said grandly. "I own all this," he said, waving his hand in an encompassing sweep to the south.

"No. Seriously," Jackie said. "What Revbo said back there. About you being rich."

"Just liquor talk," Elijah said dismissively.

"What was that about you not hanging on to it?" Jackie persisted.

Elijah walked in silence. He stopped abruptly and looked back down the tracks. An SP freight was pulling out of the K-Falls yard, heading out across the causeway to start down the Klamath River Canyon toward Weed and Dunsmuir and Redding. Elijah turned and stepped along more quickly to clear the causeway to step through a barbed wire fence and move up into a field. He settled on one knee under an oak for a moment, pausing to let the train pass. He pulled out the makings for a smoke. Deftly, he crafted one of his perfect, hand-rolled cigarettes and put it between his lips. He studied the boy, who had taken a seat in the grass but was staring intently at him, as though waiting for an answer. Elijah looked off at the approaching train as he flicked a match and lit up.

He exhaled. "Long time ago. Before any whites. My people lived here for a long time. Hundreds of years. Thousands. Nobody knows how far back. Long time." He inhaled another drag on his cigarette and studied the boy.

"We didn't know how rich we were. Didn't think in terms of rich or poor." The rumbling of the approaching train grew louder. As the string of locomotives pulled past, the ominous drumming of the big engines filled the air, flowing over them like the breath of terror. Elijah and Jackie watched the orange and gray SP locomotives glide past, gathering momentum as the train cleared the junction that turned into the BN yard. The roar of the engines grew more subdued, replaced now with the squawk and squeak and groan of boxcars gathering speed.

"As far back as anyone could remember, this was home to The People, to the Modoc. Then the settlers came. They wanted our land to raise cattle. Grow hay and potatoes." Elijah studied a string of old battered boxcars, looking for monikers drawn by tramps he might know.

"It's a long story," he said distantly. "What matters in the end is we lost our land. The government took it. Eventually gave us some money. But only if we'd give them everything. Including our right to call ourselves Modoc. I suppose to some it looked like riches. Must have, I guess. We took the money. Gave away our name."

"Your name?"

Elijah nodded. "Don't that beat all?" he said, shaking his head.

"Why'd you sell?" Jackie asked.

Elijah smiled wearily and eyed the boy. "To be honest, we never thought of it as ours to sell. But the government took the land and told us we had to leave, and we took the money." Elijah crushed the smoke against the heel of his boot and buried the butt in the dirt.

"Come on," he said, pushing himself to standing. "Let's see about getting us some firewood and getting back before dark."

It was only a hunch, but it was the only thing he had to go on. Bud Keaton had kept the accelerator of his big truck pressed hard, keeping the needle hovering around eighty. He was road weary, and his leg ached from ten hours behind the wheel traversing the length and half the breadth of Oregon since sunup that morning. *They've got to be going south,* he told himself, even though south was still a mighty big place on the map. South could just as easily be through Boise to Ogden and Salt Lake City, as Bend to Klamath Falls and Redding.

This was either the biggest wild goose chase or a true inspiration, he didn't know which. But something in the back of his mind kept prodding him to think about K-Falls. Either way it felt good to be out of the office, on the road, letting the miles roll under him in pursuit of his one best—if not only—hope of putting an end to the killings and this asinine assignment.

Keaton had left Portland as the first commuters began to fill the freeways flowing into downtown. He'd selected Route 26 across the shoulder of Mount Hood, down through the Warm Springs Indian Reservation to Madras, where he picked up 97 South through Bend, Gilchrist, and Chemult. He'd stopped briefly in Bend to ask around the yard if anyone had seen a boy and an old man, and had been encouraged by vague recollections of both from a couple of different people. Even though his optimism was dampened in Gilchrist and then Chemult, with no mention from any of the track hands about seeing the pair, the only direction that made sense from Bend was still south to K-Falls. K-Falls held the promise of his picking up the trail again. Or so he certainly hoped.

Keaton stopped first at the tower in the SP yards on the edge of downtown Klamath Falls. The chief of security was still at his desk. The man was thickset of body and seemingly of mind, as well. He was cordial, but barely. He hadn't seen any of the bulletins Keaton had posted on the wire in the month Keaton had been on the detail. Though he hadn't seen an old man and a boy, he had seen a Negro tramp earlier in the day, he said, crossing through the yard. Keaton gave him a set of bulletins and asked that he circulate and post them, though he wasn't hopeful the man would do either. If this man's attitude was indicative of the type of cooperation Keaton was getting across Western rail lines, his job was a whole lot bigger than he'd feared.

He stopped at the Quality Inn Motel to get a room for the night, and then went next door to wolf down a steak dinner before heading out to the yard. The 171 out of Pasco, the freight tramps called the California Man, was due through sometime around ten, and he wanted to be out there before then to be sure the switchmen knew to keep an eye out for Elijah and the boy. After eating and paying, he stopped by his room to call his daughter, but she wasn't home. He left her what he hoped was a cheerful message, saying he was on the road and would call again in a few days.

The security lights high over the rail yard, visible from more than a mile away, helped guide Keaton's approach to the big switching yard on the southwest periphery of town. Keaton parked in a no-parking space and went into the main office and introduced himself, asking to see the yardmaster. He was directed to a barren lunchroom where a big man wearing a canvas coat was sipping soup he'd poured from a thermos. The man had close-cropped gray hair and a mottled complexion with the telltale explosion of red webbing at the temples that marked a serious drinker. His eyes came up with the lift of the spoon to his mouth, and he gave Keaton a long, hard stare as Keaton crossed the worn linoleum floor to greet him. The man's expression didn't waver. It was flat, without emotion. He assessed Keaton's presence without a hint of warmth.

"You Tom Prescott?" Keaton asked, pulling up slowly to stand in front of the man.

"Yup," the man answered curtly.

"Bud Keaton. Special Investigative Unit of the Union Pacific."

The man nodded, inviting Keaton to take a seat at the table as he lifted another spoonful of chicken soup to his thick lips. The man was laconic to the point of being mute. Keaton unzipped his jacket against the stifling heat in the room as he sat down opposite the big man.

"You know anything about the investigation into this series of tramp killings that have been going on? Past eight, ten weeks?" Keaton asked, deciding to back into his inquiry rather than appear presumptuous or autocratic. Rail yards were points on an endless circle of tracks, each a small fiefdom of local prerogative.

"Some," the man said, wiping his mouth with a paper napkin. He opened a metal lunch box and extracted a roast beef sandwich in a plastic baggie. "Don't mind if I keep eating, do you?" he asked, taking a bite of his sandwich.

"Not at all." The two men sat in silence for a long moment as the man chewed meditatively. "Ever hear of a tramp named Elijah McCloud?" Keaton asked. He watched the man closely for any hint of wayward expression.

Tom Prescott looked at Keaton as he chewed, then nodded, half shrugged, admitting some knowledge of the man.

"Did you know he's wanted for questioning on these killings?" Keaton asked neutrally.

"Yup," the man said, putting his sandwich down and wiping his mouth with his napkin again.

"You haven't seen him, I take it?" Keaton asked.

"Nope."

Keaton nodded slowly, as though registering an offhand remark about the weather. Silence rose up between them again as Prescott picked up his spoon to raise another mouthful of soup to his lips. Keaton closed his eyes and reached up and rubbed the bridge of his nose with his thumb and forefinger. He was tired; what he wanted most was to sleep.

"The one seventy-one. You got notice on its arrival yet?" Keaton asked.

"About eleven. Eleven thirty," the man said.

"After the swing shift comes on?"

"About then," the man said.

"You got a good crew of men in the yard that time of night?"

"Yup."

Keaton raised his eyebrows as if to elicit some further confirmation.

"O'Malley's the night bull," Prescott said, turning his eyes up to stare at Keaton as he spooned the last mouthful of soup. The man arched his eyebrows, providing both an exclamation point and question mark to his statement. Keaton nodded back.

"I've heard of him."

"Be surprised if you hadn't."

"Oh yeah," Keaton said with a bit of enthusiasm, working to establish rapport wherever he could find it.

"He don't much like tramps."

"So I heard."

"Has a sense for 'em," the man said, picking up his sandwich, starting to take a bite. He hesitated, fixing Keaton with a telling look. "If they're around, he'll know it. And if he knows it, well . . ." He let the uncompleted thought hang between them.

"Make yourself at home, if you care to," the big man said, deciding he was finished eating. He bagged what remained of the sandwich. "I gotta get back to work." The man dropped the bag into his lunchbox and closed the lid. He lifted the thermos lid to his lips and drained the last of the soup, then secured the lid on the wide-mouthed container. He exited without saying anything more, leaving Keaton to his thoughts and the silence of the lunchroom.

Ol' Dirty Face and the Bull

The wind quickened. It rattled the branches of the barren willows at the edge of the tules and stirred a shower of sparks from the fire. A roll of thunder broke over the whine of the wind.

"Sweet Jesus," Revbo moaned bitterly, studying the darkening sky. The last light of day was fading fast, with only enough left to see that the clouds had thickened considerably, were pressing closer to the earth. Holes of light shifted and disappeared, mixing with dense black patches of sky.

Elijah studied the sky and rose, smiling, standing to stretch and draw in the full threat of the storm in a deep breath of air. "Nothing like stormy weather to make a man know he's alive," he said joyously.

"You a damn fool," Revbo spat, knocking the coffeepot over to spill the dregs into the fire, creating a sizzling gray cloud of smoke and steam that rose like a phantom amidst them. The wind whipped it away almost as fast as it appeared. "Even ducks don't fly in this shit," Revbo said. "Get your ass up, Sarah, and get your things together."

The wind built in a rush of gusts heralding the coming front. A sprinkling of rain spattered in the dry dust, hissing and popping when drops struck the blackened rocks ringing the fire.

"Time to mosey," Elijah said, lifting his bedroll and bundle. He snugged his hat and adjusted his coat beneath the strain of his load. "Best be quick. It's on us now for real." He stood watching Sarah and the boy as they finished cinching their bundles. Revbo had already started down the catwalk through the tules toward the causeway. Sarah gathered up her things, lifting the pup, holding it in her arms. The boy shouldered his bedroll.

"Where we going?" Jackie asked, hunch-shouldered against the intensifying wind.

"Hurry now," Elijah said, ushering them out the catwalk in front of him. "We'll hole up down at the cattle pens till the Man comes. Be quick. Here she comes."

The dark sky opened like the parting hands of God, spilling a fury of rain in a sudden deluge. The last one out, Elijah stopped to set the dead willow in place, delaying against the blowing rain to be sure it was properly secured to cover the entrance. He turned and scrambled up the bank to the mainline and started at a trot after the others.

They crowded into a small building, a shed really, at the upper end of the stockyards that were adjacent to the mainline. It was tight and dry though the air was sour with the odor of old hay and manure. The four settled randomly where they found space inviting, shedding bundles and bedrolls, slicking water from their clothes with their hands. The rain beat ominously on the tin roof.

The rain—miserable as it was—was a blessing. Elijah welcomed it. He and the boy had learned from another tramp they encountered who'd been scouting the yard that Dutch O'Malley was back on the job. O'Malley was fully immortalized in the realm of hobo legend; stories of encounters and near-encounters were shared around jungle fires throughout the West. It was impossible to separate fact from fiction, but even exaggeration didn't seem to do him justice. He was notorious for his love of the dark side of his job as a yard bull, and played it to his advantage in keeping the number of tramps through his yard to a minimum. He seemed to relish the promise of violence, sometimes appearing hours before the night shift change if the California Man was due ahead of schedule. Tramps went out of their way to avoid the BN yard when they knew he was on duty, risking instead the inhospitable Southern Pacific despite the guarantee it was a night in jail if they were caught on the property. The Southern Pacific booked no favors: one and all went to jail. A night in jail was preferred, however, over an unexpected encounter with O'Malley.

Love this rain, Elijah thought. *Let it rain.* A patient student of the behavior of animals—and man was just another beast, Elijah passed like a shadow, undetected when it was called for, using stealth, but more, *cunning.* He exploited the quirks and nervous tics of those he studied. All men, like all animals, had a blind side. Man, being conscious and thereby assuming he was superior, made misjudgments and mistakes that created broad openings in his defenses. *Lord knows,* Elijah thought, smiling, *I'm a walking schoolroom of blunders.* But humility was both the result and the benefactor of hubris. And he had been humbled.

O'Malley had had plenty of opportunity to learn that lesson, but he hadn't quite caught on to it yet. Casual in most regards in personal attire, O'Malley had a thing for expensive, hand-tooled Western boots. He kept them spotless and well polished, dusting them frequently with a soft rag he carried in his truck while patrolling the yard. His devotion to his boots went against common sense: a rail yard is a nasty place—dirty, dusty, and soaked in corrosive powders that have leaked from old rail cars. Yet Elijah had never known him to wear anything but the finest of footwear, even when it rained. Rain was one thing O'Malley seemed to hate about the job. There was no way he could avoid getting his boots muddy. Consequently, when it rained, he stayed in his truck on prowl through the night, getting out only when it was absolutely necessary.

"You hear O'Malley's back," Revbo said in the darkness, a simple statement, but his meaning clear. The only thing O'Malley hated more than bums was blacks.

"So I heard," Elijah said.

"And they call me a criminal, hopping rides on Ol' Dirty Face," Revbo said bitterly. "Ain't nothing compared to what he done done."

"Who's this O'Malley you be talking about? And what's he done *done*?" Sarah asked mockingly. "Sounds like you talking about the devil."

"I am indeed," Revbo said. "I bet you rub his damn head, you'd feel them horns."

"What makes him so bad and nasty?" Sarah asked, irritated. She was annoyed with herself for bringing up mention of the devil, superstitious and fearful of calling down evil.

"He crippled a man," Revbo said, "for the sheer pleasure of seeing a man suffer."

"What's he got to do with us?" Sarah asked cautiously.

"He's the night bull here," Elijah said, hoping a simple explanation would suffice. He knew the story of O'Malley's suspension. The details didn't need to be repeated.

"What'd he do?" Jackie said. "How'd he cripple somebody?"

"He caught a damn tramp trying to steal some worthless piece of shit to pawn for a few dollars," Revbo said, his voice becoming sonorous, warming to the story as though preaching a parable. "A few sad, miserable dollars. Probably to get something to eat. Probably hadn't eaten in days." He paused, letting the drumming of the rain fill the silence between his words. "Now, no doubt the man was trespassing. He was where he ought not to have been. Had no right. Should have known better. But he made a mistake." Revbo paused again. Elijah sighed, wishing Revbo would merely tell the simple truth of it.

"Now, you might think his mistake was that he was trying to steal something that didn't belong to him," Revbo said. "That's true—but that wasn't his real mistake. The real mistake he made was trying to steal while O'Malley was guarding the henhouse, watching over the flock, so to speak."

"Don't be damn preaching to us," Sarah interjected irritably. "Just tell us what he done."

"You watch your mouth," Revbo shot back, rising from his seat on a bale of hay, starting to cross to confront Sarah.

"Whoa, now," Elijah said, jumping up, coming between them. The two men stood rigid, facing each other, Revbo towering over Elijah.

"Let's keep our minds on catching this train," Elijah said soothingly. "We need to stick together now." The two stood unmoving. Then slowly, Elijah stepped back, retracting himself from between Revbo and Sarah, but cautiously, ready for anything. When Revbo got in one of his moods, fueled with a little liquor, he was unpredictable.

There was a long silence filled with menace. Finally, the tall, lanky silhouette of Revbo stepped back a half step. Then another. He turned and retreated.

"You best watch your mouth, woman," he cursed bitterly as he sat down.

Nobody said anything for a long while. Then Jackie spoke. "What'd he do, this O'Malley?"

When Revbo remained silent, Elijah answered. "Crushed the man's hand with a wrench he'd been trying to steal." He stepped over to the window that overlooked the rail yard, his back to the group. "To make the point, in case anyone missed it, he took the man's hand—his other hand— and crushed it, too, winding it in a shop vise. Left him there. That's the way they found him in the morning."

"Sweet Mary Mother," Sarah whimpered.

"She ain't got nothing to do with it," Revbo said antagonistically.

"Oh hush, Revbo. Sometimes you so tiresome," Sarah shot back.

"For real?" Jackie said, spellbound, oblivious to the running feud between Sarah and Revbo.

"For real. As real as rain," Elijah said.

The dance of the rain on the tin roof intensified, sealing each of them in their own private thoughts and ruminations. Riding trains certainly had its dangers, mostly as a result of being careless, stupid, or unlucky. The tramp who'd gotten his hands mangled suffered a fate mixed of all three. For the most part, a man made his own luck, Elijah believed. The Modoc put a lot of stock in luck; it was central to their sense of the world. But if a man was careless and stupid, his luck usually wasn't worth much. Elijah had had it fall both ways, for and against him, and he had learned that lesson the hard way.

The blaring of a locomotive horn broke through the din of the storm. Revbo bounced up and rushed to crowd Elijah at the small window.

"There he be now," Revbo proclaimed joyously. "And ahead of schedule, too. The Man making things flow our way now."

"Maybe," Elijah said. "Maybe not." Revbo turned to take umbrage, but Elijah redirected his attention, nodding for him to look up into the rail yard. Dutch O'Malley's red Ford pickup was rolling along a wet tongue of road with his headlights shining directly on the switching junction that would bring the California Man down into the BN yards. O'Malley, like the train, was early.

Revbo slammed a fist into the wall. "Shit," he cursed violently. "Can't leave out now. We stuck till tomorrow."

"Maybe," Elijah repeated dispassionately. "Maybe not."

"Whatta you talking 'bout—'*maybe, maybe not?*'" Revbo barked. "He catch you, he'll put your dick in a vise, six-month suspension or no."

"That's a good trick," Elijah said, smiling. "But he's gotta catch me first." He stared intently out the window. "Don't you just love it when it rains?"

"You a crazy sumbitch," Revbo said, stomping back to his corner of the shed, leaving Elijah standing, staring out the window. Elijah watched as the train slowed to make the junction turning into the BN yard. He watched as the long slender hulk of the California Man passed in front of them for inspection, noting every open boxcar to the end of the train. "Ain't no way it's safe with that sumbitch O'Malley skulking 'round the yard," Revbo said. "I don't like it."

"Suit yourself," Elijah said, rolling a cigarette in the light from the window. He licked the seal and put it in his mouth without lighting it. He paused and stared out at the world awash with rain and possibility. He watched the red pickup turn around and head back up into the yard after the California Man had cleared the junction.

"You gonna ride this train, Mr. Elijah?" Sarah asked tentatively. Elijah stared for several long moments without answering. He turned slowly to face her dark silhouette.

"Yes I am," he said calmly. "And you can too."

"Oh Lordy," Sarah exclaimed softly. "You ain't fearful of this man O'Malley?"

"Be foolish not to be," Elijah said. "But this storm is a blessing. One we can take advantage of."

"How you figure?" Sarah asked, rising, crossing the distance to stand beside Elijah, pressing her face to the glass. She cradled the pup tenderly in her arms.

Elijah stood looking at the rain. "Rock is hard," he said. "Water, soft. Ain't that right?"

Sarah thought about it for a moment. "You right about that. But what's that got to do with riding this here California Man?"

"Nothing . . . and everything," he said cryptically.

"Elijah, would you talk sense!" Jackie complained, pushing his way in between Sarah and Elijah at the window. "What's this *rock is hard, water is soft* stuff? You're so annoying."

"Likewise," Elijah said, laughing. "Think about it: water is soft, but steady flowing water cuts rock, wears it down, carries it away."

"This some kind of Indian thing?" Jackie said angrily.

"No. Nature thing. Natural law," Elijah answered, amused with himself. "O'Malley is the rock. And the storm is water. We got us plenty of it, right? As long as it keeps up like this, O'Malley isn't gonna want to shuffle around in all this mud and muck unless he knows for sure he's got a bum on the end of the line. That puts luck on our side—if we're careful. And not stupid."

"You are so annoying," Jackie said, shaking his head.

"When I say so—for anyone that's going with me—we're gonna move up along the back side of the yard, up over there," he said, pointing out the window toward the rise of hill that stood as a backdrop to the rail yard. "The railroad stockpiles a bunch of stuff back there—railroad ties, old crates, junked equipment. After O'Malley comes back around this end of the train again, we're gonna cross over to that shed there," he said, pointing out a small utility building at the periphery of the yard. "From there, we'll work our way up the back side to about the middle of the yard where there's a run of side tracks full of idled cars. We'll cross and move down through them, making our way into the center of the yard where the main-line runs. Then we'll pick out a good, dry sleeping car, and—*all aboard*! Next thing you know, when we wake up in the morning, we'll be in California."

"You're serious?" Jackie said, his tone a mixture of incredulity and assertion. "What are we going to do when O'Malley comes along when you don't suspect him?"

"Jump for cover."

"Right. Where? In some puddle," Jackie said sarcastically.

"Exactly," Elijah answered tersely.

"Come on," Jackie said nervously, turning away from the window, crossing through the dim space to sit down in his corner again. "Can't you be serious just once?"

"I am serious. There's a ditch that runs along the back side of the yard," Elijah explained. "Probably full of water with all this rain. But before it's over, we'll be plenty wet whether we hit the ditch or not. If O'Malley comes along, we'll dive and be quick about it. O'Malley would walk through hell *and* high water if he was sure he could collar a bum."

Elijah turned to study the rail yard again. Sarah stood silently beside him, watching what he watched, her attention mirroring his. The falling rain glistened in the glare of the security lights. The rail yard looked like the loneliest, most unwelcoming place she'd ever seen.

"Best check your gear," Elijah said to no one in particular. "We'll be leaving here directly." He moved to his pile of belongings to inspect the feel of all the knots that held things secure. He lifted his bedroll and slung it over his shoulder and moved his gunnysack to the window where it was within easy reach.

"Here he comes," he said, watching the headlights of O'Malley's truck as the red Ford came down and around the end of the train, then started up the other side again. "Time to go. Be quick about it." He hoisted his bag, swinging it over his shoulder. "All aboard that's getting aboard." Elijah opened the door and stepped out into the rain. Jackie followed, then Sarah, hunched over, her massive breasts providing ample protection for the pup in her arms. Elijah waited a moment, seeing if Revbo was going to come or not. He started to pull the door shut to latch it finally, but Revbo snatched it open and came out, his hat pulled down hard on his head.

"You a damn fool," he said as he passed Elijah. "And that makes me one, too."

Elijah smiled as he pulled the door shut and secured it against the blowing wind. A loose door banging in the storm was just the kind of thing that O'Malley was likely to notice, he thought to himself, smiling as he hunched under the weight of his load, following the others in the direction he'd shown them. Elijah walked quickly, closing the gap with the others as they scurried through the falling rain.

Deep in the interior of the yard, a switch engine rumbled to life. The squawk of wheels split the night air. Elijah quickened his pace to a labored trot, overtaking the others. He led them in behind a stack of railroad ties just as the nose of the engine broke into view from behind an idle length of freight cars, pulling two boxcars. It ran out to a junction point where the brakeman threw the switch, and the engineer reversed direction, sending the cars down another track where a new train was being made up.

The group was up and moving again. They quickly traversed a brightly lit section of the yard, hunched under the beating rain and the fear of being seen. A hundred feet away, they made the shed Elijah had pointed out earlier. All four crowded in behind the back side of the building, pressing in tight under a low overhang that shielded them from the rain.

"The mainline runs through the center of the yard," Elijah said. "It's eight tracks in, counting from the first track on this side. The California Man will be sitting on the mainline, waiting to be called."

"What about O'Malley?" Sarah asked.

"Stay low, stay quiet, and move fast," Elijah said.

"And keep that damn mutt of yours hushed," Revbo spat angrily.

"*You* hush," Sarah retorted. "You so spiteful sometimes, Revbo. It's *tiresome.*"

"All right, all right," Elijah said in a commanding tone. "Stay together. No dallying." Elijah turned and broke from the shadow of the building, running straight toward the heart of the yard and the protective cover of a line of freight cars on the outside track. All four crossed open ground, completely vulnerable to be seen if anyone happened along unexpectedly. Elijah jogged at a fast trot, a dark, squat form bouncing over the muddy ground like a beast of burden beneath his bundles. He was nearly to the first track and the cover of the idle train when he caught the glare of lights intensifying, reflected in a pool of water beneath the tail of a line of freight cars. "Shit," he hissed, breaking into a sprint. He dove under a tanker and rolled up near the wheel carriage, shouting for the others to hurry. Jackie dove, then Sarah, stopping to stoop and shimmy beneath the fat belly of the car, afraid if she dove, she'd crush the dog.

"Goddamn, girl," Revbo cursed, pushing her hard from behind, causing her to strike her head on the curvature of the steel tanker as she fell sideways between the steel rails. Revbo crabbed his way under the car quickly, just as the headlights of the red truck came around the end of a boxcar, cruising slowly under the glare of the bright tower lights.

"Damn you," Sarah complained, rubbing her head and her hip, too. The pup was loose and started to wander playfully out into the rain to investigate the dance of drops in a thin puddle. Revbo snatched it with a snapping sweep of his arm, causing the pup to yelp in fright.

"Damn you, Sarah," Revbo seethed. "I told you this dog was gonna be the ruin of me."

"Gimme my dog," Sarah demanded bitterly. The two of them were squared off, ready to go at it.

"Whoa now!" Elijah commanded in a loud whisper. "Just quit it, you hear?"

Revbo fixed Elijah with a scalding look.

"I don't mean to get in your business, Revbo, but we're *all* committed now. Can't be no squabbling. You don't want to ride this train, you should have made up your mind *back* there," Elijah said, tossing his head in the direction of the cattle pens.

Revbo held his stare, then handed the pup to Sarah.

"You best keep it quiet, you hear?" he threatened.

Sarah took the pup without saying a word, cradling in it the fold of her big coat.

"Sweet mother of God," Revbo said, turning to watch the pickup roll past, not thirty feet away. They could see the dark outline of O'Malley behind the slap of the windshield wipers. The truck continued past them, down the back side of the yard, bouncing through the puddled potholes, splashing muddy water in its wake.

"That was close," Jackie whispered.

Elijah turned and eyed the boy. "We should be okay now. Just keep an eye out. And stay with me." Elijah rolled out the other side of the tanker, rising in the narrow corridor between two strings of freight cars. "Come on," he commanded, waiting for the others to roll out and join him.

"That's the first track," he said, patting the side of the tanker car. "And this is the second." He slapped a battered, old Missouri Pacific boxcar. "The California Man is seven tracks farther in. Let's go."

Elijah walked down to the end of the MoPac boxcar and scaled the ladder to cross over the coupling and jump down in the narrow corridor between the next two tracks. He stood and watched as the boy followed in his footsteps—or nearly so. When Jackie started to step out on the Gould coupler, Elijah reached quickly and caught his pant leg and jerked his foot back onto the heel of the heavy iron knuckle.

"What are you doing?" Jackie complained, unnerved by Elijah's unexpected intrusion

"Watch where you step," Elijah said. "You put your foot here"—he pointed to a space between two iron lips—"and if it's the wrong time, this bolt of steel will take your heel off if the train starts to move."

Jackie moved on across and climbed down, followed by Sarah and Revbo.

"Two down, six to go," Elijah said, turning to walk up to the next coupling of cars sitting on the inside track. He repeated the maneuver, climbing the ladder and crossing over, followed closely by the others, as they moved one track at a time, progressing toward the heart of the rail yard. They established an easy rhythm to their passage: first Elijah, then Jackie and Sarah, then Revbo bringing up the rear. Elijah was just about to grab for the ladder of a boxcar on track five when a rolling drag slammed into the head end of the string, splitting the air with an explosion of iron, causing a chain reaction to shudder down the length of the string.

"Stand back," Elijah yelled as the rippling impact passed before them, causing the boxcar in front of them to jump backward a good foot.

"Lordy!" Sarah exclaimed with fright.

Elijah crossed through the fifth and sixth string of cars, then finally the seventh, bringing them up to the mainline.

"This is the Man," he said, patting the side of a brown Western Pacific boxcar. It was shut up and sealed tight. "Come on," he whispered hoarsely as he turned and started walking down the thin aisle between the two hulking strings of cars. Nine or ten cars back, Elijah found the empty boxcar he'd spotted when the train first pulled past the cattle pens. Its door was slightly ajar. Elijah looked inside, taking inspection. It had a good hardwood floor. There was a stack of broken down cardboard containers lying up in one corner. "It's the damn Hilton," he said. He flung his sack in, then unslung his bedroll and tossed it up, and climbed up after them. He helped Sarah up, then the boy. Revbo was last to climb in. They stood in the cold, dry space, shivering with dampness but grateful for the shelter the car provided.

Revbo moved back to claim his corner of the boxcar. He siphoned off half the cardboard cartons in the pile to make himself a pallet on the floor, leaving just enough for the other three to share between them. Elijah fixed up his pallet, followed by Jackie and Sarah, who imitated him, bedding down beside him, leaving Revbo to himself. Elijah sat down and made himself comfortable and rolled himself a cigarette, but didn't light it. It was something of a nervous habit with him. Even an unlit cigarette soothed him. He sat in silence, rolling the slender white cylinder from one corner of his mouth to the other. All that was left now was the wait. And hope that their luck held.

They sat for ten minutes in tense silence. Then all of a sudden, the car jerked, slack running out between the couplers, and the train started to move.

"We going?" Jackie whispered.

"Not yet," Elijah said. "Probably pretty soon." He rolled the cigarette from the left side of his mouth to the right.

"How do you know?" Jackie asked.

"Old Indian trick," Elijah said. He worked the cigarette from the right side back to the left.

They rolled forward about fifteen car lengths, then stopped and reversed direction. They rolled slowly backward for several long moments, passing out of the congestion of idle freight cars and into the exposed glare of the open yard.

"What are they doing?" Jackie asked nervously.

"Adding a few more buggies," Elijah said. "Probably be heading out real soon now."

"About time," Revbo said. "Waiting's about to kill me. I gotta piss bad."

"Hold your ponies," Elijah replied.

"What is . . . ," Jackie began.

"Quiet," Elijah commanded harshly. "Someone's coming."

They sat in mute silence. Footsteps could be heard coming back along the train. Jackie's breath caught in his throat.

The pup growled, then barked. "*Shh,*" Sarah scolded.

The silhouette of a man passed in front of the open door. The pup barked again, and the man stopped. The four were blinded by the sweep of a high-powered lantern.

"What the hell?" a deep voice boomed.

There was a long pause. "Staying dry," Elijah said. "Ain't causing no trouble."

The light fixed on Elijah. Though the brightness hurt his eyes, he did not flinch or look away.

"You're a damn fool," the man said, not unkindly.

"This the California Man?" Elijah asked, wanting to keep the conversation to the positive.

"Damn straight it is. And this is O'Malley's yard. He's early tonight."

"I saw him," Elijah said, staring into the blinding beam of light.

"You *are* a damn fool," the switchman said, laughing.

"Been accused of worse," Elijah offered.

The man's radio crackled with a garbled voice. The light swept away. The man turned and looked up and down the track, then spoke quickly into the radio, answering the call. He stuck his head in the open door again.

"You all sit tight now," he said. "If you lay low lay and keep quiet, you just might make it out of here. The Man's been called to leave.

"Thank you," Elijah said gratefully, acknowledging the man's generosity of spirit.

"Have a nice ride," the man said, stepping back, disappearing from view.

"Hope to," Elijah whispered to himself.

"Give me that *goddamn* dog," Revbo barked at Sarah.

"Whoa now!" Elijah commanded. "Revbo, *please.* Didn't you just hear the man? He said lay low and keep quiet. And he ain't playing."

Silence rose up to engulf the space that both held and separated them all. The wait was thankfully brief. After a couple of minutes, they heard the lone note announcing the train's departure and felt the slack ripple free of the train. The wheels began to squeak. The car began to move.

They were aboard and under way. High and dry on the California Man, soon to be leaving Oregon . . . *home and not home,* and all the bitter history it held.

Two Crows

The California Man rolled south into the storm and the blackness of night. It rumbled down through the Modoc Plateau, a bleak landscape of greasewood and sage, past ancient lava flows, now dark stone, gnarled and pocked with twisted fissures, sinkholes, and caves. Elijah McCloud lay wrapped in his bedroll, rocked in a meditation of remembering and forgetting by the familiar rhythmic cadence of the train. Buried deep beneath the precision of lines on a map, between the twin rails of steel that carried the rumbling freight train, lay the heart of Modoc country.

The great roving eye of the train swept the darkness, lighting the wet steel track that lay ahead like the paths of twin shooting stars. At each isolated grade crossing, the hand at the throttle of the train rose to sound the horn, giving warning of its approach—*beWARE, beWARE, be-beWARE.*

Elijah was perplexed by the weave of the journey. But he knew that events were not random, that the pattern had been set long ago. This is what the dreaming had been trying to tell him. Even if the way ahead was not clear, the journey to this point had been filled with too many echoes of the past. The past was alive—so much so that it was almost present. It was all now like a dream, mixed and confused, but holding the weave deep within just the same.

—|—|—|—

The boy Elijah fled the Klamath Agency, the threat of the superintendent, and the inability of his uncle to protect him. He was driven like a deer escaping the hunt. The cottonwoods flamed golden in the stream bottoms, the light of day soft in mid-October as the earth prepared for the coming winter. Elijah ran through the trees at the edge of the broad grassland valley of the Upper Klamath Lake basin, keeping away from the road that connected the farms on the way toward Klamath Falls and Tule Lake beyond. His lungs ached and his legs were leaden, but he dared not rest for fear they would find him and keep him from the vision of his life. When he grew tired, he walked. He traveled for two days with only a few hours of sleep stolen when he was too exhausted to take another step.

The center of the Modoc world was the land that surrounded Tule Lake, which had birthed all things Modoc, a land that spoke to the Modoc and they to it in an ancient language only time could forge. Without their homeland, Captain Jack knew they would no longer be Modoc no matter where they moved. Elijah had never been to Tule Lake or to the Lava Beds where Captain Jack and his small band defended themselves against capture. But Elijah trusted the resonating pull they exerted on him. By late the second night of his journey, he was walking south over plowed fields, once ancient lake bottom, now "reclaimed" by the Army Corps of Engineers. Where the Modoc had harvested the meaty camas bulb that grew in the shallows of the lake, farmers now harvested potatoes. The ever-abundant tule grass the Modoc used for everything from thatched shelter to boats, hats, and clothes was replaced with alfalfa for thoroughbred horses, prized cattle, and hardy sheep.

Elijah moved steadily southward, passing out of farmland and into the sparse zone of high desert vegetation. By first light, he was well into the desolate terrain of the old Modoc world, beyond the prying eyes of strangers. Tule Lake, what was left of it, lay like a broad pewter-colored tablecloth spread for the feast of the coming day, dotted with hundreds of migrating waterfowl—geese and ducks and pelicans floating on the surface, an occasional great blue heron standing in the shallows near shore. Their chorus of cries to the coming of day rose like a wild symphony. Elijah was joyous. His being here was meant to be, he believed. He was filled with the exhilaration of imminent manhood.

Elijah greeted the coming of the morning of the third day of his quest tired and hungry, but buoyed by the success of his long traverse from the Klamath Agency, eighty miles to the north. It was a good omen to see the sun rise over the sparkling waters. He drank from the lake to quench the deep thirst he had carried through the night. He stripped and stood naked, facing the rising sun, his arms lifted overhead in welcome. He whooped finally and dove into the water. His joy sent a thousand birds into motion, rising in a deafening cacophony of wings and bird cries as they rose from the face of the great lake.

His exuberance was short lived. He still needed to find Captain Jack's Stronghold where, according to the stories his uncle told, he'd taken his people when they left the reservation. Captain Jack had returned to the ancient Lava Beds near Tule Lake, a no-man's land of its own that had long hidden and protected the Modoc from warring neighboring tribes. Here, Captain Jack defied the will of the US Army sent in the winter of 1873 to return him to the Klamath Reservation. Though barely more than a skirmish in the grand settling of the West, it captured the imagination of the entire nation. Popularly bannered in the national press as the Modoc War, the siege was the longest ever sustained against the US military by a Native population. It generated widespread sympathy among Americans— except settlers in southern Oregon and northern California. Sympathy was fleeting, however, when on Good Friday, April 1873, Captain Jack came out of his stronghold to meet with General Edward Canby under a flag of truce and mortally shot the general with a concealed revolver. There was no sympathy when Jack and three compatriots were publicly hanged at Fort Klamath that October. Beheaded, his skull shipped to the Smithsonian Museum for study, Captain Jack suffered the ultimate indignity in never being properly buried on home ground.

It was a good hiding place, the Lava Beds. Elijah wandered all day under the bright sun in search of the stronghold of Captain Jack. He searched first methodically, then aimlessly, crossing and recrossing the flat, trackless desert landscape. He only slowly became cognizant of being accompanied by two errant crows. As the sun passed its zenith and began its descent to the west, the crows became more plaintive. As Elijah's apprehension grew that he would not find the Lava Beds, he began to see the crows as the cause of his problems. He was hungry—and it was their fault. He was frustrated—their fault. He was fearful he would fail to obtain a vision, would fail in his quest to become a man. And it would be all their fault.

Elijah went down to the lakeshore and drank his fill, and splashed water on his face to relieve the despair settling over him. He lay down in the weak shade of some tall tules to rest. *What if I fail?* he worried. *What if the vision does not come? What then?* He sighed deeply and closed his eyes. He lay listening to the beating of his heart, his own labored breathing. *Pay attention,* came the whisper of a voice. *Let nothing escape you.*

The boy Elijah sat up and turned to scan the horizon. There they were, the two crows, a hundred yards distant. He rose and began walking toward them. They watched with fixed attention. Elijah saw now that they sat on an almost imperceptible rise of land in the dense sea of sagebrush. He wound his way through the rocky terrain, weaving his way up through the brush, approaching them directly.

"Caw-caw," one of the black birds cried. Elijah looked up to see it rise from the lip of dark volcanic rock.

"Caw-caw," the other cried, lifting ponderously, heavy and ungraceful in flight.

Elijah picked his way quickly, keeping an eye on the spot they had departed. The ground rose as he went. He could see now that this spot did offer relief to the otherwise flat stretch of high desert plateau. As he climbed to meet the lip of dark rock, he stumbled upon a dusty path. He began to run, letting it guide him, leading him up through ancient, massive runs of lava. He broke into a clearing of level ground and stopped abruptly. He stood transfixed. Rock screens were built up at strategic points around the perimeter of the giant scabbed boil of earth. He could see half a dozen depressions, the dark mouths of subterranean caves. This was it. It had to be. He'd found Jack's Stronghold. By *paying attention.* The two crows had led him here.

In the remaining light of day, Elijah investigated the stronghold. It was a cratered blister of volcanic rock, honeycombed with depressions and caves and meandering trails. Its presence was hard to detect from a distance, even from a few hundred feet, as it did not so much rise out of the surrounding terrain as float upon it. The Modoc lived in simple mat shelters at the lakeshore and along the Lost River during summer and retired to earthen communal lodges during winter. But always, they lived close to the stronghold, which provided them a fortress in which to defend themselves against neighboring Paiutes, Shastas, and Klamaths. The Modoc were legendary fighters and had never been routed by their ancient neighbors. Not until the whites came.

It filled Elijah with great pride to be here. "I am Modoc!" he shouted to the evening wind. "Mukaluk." The wind carried his voice away, leaving only the hush of the world. "I am Modoc," he repeated in an even voice. The empty silence of the place as sundown approached was oppressive. It caused him to feel profoundly alone. He sat on a rock staring at the deepening crimson sunset over the shoulder of Mount Shasta. He remained still as a stone through the fading light, into the coming brilliance of the stars as the world was transformed by the night. He witnessed the cooling of the air along his skin, the quieting of the earth in his heart.

"I am Modoc," he said quietly to the fullness of the night. "Mukaluk. The People."

Elijah arose from his perch and stretched. He turned and started back toward the cave he'd earlier selected as his night refuge.

—+++—

The following morning, Elijah came to consciousness slowly, the plaintive cry of crows tugging at the sleeve of sleep. He was sore, cold, and hungry. He wished not to rise to the surface of wakefulness, but to sink again into the dim murkiness of exhausted oblivion.

The call of the crows was insistent. Elijah felt an eyelid start to flutter, a small crack in the eggshell of sleep. First one, then the other. He grimaced with the pain of lying too long in one position, tensed against the cold.

"Caw-caw. Caw-caw."

Elijah started to push himself upright, but struck his head on a sharp knob of rock. The pain knocked away the last vestige of sleep. This certainly was not a dream.

"Caw-caw. Caw-caw," the crows cried again.

Elijah focused and lifted his eyes toward the bright mouth of the cave. High on the lip of the entrance, two large black birds sat perched, hunched forward, staring down at him, bobbing their heads now and again as if to get a better look.

"Caw-caw. Caw-caw."

"You? Again?" Elijah complained. "Can't you see I'm sleeping?"

"Caw-caw," the one on the right responded.

"Caw, caw-caw," the one on the left added for emphasis.

"Go on!" Elijah shouted. The two birds hopped back, spread their wings, and flapped away, disappearing from view. "Damn crows," he said bitterly. He let his eyes roam over the contour of the dim cave. He was sure this must have been Captain Jack's cave, for it was the biggest and most accommodating in the Lava Beds. This was where Jack, his two wives, and his brood of children spent the desolate winter of 1872–73. Captain Jack had first welcomed the white settlers and wished only that they and his people could live together in peace. All he asked for was a piece of ground, of

Native ground, the ground of The People, his ancestors, where he and his clan could live unmolested. He was bonded to the pull of this place just as the ducks and the geese were. It could not be otherwise. The root of that attraction lay deep in the pattern of life itself.

What must it have been like, Elijah wondered, for Jack to lie here, breathing this same dank air that tasted of earth, carrying the burden of his people, their future, their past? Elijah thought he could almost hear the muffled pop of rifle fire and the occasional whoop signifying that a brave had hit his mark. Ammunition was precious, and each shot had to count. But did the whoop gladden Jack's spirits or move him to despair at the growing futility of their fight?

As the pintails and white snow geese began to return to Tule Lake in the spring of 1873, open rebellion erupted in the ranks of braves who had followed Captain Jack into the Lava Beds. In a confrontation of tragic dimension, Jack was accused of being a coward, a squaw. A woman's shawl was thrown over him. He counseled for peace. But a contingent who'd joined his clan late in the Lava Beds, including Curley Headed Doctor, a shaman, after that band had slaughtered white settlers on the eve of the rebellion—this group would hear nothing of it. Death awaited them no matter what. Better to die fighting, they argued. "You must kill the white general," they demanded. "You must drive them away from our land once and for all. Or you are *sne-we-cas. Woman.*"

The ache of hunger in Elijah shifted during the fourth day to join with a deeper unsettling, one that had nothing to do with food. Without so much as a shadow of a dream to grace his sleep, Elijah had begun to worry that he had chosen his vision ground impulsively, or worse, was unworthy of the site he'd selected. He feared that he'd come here more out of *wanting* than *seeking.* He worried he was being defeated by his own desire.

The persistent presence of the two crows became a source of almost unbearable irritation to Elijah during the long, slow procession of the fourth day. He came to view them, their dark plumage, their hoarse cackling, as mockery of his quest. They fluttered about the mouth of the cave, walking stiff-legged like black sentries, peering in, calling out, shattering the silence with their incessant prattling. Though he chased them off again and again, they always returned.

That night, Elijah slept deeply. He plummeted, then floated, then plummeted again into the dark chasm of sleep. He was aware without being aware, sensing without being conscious. At the deepest point of descent when all was black, he floated as though cradled in the arms of some un-seen host.

A small point of light appeared, and the sleeping Elijah fixed on it. It was no bigger than a grain of sand. He sharpened his gaze and watched it grow, eroding the darkness until a shaft so brilliant it was blinding shown like a torch that swept away nearly all the darkness. Then down the column of light came two shadows, whirling, twirling, descending toward him. They seemed close, yet far away, too. One seemed to alight on a perch, a dark form that dimmed the light around it. Elijah was fearful they would come closer . . . yet was hopeful, too.

The one that blocked the light was more a shade, a specter, than a fully embodied thing. The other, when it flapped its wings to alight on another perch, caused light to spark and crackle at the tips of its feathers. It seemed to emanate a light of its own. They were both crows, Elijah-of-the-dream realized.

Who are you? Are you my shadow? Elijah asked the dark one, the one shield-ing the light.

There was a long pause, then a hoarse cackling. *No. Not your shadow. I am between you and the light.*

Who, then? Who? Elijah asked.

The question is who are you? the shade responded.

I am . . . I am . . . , Elijah replied, perplexed by his uncertainty. He knew, or thought he knew, but could not speak it. He grew afraid.

I am not your shadow. You are mine. I am between you and the light, the coarse voice spoke.

What do you mean? Elijah pleaded desperately, not understanding. He thought the dark form impatient, eager to go. *What? Tell me!*

Elijah watched as the shade first started to turn one way, then stopped and turned back the other. *In the turning,* came the voice, *all is possible.*

There was a thick flapping of wings, and the dark one lifted. *The way will be difficult,* the other crow, the one that possessed the inner light, said as it, too, rose. It flapped hard, rising to join the other. The beating of its wings stirred the crystal column of light into giant eddying whirlpools, swirling the dark sediment at its edges, mixing the dark and the light.

Caw-caw, came the hoarse cry of the winged ones. *Caw-caw.* They flapped and flapped, the light growing weaker as they ascended, the shaft of radi-ance dissolving in their wake.

Caw-caw . . . caw-caw . . . caw-caw . . .

Elijah awoke abruptly. The twilight of dawn filtered down through the mouth of the cave. He lay still. His heart was pounding. Where had the dream come from? he wondered. It seemed to come from someplace beyond him.

The way will be difficult—what did that mean? *I am between you and the light. In the turning, all is possible.* He lay pondering all that he'd heard. He rose slowly, stiffly, and climbed up out of the dark cave into the coming light of day.

At midday, sitting silent on his perch of stone near the mouth of the cave, staring out at the great expanse of high desert that surrounded him, his eyes settled on a point in the distance. His line of sight fell to the northeast across the lower end of the lake. He stared unthinking for a long while before a thought emerged. *What is that?* he wondered idly, half consciously. He blinked to clear his vision. *What is that?* he pondered again, straightening for a better look.

Elijah watched as the speck grew larger, until he could recognize it as a team of horses pulling a wagon. It was Uncle. How had he known to come here? As the wagon drew closer, Elijah saw finally the slow-floating advance of two crows before it, as if leading the way.

Elijah rose finally and waved. His uncle waved in return. Elijah turned slowly and scanned the full circle of the world, looking east and south and west and north, returning to gaze at Uncle. His uncle had stopped a distance away and sat watching him. Elijah turned for one last look into the cave where he'd passed the night. *I am between you and the light,* came the echo of the shade again. *In the turning, all is possible.*

After Elijah told his uncle of his dream, the two rode together in silence nearly the whole way home. The silence distressed Elijah, causing him to feel that he must have failed. Only in the last few miles, long after dark, did Uncle speak. He told Elijah two stories, both about Curley Headed Doctor, who was the shaman and *dream singer* who'd been with Captain Jack in the Lava Beds. Curley Headed Doctor told of a dream he'd had that showed the way that the clan would be protected. The clan was to encircle its camp with a long length of string, which would fortify it against the soldiers' attack. But in the end, Uncle said, the power of his dream failed them.

After they were defeated, Curley Headed Doctor was remorseful. He said that he'd caused the power of *dream singing* to abandon The People. He said he didn't know when it would return. Maybe never. But maybe there would be a time that Crow, the great shape shifter, the one able to pass between worlds, would come again in a dream to mark the return of *dream singing* to the people. Such a time would be marked, actually, by the appearance of two Crows.

"Crow is powerful medicine," Uncle explained to Elijah. "Very powerful. Difficult, too."

"What do you mean, difficult?" Elijah asked.

"Difficult," he repeated, nodding thoughtfully. "Crow is powerful, for it has sacred powers. Difficult, too. But two is good. One to balance the other."

"How? *Powerful?*" Elijah asked tentatively.

"Crow can be inside. Or out. In the dream, or in the world. Or both at once. Like this morning. In your dream, and outside my house. Both at once."

Elijah dwelled on this. His uncle snapped the reins and the horses started again.

"And how, *difficult?* How is Crow difficult?" Elijah asked.

"Difficult," Uncle responded. "Yes. This too. This will be your challenge, Elijah. To know the difference between the two. One the shadow. One the light. But which? That is the thing. Which? That is how Crow is difficult. How your way as a man will be difficult. To know the difference. One is the shadow. The other the light."

Anybody Home?

The storm caught Luther Gon by surprise. It was an annoyance more than a hindrance and did not dissuade him from his plan. He was close now, he was sure of it. This one they called Elijah: he could feel him, not like in a dream, but for real. It would settle him immensely to finally be done with it. But even more than Elijah, what drew him into the rain, forgoing shelter, forgoing patience, was the boy. The boy would be with Elijah, and it was the boy—more than anything—that he wanted. Gon knew what the voice did not. He did not dare dwell on thought of the boy too long, though, for the voice did not like confusion. The voice was insistent upon Elijah. Gon knew otherwise. The boy was the threat. The boy.

Yet and still, the presence of Elijah was a powerful thing, like an invisible force, like the voice. It was as if he had made the storm, had gathered the clouds and stirred the wind and caused the thunder and the rain. He was using the storm to hide in, Gon thought. He could sense it. This one they called Elijah was not like the others. He was different. He was powerful. Maybe even the One.

But first the boy. The boy first. Then this one, Elijah.

Gon had sat hunched beneath a tarp he'd rummaged up once the rain began, watching the Burlington Northern yard on the edge of K-Falls. The tarp kept most of the rain out, but it was uncomfortable squatting in the weeds, the cold wind blowing, dampness everywhere in the world. He'd sat in the weeds on the periphery of the yard for several hours now, biding his time, carefully observing the goings-on under the bright security lights. Something wasn't quite right. He could feel it. It was well past two in the morning maybe even three or four, though he knew that misery warped one's sense of time, making small moments like an eternal hell if you were suffering. Gon had learned that a long time ago. But he knew there was no point in becoming impatient. To rush would ruin things.

There was too much activity in the rail yard for this time of night. There were two trucks that seemed to endlessly circle the yard. One was white. The other was red. Sometimes they passed going in opposite directions. Sometimes they trailed each other. But they moved constantly. First one way, then the other.

Gon sat waiting for them to come around again. He was sore and cold and tired. He had been traveling for two solid days. He'd traversed the length of Oregon to reach K-Falls. He'd come close to being cornered by a railroad bull in the Eugene rail yard, but as luck would have it, the bull spotted another tramp and went for him rather than coming the last dozen steps to where Luther was hiding.

Gon's attention wavered and waned, and he began to nod from fatigue. He caught himself, slapping himself hard, angrily, with the intent of punishment as much as stimulation. Was it his imagination or lack of attention, or was there a lull in the movement of trucks? Gon shivered against the dampness and the cold, pulling the tarp tighter around him for warmth. He waited. No trucks came. He smiled.

Gon rose slowly. Patience was always rewarded for those willing to wait and suffer, to see their way clearly to what must be done. Few had that clarity, but Gon had it. He had come to count on it . . . *no,* depend on it. It was one thing that never wavered.

He stood bent against the rain staring into the rail yard, straining to sense movement. He heard nothing above the low rumble of the yard engines and the patter of rain. He grit his teeth in an animal grimace, his eyes narrowing in their scan of the night. He was wrong. It was dangerous to think that that clarity never wavered. It does. It had. In the Vancouver yard. When he'd let the boy see him.

Gon straightened to his full height, holding the tarp around him like a shawl. He let the cover slip from his head, craning his head side to side in search of the sound of danger. No mistakes this time, he told himself. Not again. Sure that nobody was coming, he stepped forward with a fast, stiff-legged gait.

He broke out of the shadows at the end of the yard and started across the distance toward two outbuildings eighty or ninety feet away. On instinct, he began to trot, then run. As he closed the distance, he saw the bounce of light beams, then heard the sound of a truck coming around the rear of a drag of boxcars not fifty yards distance. He was at a dead sprint. As the headlights broke free of the shadow of the train, he made the edge of the first shed. He ducked in under the awning. He tried the door, but it was locked. He dashed to the next building, pushed against the door, and disappeared quickly inside.

The sound of the truck grew louder, the engine suddenly accelerating. The sweep of lights filled the window of the shed with a flash of brilliance. Gon used the light to orient himself, searching for the best place to hide. The rain was loud on the roof. Light flooded the shed window again as the truck roared to a stop directly outside the door. Gon crouched. There was a stack of wooden crates near the back of the space, but they didn't offer much protection. Gon's heartbeat was loud in his ears. He noticed now the wet trace of his footsteps in the light that came in under the door. *He'll know,* Gon thought. He heard the door of the truck slam shut.

Without thinking, Gon quickly crossed the distance to the crates, then carefully backtracked to the point where he'd come in. With fluid grace, he leapt sideways, away from the swing of the door, and crouched. In one swift reflexive movement, he withdrew the long knife from its scabbard tucked in the small of his back.

The door burst open, a black shadow silhouetted in the swath of light that filled the room.

"Anybody home?" a deep voice rumbled with feigned humor. Beneath the menace of the voice was the distinct edge of pleasure. It set Gon's senses on edge; he knew that tone. It was like an echo out of childhood, from a time and place of being trapped, caged in a small place. His fingers curled tightly around the handle of the knife.

"I know you're in here, asshole!" The shadow moved a half step. "You have fucked up. Coming in here on my shift. Fucked up *big* time!"

The door crashed violently into the shadowy form, catching Dutch O'Malley by surprise, knocking him sideways. He stumbled, struggling to maintain his balance, but the fury of Gon's attack drove him to the floor. The struggle was over almost before it began. The knife flashed numerous times. O'Malley sighed a deep, withering gale of expiration, his eyes devoid of light before Gon's shadow suddenly filled the room as he rose in the open doorway that was flooded with light. In the next instance, the shadow was gone.

The storm pummeled the roof of the small shed with a steady, deafening beat. The noise of it drowned out the idling sound of the red Ford pickup, its lights burning blindly in the night.

Aha!

The four "guests" aboard the California Man stayed hunkered down against the cold until well into the morning. They awaited the warmth of the sun breaking through the thick curl of mist that draped the vast northern forest. Sarah and Jackie lay in their blankets in one corner, playing with the pup. Revbo remained motionless in his bedroll at the far end of the car. Elijah sat wrapped in his bedroll where he could take in the view out the open door. With K-Falls now behind him, he was possessed by a sense of great relief, for K-Falls marked the endpoint to the journey across "the flats." Though a hunted animal is always vulnerable, prey will seek the advantage of higher ground over their predators. Elijah did not know where this *other*, this one who was following them, was, but he felt relief in their moving back into the mountains again. Like Glacier in Montana, these mountains were familiar, almost home, if Elijah still believed in such a thing anymore.

Below Greenville, midafternoon, the trees thinned further and the mountains opened up on Indian Valley, a flat, broad grassland plain in the bottom of a bowl of mountain ridges that enfolded it. To the south, Mount Hough rose like a broad-shouldered mastiff, its face to the valley in dark shadow, which caused it to appear even larger than it was. Its summit glistened brightly, reflecting sunlight off the night's fresh powdering of snow. The train slowed as if to take in the beauty of the surroundings, the track following a shallow, meandering stream dotted with willows through the middle of the valley. Black Angus and whiteface Hereford cattle stood docilely in scattered knots all across the valley floor. Above the constant squawking of iron wheels rose the periodic trill of a meadowlark enjoying the warmth of late-autumn sunlight.

The track curved slowly to the west at the southern end of the valley and slipped through a narrow gap in the face of the mountains, following Indian Creek's gathering descent toward its eventual merging with the North Fork of the Feather River. The route zigzagged through tight turns, following the deep cut of the meandering river below. They passed through one tunnel, then another, and crossed the shoulder of a ridge into another canyon network to find themselves above an opening vista to the west. Far below, the wet welt of river threw the light of the sky up at them like a dazzling silver blade. The air was filled with the clean scent of pine and fir.

Elijah rose and began gathering up his belongings, rolling and tying his blankets, making sure everything was secure. He moved his gear to the open door.

"Best get your things together," he instructed Sarah and the boy. Revbo was already busy rolling and tying his bedroll. Sarah and Jackie moved quickly, following Elijah's example. Elijah stood taking in full measure of the cleft of the mountains that fell away before them, running to join other depressions and declivities westward, in the direction of the great California Valley that lay sixty, seventy miles to the west. Jackie and Sarah came up and stood beside him at the door, the pup's head poking up out of one of the big pockets in Sarah's coat. They rode staring out at the endless progression of ridges and thickly forested mountain flanks, drinking in the beauty and stillness of the land without need for commentary or conversation.

"Just the other side of the next tunnel," Elijah said. "Throw your stuff down first. Then sit down and slip free. Careful how you land."

The train entered a short black hole in the rock where the track pierced a column of stone that seemed to climb straight up out of the depths below. The squawk of the train wheels became deafening, then fell away again as they emerged back into sunlight. Elijah dropped his bedroll and burlap bag out, cradled his water bottle in one arm as he sat on the threshold, then kicked free of the train. The others followed.

They had made it: Keddie Junction, in the canyon of the Feather River.

The canyon bottom was deep in late-afternoon shadow by the time the four descended the ridge and reached the river. Though the air in the shadow of the mountain was cool, they were bathed in sweat, exhausted by the steep descent. The only one unaffected by the effort was the pup, who'd made the portage peering out of the top of Sarah's coat pocket. The four knelt and drank deeply from the cold sweep of the river as the pup pranced back and forth among them, barking vigorously with sheer exuberance at being four-footed on solid earth again.

"Gawd, I can't take another step," Sarah said, rolling over onto her back on the stony riverbank.

Revbo dunked his bandana and mopped his face. He eyed her with fierce contempt. "You the most sorry excuse for a woman I ever seen," he said, tying the bandana around his neck as he rose to standing. "And I seen some, too."

"You bragging? Or complaining?" Sarah retorted. She was too tired to care whether Revbo was agitated or not. She lay staring absently up into the jagged-edge sheet of blue that hung from the enclosing circle of trees.

"It ain't much farther," Elijah said, rising, shouldering the burden of his gear once again. He stood looking down into Sarah's round face. "Come on," he said, encouraging her. "You close, but you ain't in heaven yet." She smiled at him, and he smiled back. "Come on," he said, offering her a hand up. She clasped his hand and let him do the heavy work of righting her.

"Lordy, I'm tired," she moaned, picking up her bedroll.

"That's 'cuz you're fat and lazy," Revbo said, swinging his bedroll onto his back.

"Oh hush. You so tiresome," Sarah said cuttingly, her anger rising.

"I'm tired, too," Elijah said, "but it ain't but a little ways farther." He turned and started downstream, striding confidently through the clumps of willow that filled the edge of the flat river course.

"To think folk work all year long so they can come out to be in the woods for a little while. Call it *vacation*," Sarah said. "I'll tell you what vacation is. You wouldn't be finding this girl in no woods. No sir. I'd be up in the bed. That's where I'd be. In my bed, not going nowhere. That's what I call vacation."

"Where's your home, Sarah?" Jackie asked as they followed along at a distance from the others.

"My mamma, she lives in Bakersfield. I guess you could say that's where home is. But I ain't seen my mamma in nearly a year. Not since I went off with the *Reverend.*"

"You miss your mother?" Jackie said, a sad, wistful tone in his voice.

"Shoot, suga. Don't every child miss their mamma? Don't you?"

"I guess," Jackie said.

"You *guess*?" Sarah exclaimed. "How old are you, anyway? You too young to be out running 'round the world without nobody to look out for you."

"I'm old enough," Jackie said defensively.

"Old enough to get into trouble, I can see that," Sarah said good-naturedly. "Ain't that right, Pup?" she said, stopping to rub the dog's soft furball head. She stooped and picked it up, cradling it against her bosom as they followed Elijah and Revbo along the rocky floodplain that held the narrow channel of the river.

"Where's your mamma live?" she asked.

"Sacramento."

"Shoot, child. You almost home. That's just down the road a ways," Sarah said excitedly.

"Only I don't know if it *is* home anymore."

"What you talkin' about? A mamma always glad to see her children."

"Don't count on it," Jackie said harshly.

"Shush. What you saying? Your mamma don't love you?"

"When my mom and dad split up, she made me go with my dad. I didn't want to, but she made me. Said it'd be better if I did. *Yeah, right!*" he said bitterly. "Maybe for her."

"You don't know," Sarah scolded. "You don't know what she be thinking, boy. She might know something you don't."

Jackie walked in silence.

"You can't be judging her too hard, now," Sarah said. "You don't know what was in her heart."

"I don't really care," Jackie muttered under his breath, more to himself than to Sarah, his mood darkening. He didn't care to dwell on thoughts of the past, though it was always just below the surface, waiting to push through.

Jackie quickened his pace. "Come on. Let's catch up with the others."

Jackie and Sarah pushed through a screen of yellowing willow brush and came out on a long gravel bar that fanned the river into a wide, shallow ripple that caught and reflected the afternoon light in a thousand fractured shards. Elijah and Revbo were already wading through the middle of it, the current wetting the bottom of their pants to boot-top height.

"*Ah, great,*" Jackie stammered cynically, stopping at the water's edge. "How much farther?" he called out to Elijah, who was tracking across the exposed dry stones on the far shore.

"It's right here," he said, turning back to beckon to the boy and Sarah. "Just up in these trees." He stood waiting for the two stragglers, Revbo coming up past him, climbing the short bank and disappearing in amongst a weave of cedars and pines.

Jackie sat down to kick his shoes off and roll his pants up as Sarah scooped up the pup and started across in her ankle-high boots.

"Come on," Elijah yelled, shaking his head, watching the boy tie his shoes together and sling them over his shoulder with his bedroll. "Barely enough water through here to stop a grasshopper," he complained, eyeing Jackie picking his way delicately through the slick cobblestones that lined the river bottom. Jackie made the crossing and started barefoot up the bank to join Elijah waiting for him at the edge of the trees.

"I'd put my shoes on if I was you," he said as Jackie came on, picking his way carefully over the big stones. "There's likely to be some broken glass around. A few rattlesnakes, maybe."

Jackie halted in midstep. "You're kidding me?" Elijah didn't bother to answer, just turned and headed on into the trees.

"*Now* he tells me," Jackie said, finding a spot to sit down and put his shoes on hurriedly, eager not to be left behind.

A broad, flat bench of land ran back away from the river a hundred feet or more before meeting the rapid rise of the canyon slope. Cedars, ponderosa pines, hemlocks, and spruce grew in scattered profusion, shielding more of the afternoon light, making the forest glade seem dim and unwelcoming. A large clearing in the middle of the trees was littered with rusted cans, broken bottles, and two hapless fire rings that stared unblinkingly at the narrow patch of pale blue sky overhead like a pair of black eyes. Elijah threw his bedroll and bag down in the center of the clearing. "Not much to brag about, but I guess it'll do," he said, kicking a stray can or two into thick undergrowth at the periphery of the clearing.

Revbo laughed mockingly. He dropped his bedroll and sat down atop an old stump to survey the sight. "Every damn tramp on the High Line know about this place, Elijah. This ain't no special place. And you bragging how sweet your place on the Feather River is. You can't teach no old dog any new tricks."

"It's tough," Elijah conceded. "Especially when the dog's so dumb."

"Who you calling dumb?" Revbo demanded, stiffening visibly.

"Nobody," Elijah said with a sly smile. "I thought we were talking about dogs." Elijah bent and picked up a tattered trash bag that was in half-decent shape. "Come on, boy," he said, gesturing to Jackie. "Give me a hand and help me straighten up a bit, make ourselves comfortable 'fore dinner."

"Dinner?" Jackie said enthusiastically, bending to pick up two empty wine bottles at his feet.

"Oh yeah," Elijah said cheerfully. "You hungry? How about you, Sarah? Now, I know Revbo is hungry," he said, bending to pick up a ripped sheet of clear plastic too far gone to be of utility to anyone anymore.

"Depends," Revbo chortled mirthlessly. "Seeds and berries, no thanks. Now, you got a couple of nice pork chops, a pile of mashed potatoes, some butter beans and collards, and a splash of gravy—now you talking hungry."

"Could be a problem," Elijah said earnestly. "Don't think I got any butter beans."

Revbo's chortle darkened. "Who you kidding?" he challenged. "You expectin' crows, like the prophet Elijah in the Bible? Swoop down and feed you in the desert? I don't think so," he smirked.

"Crows? You don't say?" Elijah said, amused. "Never heard that story."

Revbo stooped, picking up his bedroll, and walked off a distance to stake out a private corner of the glade for himself. "You call me, now," he said curtly, "when supper's ready. I'll be napping till then." He unrolled his blankets and stretched out as Jackie, Sarah, and Elijah finished picking up the worst of the trash.

"Sarah, you think you could manage a fire while me and the boy go shopping?" Elijah asked cheerfully.

"You go 'n get that food and I'll take care of building a fire," Sarah said. "But don't you disappoint me now, Mr. Elijah. That pork chop sure sounds mighty fine." She watched Elijah lead Jackie from camp. "I can taste it already."

"Better get that fire going, 'less you like your pork chops raw," Elijah called over his shoulder. And the two disappeared into the willow brush and were gone.

They worked their way upriver through the cool shadow of the mountain, the sound of the play of water over rocks a soothing balm to their exhaustion. Across the river and up into the tree line that ascended the slope, the golden light of late afternoon bathed the dark, mixed conifers in soft light. The river swept away to the far bank, around a broad alluvial bar that had gathered the sediments of countless floodings, where now it was built up almost into a meadow of thick, tall golden stalks of grass. Elijah broke from the shoulder of the slope, out into the grassy expanse of level ground, and stopped abruptly. He stood and surveyed the lay of the land.

"Been a while," he ruminated. "Now we'll see if the ol' dog can remember where he buried his bone." He stepped forward tentatively. He turned a quarter turn to the left and took two steps toward a cluster of stones lying in the grass. He stooped and turned the largest capstone over. Nothing but more stones and little crawly creatures that scurried madly at being disturbed. He reset the top rock much as it had been and moved on again, rubbing his chin whiskers, deep in thought.

"What the *hell* are you doing?" Jackie said, standing back a ways, observing Elijah curiously.

"Be a little patient," Elijah said, moving forward another couple of paces, stooping again, turning yet another stone and then replacing it.

"I thought we were looking for dinner," Jackie complained.

"We are."

"What? Gophers?"

"Just hold your horses," Elijah said coolly. He meandered several more paces, then stooped and turned over yet another large stone. "Aha!" He knelt on one knee. Jackie moved through the grass to stand beside Elijah, who was bent over a deep hole.

"What's that?" Jackie asked, his curiosity rising.

"*Damn,*" Elijah said, peering into the dark hole. Jackie stooped to inspect the find. He saw that the hole had symmetry and craft to it, and was lined with willow branches to hold its form.

"What *is* that?" Jackie asked earnestly.

"It's what you call a *cache.*"

"A cash? Like money?"

"No. Not like money," Elijah said, turning the stone back. "*Cache.* From the old French explorers. A place to hide things."

"How'd it get here?"

"It didn't *get here*. I made it."

"What for?"

"Damn, but you're full of questions."

"And you're weird," Jackie said curtly. "Walking around, saying '*aha*' like a pirate or something."

Elijah straightened, a faint smile growing at the corners of his mouth. "A pirate? That's good," he said absently. "Nobody's ever called me that." He surveyed the bench of land. "I know there's gotta be something around here somewhere. I can *feel* it." He strode forward purposefully. "*Aha!*" he exclaimed again with dramatic flair as he knelt down in the grass. Jackie shook his head as he followed along behind him.

Elijah turned another flat stone back, peered inside, then straightened slowly. Jackie bent and put his face to the opening in the ground.

"*Oh shit,*" he said, recoiling. He stumbled and fell and scrambled backward. Elijah watched in amusement, laughing at Jackie's antics.

"You think that's funny?" Jackie screeched. "You think it's funny I almost got bit in the eyeball by a snake?"

Jackie's reaction only made Elijah laugh harder, to the point he couldn't catch his breath and started coughing. He hacked and coughed vigorously as he struggled to breathe.

"Hope you choke," Jackie said, collecting his composure.

Elijah expelled a bull roar of air and squared his shoulders. He had tears in his eyes and a big grin on his face. He replaced the stone with care. "How was I to know you were afraid of snakes," he said, chuckling softly.

"Very funny," Jackie said.

"Really. I had no idea," Elijah said more earnestly, though still enjoying himself.

Jackie stood and walked off a distance, his back to Elijah. He stood stiffly, defiantly.

Elijah dried his eyes and shook his head to dispel his mirth. He scanned the flat sweep of ground again. Slowly, methodically, he stepped half a dozen paces to yet another small rock pile and rolled back the capstone. "*Aha!*" he exclaimed loudly, reaching into the hole, extracting a lumpy burlap bag. "We're in luck."

Jackie raced over to watch as Elijah untied the top of the sack, forgetting his hurt feelings. Elijah pulled the sack open as he lifted it, dumping its contents onto the ground. Half a dozen quart-size cans tumbled out in a pile. All were without labels.

"What is it?" Jackie said, lifting one to inspect it. It had clearly been buried and left for a period of time, but the integrity of the can was still good.

"Don't know," Elijah said, lifting one to shake at the side of his head. He listened intently. "Peaches, maybe. Stewed prunes. Hard to say."

Jackie gave him a look of incredulous despair.

"Does it matter? Hungry is hungry." Elijah bent and gathered up the cans, replacing them in the burlap bag. "And whatever it is, it's dinner. And not only that, but I guarantee you'll relish it."

—|——|——|—

Dinner made up in variety what it lacked in protein. Elijah prepared four of the eight unmarked cans, having selected them at random since there was no way to do otherwise. The main course was a mixture of creamed corn, candied yams, and beets. Dished out, it wasn't all that appetizing in appearance, but it was hot and it garnered no complaint, even from Revbo and the pup. After they'd completed the main course, Elijah built up the fire again and brewed a pot of camp coffee. The fire crackled and hissed as the darkness of the evening settled fully around them. They shared the last can over coffee: sliced pears in thick syrup.

The four sat in subdued, sated silence for a long spell. The boy lay on his unrolled blankets, staring at the fire. Sarah sat Indian-style, the pup nestled in the pit of her folded legs where she could stroke it absently as she dreamily watched the dancing of the flames. Elijah sipped coffee and smoked, content and satisfied in being there, the shoaling song of the river playing delicately to his ear. Revbo marked the evening with slow sips from a pint of whiskey that materialized as if out of nowhere. Elijah and the boy pretended not to notice. Sarah pretended not to care.

Revbo rose unsteadily. He stared into the darkness, then turned and started to walk away from the fire and the circle of people around it.

"Little more coffee left," Elijah called. "Care for a last swallow before bed?"

"I done had my last swallow," Revbo slurred. "I be turning in."

The three let their eyes follow him out of the circle of light, the boy turning his gaze finally on Sarah at the last, studying her composure. Elijah threw another couple of sticks on the fire. The three remaining settled in the wake of Revbo's departure. They seemed to breathe a collective sigh of relief.

"Sarah . . . ," Revbo called from the darkness. "You coming . . . ?" It was less a question than a demand.

Sarah closed her eyes and stroked the pup's head, rocking meditatively to an inner rhythm.

"Sarah . . ."

"I be along directly," she said evenly. She rocked back and forth, her dark round face glowing softly like the soft penumbra of an eclipsed moon, her mouth the lone thin crescent of light.

"Sarah . . . ," Revbo hollered impatiently.

"Okay, okay," she bellowed, sighing deeply, a tired sorrow rising out of her like a fog. She rose and brushed herself off. "Guess I be turning in," she said wearily.

"Night, Sarah," the boy said kindly.

"Night, suga," she replied as she turned to wander off into the darkness of the trees. Elijah raised his eyes to appraise Sarah's retreat. His gaze caught that of the boy's for an instant. The boy's expression seemed to beg intercession. Elijah turned to stare at the fire again.

Elijah reached back into the pile of wood he'd gathered and collected three hefty chunks to throw onto the fire. He set to rolling one last cigarette for the night. He lit it with a burning ember, then tossed the ember back into the flames as he inhaled deeply.

"Don't . . . ," a plaintive cry came from the edge of the darkness. "You're hurting me."

Jackie stiffened and turned to stare at Elijah.

"*Goddamn it,*" Revbo complained. There was a sharp smack, followed by a short yelp from the dog. "Git the fuck outta here!"

"Don't, Revbo," Sarah's voice pleaded meekly.

The boy stared at Elijah. Elijah stared back for a long moment, then dropped his eyes. The pup came sidling out of the darkness, looking for a friendly welcome. He waddled up to Elijah.

"Feisty little devil, ain't you?" Elijah said, letting the dog chew on his fingers as he rubbed its snout. The pup grew disinterested after a bit and wandered over to the boy, climbing up into his lap to lie down. Elijah smiled at the boy, who stared wondrously at the pup, then up at Elijah.

"Cute little son of a dog, ain't he?" Elijah said lightly.

Over the dulcet murmuring of the river and the soft crackling of the fire, the faint sound of strenuous breathing floated up out of the darkness with a pervasive insistence.

Elijah looked up, staring out into the darkness in the direction where Revbo and Sarah had disappeared. The boy looked at Elijah quizzically, his face deepening into embarrassed disgust as he realized the nature of the sounds.

"Guess I'll turn in," Elijah said evenly, pushing himself to standing. "You be turning in soon?" he asked casually.

"Yeah," Jackie said distantly. "Pretty soon."

"Sleep well," Elijah said. "Should be sweet dreams all around. We're in the mountains now."

A Longing

Tired though he was, Elijah slept fitfully, unable to dissolve conscious at-
tachment to the world. He tossed under his blankets, trying to find the
groove, the passage that led in and down into timeless sleep. He was on the
edge of it, but couldn't find the opening. Then, there it was. But just as he
was about to slip away, he awoke fully and sat upright.

The sound of the river was constant. There was a faint, almost imperceptible night breeze pulling at the branches of the willows along the river's
edge. The brightness of the moon glow was diffused through a layer of mist
that had risen off the river, filling the canyon with a shimmering diapha-
nous haze that half concealed trees along the summit of the ridge, causing
them to appear ghostlike. It was hard to distinguish shadow from shape,
substance from illusion, especially under the towering evergreens that filled
the narrow bench of ground between the river and the abrupt rise of the
mountain. Elijah's gaze swept the muted landscape, finding the boy curled
near the fire, now just a glowing eye of heat. Elijah turned and looked off in
the direction Revbo and Sarah had departed, but was unable to determine
where they lay.

He rose soundlessly, slipped on his boots, and walked out from under
the trees to the river's edge. The river poured steadily, conversing with the
stones that shaped its sound, quieting in pools, then pushing forward in a
singing rush. Elijah reckoned it was well past midnight, but nowhere near
dawn. He could not see the moon, but like a sailor who knows the tide even
when he is not near the water, he knew it to be nearly full. He squatted beside the river and scanned the dark shadow of the opposite bank. He bent

slowly and scooped a cool handful of water and drank cautiously, his eyes ever alert to movement of shadow. Something had disturbed his sleep, he was sure of it. He splashed a handful of the cold water on his face and rose. He watched the flow of the river, transfixed by the endless drift, marveling at the sound of flowing water, its ability to soothe and quiet the most troubled spirit.

Had he heard something? he wondered. Or only imagined it? There was only a faint breath of air. *So different*, he thought, *from the night in Montana.* He thought of Ol' Icy Eye, the grizzly. *One in a hundred*, he ruminated. The bear had attacked with fierce purpose, had batted him like a toy. He could hear the echo of its deafening roar, *Go.* What were the odds of that? he wondered. One in a million, one in a billion? And what were the odds that his path would intersect with that of the boy's? In the world that lay half revealed in dreams and half concealed in wakefulness, it was not a matter of odds at all. It was, he had learned long ago, merely a matter of paying attention.

Elijah knew Jackie's mother lived in Sacramento, less than a day's journey by trail. The boy could be sleeping in his own bed this time tomorrow night, Elijah speculated. But how safe would he be? Would the danger disappear? Somehow he suspected not. No, not suspected: *knew.* And he knew, too, that this wasn't just about the boy anymore. There was far more to it than that. But what? Now more than ever, it was vital that he pay attention.

Elijah wandered back beneath the mantle of trees to lie down and wrap himself in his blankets again. He rolled over and squirmed, seeking the groove of sleep. In this cycle, the one between him and the boy coming together, something remained to be completed. He did not know what it was. Part of it filled him with apprehension. But part of it was edged with regret, also. He sensed this only as a longing, a pull that tugged at him without language. It was a longing. A longing.

+ + +

Elijah awoke to the smell of pine smoke and coffee. He blinked his eyes against the morning light, imagining at first it was only the faint lingering impression of a dream.

"Here ya go," Jackie said, inviting Elijah fully into the world, a cup of fresh coffee extended as greeting.

Elijah stirred, rising on one elbow, sure now it was not a dream. He took the cup and stared at the steaming black liquid, then at the boy. Smiling, he took a sip. He sighed appreciatively. The boy had made a decent cup of camp coffee. "That's pretty good. You got any bacon and eggs to go with that?" he asked hopefully.

"In your dreams," Jackie teased.

"That's what I was afraid of," Elijah said, taking another sip.

Jackie sat down on a log near the fire and took up a cup of his own. He sipped thoughtfully.

"How long you been up?" Elijah asked.

"'Bout an hour, maybe," Jackie said. "The pup got frisky, wanted to play."

Elijah sat up and looked around the campsite. He saw the hollow dip between three big trees where Revbo and Sarah had bedded down. He turned back to the fire, saw the pup curled asleep on Jackie's blankets.

"Must have worn him out," Elijah said, laughing, nodding at the dog.

"Dirty son of a dog," Jackie cursed mockingly, imitating Elijah. "Woke me, then decided he wanted to sleep some more. So I made a fire. Some coffee. Hope you don't mind me using your stuff."

"Something a tramp could get used to—coffee in bed," Elijah said.

"Sorry there's no eggs and bacon."

"I reckon we'll eat all right."

"Find some more caches?" Jackie said, half statement, half question.

"Oh, no doubt. I been squirreling things away for a long time. A *long time* now. Just got to remember where."

"Wouldn't hardly call it fast food," Jackie said.

"How's that?" Elijah said.

"You know, ready when you are. Gotta find it first."

Elijah wasn't following Jackie's humor. "Fast food?" he said curiously.

"Forget it, Elijah," Jackie said. "It's a joke."

"Joke?"

Jackie took a sip of coffee and shook his head. "I guess ya gotta be there," he said absently.

"How's that? Be where?"

"*Jeez*, Elijah," Jackie said, exasperated. "It's an expression!"

"*Right, right,*" Elijah said, catching on finally. He took another sip of coffee. "This is pretty damn good. You'll make somebody a good wife someday."

"Unless I decide to be a tramp."

Elijah studied the boy. "Ought not to do that. Ain't a life to take pride in."

"You seem to enjoy it," Jackie said.

"I don't think I'd go that far. I tolerate it. I'm too ornery to live civilized."

The boy wasn't listening, lost in thought. Elijah sensed something of the struggle Jackie was dealing with, family splintered apart. *Tough*, he thought. He wondered about the struggle he'd bestowed on his own children.

Elijah threw his blankets back. "Hey, hey," he said with rising enthusiasm, causing the pup to lift its head, blinking at the world. "Let's see about rustling up something hot for breakfast."

The pup rose and stretched and sauntered over for a pat and a scratch behind the ears from Elijah. "And how you doing this morning?" Elijah said. "Chase any rabbits in your dreams?"

The pup turned its head under Elijah's hand and began to gnaw on his fingers. "Hold your ponies, now," Elijah said, holding the dog's lower jaw and shaking it gently as it chewed on the weathered flesh of his hand. Elijah let go and stood up, stretching with a muffled growl. Peripheral movement at the edge of camp caught his eye, and he turned to see Sarah lift her head from beneath the tangle of blankets where she lay. She smiled sleepily, waving a halfhearted hello.

"Sleeping Beauty awakes," Elijah said, nodding toward Sarah. Jackie turned and, seeing Sarah waving, waved a greeting in return.

"Fresh coffee if you want it," Jackie said with pride, lifting his cup in a gesture of invitation.

Sarah sat staring at them, still seemingly half-asleep. She blinked and rubbed her face, then blinked again. She stretched and slipped from the covers, pausing to put her boots on, leaving the laces untied. Jackie found her cup next to the fire and filled it. He rose and carried it toward her, meeting her halfway in her slow, sleepy amble toward the fire.

"Thank you, suga," she cooed softly, taking it. She patted Jackie affectionately on the arm. "You too good to Sarah," she said tenderly. Jackie blushed, embarrassed in remembering the sounds from her and Revbo in their blankets the night before.

"How'd you sleep?" Jackie asked, turning back toward the fire.

Sarah stretched and farted, and giggled. "Excuse me," she said shyly.

"Probably got a bunch of fleas like I did," Jackie offered quickly, scratching at his raw places.

Sarah laughed. "What I got would snack on fleas," she said, rubbing her hip.

Elijah chuckled.

"What you guffawing about," Sarah said.

"Old joke I just remembered," he answered quickly. "How'd the preacher there sleep?" he added, nodding in the direction where Revbo lay.

"*Hmmpf.* He ain't got no problem sleeping, what he drunk. Mean and hateful, that man. When he be drinking."

As if summoned by mention of his name, Revbo stirred. The three at the fire made busy to ignore him as he rose to amble over and bum fixings for a cigarette from Elijah. He barely spoke except to make his needs known, ignoring Sarah and the boy completely. As soon as he had his smoke lit, he returned to his little encampment and began slowly gathering up his belongings as though preparing to go. Without a word from Revbo, Sarah got up and went over to help him. Jackie watched the two of them out of the corner of his eye, angry with Revbo, wishing he'd treat Sarah with the respect she deserved. He watched Revbo finish tying up the last of their belongings, then grumble something to her under his breath. He rose and shouldered his gear and came back over to the fire.

"Be catching you somewhere down the road," he said to Elijah. "We be heading out now." He turned and started down the path toward the river, the way they'd come the previous afternoon.

"Remember: don't piss into the wind," Elijah called out in farewell. Revbo didn't turn or even raise a hand of acknowledgment or farewell.

Sarah shouldered her sack and picked up the pup, cradling him in her arms, hugging on him hard as she came back to the fire.

"Revbo say I got to leave the pup," she said, her voice soft, without force of will. She stroked the dog's downy fur, unable to look up and meet Elijah and Jackie's gaze. "I was wondering, Jackie, since you seem to like him so much—and him you—if you'd mind looking out for him. I know I shouldn't ask it, but he's so little . . ."

Jackie looked at Sarah in disbelief, a mixture of sorrow and joy welling up to catch in his throat. "Sarah . . . Sure. But don't you want to keep him?" he managed.

Sarah kissed the pup on the top of the head and then held him out to Jackie. Jackie took the pup with grave reluctance.

"You take good care of him, you hear? He don't have no mamma to look after him. So you gotta be the one to do it." She looked up at Jackie, then at Elijah. Tears pooled in the crescents of her big eyes.

"I will. I promise," Jackie stammered.

Sarah gave a brave smile and turned. She took a half step, then stopped and turned back to Elijah. "Mr. Elijah, you're a good man. You got a good heart. You take care of Jackie here. Make sure he gets home to his mamma."

Elijah nodded affirmation. "And you, you take care of yourself, too. You make sure you get back by to see your mamma as well. I know she wants to know you're all right."

Sarah started to say something, her lip quivering, tear streaks starting to glisten on her dark face. She turned quickly and started off again.

Jackie stared mutely, watching her broad form make its way down the trail under the weight of her load, one foot after another, shoelaces dragging in the dirt. "Elijah, we can't just let her go like that," he said. "Can't she stay with us?"

"Nobody's decision but her own," said Elijah, continuing to stare after her, watching her move deeper into the thicket of willows along the river.

"Elijah . . . ," Jackie pleaded.

"She's the only one who knows what she's got to do. Just like anyone else," Elijah said with finality.

Jackie turned to catch a last glimpse of her, but she was gone. He buried his face in the scruff of the pup's neck and squeezed tight. "Don't you worry," he whispered to the dog. "I'll take care of you. I promise. I promise."

Elijah emptied the contents of the coffeepot into the fire, then kicked dirt and cold ashes over the smoldering pile of coals.

"Better get your things together," he said as he turned and walked over to kneel at his bedroll.

"What? Where we going?" Jackie asked, hopeful that they, too, were heading out after Sarah.

"Moving."

"Why? Where?" the boy quizzed.

"To my camp."

Jackie's face wrinkled with confusion. "Your camp? I thought this was your camp. Yesterday you said this . . ."

"No," Elijah interjected. "Revbo said."

"But you didn't say anything."

"Why? You tell somebody about something special, it's not likely to stay that way long." Elijah rolled his blankets and tied them with a deft twist of cord. "Come on. It ain't far, but it's far enough. Hurry up now. We'll worry about breakfast later."

240

One Standing

The two traversed upriver the way they'd gone the evening before in search of Elijah's caches, then crossed the shallows to the other bank to move through thick brush. Jackie had to dovetail close on Elijah's heels to keep sight of him in the overgrowth.

"It was way easier on the other side," he complained, thrashing his way through a dense clump of willow.

"I know," was all Elijah answered, pushing forward, letting a long, limber branch snap back and swat the boy in the face.

"Watch it," Jackie called out.

"You watch it. You're the one following," Elijah said, letting go with another one.

"You're lost, aren't you? You trying to find a trail or something?" Jackie said, struggling to keep up.

"There ain't no trail." Elijah halted, holding a branch so the boy could catch up without getting batted again. "Move more like water," he said, watching the boy bulldoze his way through the growth. "Like a lizard—like a snake." He grinned, teasing the boy. "Bend, slide, like you're slithering through the branches. You'll find it much easier than fighting your way through."

"When are we gonna get there?" Jackie asked impatiently, barely considering Elijah's advice. The pup stared up into Jackie's face from the press of his arm where he held it firmly to his chest. The dog licked the boy's neck, then turned to consider Elijah.

"Soon," Elijah said simply, ruffling the pup's ears. He turned and started out again.

They moved out of the shadow of the mountain, into the morning sunlight, the air appreciatively warmer. The rise of the slope grew more precipitous as they worked their way upriver toward a vertical outcropping of dark rock, where the rush of water narrowed and deepened into large cascading pools pouring over carved stone. Jackie stopped to admire a stretch of the river, the way the water spilled in long white scarves, one pool to the next. When he turned to take up after Elijah again, Elijah was nowhere to be seen. It was as if he'd dissolved, disappearing into thin air.

"Elijah!" Jackie bellowed, flooded with panic.

Elijah stuck his head out from behind a slab of rock nearly ten feet off the ground. "What," he responded, struggling not to show his growing annoyance. Jackie raced forward a half-dozen steps and looked up to find Elijah working his way up a narrow crack in the rock. He watched as Elijah slipped past a sinewy branch of madrone, its smooth, polished red bark looking almost like flesh. He disappeared completely from sight.

"Elijah?" Jackie called tentatively.

Elijah appeared to the right, out on a ledge of rock fifteen feet overhead.

"It's easy going," he called down. "There's handholds in the rock—you'll find them. But keep a good grip coming up under the tree here." He pulled on another branch of the madrone, shaking it, making the sunlight filtering through its leaves dance along its smooth surface. "Watch your bedroll, or it'll knock you on your ass."

Jackie inspected the narrow chute of light-colored rock sandwiched between two uplifted dark panels. The lighter rock, a vein of quartz, was notched almost like a giant saw blade, creating a series of natural steps. It was more a ladder than a staircase, and Jackie began the slow, careful climb, finding each foothold and handhold as naturally as if they'd been carved purposefully. He advanced cautiously, careful not to let go of the pup or lose his balance. He ducked his head and slipped under the overhanging tree, maneuvering carefully, and emerged on a flat shelf of rock. He set the dog free, then crawled forward to finally rise from his hands and knees, wanting to turn and take in the sweeping view of the river below.

Still in a half crouch, he froze, his gaze staring straight ahead into the mountain. He eased himself slowly to standing as he studied the twin rock vaults, almost caves sculpted into the face of a second outcropping, this one set back fifteen feet, creating the broad ledge where he stood. In the strong sunlight, it was impossible not to notice the primitive pictographs painted on the wall of the largest vault.

"*Jeez,*" Jackie exclaimed under his breath. He stood transfixed. Elijah watched from an oblique angle. Jackie's reaction was pretty much what his had been the first time he'd stumbled upon the spot, quite by accident, two years before. "*Oh my God.*" The boy moved forward, drawn by the distinct outline of a dozen red-and-black drawings. Jackie moved to the dominant figure, a stark reddish-brown silhouette of a human form drawn at the center of the largest vault. It was long and slender, more totem than realism. There were no discernible facial features—only elongated legs and torso and arms, both raised high overhead. It was a triumphant, defiant figure, standing amidst a swirl of lesser figures and designs.

"Are these for real?" Jackie said, stepping closer to inspect the rock art. There were three smaller figures gathered in the lower right corner, dwarfed by the central one. They were in black. There were two orbs dominant in the upper left quadrant: the larger one with four spurred points, the other with a spiral winding inside it. A pair of long, sawtooth lines, one black, one red, ran parallel to each other.

"Oh, they're real," Elijah said. "The question is what do they mean?"

"What do you mean?" Jackie said.

"Why were they put here? What's this fella here?" Elijah said, stepping forward, pointing to the larger-than-life character with his hands outstretched overhead. "What's his story? I call him One Standing."

"One Standing," Jackie said, ruminating. "You think he's got a story?"

"Don't you? The pose is common to many tribal people, a symbol for 'man.' But his size is what makes me wonder about him. Gotta mean something."

"*Wow,*" Jackie whispered. "I wish I knew."

"You and me both."

Jackie stepped back to take it in more fully.

"Careful you don't backpedal over the edge," Elijah said, kneeling, opening his traveling bag. He fished out two large Gravenstein apples and shined them on his shirt. "Here," he said, extending one toward the boy. "Sort of a light breakfast this morning. There's a handful more, but we'll rustle up something else by dinnertime."

"This is your camp?" Jackie said, biting into the apple, walking around the broad ledge in the warm sunlight.

"This is it."

"Cool," Jackie exclaimed.

Elijah laughed. "Yeah, cool. I suppose it is." He momentarily studied the pictographs anew.

The boy sat down on his bedroll and let the pup curl up in his lap. He looked down at the dog and grew quiet. "Wish Sarah had stayed," he said quietly. "She'd have loved this."

"No doubt," Elijah offered, taking another bite of apple. "But she'll do all right by herself."

"Revbo's mean," Jackie complained. "He doesn't treat her right."

"No, he don't. But she's got to get clear on that for herself." Elijah sat munching his apple, remembering again how he'd stumbled upon this place, cold and shivering after a long night's ride from K-Falls one November. He finished his apple and set the core on the ground for the pup. He unrolled his bedroll and lay down, tipping his hat to shield his eyes from the sun. He suddenly felt immensely tired, ready for a nap. A nap was exactly what he needed.

"I'm gonna rest my eyes awhile," he muttered in a muted voice, his face shielded by the cant of his fedora. "Wake me when room service brings lunch."

Jackie watched silently, stroking the pup lovingly as Elijah adjusted the curve of his body, finding a groove to settle into. The boy sat without moving until Elijah began to snore sonorously.

The boy sat in the sun for a long time, soaking in its heat. The pup snoozed easily, curled in a little ball. Jackie rose finally and walked to the edge of the broad shelf and stared down at the dance of sunlight on the river. He felt the breeze tease the hair on his neck and arms. He went over to the madrone and slipped beneath it, descending the rock staircase. At the river, he turned and began working his way farther upstream, jumping from boulder to boulder. Fifty feet on, he climbed out on a large domed rock with a long view of water. He sat and became quickly transfixed by a ripple.

Sarah's departure had touched him deeply, opening a wound of sadness. He let his mind go with the flow of the river, allowing the sadness to rise and course through him.

—+—+—+—

Elijah awoke from a sound sleep to the heat of midday. He pushed his hat back and cracked an eye as he turned his head to account for the boy. The cave mouth was vacant, the ledge empty except for the dog.

He rose and inspected the sweep of the river, easily spotting the boy sitting alone on a big rock that jutted into the current. He stood watching him for several moments. Jackie barely moved, as though sleeping sitting up. An echo of the dream in Bend the night the boy ran off floated back to mind. The warning that had come in the dream as the stranger ascended the knoll where he'd sat: *be careful . . . be careful.*

Elijah stepped to the edge of the shelf, slipped under the madrone, and descended the stone staircase. "Hey now," he called as he approached Jackie from behind. Jackie turned, stared vacantly, then turned back to the river.

"What's up?" Elijah asked nonchalantly, taking a seat beside him.

Jackie shrugged.

"Turned out to be a beautiful day, don't ya think?" Elijah offered, staring out across the river, letting his gaze rise to the top of the far ridgeline. Getting no response, he directed his gaze back to the boy. Jackie sat with his head tilted forward, his eyes closed. "Kinda day that makes having nowhere to go a small blessing. Nowhere I'd rather be than right here." The boy said nothing.

"You all right?" Elijah asked.

The boy shrugged again.

"You feeling okay?"

The boy slowly raised his head to stare out at the river. "You ever feel sorry for yourself?" he asked flatly.

Elijah snorted a laugh, working to lift the sullen mood that hung over both of them. "I suppose. Sometimes," he said. "I suppose you could call it that." He pulled out his rolling papers and tobacco and started to make a smoke. "What about you? You ever feel sorry for yourself?"

The boy shrugged again.

"I live with myself all right most of the time," Elijah said, turning to gaze at the river. "Or at least try to. But when I was younger, I did some things . . . things I later regretted."

The boy lifted his head again, drew a big breath. "I feel, you know, bad sometimes," he said. "Real bad. About the way I've acted . . . things I've done. You know, to other people." He hesitated. "You know—to my mom. Even my dad, sometimes. I think he's mostly an asshole, but I still think I could've been nicer. I feel so bad sometimes, I start to feel sorry for myself. I mean—here I'm the one that's done something wrong, but I'm the one who feels sorry for himself."

Elijah considered. It was not easy being young—now or ever, he thought.

"Yeah," he offered. "Sometimes I suppose I do feel sorry for myself. Crappy feeling, ain't it?"

Jackie sat with his head bowed, his shoulders rolled over. He sucked a breath, began to silently cry, his shoulders shaking. The crying grew harder.

Elijah sat mute, staring at Jackie, paralyzed by the tide of grief and pain that poured out of the boy. He lifted his head and glanced nervously out at the landscape, as if looking for someone who could help. The raw sound of the boy's pain wrenched Elijah's heart. Almost involuntarily, he found his arm rising, moving in an arc, encircling the boy to pull him gently to him.

The boy resisted instinctively, then eased and surrendered, allowing Elijah to pull his weight over against him. Jackie turned to curl into the curve of Elijah's chest. The crying continued, but after a bit, Elijah felt it abating. He kept a soft but steady hold on the boy. Elijah realized he was oddly grateful for the opportunity to hold him. It was soothing to his spirit as well.

As the afternoon light shifted and Jackie collected himself, Elijah sat to give witness to the boy's whole long story of woe. It came out in rambling circles that led to short, sharp points: the death of his brother; the dissolution of his family; the neglect of his father; the haunting image of the wounded horse, the one he called Star. The story of Star naturally stirred the memory of Smoke, the dappled gray stallion Elijah had so loved.

"I didn't mean to," the boy said, his voice cracking. "I didn't mean to hurt anyone . . ."

Elijah had little experience consoling the grief of a child, so he offered a gentling hand on the back like he would offer a colt to quiet and settle it. "I believe you," he intoned. "I believe you, Jackie." He sensed a slow easing of the tension in the boy's body. "It's hardly fair sometimes. The way the world is. Sometimes things just happen. But it doesn't mean we're bad. That we're bad people. It just *feels* that way. Especially if it's something that happens to someone . . . we love."

The dulcet sound of the river enveloped them, the dappled sunlight soft about them. Elijah sat with his arm around Jackie for a good, long while.

Spo-klis

Jackie slept the sleep of a stone: heavy without buoyancy. On the ridge crest, the waxing moon rose into the trees, then sailed like a bright jewel along the curve of the mountain, never quite leaving the touch of the trees. Here and there where the trees thinned, its light spilled shadows everywhere.

Elijah lay in his blankets, marveling at the radiance of the three stars in the constellation of Orion, marking his belt, visible despite the brightness of the moon. He had viewed this constellation from a thousand different places, and it always caused him to think of his uncle. It had been Uncle who'd first shown him the pattern in the stars. When Elijah was a small boy sitting before the fire in the cabin on the Sprague River, Uncle extracted lumps of glowing coals from the embers and laid out the outline of Orion on the stone hearth. Then the great bull, Taurus, who confronted Orion. Lulled by the husky voice of his uncle, Elijah easily imagined the endless contest between the two. Uncle then did a most magical thing, and showed Elijah how the stars in the bull's head depicted Coyote, and how those in Orion's belt were the shaft of perfect Arrow. Uncle then took him outside and showed him the same magic right there in the sky, and sure enough, it was a trick of the eye that permitted you to see what the different stories told you to see.

"Things of this world go by many names," Uncle said. "Some given by whites. Some by The People. From this ground where we stand, these stars have been Coyote and Arrow much longer than they have been Bull and the hunter Orion. To say they are Bull and Orion does not mean that they aren't Coyote and Arrow also. You only have to look, and know what to

247

look for, to see what The People saw."

With the sky finally lightening along the ridgeline, Elijah rose and kindled a fire over the ashes from the night before. He fed it the biggest wood he could find. The blaze chased away the darkness, pooling it in eddies behind stumps and boulders and trees. While the light of the flames danced on the rock wall of the overhang, Elijah made preparation for the day. It had come to him in the night that it was time for purification. It had been many months—well over a year now—since Elijah had entered a *spo-klis,* the sweat lodge. Not since the anniversary of Emma's death. It was time. He knew to heed the urging, sensing something pending, a premonition of change like a shifting weather front.

Elijah cleared away the face of the brush pile on the periphery of the ledge, exposing a small, rough-hewn structure. It was made of weathered scrap planking, cobbled together to form a small, crude hut. A drape of old canvas tarp was hung over a small opening. Elijah crawled forward on his hands and knees and disappeared. Out rolled a large round stone. After a moment, another. Then another. When he emerged finally, there were nearly a dozen stones at the door of his sweat lodge.

The light grew steadily in the east. Elijah added another armload of wood to the fire and began to set the stones in the blazing embers, one atop the other. The commotion roused Jackie from sleep. He lifted his head to peer from his covers in the direction of the fire.

"What are you doing?" he asked, curious but annoyed.

"Nothing," Elijah answered, continuing to tend to his task. "Go back to sleep."

"I would if I could. You woke me up with all your damn banging around."

"I'll be done in a little bit," Elijah said. "Go back to sleep. It's early yet."

"What are you doing?" the boy asked peevishly.

Elijah didn't answer. Jackie stared in annoyance, then flopped down again, covering his head with his blankets.

Elijah stepped back to take in the fire, the sweep of the cave mouth, the ledge overlooking the river, the thinning of night. He took inventory of what yet needed to be done. He stooped and entered the hut again and retrieved three mismatched, battered buckets. He set one by the fire and carried the other two to the river. He worked steadily, without rush. He placed the two pails of water in the hut, one after the other, then used an old deer antler to roll the glowing stones into the third pail, one at a time, carrying each into the small chamber as well. When this was done, he put yet more wood on the fire, covering the stones that still remained. He stood silently for several long minutes, staring at the blaze. Slowly, he turned and faced the entrance to his sweat lodge.

He disrobed quickly, making a neat pile of his clothes, his hat the last item he removed. The stack of articles presented itself like a compressed human form: boots, then folded pants and shirt, his hat settled securely on top; the remnant of his presence, an empty skin, like the shed skin of a snake.

Elijah stood naked in the dawn light, his squat form and dark features making him appear like an aboriginal specter. He knelt and crawled into the lodge, entering the mystery of Mukaluk, The People.

The sun broke above the ridge and filled the canyon with sharp light, giving promise of a good day. A slight breeze began to rise up out of the canyon, warming its walls. Birds—fat Steller's jays, chickadees, and wrens—darted through the Jeffrey pines around the camp. The growing warmth of the morning and the chatter of birds brought Jackie slowly up from his dreamless sleep. Now and again, Elijah threw back the canvas flap to emerge from the lodge, his dark body glistening with sweat, to retrieve another fire-heated stone and lay more wood on the blaze.

The second time Elijah emerged, Jackie sat up fully to stare at the naked apparition coaxing a stone from the fire. He watched as Elijah rolled the stone into the bucket and then walked to the hut and started to disappear inside.

"Elijah?"

Elijah slipped like a snake into his hole, pulling the flap closed after him.

"What the hell," the boy whimpered. "Elijah!" he called out loudly.

Nothing. The boy threw back his covers and rose. The pup rose also from its nest at the bottom of the blankets, waiting expectantly. The boy, followed closely by the pup, stepped soundlessly toward the odd structure at the far end of the ledge.

"Elijah," Jackie called out, pulling back the flap, bending down to peer into the hole. His query was met with a blast of hot, moist air. "Elijah," the boy called desperately, withdrawing rapidly from the cloud of steam.

"Come in or stay out. But close the damn flap," Elijah retorted gruffly. "You're letting the heat out."

The boy dropped the flap. He squatted on his haunches, trying to decipher the disparate images of the morning. The pup pawed at his stocking feet.

"Go on," Jackie commanded. "Go lie down." He quickly lifted one corner of the flap and disappeared inside. "What are you doing?" he spoke into the darkness, his voice both sullen and curious.

"Sweating," Elijah said solemnly.

"Sweating?" the boy repeated, incredulous.

"Yeah. You know. Sweating."

"What for?"

"What do you mean, what for?" Elijah growled. "I'm sweating to sweat."

"Jeez, it's hot in here," he complained.

"Supposed to be."

"Where are you?" Jackie asked, agitated.

"In the dark, like you."

Jackie heard a light splash of water followed immediately by an insistent hissing. The small, tight space filled with moist, superheated air. Jackie coughed fitfully, nervously, frightened by the invisible attack of steam. "What are you doing?" he begged.

"Making steam. Here, give me your hand."

"I can't see a thing," Jackie protested hoarsely.

"Just reach out. I'll find you," Elijah replied evenly. The boy did as he was told. Their hands touched, Elijah's closing over the boy's.

"Easy now," Elijah said calmly. "Relax. Come in a little more where you can sit." He guided the boy with the pull of his hand. "Get comfortable."

"Comfortable?" the boy complained. "The air in here burns the shit out of my nose."

"Quit whining," Elijah said. "Relax. Breathe. You gotta breathe anyway, so relax."

Elijah let go of the boy's hand. He felt the boy as much as heard him as Jackie adjusted to the unfamiliar contour of the space. He heard the boy sigh. Elijah smiled, taking a deep breath of the moist air. The heat penetrated deeply. He sat silently, his body relaxed, his eyes closed lightly, inviting the blackness of the closed space into his soul. He sighed now, letting go of a layer of tension stirred by the disturbance of the boy's arrival. He sat and let the natural rhythm of his breathing carry him.

"Elijah," Jackie whispered.

"Yeah."

"What are you doing?"

"Breathing."

"I mean sitting in here in the dark. Why is it so hot?"

"So I can sweat."

"Why?'

"You're full of questions this morning," Elijah said without rancor.

"I mean . . . it's just a little weird, you ask me. Sitting in the dark. *Breathing*," he intoned. "What do you mean, *sweating?* Why are you sweating?"

"'Cuz it's hot in here," Elijah said with a chuckle. "To cleanse Body. And Spirit."

The boy sat silent for a moment. "You ever hear of a bathtub?"

"That an attempt at humor?" Elijah asked dispassionately. "I'll ignore it." The tone of his voice conveyed an earnestness the boy was unfamiliar with.

Jackie sat chastened but confused. He paused for a moment. "But *why* are you sitting here in the dark? I don't get it."

"Old Modoc custom," Elijah answered. "Enter the *sko-plis*—sweat lodge—to cleanse Spirit and Body. Helps you see things clearly. Helps you walk the Straight Road."

Jackie said nothing. He sat straining to see in the darkness. He couldn't even see the end of his nose.

"Relax," Elijah said calmly. "Just sit and breathe. That's all there is to it." He ladled on yet another dose of water. The water sizzled and hissed as it was transformed into steam by the superheated rocks. The temperature in the dark space rose again, filling the canopy above them, curling over to follow the outline of the space, engulfing them in a wave that seared the tender flesh inside the nose. Jackie tensed, doubled over, and pressed himself down into the cooler stratum of air near the floor. Slowly, as the heat moderated, he rose, testing his tolerance carefully. He pulled his shirt off over his head and laid it by the entrance. His skin was growing slick with sweat.

"This is torture," he complained. "I mean, if you want to take a bath, get cleaned up, there's a river right outside."

Elijah laughed, laying a sprig of sage on top of the hot stones. The pungent aroma of sunbaked sagebrush swirled up around them. "Mukaluk use *spo-klis* for cleansing. Don't bathe in rivers."

"Who?" Jackie asked.

"Mukaluk. The People. Modoc."

"Mukaluk?"

"Yeah. Mukaluk."

"Were they like, you know, real Indians, these Mukaluk?"

Elijah laughed. "As opposed to what? What you see in the movies?" He laughed jovially, filling the small space with sound. "Yes, they were real Indians. At one time, they were the most feared among all their neighbors."

"I never heard of them—Mukaluk," Jackie said with finality, feeling that Elijah was laughing at his expense.

"No, I suppose not. But if you'd been alive a hundred years ago, they were all the news. Every newspaper in the country had them on the front page."

"What'd they do?"

Elijah sighed. "It's a long story," he said slowly. "Mostly, they just wanted to be left alone. Be themselves. Live the way they had always lived. But the government wouldn't let them. Made it against the law to be Modoc. My uncle, he didn't care. He raised me in the old way. Had me enter *spo-klis*. Had me seek my vision. I still remember. Not everything. But some. A little. My uncle always told me it was important to remember. So I try. That's why I sweat. It is the old way. It helps me remember."

Jackie sat up, folding his legs Indian-style in front of him. "I've heard of that, the Vision Quest. How old were you when you went on yours?" he asked earnestly.

Elijah chuckled softly in the dark. "About your age, I guess. Just about the age you are now."

"How do you know where to find it?"

"It finds you," Elijah said. "If you're lucky. And have a good heart. A good heart is important. Most important. One must seek without wanting. Very important."

"Did it find you?"

"It did," Elijah said solemnly, remembering the time in the Lava Beds. "It certainly did."

"What was it like? What did it mean?" Jackie asked tentatively.

Elijah dipped his hand into the cool water, held his hand over the stones, letting the drops fall away to sizzle into steam. The stones hissed softly, their heat tempered now by the length of time they had been out of the fire.

"A Vision Quest is a sacred thing," Elijah said simply, letting the silence speak for itself. Neither spoke for several minutes.

"You never told anyone?" Jackie asked hesitantly.

"Only my uncle. Uncle was, you would say, my Helper. He was wise in the old ways and still practiced them, even though they were outlawed."

"But it was okay to tell him," Jackie said, working another angle.

"Yes."

"And what'd he say?"

"He said the way would be difficult."

"And?"

"And what?"

"And was the way difficult?

"You *are* full of questions," Elijah said, laughing. He said no more. Silence filled the darkness again. Elijah sat lathered in sweat, relaxed and gentle in his breath.

"Elijah?" Jackie asked quietly.

"Yeah," Elijah said softly.

"Nothing. I thought maybe you were sleeping." Jackie paused, pondering whether to ask more. He desperately wanted to know more. After a long while, he gathered his courage.

"Elijah?"

"No. I'm not sleeping," Elijah answered softly, without annoyance.

"That wasn't what I was going to ask."

"I'm sure I don't have to ask what you were going to ask," he said with mirth in his voice.

"What do you mean?" Jackie said, caught off guard.

"Only that if I wait, you'll have no trouble finding your way to the question on your own."

"Sorry," Jackie said, chastened.

"Ask."

"You sure?"

"Sure."

"Can't you tell me anything about your Vision Quest? I mean, it might help me and all. You know."

"No. I don't know."

"Well, you know. Me being the same age and all. Maybe I should know something about a Vision Quest."

Elijah sat in silence, pondering what Jackie had said. It made sense, in a way. One could retell his vision to a wise one, to ask for help in knowing what it meant. And if Elijah had learned one thing in life, it was that it was not always easy to determine who was wise from who wasn't. That was one of the tricks of wisdom: it did not wear a common face. Maybe the boy would know something that had long escaped him.

"I will tell you one thing," Elijah said solemnly. "But do not ask me to tell

253

you anything more."

"I swear," Jackie said eagerly. "Promise."

"It is a song. A song my uncle gave to me when I told him the dream I had on my quest." Elijah sat remembering the words, picturing again the image of the dream.

"Two crows calling.

"Two crows. Two crows."

Elijah's voice rang deep, richly modulated, his song filling the small chamber with sound.

"Two crows calling.

"One the shadow. One the light."

Elijah drew a deep breath and exhaled slowly.

"What does it mean?" Jackie asked.

Elijah chuckled wearily. "I was hoping maybe you could tell me."

"Come on!" Jackie said incredulously.

"No really," Elijah said. "All these years. Sometimes I think I know. But it never stays with me."

"Jeezzz," Jackie said, disappointed. "You had a dream back when you were a boy and you still don't know what it means? What good is it?"

"Good question," Elijah said. "But sometimes it is better to have a good question than a good answer."

Elijah groaned loudly as he rolled forward, out of a sitting position, onto all fours. "Time to take a break," he said, reaching out, finding the boy with his hand, tapping him, prodding him gently to move, to crawl forward to the chamber's opening. "Get some air, some water. Some more rocks. Then we can sit some more."

The day was warm, the sky almost cloudless. The chill of dawn was long gone, but the sharp contrast of the open air to the tight enclosure of the superheated hut made Jackie feel as though every nerve ending had been ignited. He could feel the slightest breeze, sense the faintest puff of air across the flesh of his arms. He felt more alive, more truly *in his skin*, than he could ever remember feeling before.

Elijah took a long swallow from his water jug and extended the jug to the boy, encouraging Jackie to drink. Jackie took the jug and tipped it up quickly, taking a small sip.

"More," Elijah said. "You dry up from the inside out in a sweat. Drink more."

The boy tipped the jug up again as Elijah retrieved another stone from the fire. He carried it in the pail over to the entrance of the small hut and stooped and went inside. Jackie watched as Elijah repeated the process two more times. He was both amused and embarrassed by Elijah's nakedness. He'd never seen a grown man walk around without a stitch of clothing. Elijah paid Jackie's sidelong glances no mind, until the awkwardness the boy felt was palatable.

"A great day to be alive," Elijah said, stretching his arms over his head, oddly mirroring the pictograph of One Standing on the wall of the cave. He drew a deep breath of air and expelled it loudly. He took the jug from the boy and raised it for one last long pull of water.

"You might want to strip off them pants yourself," Elijah offered, "if you're crawling back into the lodge. Otherwise, they'll be completely soaked before we're done." He saw Jackie make a squeamish face.

"Suit yourself," he said, handing the jug to the boy and turning back toward the entrance to the lodge. Jackie watched as Elijah's dark hide disappeared from view. He took another long swallow, stripped down to his underpants, and dashed on tender soles to the entrance. He bent and scurried inside, pulling the canvas flap down behind him.

The water striking the hot stones hissed again and again as Elijah poured more on, intensifying the volume of superheated air. Jackie stiffened under the stinging assault as Elijah ladled on yet more water. The air grew so stifling the boy bent clear to the floor in search of air that did not burn his lungs. Elijah sat stolidly, breathing deeply. He heard the boy gasping for breath, then poured on yet one more scoop of water.

"It's too hot. Too *hot!*" Jackie said plaintively, fighting an urge to flee. "I can't breathe."

"You'll be fine," Elijah said calmly. "Just breathe."

"It's too hot," Jackie complained, his voice filled with rising fright.

"It's okay, Jackie," Elijah said soothingly. "When you feel the sting deep in your body, the pulse of fear beating in your heart, the steam is working. Driving out the poison, cleansing your spirit."

"It's burning the shit out of me," Jackie said, his voice less desperate but still plaintive.

"Good. That's good," Elijah said. "Fear—shit . . . bad stuff. That's why we enter the sweat lodge. To know it for what it is. Something that we can rid ourselves of, if only we are willing to sit calmly in the face of it."

Silence settled over them with the rise of the scent of sage sprinkled on the glowing rocks. The fragrance was pungent, but soothing too. Jackie lifted his head, straightening, rising in the heady dome of moist, hot air that hung over him in a cloud. He breathed tentatively, taking small sips of air, teasing the heat into his body, feeling the sting. The fear was there, but it was subsiding. He could feel it. He sipped deeper breaths, pulling more and more of the moist heat into his lungs. The silent darkness of the sweat lodge was total. He rolled his head around his shoulders, surprised at the tension gathered in his neck. He took another deep breath and sighed.

Time passed. As he relaxed, the boy grew sleepy. His head dropped, startling him into wakefulness again. He had almost forgotten that Elijah was there with him, but now could plainly hear the old man's breathing. Elijah's breath was even, steady, unstrained. Jackie wondered now if perhaps Elijah had, indeed, fallen asleep this time.

"Elijah," he said lightly.

"Yes," Elijah murmured, alert and focused, present and clear.

"Oh," Jackie said.

"Oh what?" Elijah said, dipping his hand into the bucket, then letting the water run off his fingers onto the heated stones. The hiss of steam was like a whisper in the darkness.

"I thought maybe you'd gone to sleep."

"It happens. Especially by yourself. Kinda nice, isn't it."

"Kinda hot," Jackie said, trying not to sound like he was complaining.

"Has to be hot if you're going to sweat."

Elijah drew in a deep, slow breath, then exhaled.

"In the old days, how often would people do this?" Jackie asked.

"Whenever they wanted. Sometimes once a day. Sometimes maybe only every now and then, when they felt they needed to."

"And they'd just sit in the dark?"

"Yeah. Sing sometimes. Tell stories."

"Sing what?"

"Old songs."

"Like having a party?"

"No. Like praying."

"Did you ever do that?"

"With my uncle."

"And you know the old songs?

"Not too many," Elijah said, a touch of regret in his voice.

"Do you still remember any?"

"Not really. Just that one. *Two Crows*."

"*That* was a song?" Jackie said. It hadn't sounded like any song he knew.

"More or less," Elijah chuckled, more mirth in his voice this time. "But more a prayer."

"And your uncle made up that song for you?"

"Didn't *make it up*. He *heard* it. When I told him about my dream."

"He *heard* it?" the boy said.

"Yes. Is that so strange?"

"No. I mean . . . I don't know. It's *kinda* strange."

Elijah splashed more water on the fire. "Don't you ever hear things in your mind?" he asked solemnly.

"You mean, like voices?"

"Whatever."

"I *don't think so*," Jackie said.

"Too bad," Elijah retorted evenly.

"You mean you do?"

"Oh yeah. If I pay attention, I do."

"What do you mean? Voices like little men telling you what to do?" Jackie teased, thinking Elijah was pulling his leg.

"Yes," Elijah said seriously, an edge of sternness in his tone.

"You hear voices?" Jackie asked.

"Yes. You know, when you're doing something. About to do something, and you get a feeling, as if someone were prodding you to be careful. To watch out. That never happens to you?"

"Yeah," Jackie said. "But I don't actually hear voices."

"No? How would you describe it then?"

"I don't know. It's kind of a feeling, I guess. Kind of weird like."

"Do you pay attention to it?"

"Not usually," Jackie said, embarrassed to think of himself listening to voices, whether he paid attention to them or not. Either way, it was weird.

"And did you ever later have the feeling that you wished you'd listened to that *feeling*?"

"Yeah," Jackie said, laughing. "Most of the time. I usually end up getting into trouble."

"*Voices. Feelings.* Whatever you call it, it's wise to pay attention."

Jackie sat considering it. He knew there was something to what Elijah was saying. He did indeed usually regret not following the urging of such feelings. Almost unfailingly.

"Who do you think does the prodding?" Jackie asked, now fully curious.

There was *something* to it, but he couldn't fathom it.

"Depends. Sometimes it's your Spirit Helpers. Sometimes maybe just the wind. It can come from many places if you're open to it."

"The wind?"

"Sure. Wind is one smart fella. Tell you a lot if you listen. Big Wind, Little Wind, No Wind. They all got plenty to say."

"And Spirit Helpers. What are those?"

"Whatever has come to guide you."

"Like ghosts?"

"No. *Spirits.* Like an animal. The call of a bird can carry a message. Even a feather. Especially a feather. It is a special thing. It is like magic, only better. For it's real."

"You're just telling a story now, right?"

"Most definitely," Elijah said enthusiastically. "Stories are great teachers, like dreams. Long ago, Modoc loved to tell stories. Winter was time for storytelling. When the nights were long, they loved to tell stories. That is how they shared what they had learned with their children, how to live in the world, what had been taught a long time ago by the First People, the Stone People, and the Animals, when we could still understand what they told us. That is how we learned how to clothe and feed ourselves. How to build shelters and survive the winter. We learned all this from the stories the Stone People and the Animals told us. Now, we have to listen especially hard to hear what they say. They speak to us as spirits. But they still talk to us. Telling us stories."

Elijah ladled more water on the stones, filling the tight space with more heat again. Jackie fought the impulse to tense up, to fear the sting of the hot, moist air. Elijah sprinkled more sage, and the two could see the brief incineration of the leaf on the stones, tiny sparks, popping light.

"Like what?" Jackie said. "What stories?"

"I forget mostly," Elijah said soberly. "My uncle told me stories, but not like they did in the old days. It was discouraged, but he told me anyway. But that was a long time ago. And I forgot to pay attention, I guess, 'cuz I can't remember them."

"Not even one?" Jackie said, disappointed.

"Doesn't seem like it," Elijah said sorrowfully. "That is why it is always important to pay attention. So that nothing is lost. There are lessons everywhere, if we only pay attention. I try to pay attention, but the old stories are gone." Elijah thought of all that had slipped away in his life: his hope as a boy to be the pride of his people; his pride in being at Emma's side, having her at his; their dream of land of their own at the center of the Old World. "Maybe I am not worthy," Elijah said softly, speaking to the darkness that enveloped them. "Maybe it is simply because I am not deserving of the memory. It is not easy sometimes to know the meaning of things."

Ciya-las

The river was bracing after the swelter of the sweat lodge. Elijah and the boy swam in the deep pool below the big rock, jumping in to ride the current where it poured over quick rapids at the upper end, letting it carry them past the rock, angling into its eddy where they thrashed to escape its chill. Rising from the water, they rubbed themselves vigorously to rekindle warmth.

"Fine day to be alive," Elijah bellowed, jigging on one foot, then the other, his leathery brown skin dimpled with goose bumps from the kiss of the river.

"*Elijah,*" Jackie screeched, sloshing through the narrow chute of roiling water at the upper end of the pool. He spilled between two large, semi-submerged boulders. The rush jettisoned him into a calm run of water. Elijah laughed heartily. They had been together not quite ten days, both an eternity and an instant, and a transforming touch of lightness, if not hilarity, felt like a wonderful counterpoint to what they'd been through.

"It's *cold,*" Jackie said, shivering, hugging himself as he danced naked up the edge of the big flat rock to join Elijah. He heaved himself flat against the broad surface of the stone, seeking to suck out the sun's heat. Elijah eyed the boy, excepting for his face, pale as the stone itself. The boy's abandon warmed Elijah, and he drew a deep breath, raising his gaze to stare at the river, to follow its undulating line down the canyon to where it disappeared around a bend. He closed his eyes and listened to the fluted sound of the river and the boy's chattering teeth, and the soft, faint whispering of the wind in the big pines on the far bank. A very fine day to be alive.

The two let the sounds of the Feather River Canyon and the warmth of the late-afternoon sun soothe them. Elijah couldn't remember the last time he had felt so satisfied with his place in life. There was, at this moment, truly nowhere else he would rather have been. He sat with his eyes closed, smiling at the thought of how he must look like some dark elfin creature, a figment of someone's fantasy; the boy, a water nymph, thrown up on the rock beside him to dry his wings. The residual tension of the last several days had been drained out of them, loosened by the sweat, teased free by the flow of the river and the heat of the sun. Elijah was on the verge of dozing when the sharp bark of the pup startled him.

The pup bounced and pranced, yapping up a fit. Elijah and Jackie both were instantly alert to the presence of some unseen danger, their eyes scanning the river, the far bank, searching the shadows at the base of the ridge.

"What is it?" Jackie said, stroking the dog, trying to soothe it. He tried to follow the dog's line of sight, but saw only the river. He scanned the rocks along the opposite bank. Then a slight splash in midcurrent caught his eye at the same time the dog exploded with renewed vigor. "There," Jackie said, directing Elijah's attention to the river's flow. Another splash, another flash of silver light, then another. Now both Elijah and Jackie could make out twin shadowy forms schooling in the current.

"What is it?" Jackie asked excitedly.

"*I be damned,*" Elijah said solemnly, staring at the dark shapes. Slowly, in fits and starts, the twin torpedoes advanced toward the upper end of the pool, toward the shallows of a quiet eddy behind a finger rock that jutted out from the bank.

Jackie could now make out two of the biggest fish he'd ever seen. One shadowed the other as they moved forward, then stalled, moving like dancers. Their large dorsal fins carved quick tracks in the glistening face of the river as their tails powered them forward.

"What kind are they?" Jackie asked.

"Phantoms," Elijah answered, unable to tear his eyes from their courtship in the quiet shallows.

"What do you mean, phantoms?" Jackie asked, thinking Elijah was toying with him again.

"I wouldn't believe it if I didn't see it with my own eyes."

"What?"

"An act of magic," Elijah said, shaking his head. "Pure and simple. *Ciyalas.* Their being *here* is damn near impossible. Not just *damn* near," he corrected himself. "Completely impossible. Yet here they are."

"What's *see-ya-less*?" Jackie asked, staring at the fish.

"*Ciya-las.* Salmon."

"What's so impossible about that?" the boy asked, his attention riveted on the play of the fish. One set to pulsing vigorously, fanning its powerful tail, sending up a spray of water. "They're fish. Where else would they be?"

Elijah ignored him. "That's the female, the one making all the fuss. She's preparing a bed for her eggs. The other one, behind her there. He's the male. He's waiting for her to finish her business so he can do his. She'll lay her eggs, and then he'll move in and fertilize them."

Jackie stared mesmerized, as though witnessing a secret rite. "Why's it so impossible?" he asked, his eyes fixed unwaveringly on the fish.

"Salmon are oceangoing fish. Weren't always. But the last several thousand years or so, they have been. Born in fresh water—swim to the sea. One day they sort of get a calling, and they find their way back up the same river to where they were born. They spawn a new brood . . . and die."

"So? What's so impossible in that?" Jackie asked, turning quickly to consider Elijah, then turning back to stare into the shallows. The two watched as the female slowly pulled ahead, then slipped back over the depression she'd sculpted in the gravel. She convulsed three or four times in quick succession.

"There she goes," Elijah said. "Laying down her eggs."

"So what's so impossible?" Jackie persisted.

"There's no ocean to get to anymore. Not from this part of the river, anyway," Elijah said. "Been dammed for well over forty years."

"So how'd they get here?"

The two watched as the male moved into place over the watery nest as the female pulled ahead again.

"There he goes, doing his business," Elijah said.

"So how come," Jackie said distractedly. "How come they're here?"

"Must have caught a northbound out of Sacramento."

"Seriously."

"They must be descendants of some tough old mamma who went down the river, found a dam in her way, and just decided she was going to be a salmon whether she got to the ocean or not. These two aren't as big as you'd find down, say, on the American River. But *damn* the dams, they're salmon just the same. Doing what salmon do."

Elijah rose and retreated down the back of the rock, came around the base to the river's edge, and began to slowly wade into the current, moving cautiously, without threat or hurry.

"What are you doing?" Jackie called.

"Shh," Elijah hissed softly, raising a hand for silence. He waded knee deep and stopped, staring upriver to watch the last of the mating dance. The female schooled in the shoals beside the male, her vigor waning perceptibly, her tail stroking the pull of the river in shorter, weaker bursts. Little by little, she began to slip in the current, the distance between her and her mate and the precious deposit she had laid down lengthening. The male fanned his tail, laying down a ragged jet of milky substance, tossing gravel and the eggs and the one million tiny swimmers he'd released all together, surrendering their destiny to the stream. As the female slipped farther away with the current, Elijah waded deeper, correcting his position to the trajectory of her descent.

The boy watched spellbound as the rhythm of one cycle, of one dance, was replaced with that of another. Elijah entered the sacred descent at the end of the line of the mother's journey. As the distance between them narrowed, Elijah made small adjustments, his arms rising in front of him, preparing a cradle with his hands. The female let go a little more, letting her tail slip within reach of Elijah's fingers. His touch spooked her, causing a brief thrashing, but only for a moment. Gentle as a midwife, he let the female slip back yet another few precious inches before tenderly enclosing her in his dark hands. She shuddered once at his touch, surging forward briefly, then surrendered, accepting the inevitable. She glided backward again, into his embrace. His hands closed over her and held her, buoying her against the push of the river. She fanned her tail once, twice, then ceased to kick and flutter any further.

Elijah bent low over the fish and whispered to her, letting her feel the current rush around her for one last lingering moment. Then assuredly, with deliberate speed, he waded ashore. He emerged carrying the big fish in his hands. The boy watched as Elijah knelt and laid the fish gently on dry river stones. He paused a moment, bent and whispered gently to the fish again, then reached and clasped a large, fist-sized stone in one hand and extinguished her life with one sudden blow. A splash of blood sprayed his face.

Without lingering, Elijah rose and stepped back to the river, wading into the depths to prepare to accept the retreat of the male. Slowly, he, too, surrendered to the pull of the river, slipping finally into Elijah's waiting embrace.

—+—+—+—

Dinner was a final gift of life, made not so much as a sacrifice as simply an exchange of energy, one form being consumed by another. Elijah slow-roasted the two fish stuffed with leaves of wild mountain laurel and pine nuts, sweetened with a glaze made from the syrup of canned peaches. To the basic fare of fish and fruit, he managed to add a serving of canned artichoke hearts for each of them from a special cache he delighted in finding. The pup shared royally in the meal, begging for more all the while but having to settle finally for only his portion. Dinner was complete with a pot of strong coffee. The two sat up late, watching the near-full moon climb into the vaulted dome of night sky framed by the summit of the canyon.

"What were salmon in the beginning?" Jackie asked, studying Elijah as he rose to throw another couple of sticks on the fire.

"What do you mean, in the beginning?" Elijah said, stoking the fire.

"You said they weren't always oceangoing. What'd they do before that?"

"Adapted."

"God, Elijah," Jackie said, part amused, more annoyed. "Can't you ever give a straight answer to a simple question?"

"They were freshwater, so I'm told," Elijah said, settling back again on his blankets before the fire. "Met a man on a freight one time. Coming up out of Portland, up the Columbia. Said he knew everything there was to know about salmon. Said he'd studied them. Had some kind of college degree. Said salmon used to be strictly freshwater. Didn't know the ocean. Lived so far inland, they couldn't have found it with a compass. Then the glaciers came, filled the valleys where the rivers ran, pushed the fish downstream, all the way to the sea."

Elijah reached out and stirred the fire, settling the wood to burn more slowly. "Don't suppose they liked it much, the salt and sharks and all," he said. "Not at first. But they adapted. And they *remembered*. That was the thing. They *remembered*. And all those years later, when the ice melted and the river valleys were free again, I guess it must have been their children's children's children, or some such, that returned up the river to where Grandfather and Grandmother had come from. And it was *there* they spawned. Exactly as before."

"*Come on,*" Jackie protested.

"Seriously," Elijah said. "Cross my heart. That's what the man said. And

I believe him. To this day, now, when the fish hatch in freshwater, they get naturally restless. Gotta move. And they do just like their ancestors that got run off by the big ice. They hightailed it out of the mountains, downstream to the ocean. Same as before. Then back again to lay eggs and die."

Elijah pulled out the fixings for a smoke. "What we ate for dinner tonight was just another turn in the story. These fish, I'm telling ya. They're smart. And they got a memory like an elephant. They remember."

Jackie didn't know whether to believe Elijah or not. He stared into the fire, then up at the moon, a silver saucer adrift in an inky sky. "Full moon tonight," Jackie said thoughtfully. "Know any stories about the moon?" he asked facetiously.

"Oh yeah," Elijah said. "This is the moon they call the Hunter Moon. The full moon of October. But this one is not quite full, I suspect. Tomorrow, what I think." He stared up at the glowing orb. He remembered his encounter with Ol' Icy Eye beneath the summit of Red Crow Mountain. *Odd how things work out,* he thought. *Here I am, sitting a thousand miles away the way the crow flies, but leagues farther, given the circumstances of all that's happened in the journey.* Elijah smiled ruefully. *Kind of like the story of salmon. Like the Mukaluk, The People, too. Those that adapt, survive. Those that don't, die out. That's the thing.* He stared at the moon.

"What's the Hunter Moon?" Jackie asked, staring up at the glimmering sphere.

"The Hunter Moon's when the fate of The People was set," Elijah said, remembering a fragment, a thin thread of an old story his uncle had told him. "They called it the Hunter Moon, because this was the last moon before the Moon of the Long Snows, when winter ended the time of gathering. Winters were always hard. On the old and the young especially. This was the moon that blessed or cursed them. Their fate was told in the passing of this moon."

"Is that just a story?" Jackie asked, staring at Elijah as if seeing him in a light he'd never considered before, a light flickering out of the long, dark past. "You think this is, you know, *really* the Hunter Moon?"

"I've lived long enough to know that there is truth to much of what the Old People used to tell. Truth and wisdom. Now the old way is mostly a memory, almost forgotten."

"It's kinda sad," Jackie said. "How everything had to change. How the Indians weren't allowed to continue living the way they wanted."

"Sad?" Elijah said meditatively, staring at the fire. "Yes. But it isn't just from the outside that things changed. It changed on the inside, too." He sat watching the shimmering of the embers. "That's the saddest thing, I think. It's not just the world that limits and restricts us. But our own dark selves, what's inside us that we fear knowing, that we do not want to face and call by name. If I've learned one thing, it is this: you must come to know the darkness in your own heart. This you must do to be a man. There is no other way."

Jackie stroked the pup, watching the dance of flames. "What do you mean, Elijah? You have to know your own heart?"

"The worst lie," Elijah said gravely, "is the lie you tell yourself. That is the root of it. It is the seed of all darkness," he heard himself say, aware of the sound of the words, as if listening to someone else speak. "It is why the moon dims, to remind us. And why it grows bright again. So that we can remember. *Remember.* To know that the truth is ours to know. It is in the light all around us. And in the power of darkness, too. We think that they are separate. But they are not. They are one. They only look like two. *One the shadow. One the light. But not two. . . just one.*"

Elijah sat peering into the fire without seeing the flame. He felt hollow, light-headed, as if the air were too rich with oxygen. It had been his voice, but he did not know the source that stirred it. It was as if he'd slipped through a doorway into a chambered vault in the earth where the air itself whispered it. *One the shadow; one the light. But not two, just one.*

"You must find power to save yourself.
Find men to go and ask the mountains for help.
Those who go must ask to be wise or brave . . .
They must swim and dream."

—From Modoc creation myth

Remember the Children

Passing trains throughout the night filled the canyon with sound. First, there was a faint drumming of locomotives under stress, growing loudly quickly. Then they flooded the whole canyon with their deep drone. After the locomotives, the wail of wheels pinching steel rails rose as long strings of boxcars snaked through flowing curves. Gradually—then all of a sudden—the canyon swallowed the sound almost whole. Again the fluted notes of the river rose, an enduring counterpoint. From a great distance, the haunting call of a great horned owl pierced the darkness.

Elijah awoke, pulled by the insistence of needing to pee. He got up without debate. He moved to the edge of the ledge waiting patiently to finish. He wondered whether it might rain before morning. He padded back to his blankets and lay down again, thinking it was not likely.

Elijah sank to the depth of deepest sleep, then rose into the chamber of dreams. Dream images came fully formed. In his dream he felt himself gasp: *Emma.* His Emma. She approached where he stood at the edge of a throng of dark strangers. She came and stood before him. He ached to reach out and hold her. He waited, but for what, he didn't know.

I knew you were different, Emma-of-the-dream whispered. *Do you remember our meeting?*

I do, he answered. *Like it was yesterday.*

You tease, she laughed lightly. *It was a long, long time ago.*

Have you come to stay?

I cannot, she said. *But know that I chose you, knowing what lay ahead. I knew. I knew.*

What? Tell me what you knew, Elijah-of-the-dream asked, confused. Without answering, she began to drift away.

What did you know? he pleaded. *Tell me. Stay!*

Emma-of-the-dream walked to the edge of a stone staircase that wound downward into a yawning pit. Elijah-of-the-dream knew he could not follow. He watched as she passed vaulted windows down along the passage of the staircase. He grew fearful, watching her descend.

Remember the children, she called back to him. *Remember the children . . .* Her words lashed him. Elijah-of-the-dream knew not whether it was an admonishment for his past failure as a father or an invocation for the future.

He watched as she passed before a window through which he saw the bend of a deep river canyon, saw a dark shadow pass over her. It was that of the great horned owl, the shadow that rules the night. The shadow closed over her, and she was gone.

Elijah bolted upright. He sucked a deep breath as though he'd been drowning. "*Emma,*" he whispered. The dream seemed so real. He was gravely shaken by it—by the appearance of Emma, but also because he knew that for a Modoc to dream of the dead was a bad sign, for after people die, it is best to let go of them to continue on their journey.

Elijah sat there wondering what the dream meant, and then he heard the hollow, haunting call of an owl.

His eyes swept the ridge where a thin crack of light lay along the jagged traverse of the mountain, a hairline crack in the dark egg of night. He turned suddenly, searching to find the outline of the boy. He rose again and went over to Jackie's mound of blankets to be sure he was actually there. He bent and listened to the mixed cadence of Jackie's breathing overlaid on that of the dog's. He straightened again, studied the timbre of the light on the eastern summit. Another hour before true dawn.

Elijah patted his pockets in search of fixings for a smoke, retrieved his papers and tobacco, and fumbled together a slender, sloppy roll in his nervous fingers. He lit it and drew deeply as if for strength. He listened intently to the night. Had he actually heard it, the call of the owl, or had it merely been part of the dream?

At risk, the familiar voice within whispered. *At risk . . . Pay attention.*

There was a freight due soon after sunrise. Should they be on it? He paced, drawing ragged puffs on his cigarette. He stooped and busied himself with laying a fire. After he got it going, he wrapped himself in his blanket and sat down before it. He watched the flames dance, hoping their light would help him see what was to be done.

Calm yourself, the voice bade him. *It is important.* He drew a breath and settled himself. *What you intend is what happens. Put not yourself first. In the turning, all things are possible. But you must choose. One the shadow, one the light. But not two, just one.*

Elijah considered this. How could one be the shadow, one the light, and yet there be *not two, but one?* He heard again, *in the turning . . .*

They were, in truth, he realized, indeed one within you, but you had to choose *in the turning . . . what you intend.*

Elijah found his boots and slipped into them. He went over to the boy again and stood looking at him for a long while, contemplating what to do. He bent finally and shook him firmly. The boy barely stirred. Elijah shook him hard.

"What is it?" Jackie said, coming awake, sitting up, alarmed.

"I'm going up to Keddie Junction. I have to make a call."

"Now? Who are you calling? What for?"

"Don't go anywhere. I won't be gone long."

"Where are you going?" Jackie asked as Elijah turned away. "Elijah . . ."

"Keddie Junction. It's a little bit of a place a mile or so downriver. There's a phone there. I have to make a call. I'll come right back."

"Who? It's the middle of the night," Jackie exclaimed.

"It'll be light soon. Don't go anywhere."

.At the end of the ledge, Elijah started to climb up the steep slope toward the BN track above.

"Keddie what?" Jackie said, grasping at anything that might explain Elijah's sudden impatience.

"Keddie Junction. I'll be back in less than an hour."

Elijah disturbed the sleep of two irritated strangers before he correctly dialed the number for his daughter's house in Sacramento. He didn't want to wake her, but couldn't risk missing her. Waiting for her to wake up on her own held no better promise of a welcome reception than waking her himself. He stood at the pay phone that hung on a wall of the long porch at the Keddie Resort Lodge, nervously tapping his fingers on the side of the coin box. On the eighth ring, he heard a familiar voice. Marna sounded so much like her mother, it unnerved him, remembering the dream.

"Marna?"

"Who's this?"

Elijah didn't know how to start. She was the only person he could think to call.

"Who is this," she asked insistently, annoyed.

"Elijah," he said hesitantly. "Your father."

There was a long, stony silence on the other end of the line.

"I need your help."

"You have the wrong number. Please don't call again."

Elijah heard the sharp click as the line went dead.

"*Shit,*" he hissed, slamming the phone down. "Son of a dirty dog," he moaned, pulling at his whiskers, trying to think. He fingered the last few coins in his pocket. He dialed her number again. Nine, ten, eleven rings. No answer. He jammed the handset onto its hook and pounded a fist against the wall. He paced the lodge's porch, the light of dawn growing brighter along the eastern ridgeline. He sat down on the steps and watched the light of day rise. He rolled and smoked two cigarettes in quick succession, without even being aware of it. He went back to the phone and dialed again. All he got was the steady pulsing of a busy signal.

"Stubborn son of a dog," he muttered, setting the receiver back in its cradle, gently this time. "Like her mother." He turned and walked over to sit on the broad wooden steps at the entrance to the lodge again. *Let her cool down, get over the surprise. Explain why you're calling. That it's not for you.*

—|—|—|—

Jackie awoke to the pup licking his face. The pup had risen to relieve himself, then gone looking for food. Finding only the scorched tins from the evening's meal, he'd come back to Jackie to roust a little company.

Jackie tried to cover his face with the curl of his arm, but the dog was persistent. He batted the dog away, but he sprang back. Jackie finally sat up. "What the hell?" He turned to look for Elijah. All he saw was empty blankets. Then he remembered: Elijah had gone somewhere downriver to make a phone call. *A frigging phone call?* He scanned the slope leading up to the curve of the railroad track high above camp. Nothing but trees and the lightening sky.

Jackie called out Elijah's name two, three times. He threw back the covers and rose. He yelled out Elijah's name as loud as he could, raising an echo. Nothing.

"Where the hell are you?" he cursed, dropping to his blankets to put his shoes on. A quiver seized him as he tied his laces, the memory of Elijah's disappearance in Bend returning. Jackie looked around nervously, spooked by the thought he was in the middle of nowhere—and with no idea where that was.

"Come on, boy," he called, starting out across the slope, working his way upward toward the track, following the route Elijah had taken. The pup scampered eagerly in his footsteps.

They found their way up to the railroad track and began to follow it downriver through a series of snaking turns that hugged the mountainside. "He said downriver," Jackie muttered, trying to reassure himself that he was going in the right direction. The dawn grew brighter.

A towering iron trestle came into view as they rounded a sweeping turn, the bridge gleaming in the early morning light. The fork of another river coming through the mountains from the opposite direction ran beneath it a hundred feet below, joining the river Jackie had been following where it turned sharply to run more westerly through the canyon. Another set of tracks that traced the other fork junctioned at the trestle with the track Jackie was on, the two flowing into one to cross high above the rushing water. On the far side of the towering bridge, the track disappeared into the face of the mountain, entering a dark tunnel.

Jackie was so taken by the sight of the gleaming trestle that he was unaware of the broadening of the shelf where the track ran, permitting a short spur line for holding shunted rail cars. He hoped he didn't have to cross the trestle and go through the tunnel to find Elijah. All of a moment, he felt terribly alone.

"Come on, boy," Jackie called anxiously, impatiently, turning to encourage the lagging pup. The pup stood resolutely, unmoving, staring at a lone figure standing in the shadows of the shunted boxcars on the spur line twenty yards away. The fur on the dog's neck was raised. Jackie stepped back impulsively, startled in seeing the stranger. The man bore the unmistakable stamp of a tramp. His clothes were worn and grimy. His face was deeply weathered. He wore a brown fedora that seemed to sit atop his head for being too small.

Jackie's startled movement, taking a half step back, set the pup off. The dog bounced up and down as it began barking at the stranger.

"*Shh,*" Jackie scolded. "Come here, boy," he called insistently, caught between the impulse of fright and embarrassment. "Come on, come here," he called forcefully, finally getting the dog's attention. The pup scampered toward him, yapping back over its shoulder.

The stranger merely stared, unnerving Jackie. Jackie studied him intently, clapping for the dog to be quiet. The stranger's gaze was fixed, Jackie could see in the coming dawn light, but one of his eyes was alive, the other unresponsive.

"Sorry," Jackie said, kneeling, pulling the pup up against him, trying to quiet him. "I think you just surprised him."

The man smiled a wan smile. "Sorry to scare you," he said as he stepped hesitantly forward. The pup continued to yap and growl, broke away, halved the distance again between the boy and the stranger.

"Quiet," Jackie commanded sharply.

Out of the distance rose the low, slow drumming of a train making an approach to the junction. Both the man and the boy looked back the way Jackie had come. A dark lead locomotive rounded the bend, coming into sight. The two stood and watched it as it lengthened car by car around the bend, filling the long curve. The man stepped forward and crossed the track to be on the same side of the oncoming train as Jackie. He turned to the boy, fully in his line of sight now. He grinned. Jackie smiled weakly in return. The man began to saunter slowly down along the track toward him. The pup started howling.

"Stop it," Jackie called, fully embarrassed now. "Come. Come now!" The pup ignored him, continuing to bark. The man came forward as if he intended by his slow advance to calm the dog.

"Sorry," Jackie said, moving toward the pup.

The stranger said nothing, closing the distance to the dog. The train came on. The man knelt and held his hand out, only a foot separating him from the pup. He leaned forward. The pup snapped out and closed his needled teeth on the man's fingers.

The man sprang backward, jerking his hand away. The suddenness of his move caused his hat to topple from his head. "You s-s-son-of-a-b-b-bitch," the man growled.

Jackie stiffened, hearing the faltering speech. He watched the man step forward, kicking violently at the dog. The terror of the night in the Vancouver yard filled Jackie once again.

The engineer blew a long warning note on the train's horn. The sound enveloped them as the pulsing locomotives rolled past. The earth shook underfoot. Jackie acted more on impulse than thought. He turned and sprinted, trying to match the pace of the train as it drew down to make its crossing at the trestle.

Taking a quick glance back over his shoulder, Jackie looked for something to grab hold of. He saw the stranger striding fully after him, his loping gait filled Jackie with terror, spurring him on.

The distance to the edge of the chasm and the start of the trestle closed rapidly. Jackie threw a glance to his side, saw a ladder on the end of a car come into view. He committed without thinking. His hand rose and his fingers curled around the iron ladder that ran up its side. The speed of the train sucked him off balance. Falling forward, stumble-stepping, he pulled with all his might, slipping dangerously toward the vortex where the rolling wheels spun. He brought his other arm around to catch hold of the ladder rung. The trestle loomed directly ahead. He pulled hard, raising his body, lifting his feet off the ground, seeking to snatch a higher handhold. He pulled again, his feet finding the ladder as the car rolled out over thin air. He glanced back. He saw the stranger hesitate, then commit also. The man's hand found its grip, but he stumbled hard. His feet bounced over the rocky ground. His legs swept inward, toward the track. Jackie held his breath, hoping, hoping. The man's form took a hard bounce that lifted him, allowing him to gain his footing. He took two running steps and pulled himself up and swung onto the platform at the end of a tank car, disappearing from view.

—+—+—+—

Elijah kicked along the track, heading back toward camp, having given up on out-waiting his daughter. As he rounded a curve above the trestle on the track coming down the other river fork, he could see the leading end of the early morning freight as it shuttled out onto the Keddie Junction trestle. It was ahead of schedule. The big locomotives spewed smoke into the lightening sky, then disappeared into the dark mouth of the hard-rock tunnel on the other side. It was certain now that he and Jackie wouldn't be catching out on the first freight of the day. He quickened his step.

He stopped abruptly, brought up short by the faintest of sounds that rose over the clatter of the train. "*Elijah.*" Someone calling his name.

The caboose rolled out on the trestle, then disappeared into the tunnel. In an instant, the scene grew serenely still again, the mouth of the tunnel swallowing the train whole.

The boy, he thought with a shudder.

Elijah ran toward the trestle. He stared after the passage of the train. That was when he heard the barking of the dog. He stared up the track the way the train had come, in the direction of camp. The pup stood bouncing back and forth, barking wildly at a small dark object on the ground. Elijah called for the pup as he moved quickly toward it. He called the pup again, catching its attention. The dog stopped and stared, then turned back to the dark object and began barking again. Elijah could see now that it was a hat. A hat very much like his own. He felt his head to be sure his was in place.

He stopped abruptly. He turned and stared at the Keddie trestle, peering fiercely into the dark tunnel on the far side.

His gaze fell to the bottom of the canyon. An image from the dream appeared. It was the bend in the river that had appeared through the last window in the staircase that Emma had descended. Before the shadow of the owl darkened the dream.

The boy was in trouble. No question. He heard again the haunting echo of Emma's voice, the last thing he heard her say . . . *Remember the children.*

In the Turning

It was well after sundown when the BN freight coming down from K-Falls to Oakland rolled through the last of the forty-three hard-rock tunnels on the Feather River route and rounded the curve to approach Oroville. The train rolled through the dry grasslands that fell away to the unbroken flatness of the upper Sacramento Valley, gathering speed now that it was free of the tortuous twists and turns of the canyon. Elijah cradled the pup in the flap of his coat against the raw bite of the wind. He'd had a time of it, catching out from Keddie Junction, one hand ready to swat the pup back down into the pocket of his coat while trying to concentrate on seizing hold of the ladder on the freight car. He grabbed the first thing that looked promising. He and the pup had made the trip pinched into the tight space over the wheels at the end of a grain hopper. It could have been worse; it could have been raining. It could have been snowing, or blistering hot, or riding above a wheel with a flat spot that pounded like a jackhammer at every rotation. There was plenty to be grateful for, though what Elijah felt most was far from gratitude. He was worried about the boy.

The train crossed the Feather River for the last time below the Oroville Dam, entered fully under the nightglow the city lights threw up against the cloudy night sky. After a bit, Elijah felt the pressure fall in the brake lines, the train easing its way down the long straight run of track into the Oroville yard.

It was an equipment and repair yard, mostly; two tower lights gave dim dimension to the lay of tracks. Elijah stroked the pup, then deposited him in one of his coat pockets and moved out to stand on the back platform, gripping the ladder with one hand, securing the pup with the other. He slowly worked his way around to the outside of the ladder, then down to the bottom rung. He took a breath and then dropped free of the train.

He moved quickly off the shoulder of the mainline into the weeds. He turned and paused, watching the dark train glide past, the great length of it slipping deeper into the center of the yard. He sniffed the air and raised his eyes skyward. The overcast was more mottled here, broken into huge, drifting clouds, bumping and jostling one another like sheets of ice in flow. The cast of the moon gave a white wash of light to the cloud cover near the eastern hills. Now and again, its radiance broke through shifting seams, and then was swallowed again. Normally, this was exactly the kind of night Elijah liked for moving in and out of rail yards, timing movement to the shuttering of moonlight. But tonight a little light would be useful. No telling where the boy might be—if the boy was even truly here. Elijah was betting the boy would go with what he knew, and be drawn by the lights of a city. It was only a hunch, but it was all he had to go on. He worried he might already be too late.

A small speck of light shimmering in a dark field caught his eye. Elijah knew that there was always an old tramp or two in semi-permanent residence on the periphery of the yard, typically encamped near an industrial operation with easy access to water. But this light was in the middle distance, well within railway property. This tramp was bold, Elijah mused, heading toward the light. A fire during the day was one thing, but one at night, out in plain sight, you were just asking to get hassled. Elijah used the wavering light of the moon to carefully pick his way across the field toward the glowing campfire. The site was adjacent to a sparse scattering of trees. As he drew nearer, he could make out the silhouette of a man sitting hunched over the fire. The pup stirred, catching sight of the outline beside the fire. A low growl rose in the dog's throat. Elijah slipped his hand into his coat pocket and stroked the pup. "Easy now," he whispered soothingly. "Easy."

Elijah slowed as he drew closer. He guessed the man to be roughly his own age, maybe younger; it was hard to tell with so little light. He could hear him humming softly to himself.

Elijah moved closer still. Looked to be younger, for sure, he thought, watching the man languidly stir the fire. Impatience drove him forward. Time was wasting. The boy could be in trouble.

"Ho now," Elijah called out, sauntering slowly in from the dark, into the circle of the light from the fire.

"*My G-Gawd,*" the man exclaimed nervously, turning to appraise the sound of the voice. "Scared the p-piss out of me, sneaking up like that." The pup snarled and snapped a yappy bark.

"Hush now," Elijah said, moving into the clearing around the fire ring. The pup barked again. "*Shush,*" he commanded harshly. "Sorry to scare you," he said to the man. "Saw your fire."

"Cool night for riding," the man said slowly, carefully enunciating each word.

"Where you headed?" Elijah asked, studying the man, keeping one hand in motion stroking the top of the pup's head, hoping to keep the dog calm. The man looked pretty much like any of a thousand other nameless men Elijah had encountered over the years—except there was something funny with one of his eyes. It was unfocused, a pale orb in the road-worn face. It made him think of Ol' Icy Eye. *One in a hundred,* Elijah thought humorously, remembering the old bear's charge.

"Don't matter to me," the man said, throwing another stick on the fire. "You?"

"South," Elijah replied. The draw of the fire did feel good after the chilly ride. He stepped a half step closer to let the heat warm the scruff of his boots, the folds of his pant legs.

"You ain't seen a boy? Twelve, thirteen years old?" Elijah asked. He tried to make it sound casual.

"A boy?" the man repeated. He considered it, staring at Elijah with intensity. "Nope." He lowered his gaze briefly to appraise the fire, then looked up at Elijah again. "Some kin of yours?"

Elijah weighed the question, how to answer. Maybe the stranger knew something about the boy.

"A friend. I've been looking for him, is all."

The man shifted his eyes—or rather, his one eye—out across the darkness beyond the fire. A small noise in the dark, out near a small stand of trees, drew the attention of both men, setting the dog off in a scolding yowl.

"Quiet. Quiet, now," Elijah said insistently, straining to simultaneously silence the dog and peer through the blackness to see what had caused the noise. He felt as if he were standing on a precipice. Something wasn't right.

"Jackie," Elijah called instinctively. He waited, straining to see, straining to hear. He started to form the boy's name again to call more loudly.

"*It's him!*" a voice cried out. "Elijah, it's him. *It's him!*"

Time slowed. Almost to a stop. Elijah was aware of turning, or starting to turn. He had the sense of his body, of muscles tensing, working to come around to face the stranger. Elijah felt as though he'd been turning toward this moment since waking from a troubled sleep the night before—even longer, since his encounter with the old bear back in Glacier.

Pain detonated at the axis of his turn, exploding through his left knee. It was searing, like a stabbing white-hot iron. He cried out and crumpled over the pain. He collapsed in a pile beside the fire, the pup tumbling free, scampering away.

Elijah writhed, the impulse for survival stalled in the overload of agony that filled him. He saw movement, rolled away. A lethal percussion vibrated in the earth, the club of firewood wielded by the stranger. The length of wood snapped on impact. Elijah sensed more than saw the man's foot rising with murderous intent. He rolled again, taking only a glancing blow along his forearm. He flopped onto his back and raised his good leg. He fired the sole of his boot into the man's belly, doubling him over, propelling him backward over the short log he'd been sitting on. The stranger went down in a flurry of waving arms and stuttered oaths.

"*It's him,*" Elijah heard Jackie cry again from a distance.

Elijah struggled to roll up to where he could gather himself to rise. He made it to a half crouch and stalled, the pain too great to lift himself further.

"*Run,* boy. Run. *Now!*" he barked, turning to sweep the darkness for sight of Jackie.

The stranger drove into him just as Elijah spun back to face him. The two went over, bouncing in the dirt, Elijah underneath, breaking the other man's fall. What Elijah paid in being the underdog, he taxed by bringing his good knee up hard, smashing the crevice between the man's legs. The man expelled a foul explosion of breath, curling and rolling off of Elijah in one motion.

Elijah fought to muster enough strength to roll and try to rise again. Again he managed only to get to a half crouch, stumbling, going down, catching himself on his hands. He raised his head, sure to see the man coming to finish what he'd started. Instead, he saw him limping away in a crazy-legged run, following after the boy, the boy a faint form running hard toward the heart of the rail yard.

"Run, boy!" Elijah cried. "*Run!*"

Elijah dropped fully to the ground again. He was breathing hard, but could hear the pup yapping in pursuit.

"*Shit,*" Elijah squeezed out through clenched teeth. He forced himself to standing, the pain in his leg pulsing in spasms through his body.

"Jackie," Elijah whimpered. "*Jackie!*" he cried, filling the night with his lament. He hobbled forward, half dragging his injured leg. It was painful to move, painful to stand, painful to breathe. He swung his bad leg under him and stepped forward, groaning with each step, pushing forward, stride by stride. *What you intend will happen,* he heard the voice within whisper. *In the turning, all things are possible.* Elijah gritted his teeth as he hobbled forward. *But you must choose. You must choose. One the shadow, one the light.*

"Damn it all!" Elijah seethed through clenched teeth. It might be *not two, just one,* but he knew, indeed, he had to choose.

He moved through a thin line of digger pines to where he could see the rail yard in its entirety. A solid line of idle railcars on the first track sealed the interior of the yard from view. There was no sign of the boy, the dog, or the stranger.

"Jackie," Elijah called, continuing his advance toward the first line of cars. "Jackie!" he called fiercely. "*Jackie!*"

Elijah caught sound of the low rumbling of a freight engine idling up, then down, moving lengths of cars onto different tracks, building a new string out of something old. The rumble of iron banging iron thundered as couplers locked together.

"*Jackie!*" Elijah bellowed again.

From somewhere down to the south toward the heart of the yard, Elijah heard the unmistakable barking of the dog. He moved in that direction, coming down to the end of the first idle string of cars, crossing over the track to move down the length of the next string of cars.

The pain was unrelenting. He walked favoring the right side, his boot planted for stability, then stepped through the intensifying of the pain. He wove his way through broken lengths of boxcars and tankers and gondolas. He cursed himself for being careless, for not being more wary in encountering the stranger. For not paying attention.

The sound of iron against iron exploded again as boxcars coupled. He reminded himself to be alert to the movement of silent, rolling cars, always a danger when walking a yard, especially at night. He cut through a narrow gap between uncoupled cars, moving quickly, forcing the pain from his mind. He made his way through two other openings, these gaps much larger than the first.

The yelping of the pup pierced the night, more a sound of fright than pain.

"Leave him alone!" It was Jackie's voice, urgent and frightened. It sounded like it was just the next track over. There was a scuffle, a kicking of feet in the gravel.

"Lemme go," Jackie wailed. Elijah shuffled forward to the end of a tanker and slipped through a narrow slot between open couplers.

Jackie stood kicking and struggling in the grasp of the stranger. The stranger had one arm wrapped around the boy's chest, drawing him tight against the length of his own body. He fumbled for the handle of a knife, caught up in the tangle of his coat.

"Let him go!" Elijah commanded.

The agitation of the fight ceased. Jackie continued to wiggle, but not as fiercely. Both Jackie and the stranger turned their attention fully on Elijah. The boy's pause gave Luther Gon the opportunity he needed to slip his knife free. He whipped his arm around, spinning the boy in front of him like a shield, the long silver blade glistening.

"Let him go," Elijah said again, more evenly, though still commanding.

Luther Gon smiled triumphantly, twisting the angle of the knife, the glare of the yard lights flashing off the blade. He flicked the knife playfully, pretending to draw it across Jackie's throat. Jackie winced audibly as the back of the blade touched the smooth flesh of his neck.

Elijah hobbled a step closer, not directly, menacingly, but diagonally. Luther Gon grinned appreciably, seeing the difficulty with which Elijah moved.

"Let him go," Elijah said for the third time. "It's not him you want. It's me." Elijah spoke slowly, words not quite his own finding utterance through his lips. He saw the power of the words register in Gon's eyes. Elijah knew not to question the truth or the source of the words coming through him. Like with the light of dreaming, he was but the lantern glass that amplified the burning flame. "You know it's me. It's been me from the beginning. Not the boy." Elijah studied the strange contortion that puzzled Gon's face into a mask of uncertainty. His brow tightened, his smile faded. He stood as if reckoning with the truth of what Elijah was saying.

An absolute calm settled over Elijah, as though in the eye of the storm, the wind had gone slack.

"It's me you want," he said, stepping diagonally again, forcing the stranger to step back a half step, over a rail. Elijah was aware of the low throttling of a switch engine. He kept his gaze steady on Gon. He realized, even in the dimness of the light, that one eye was lifeless, as sightless as a stone. He knew he had to entice the man to let Jackie go. It was the only hope for the boy. One-on-one, Elijah doubted he could take the stranger. Not now. But it didn't matter. What mattered was getting him to let go of Jackie.

Elijah took another half step, wincing from pain. He watched as the man turned slightly, keeping the boy between the two of them, stepping back more fully into the center of the track. Elijah realized that even with a knife in hand and the boy to cover him, the stranger was afraid of him. Had they met somewhere before? Was that it? He didn't think so. But he knew the man's fear was deep, primal—of long standing.

"Let the boy go. He's done nothing to you," Elijah said calmly.

"Like you," Luther hissed, his words spewing the venom of a lifetime of hatred. "The way you t-t-teased me. T-t-taunted me."

"Yes," Elijah answered, playing the only hand he was dealt.

"I s-s-s-swore. One d-day I'd s-s-see how you l-l-liked it."

Elijah stood steady, staring intently into the single orb of light, into the stranger's soul. He had to get him to let the boy go.

"Here I am," Elijah said, starting to raise his hands, to lift them over his head in an act of complete surrender. He started to turn one way, then hesitated, troubled by some inarticulate tic of the mind. *In the turning, all things are possible.* He remembered now where he'd heard that line for the very first time: in the Lava Beds, during his seeking of a vision, what seemed like a lifetime ago. Elijah saw again the sweep of dark shadow from the dream only the night before, how it had engulfed Emma. *Remember the children,* he heard her call again. He tried to remember which way she'd turned. It was important.

His hands high overhead, Elijah closed his eyes and let his body move as it must. He continued turning in the direction he had started. He spun slowly in a half circle. He took a deep breath. He opened his eyes.

The full moon behind him had slipped free of the clouds. His gaze fell to the ground to stare at his own shadow with his arms raised as if in celebration. He stood transfixed by the sight, struck by how it mirrored the pictograph on the wall of the cave in the canyon of the Feather River. One Standing. *Standing one's ground.*

The sound of steel on steel exploded like a bomb, nullifying the night. Elijah spun back around, hoping he would get one last glimpse of Emma-of-the-dream before the light in his life expired.

He saw Jackie rush frantically forward, nearly knocking him over. The boy embraced him fiercely, shuddering with fear. Elijah's arms fell to encircle the boy, to draw him tight against him. He stroked the boy's back. He lifted his eyes to search for the stranger. He drew a breath in horror and amazement.

The stranger stood stapled in the iron lock of two couplers, caught between boxcars where he'd carelessly stood his ground, standing between steel rails. A single boxcar had rolled down the track, approaching on his blind side, sinking steel talons through the center of his chest. He hung lifeless, his knees buckled, his head slumped, but unable to fall.

Elijah sagged against the boy, the force of his will fading. He crumpled. The pull of gravity draining the last of his power to stand.

"*Ohmygod,*" Jackie cried, clutching Elijah as he slipped to the ground. "Are you all right? Are you okay?"

Jackie knelt, holding Elijah in his arms.

"I'm okay," Elijah said weakly. "I'm still alive."

"I was *so* scared," Jackie gushed, the rush of release from terror overwhelming.

Elijah raised an arm and drew the boy to him. "So was I, boy. So was I."

"It was like a dream. Like a nightmare."

"I know. I know. But it's over now."

"You're not gonna die, are you?" Jackie pleaded.

"No. Not yet. But you better see if you can find somebody to help me. I don't think I can walk."

Jackie pulled back, stared into Elijah's eyes. "He really whacked you hard."

"Yeah, he did," Elijah said. "But he got whacked pretty good himself." They both turned to look at Luther Gon hanging lifeless between the couplers.

"Go on," Elijah said. "Find somebody to help me. Be quick. I don't want to be near this terror longer than I have to."

The Understream Road

Elijah passed the first night on a concrete bunk in the new Butte County Jail on the north side of Oroville, struggling to let sleep carry him away. He hadn't been given as much as an aspirin for pain. He lay on his right side, cushioning his bruised and swollen left knee with his other leg. He lay motionless, seeking only stillness and the forgetting that comes with dreamless sleep.

Jackie had protested valiantly when the sheriff's deputies manhandled Elijah into handcuffs and started to stuff him into the back of a patrol car. Blind with fury, he had pummeled one deputy and managed to knock the other into the dirt. The boy was subdued with a chokehold, which inflamed Elijah. He sought to wiggle out of the backseat, but was likewise subdued when one of the deputies grabbed his damaged leg to jam him back into the car. Elijah's fight dissolved instantly.

Elijah lay listening to the muted voices coming from the guard office down the hall. The memory of his stay in the Oregon State Prison came back to him like a bad dream. The approach of day was punctuated with the jangling of keys, the slamming of doors, the rowdy exchanges of the guards rousting inmates. A jailer brought a tray of food at seven, inquired how he was feeling, but didn't press for an answer when Elijah ignored him. At nine, he was visited by an aged, white-haired doctor with a thick cough who prescribed Empirin for the pain.

Bud Keaton appeared with boisterous clamor in midafternoon, escorted by a big, burly sergeant. The sergeant fumbled with his keys to unlock Elijah's cell door.

"Our paths cross again," Keaton declared. Elijah stared at him, blinked twice, and pushed himself into a sitting position. Though he tried to conceal any semblance of emotional response, his grimace from the pain did not escape Keaton's eye.

"Heard you got banged up. You okay?" Keaton asked.

Elijah nodded.

"Seems you're in a shit pickle here," Keaton said. "Don't know how this is going to play out, McCloud. But if there's anything you want to tell us, now would be a good time."

Elijah held Keaton's gaze without wavering, to the point of discomfort, forcing Keaton to shift his eyes away, arching his eyebrows to the sergeant as if passing some silent communication.

"The boy," Elijah said.

Keaton turned back to Elijah.

"Where's the boy?"

Keaton stared, then canted his head enough to eye the sergeant again. The sergeant nodded mutely.

"He's safe. His mother picked him up," Keaton said.

Elijah sighed, letting his gaze fall, his head drop. He felt very old, tired beyond exhaustion, admittedly way past his prime riding trains.

"The boy gave a statement, of course. Seems he was the only living witness—other than yourself," Keaton said.

Elijah remained silent.

"I'll be working with the county authorities to bring the investigation to a close." Keaton paused. "I want to thank you, Elijah. I'll see what I can do to get you out of here as quickly as possible."

Elijah eyed Keaton fully, then nodded. Keaton stood a moment, then turned to the jailer, and they both exited the cell.

Elijah slowly eased himself back down. He had no idea himself how it was all going to play out. In the meantime, he was left to deal with the pressing weight of time in a small, locked room. He endured the long monotony of hours lying on his side on his bunk, trying not to think. He ate very little, rose only to relieve himself, then returned to his berth.

Late into the night, long into the longest stretch of slack time that had to be endured, Elijah grew so weary that he drifted into a light doze. He was neither awake nor asleep, but strangely aware of being tethered to both worlds simultaneously. He became entranced by his slow and steady breathing.

The ever-renewing cycle followed its own command. It seemed to tug at him, drawing him downward. He fought the sensation at first, then surrendered to it. He didn't have the strength.

He descended what seemed forever, until he found himself at a juncture. *Which way?* he wondered. He heard a voice reply: *it's yours to choose.*

Elijah considered it. *Does it matter?*

It always matters. The choice is always yours.

Elijah-in-descent made a slight move to the left, saw the path to the right dissolve. *Not two, but one,* he thought, continuing to drift, pulled along by some unseen compulsion. And then he seemed to reach a point beyond which he could not pass.

He seemed to be in a large, cavernous chamber. There was nothing there but shadows. Shadowy forms.

Where am I? he wondered.

This is the Understream Road, the place that holds all your shadows, those that whisper to you.

My shadows? Why mine?

Because you are between them and the light.

Elijah stood staring, disbelieving and believing at the same time. He saw a shadow begin to emerge and take form as it approached him. Was it possible? Emma? She was as beautiful as the first time he saw her.

Emma . . . ? he whispered.

She came forward to stand before him.

He wanted to speak, but did not have a voice. He wanted to tell her he was sorry, how very sorry he was for all the pain he'd brought to her world.

I know, the shadow replied. It knew what he could not say, what he'd needed—wanted—to say all these many years. *I knew then. As I know now.* She stood gazing at him though he could not see her eyes clearly. But he felt them. *Remember the children, Elijah. Remember the children.*

She began to fade back into the darker shadows. He wanted to call to her, to tell her to stay. But he had no voice. Watching her dissolve was like a knife in the heart.

"McCloud." The sound of his name was loud and harsh. The shadow dissolved completely.

"McCloud!"

Wait, Elijah cried.

"McCloud. Wake up!"

And all of a moment, the *Understream Road* dissolved. He was back in his cell in the Butte County Jail.

"Hey, McCloud. Wake up. Someone's here to see you. Get your ass up."

"What?" Elijah muttered, surprised to hear his own voice.

"Someone's here to see you," a deputy said.

"To see me?" Elijah mumbled, pushing himself up onto one elbow. He was definitely back in his cell. "It was a dream," he said to himself.

"Whatever," the deputy said. "Get your shoes on. You're wanted out front."

—+—+—+—

Elijah followed the deputy down the narrow corridor awash with fluorescent light. The deputy pushed open and held a heavy door for him. He moved through it into a large room flooded with early morning sunlight. It gleamed and shimmered on the highly buffed tile floor. It was so bright, he had to bring his hand up to shield his eyes.

"*Elijah*," Jackie screeched, jumping up from his seat on the far side of the lobby. He rushed forward through the pools of sunlight. Elijah struggled to comprehend what was happening. The boy crashed against him, threw his arms around his waist, and squeezed. This was no dream, he was sure of it.

Elijah's arms rose to encircle the boy, his eyes accommodating the light. Jackie pulled away, stepped back to stand, smiling brightly at him.

"Are you all right? Did they treat you okay? How's your leg? Does it still hurt?" Jackie pleaded to know.

"Whoa now!" Elijah said slowly, chuckling in spite of himself, taking hold of the boy to steady himself against his exuberance.

"Are you okay?" Jackie asked, overjoyed to see Elijah despite whatever he might answer.

"I'm okay."

"Look," Jackie said, turning, gesturing with his arm across the room. Two women were standing side by side. It was difficult to make them out clearly through the glare from the floor. They started toward him. Elijah sucked for breath. *Emma?* They came closer. No. Not Emma. *Marna.*

Elijah stared transfixed by his daughter's gaze. Her eyes were gray, like his. They gave nothing away as to what lay behind them.

"This is my mom," Jackie said, grabbing his mother's arm. Elijah turned to her. Clearly, it was. They shared the same dark good looks.

"I told her what you did. That you saved me. That he would've killed me if it hadn't been for you." Elijah looked down at Jackie, then up at his mother, then at Marna. He couldn't believe she was standing before him.

"Look at this," Jackie said, dashing across the room, snatching up something, dashing back. He held a copy of the *Sacramento Bee*, showing him the front page. The headline declared "Youth Riding Rails Nets Killer."

"Can you believe it?" Jackie beamed. "It's all about us. About you and me."

"Whoa, whoa," Elijah said, flustered. "You're moving too fast for me." The two stared at each other, their faces alight with the joy of seeing each other again. Elijah slowly broke the gaze to look back at his daughter.

"Look who came with us. It's your daughter—I mean, of course you know that. She saw the story. And called us. She wanted to come with us to see you."

Neither woman had said anything. Jackie's mother stepped forward. "Hello, Mr. McCloud. I'm Susanne Logan. Jackie's mom."

"*Mom!*" the boy protested.

Susanne Logan looked at her son and smiled. "Sorry," she said. She turned back to Elijah. "I'm *Jack's* mother," she corrected, bemused and delighted at once.

Elijah studied her, then the boy.

"I'm *Jack* now," the boy said, standing a little straighter.

Elijah's eyes narrowed as he puzzled the meaning in this. Then he, too, smiled.

"Jackie's a little kid's name," the boy asserted.

Susanne Logan put a hand on her son's shoulder and extended the other to Elijah. Elijah reached out and took her hand. It was warm and delicate. It embarrassed him, knowing how coarse his hand must feel, how coarse his appearance must strike her.

"I'm so grateful for what you did. For Jackie . . . *Jack.*" It was clear that she wasn't ready to let go of the fixed memory of her son. Her face darkened, her mouth quivered. "For saving his life," she added, her voice breaking. She bit her lip, pulled her son to her side, and squeezed Elijah's hand. "I'm so grateful you brought my son back to me." Her eyes brimmed with tears. She raised her arm from Jackie's shoulders and stepped forward, startling Elijah by taking him in a gentle embrace, kissing him on the cheek. "Thank you," she whispered.

Elijah drew a breath and exhaled slowly. He smiled a knowing smile and nodded. "It was my pleasure."

Susanne Logan stepped back and pulled her son close to her side again. The room seemed to fall silent as Elijah turned his eyes to his daughter. The two stood staring at each other for a long moment. Elijah was speechless; he could not find the words to express his surprise, his sense of gratitude that she had come. He'd given up the thought back in Keddie of ever seeing her again.

"Hello," Marna McCloud said solemnly, stepping forward. She raised her hand awkwardly, and Elijah took it.

"Hello, Marna," Elijah managed. Her hand was warm also, but her clasp was firm, unwavering. He squeezed her hand gently, then they both let their hands fall back at their sides. "How are you? How are the boys?"

Marna McCloud smiled. "They're fine. They're away. With their dad this week."

Elijah hadn't known that she and her husband, Tom, were living apart.

"I miss 'em," she added.

"I bet you do," Elijah said quietly.

"McCloud," a voice boomed behind them. Elijah turned. A desk sergeant at the counter beckoned him over. Elijah turned back to eye the three before him apprehensively, then turned and walked slowly over to the counter. The sergeant unsealed a large manila envelope and poured out its contents. It contained Elijah's knife in its sheath, his tobacco pouch and packet of rolling papers, a handful of loose change, two plastic lighters, and his leather pouch on a lanyard. From under the counter, the sergeant retrieved Elijah's hat and jacket and handed them across to him.

"Sign here for these," the sergeant said. "Says everything is here." He handed Elijah a pen.

Elijah looked at his belongings, then at the sergeant, not quite comprehending what was happening.

"You're free to go," the sergeant said. "You've got a court date next month on trespassing charges. Being on railroad property. But all the other charges have been dismissed. The boy's story checks out. You a lucky man—that you weren't one of that nut's victims."

Elijah took the pen and slowly inscribed his signature on the form.

"Just make sure you're back in Oroville next month for the court appearance."

Elijah slipped the lanyard over his head and dropped the pouch down the front of his shirt. He started to slip his coat on, but took in how shabby it truly was. He folded it over one arm, found one of its front pockets and deposited the rest of his belongings in its deep hold. He still couldn't quite believe it wasn't all just a dream.

"Let's get out of here," Jackie-cum-Jack said excitedly.

Elijah turned to him. No, it wasn't a dream. He followed Jackie to the door, striding slowly so as not to limp too much. He caught and held the door for Jackie's mom and his daughter. They all stepped out into the clear October morning light.

"Jails are creepy," Jackie said, leading Elijah across the parking lot toward his mother's Toyota.

"Yeah. Creepy," Elijah said, slipping in beside the boy in the backseat of the small compact. The women got in front and buckled up. Jackie's mother started the engine and backed out.

Highway 70 south toward Sacramento ran down a narrow corridor, between old orchards—olives and apricots, almonds and plums, the dull green of late season coated with a heavy patina of dust unwashed since the last spring rain. Elijah sat looking out the window, spellbound by the dark blur of row upon row of trees. He struggled to make sense of what had just happened. Periodically, he would turn to nod acknowledgment at the boy, who jabbered incessantly at him.

"And you know what's really cool?" Jackie said, tugging on Elijah's sleeve. "Stardancer is okay. They didn't shoot her. And she didn't lose the foal," he gushed. "Isn't that amazingly cool?"

"Cool," Elijah said, smiling. Yes, it was cool. It was one less loss the boy would have to endure. "That is very cool," Elijah said, laying his hand on the boy's knee. It was hard to think of the boy as anything but "Jackie," but in that moment Elijah promised himself that he would at least try to call him properly by the new name he had earned. Elijah, more than anyone, knew just how deeply the boy had been changed by the events of the last few weeks.

They crossed under a railroad trestle and entered the outskirts of Marysville. Jackie's mom slowed, pulling up at a stoplight.

"There's a McDonald's, Mom," Jackie said. "Can we stop? I'm really hungry."

"You just ate a little while ago," his mother said, half turning to consider him over the seat back. "How can you possibly be hungry? You haven't done anything." The light changed and she started forward again. "We'll be home in another forty-five minutes."

"*Aw,* Mom," Jackie lamented, settling back in his seat again.

"Boys are tireless feeders," Marna said, easing the tense silence in the car. "Mine are, anyway."

"How old are they?" Mrs. Logan asked.

"Eleven and nine. They're great kids. I'm lucky."

"Yes you are," Jackie's mother said, giving Elijah's daughter a quick glance.

The silence blossomed again.

"How many children do you have?" Marna asked.

"Just Jackie. I mean Jack," she corrected herself. "Terry, my other son . . . he died."

"I'm sorry," Marna said, her hand rising, touching Jackie's mother's arm. Jackie's mother turned and smiled wanly, nodding.

"Thanks," she responded. Elijah eyed the boy, who was suddenly slack of enthusiasm.

"It's hard sometimes. To believe he's really gone. He was a good kid."

"It must be hard," Marna offered.

"It is. You have your dreams . . . for yourself, for your kids." She fell silent as she navigated through town. "We lived in River Park, on the east side of the city. You know where that is?" Mrs. Logan asked casually, grateful to have the opportunity to leaven the conversation.

"That's a lovely community," Marna said.

"It is. It's like a little private enclave—the bustle of the city so near, yet the river right in your backyard. It felt like we were living in a small town. Between the river and the railroad tracks, there's really only one way in or out. It felt really secure." She glanced again at Marna, unspoken understanding linking them. "Goes to show," she said, "you can't take anything for granted. Especially with your kids."

"No, you can't," Marna concurred. "Not that every parent doesn't."

"Mom!" Jackie blurted. "There's another McDonald's. Can we stop? Please? I'm dying."

Mrs. Logan slowed for the traffic light in the middle of Lincoln, a small community just north of Sacramento. She sighed and smiled. "Oh, why not? I could do with a cup of coffee myself. How about you," she said, turning to Marna.

"Why not," Marna said, laughing, tossing her head, which caused her dark hair to shimmer.

"You hungry, Elijah?" Jackie asked eagerly as his mom turned into the lot, pulling to the back to park along a wooden plank fence.

"Why not," Elijah said, shrugging, making it unanimous.

The boy's mother turned in and parked the car.

"All right!" Jackie crowed, throwing his door open, bounding out in a flash of energy.

"*Jackie*, be careful!" Mrs. Logan cried sharply. "You could get hit by a car."

The boy made a fierce face of protest at his mother. He wanted to complain about her calling him "Jackie" again, but let it go. "This is on us, right, Mom?" he said earnestly, going to hold the side door to the restaurant for everyone.

"Of course," his mother responded quickly, stifling Marna's impulse to refuse before she could fully form it. "It's my treat." Elijah let the two women enter before him, caught the door, and ushered Jackie in as well.

Jackie ordered a Big Mac with fries and a milk shake. Everyone else simply ordered coffee. Sitting in the tight space of the booth next to Jackie, opposite his daughter, Elijah was fitful and discomforted. He kept his eyes on his coffee in front of him, letting the women make small talk while Jackie worked fervently on his hamburger.

"You okay?" Jackie asked, noticing Elijah hadn't touched his coffee. "You're awful quiet."

He smiled at the boy. "I like quiet, remember?"

Jackie laughed at their private joke before biting into his burger again.

"Think I'll use the men's room," Elijah said. He slipped out of the booth and crossed the lobby slowly, gentling his injured leg. It was stiff, but the intensity of the pain had receded. He pushed through the men's room door and stepped to the sink. He ran cold water, splashing it on his face, rubbing his neck and ears. He steadied himself with one hand, scooping water with the other. He raised his eyes and stared at his reflection in the mirror. He couldn't remember the last time he'd gazed intently at himself. He was shocked at how old he looked. He ran a hand over his mouth and chin, smoothing down the mat of his whiskers.

He was a sight to behold. He was embarrassed that his daughter had to see him so . . . He couldn't find the words for what she must have thought in first laying eyes on him after such a long while. She must have felt embarrassed—among many other feelings. He set his hat on the vanity and, wetting his hands, ran his fingers through the tangles of his graying hair. He put his hat back on.

I am what I am, he thought as he turned to exit. *I'm a bum.*

Emma's "Visit"

"This is it," Marna remarked. Jackie's mom pulled up at the curb. Everyone was nervous in saying goodbyes, no one more than Elijah. Jackie's mom thanked him again; Jackie made him promise that they'd get together. "Soon. Seriously," Jackie said. Elijah agreed. Marna thanked Jackie's mom for picking her up, taking her with them.

Marna's place was a pale, two-story stucco house with dark brown trim and a tiled porch. It had a distinctive, early-Californian flair to it. It stood on a corner lot, with a weathered wooden fence enclosing the back and side yards.

Elijah stopped to take in the open space and big trees of South Side Park, a community park directly across the street. The big hardwoods and giant evergreens cast pools of dark shadows in sharp contrast to the sunny open spaces. People strolled languidly, sat on benches, lay out on the grass.

"You want to come in?" his daughter called from the walk leading up to the arched entrance of her home. Her voice broke his reverie, and he turned toward her. For a moment they stood looking at each other. The pause captured everything about how new and uncharted this all was—for both of them. Elijah recalled the little girl he'd taken long walks with years ago during interludes when he was home. He'd always loved that they could be in each other's company without need for talk. It was enough to be together.

"Or we could go sit in the park," she said tentatively, unsure how to read her father's mood.

"No," he said, smiling, starting up the walk. "I'd like to come in."

She held the door for him. He came in past her and stood at the edge of the foyer, remembering again the spaciousness of the room. The only other time he'd been here was almost ten years before when Emma celebrated her forty-seventh birthday. The room had a vaulted ceiling of dark wood, rising fifteen feet. A brick fireplace fronted most of the opposite wall. The room was sparsely but pleasantly appointed. A large handwoven rug commanded the center of the room. Indian artwork—baskets, small weavings, and beadwork—decorated the buff-colored walls. A large arched picture window with tan drapes framed a view of the park across the street.

Marna put her purse on a chair and her keys on the mantel. "Something to drink . . . a glass of juice, water?" she asked nervously.

"Nothing," Elijah said, gathering his attention, turning it from the objects on the walls to her pensive expression. He smiled, embarrassed at feeling so awkward, so out of place, not knowing what to say. "It's nice," he managed. "Your place. Very nice."

"Want to see the rest of it?" she said. It was painfully obvious they both were struggling with how to navigate the moment. "Or we could sit and talk." His daughter grinned, giving her arms a small flap, slapping her sides. She gave her father a quizzical stare, her head slightly canted to one side.

"This is hard, isn't it?" she said quietly.

Elijah nodded.

"Why is it so hard?" she asked rhetorically, letting go any pretense of control, slouching into a large overstuffed chair. She gestured toward the couch. "Make yourself at home. Have a seat, Pop. Might as well be comfortable in the great uncomfortableness of the moment."

Marna possessed the direct frankness of her mother. It served to put Elijah at ease. "I can fix dinner in a bit. But let's talk. For a little while, anyway." She watched her father walk tentatively over to the couch, turn slowly, and lower himself stiffly into the soft folds of its cushions.

"You looked pretty surprised to see me," she said, grinning. "This morning. At the jail."

Elijah smiled, relaxing visibly. "You could say that," he said, leaning back, settling more leisurely. "I thought you'd never talk to me again. After the other morning."

"Yeah, me too. I was pretty pissed," she said, her jaw muscles flexing as she fixed him with a hard, assessing stare.

"You have a right to be. You and Toby both," Elijah said. "Your mother, too."

Marna shook her head slowly, her expression softening. "That always amazed me," she said almost reverently. "I never understood how Mom could be so . . . forgiving. She always made room for kind words about you. Used to piss both Toby and me off. More Toby, though," she added. "Mom never spoke ugly about you. Not to us anyway. I used to think it was an act. Some sort of martyr routine. She used to get furious with me—with me!" she said incredulously, "when I accused her of it." She looked steadily at her father, her gaze unwavering. "But I came to believe she really didn't hold any ill will toward you. Only love."

Elijah lowered his eyes, pursed his lips, staring at his deeply creased, heavily calloused hands lying in his lap.

"It would be difficult to say which one of us was more surprised this morning—you or me," Marna finally said. "I was *at least* as surprised as you were to see myself standing there. It wasn't something I could have predicted this time yesterday."

Elijah's gaze rose and focused again on his daughter. She looked—and sounded and acted—so much like her mother.

"Why did you come?" he asked, as though he was unsure whether he really wanted to know.

She shrugged and pushed herself up out of her chair. "To tell you the truth, I'm not sure. It's rather bizarre, really." She turned and started toward the back of the house. "I need a cup of coffee. You want one?" She slipped through a doorway into the kitchen. It had big windows looking out on the fenced backyard. "We can sit out back and enjoy the afternoon light."

Sitting in the cool side yard, Elijah's daughter recounted the story of her life the past few years. She was divorced now, had retaken her maiden name, and was devoted to raising her young boys. She had also completed her master's degree in sociology, having focused her studies on the dynamics of cultural displacement. She taught one course at Sacramento City College, which was only blocks away, and was a lecturer at Sacramento State University across town. She existed in professional limbo without permanent appointment, but had made peace with it, accepting the uncertainty of it all as a lesson, she said, an opportunity to grow stronger in a world where, in truth, there were no guarantees.

She and her husband had separated in the middle of her writing her dissertation when she learned he was having an affair. He'd felt neglected. Or so he said. She'd thrown a crystal bowl at him, a wedding present from his parents, before throwing him out. They got along amicably enough now; she was even friendly with the woman he'd been involved with and whom he subsequently married. They lived in the same neighborhood, only a half-dozen blocks apart, making it easy for the kids to come and go between the two households. The boys were due back the next day.

"It works out pretty well for everybody, I think, including the kids. They stay here, or at his house, and can walk to school from either place," Marna said, cradling her coffee mug in her hands. "It's a pain sometimes, being single, but to tell you the truth, I'm kinda relieved not having a man underfoot. I like my privacy. I like my house, my backyard. I spend a lot of time out here," she said, casting her gaze around the enclosed yard.

The yard was small but inviting, with a simple rock garden at one end, a patch of grass for the boys to play on, and a concrete patio underneath a redwood lattice canopy. Elijah was amused by the stone fire ring in the middle of the small lawn, the river stones well charred from numerous fires. Marna saw her father eyeing the ring of stones, the light of a small smile on his face.

"I always enjoyed making fires with you," she said, smiling. "We bought this place in large part because of the lovely fireplace inside. But I hardly ever use it anymore. If I want a fire, I come out here."

"You never had to press me very hard to build a fire when you were little."

"No. I didn't. But we didn't live in the middle of a city, either. The first time I laid a fire here, one of my neighbors called the fire department. That was interesting —a dozen men standing around in firefighting gear, me and the boys roasting hot dogs."

Elijah sipped from his mug and studied the soft light in his daughter's eyes. There was no question that she was both strong and tender, a fierce protector of her children and a nurturing presence. It couldn't be easy raising children alone, even with a father who lived only a handful of blocks down the street. Elijah was grateful to this man, the father of his grandchildren, that the choices he'd made had not been an excessive burden on his daughter.

"You said it was bizarre," Elijah said tentatively.

"What's that?" Marna said, perplexed by the non sequitur.

"Your coming to see me. In jail." It was hard to believe it had only been that morning.

"Really strange," she said, taking a sip from her mug, drawing a deep breath, settling back against the chair cushions. She stared distantly into the trees beyond the fence, along the street at the front of the house. "I dreamed about you last night," she said, taking another sip, ruminating quietly for a long moment. Elijah said nothing, reflecting on the strangeness of his own dream the night before.

"Actually, it was a dream about Mom," Marna said, her voice soft, muted, wistful. "I find I dream about her now and again, usually when I'm feeling troubled. It always calms me." She looked directly at her father and smiled wanly.

"We were talking," she continued. "She and I. She told me forgiveness meant accepting that the past would never be any different from what it was. That everybody had a choice. That everybody had to choose which path they were going to take."

Marna stared, her gaze fixing her father with piercing intensity. "I was angry. I was angry for a long time. I always loved you coming home, being able to see you. But I hated you when you always left."

Marna shifted, her eyes downcast. Her mouth worried. "And then I woke up. I lay there for a while, thinking about the dream. Wondering what it meant. I got up finally. Went in to make some coffee. I don't teach on Friday, so I was looking forward to a leisurely morning around the house. I went out to get the newspaper. And there was the story about Jackie, about what happened in Oroville. Jackie relating the story about how you saved him. How he was worried about you now. How unfair it was that you were in jail."

Elijah watched his daughter bring her gaze back up to meet his. They sat silently in each other's presence. "And I knew I needed to see you. So I looked up Jackie's mother's name in the phone book and called. I told them who I was, and she invited me to come with them. I couldn't get it out of my mind. What Mother had said. That each of us has to choose the path we take."

Elijah didn't know if he should tell her about his dream. He didn't know if he *could*. The ache of seeing Emma was too raw.

Over the next several hours, through dinner and early evening, neither Elijah nor Marna ever broached the question of the future. Marna fixed a simple, delicious meal of chicken piccata and roasted vegetables. They retired to the backyard again where they could view the late moonrise over the fence, out over the treetops in the park. The moon was clearly diminished, its curvature flattened on its northern face where it had begun to turn away from the solar light. *Growing shy* was how Emma had always spoken of the waning moon.

Marna made a bed up for her father on the cot in the small sunporch off the living room. She showed him where the coffee was, and how to brew a cup with the small coffee machine on the kitchen counter. She bade him good night.

Elijah lay awake for a long time in the light of the moon that filled the porch, listening to the sounds of the house and the city beyond. Police sirens rose to declare alarm, then faded beneath the steady, distant hum of traffic. Footsteps on the sidewalk out front seemed to appear out of nowhere, pass, and dissolve slowly. The house creaked softly as floors settled. The day was beyond comprehension, a kaleidoscope of fractured images. Elijah lay there wondering if it was possible to fall asleep here, in his daughter's house, knowing she was there, only a few feet away. How had the miracle of this happened?

He finally drifted into sleep, never fixing on an answer that explained it. It was enough that they were together.

Where to Begin

The house was filled with noise when Elijah stepped from the upstairs bathroom after a shower and a long soak in the tub the next morning. He felt awkward, as though he had misplaced himself, standing in the dim light of the hall, listening to the raucous din coming from downstairs. He stared down at himself, dressed in a store-bought flannel shirt and a new pair of Levi's his daughter had set outside the bathroom door while he was soaking. She'd called in that she'd gotten him a couple of things that he could wear so she could wash his other clothes. The shirt was western-cut, light green. *Cheerful*, Elijah thought. The pants fit well in the waist but were long in the leg, requiring that he cuff them.

Jake and Jesse, Marna's two sons—Elijah's grandsons—had transformed the entire energy of the house with their arrival. Elijah had felt as much as heard them come in while he was soaking. He heard the television competing against their voices. It sounded like they were engaged in a war dance, stomping around downstairs. Elijah drew a deep breath to steady himself, then started for the stairs to meet them.

"Mom, when are they gonna get here?" Jesse screeched, bouncing up and down on the couch. "I can't wait I can't wait." Jesse was nine, dark complexioned with a shock of jet-black hair flopping over his eyes. Jake was eleven, more fair, with light brown hair and pale eyes. Jake straightened visibly, sitting in an adjacent chair, when he saw Elijah enter the room. He seemed apprehensive seeing his grandfather.

"Quiet," Jake scolded. Jesse continued to bounce up and down as Elijah and Jake stared at each other. Jake finally reached over and popped

302

his younger brother on the thigh. "Jesse," he said insistently. Jesse turned to complain, but froze upon seeing Elijah. The room went deathly silent. Marna stepped in from the kitchen, drawn by the sudden silence. She saw the three of them staring at one another.

"Jesse, Jake, this is your grandfather. You may not remember him," she said simply, without accusation, "but he met you when you were little."

The boys sat silent and still, leaving it to Elijah to make the first move. He stepped forward, entering the room fully. He straightened, and smiled at them a bit sheepishly, but he was gladdened, too.

"Hello. You must be Jake. You're Jesse," he said, getting the names properly placed. "I'm Elijah. You can call me Elijah if you want." He stood, waiting for some response. Jake looked down, breaking the stare. Jesse began to bounce nervously—more wiggle now than jumping. He stared at his grandfather.

"Are you a hobo?" Jesse asked timidly.

"Shut up, Jesse," Jake said, punching his brother.

"You said he was," Jesse complained.

"Didn't."

"Did too."

"Boys," Marna snapped. Both fell into stony silence.

"You might say that," Elijah answered. "I guess it's *one* of the things I am."

"What else are you?" Jesse asked, starting to bounce a bit again.

"Well," Elijah said, chuckling softly.

"He's your grandfather," Marna said, her tone soft but affirming.

Elijah and Marna eyed each other. Elijah nodded. "Yes. I'm your grandfather."

"You're my mom's dad," Jake said.

Elijah looked back at Marna.

"Yes," she answered. "He's my father, which makes him your grandfather."

"And Elson's grandfather, too," Jesse said, starting to bounce vigorously. "When are they going to get here? When? I can't wait."

Elijah stared at Jesse, then at his daughter, the question obvious in the blank face he gave her.

"Toby is bringing Elson down," Marna said simply.

"Toby is coming? Here?" Elijah asked.

"Elson insisted," Marna said. "I called them yesterday, before I went to

Oroville to see you. Toby called this morning."

"Toby is coming here. To see me?"

"Elson is," Marna corrected.

"They're gonna spend the weekend," Jake offered, glad to have something neutral, something that didn't reference him, to offer up in conversation.

"Elson is staying the weekend," Marna corrected again, a certain stiffness in her tone. She looked at her father, trying to assess what he was feeling. "Elson has a vacation day from school on Monday. So Toby decided to bring him down and let him stay over. Toby's gonna see a friend in the city. They'll be going back on Monday."

Marna turned to go back into the kitchen. "I was making the boys a snack," she called out. "Would you like anything? Some coffee?"

"That would be nice," Elijah said, wanting to be accommodating, to somehow diminish his presence, standing like he was on display before his two grandsons.

"I invited Jackie and his mother over for dinner tomorrow night," Marna called from the kitchen. "I thought we could have a barbecue, have a fire outside."

Elijah eyed the boys, raising his eyebrows in an expressive inquiry.

"We sleep outside sometimes," Jesse said, bouncing up and down. "Mom says you like to sleep outside."

"Jesse," Jake said, flicking his fingers, stinging his brother's shoulder.

"Well, she did," Jesse said.

"And I do," Elijah answered, settling the question. "But I like sleeping in a bed, too. That bed on the sunporch is pretty comfortable."

"That ol' thing," Jesse said. "Mom won't let me sleep in it. Says it'll ruin my back."

Elijah smiled. "I don't think anything can ruin a back at my age. I find that ol' thing pretty comfortable."

They managed to get through the snack and the afternoon that followed, Elijah answering an endless barrage of questions about the places he'd been, the things he'd seen. Marna kept to the background, letting the three get acquainted. She marveled at how easily her father related to the boys, something she would never have guessed. And yet, it had been obvious that Jackie Logan was very fond of him, and that he was fond of the boy as well.

Behind the easy flow of exchange between her boys and her father, however, was the tension of the anticipated arrival of Toby and Elson. Elson was between Jake and Jesse in age; the three were close, like brothers.

At quarter to four, the doorbell rang. Elijah was sitting with the boys in the backyard. The sound of the doorbell had them up and dashing for the front door. Marna caught the back door to the kitchen as they dashed through, and held her father's gaze. His apprehension was unmistakable. She smiled, and waved him forward, then turned to go into the house.

Elijah came to the doorway between the kitchen and the living room and paused. He watched as Marna gave Elson a hug, then straightened to embrace her brother. Toby caught sight of Elijah just as Marna's arms encircled his neck; he let his head fall, his eyes close as he hugged her. Elson and his two cousins stood mute, staring across the distance at their grandfather. Elijah smiled at the three of them, focusing finally on Elson. He raised the tips of his fingers on one hand in an awkward, almost involuntary little wave of greeting.

Elson stepped forward and crossed the room. He held out his hand. "I'm Elson, your grandson," he said formally. He was confident and self-assured, but relaxed, too.

Elijah reached out and grasped the boy's hand in his. "It's a pleasure to see you, Elson," he said softly, looking the boy full in the eye. "And I'm sorry it's been such a long time since I last saw you. You were very small."

Elson stared quizzically at Elijah, then turned to stare at his father, a question implicit in his look. Elijah looked up to meet Toby's gaze from across the room.

"Hello. Again," Elijah said solemnly.

"Hello," Toby responded simply.

"How was the drive?" Marna interjected. "You must be exhausted. Want some coffee? Something to eat?"

"No thank you," Toby said. "I just wanted to drop Elson off. I'm gonna run. If you need me, you can reach me at Kenny's in the city."

Elson stood next to Elijah, staring up at him, then across the room at his father. Elijah stood rooted where he stood as if he'd been set there at creation.

"Come here, son," Toby said easily. Elson crossed the room to his father. Toby put a hand on his shoulder. "I want you to do what Aunt Marna says, okay?"

"You're really not gonna stay," Elson said, disappointed.

"I told you. This is your trip. I'm just the driver. I'll be back early Monday morning. About eight. Be ready. We've got a long drive home."

"Okay," Elson said. "But I thought maybe you'd stay. At least a little while."

"I gotta go," Toby said, giving his son a hug. He stood and ruffled the heads of both his nephews.

"Sure you won't stay?" Marna asked.

"They're expecting me for dinner," Toby said. "Call me if you need me." The two hugged, and Toby turned and went out the front door.

Elijah stood stiff as a stick, barely breathing. He blinked at the vacant spot where his son had just stood. He looked at his daughter, confusion and remorse clouding his eyes. She returned his gaze and shrugged, as if to say *What did you expect?*

Elijah crossed the room, stopped at the front door, and turned back to the three boys. "Don't anybody go away," he said with a small smile. "I'll be right back."

Elijah crossed down the walk quickly, following his son with his eyes as Toby stepped around the bed of his truck parked at the curb and moved toward the driver's side of the cab.

"Toby," Elijah called as Toby opened the door to the cab and started to get in. Toby halted, straightened, as Elijah came around the back end of the truck.

"Where are you going?" Elijah asked.

"I told Elson I would bring him. I did. I told him I wasn't going to stay. I'm not."

The two stared at each other, neither looking away. Elijah was aware of the drumming of his heart in his ears.

"Thank you for bringing him," Elijah said. "But I wish you'd stay."

"I brought Elson because Elson wanted me to bring him. It wasn't something I did for you." Toby started to slip into the cab.

"Toby," Elijah called earnestly. "I'm not asking you to forgive me," he said, collecting himself as Toby turned back to face him. "I gave up that right a long time ago."

"You're right," Toby said. He turned and slid in behind the wheel and shut the door. He turned the key in the ignition, bringing the truck engine to life. He put the truck in gear and eased it away from the curb, disappearing around the corner.

+ + +

Elijah was delighted to sit with the three boys out in the backyard. They played and teased one another, and regaled him with questions. They offered no harsh judgment on his replies. They saw him as mysterious and exotic, ideal qualities for a grandfather of young boys. Marna gave the boys—which now included Elijah—their space, interceding only occasionally to make sure they weren't in need of a snack or some refreshment, and to ensure that her father wasn't trapped without an option for a polite escape. Elijah always just smiled, savoring the simple joy of watching his grandsons play.

It was fascinating to observe. Both Jake and Jesse deferred to Elson in most matters, but each had his own area of expertise the others respected. Jake was the certified sports statistician, Jesse the expert on Guinness world records. Elson's primacy was with things natural. Even Elijah was impressed by what he knew, from the courtship ritual of lizards to the way wolves marked and defended their territories.

"You seem pretty comfortable with the boys," Marna remarked after dinner while she and Elijah sat out back and the boys watched a movie on television.

"That surprise you?" Elijah said.

"Well . . . no. I mean, I guess," she said, surprised at her father's directness. He seemed to have grown more relaxed with her as well. She liked that. "It's just that you haven't had a lot of exposure to it, the way boys are."

Elijah chuckled. "I just got a crash course in it—traveling with Jackie," he said. He took a sip of coffee. He paused, appraising his daughter. "They're fine boys. All three. Not that they wouldn't be," he added. "You've done an incredible job." He fell silent a moment. "Toby, too."

"Elson's a great kid," Marna said. "He's a lot like Toby."

Elijah drew a breath. "You think he'll ever . . ." He left the sentence hanging.

"I don't know," Marna answered. "Toby has always been one to hold a grudge. It's hard for him to let go of things."

—+—+—+—

Dawn filled the sunporch with gray light, the sound of birds distinct against the silence in the house. Elijah rose and made a small pot of coffee and took a cup into the backyard. A thin sheen of dew covered the grass, sparkling brightly in the growing light. He studied a colony of ants scurrying in a hectic maze around the mouth of an opening to a tunnel where the lawn and the patio met. They were small, dark-bodied creatures, not much bigger than a freckle. They moved as one, a swirling pattern, some coming, some going, some entering the shaft into the earth, some exiting.

"What are you looking at, Grandpa?"

Elijah looked up, surprised. Elson stood on the back step, as if unsure he was welcome.

"Morning, Elson. Sleep well?" Elijah said warmly. Elson stepped off the step and came over to take a seat beside his grandfather.

"You watching the ants?" Elson said, nodding at the ground.

"Yeah. I guess I am," Elijah said.

"Know what kind they are?"

"Actually, no. I guess I just thought they were ants."

"They're honeypots," Elson said. "Did you know that when they fight other ants, sometimes it's all just a ritual? Nobody gets hurt. But sometimes, they do. When they attack another honeypot colony, sometimes they kill the queen and capture the colony. But all the ants that got captured, the others let them live. They let 'em join with them. No hard feelings."

"Is that a fact?" Elijah said, amazed. "And how do you know all this?"

"I don't know. Read a lot," Elson said, shrugging. "I like watching ants. They can make you dizzy, you watch a bunch of them too long."

"I bet they can," Elijah said, laughing.

"Did you know that some ants like to be solitary? Most don't. But some prefer it. You know where they come from?" Elson asked seriously.

"The ants?" Elijah asked with an arch of his eyebrows. "Out of the ground, I guess."

"Well, yeah, most of them do. Some live in wood, or make mud huts, kinda. But you know, mythologically?" Elijah was impressed with his mastery of the word. "They come from the Understream."

"The *what* . . . ?" Elijah asked, incredulous.

"The Understream. You know. Below. Their job is to bring things that are buried into the light. Did you know that?"

Elijah sat stunned. "No. I didn't know that." He took a sip of coffee, thinking about it. "But I can see how it makes sense. What'd you call it again?"

"The Understream. At least that's what *I* call it. Ants were real important to the Modoc, in their dreams. Did you know that?" Elson asked proudly.

"Well . . . not exactly," Elijah said. "How do you know all this?"

"I read about it. And my dad tells me stuff, too."

"Is that right," Elijah said in amazement. "Now, that is something I never knew."

"Yeah. He knows all kinds of stuff about the Modoc. We're Modoc, did you know that? Part Modoc, anyway. You know who the Modoc were?"

"I do," Elijah said, reaching out, brushing a shock of hair out of Elson's face. "Yes. I certainly do. I'm Modoc, too. Did you know *that*?"

"Not really, but it makes sense, I guess," Elson said, mimicking his grandfather's reflective tone, an unself-conscious emulation. "You being my grandfather and all."

"It does, doesn't it," Elijah said, smiling.

"Why is my dad so angry with you?" Elson asked, conveying some inexplicable yearning.

Elijah was startled by the boy's directness, a directness that was both disarming and charming. He sat staring into the boy's eyes. He drew a breath and sighed deeply. He looked out across the lawn. "It goes back a long way, Elson." Elijah understood that this was something that was both troubling and mysterious to the boy.

"It just doesn't seem right," Elson said sorrowfully. "You're his *father*." He stared earnestly, uncomprehendingly into his grandfather's eyes.

"I wasn't such a good father," Elijah answered.

Elson puzzled his face and shook his head in confusion. "It doesn't make sense to me," he said. "My dad always tells me life is short and you have to know what you want, or it'll pass you by."

"Your dad is one smart fella," Elijah said. "Life *is* short. Too short. And it is important to know what you want. Sometimes it just takes a while to understand that. Even when it's right under your nose."

—+—+—+—

If Jake and Jesse showed deference to Elson as the leader of their small tribe of three, all of them deferred to Jackie Logan once Jackie arrived later that day. Jackie drew the three cousins to him like a magnet. And they all delighted in the presence of the pup.

"He isn't The Pup anymore," Jackie announced to Elijah when Elijah bent down to ruffle the dog's head.

"No?"

"His name's *Elijah*."

Elijah laughed out loud. "I suppose that's fitting," he said. "Plenty of people have called me a son of a dog."

Jackie protested. "I wanted to remember our time together—the three of us. You, me, and the pup. That's why I named him after you."

The four boys played with the dog in the backyard until dinner, all the while the three cousins peppering Jackie with questions about his adventures with their grandfather. After dinner, the boys made a fire in the fire ring and sat roasting marshmallows while the waning moon rose over the trees in the park across the street. Elijah, Marna, and Susanne sat back in a semicircle beyond the boys, enjoying the firelight and the moonlight and the boys' chatter.

At ten o'clock, Susanne rose to take her empty cup into the kitchen and came out again, standing beside the other two grown-ups.

"I hate to break this up, boys, but Jackie—*Jack!*—we probably ought to get home. You have to register at school tomorrow morning. It's already past your bedtime."

"Just a little while longer. Okay?"

"Actually, my boys need to get to bed, too," Marna said gently. "Elson's leaving to go home early in the morning."

"Aw, Mom," rang a duet of voices.

"Aunt Marna, how about letting us have one story," Elson said. "Let Grandpa tell us one story around the fire. Like you let us when we're camping. Just one. He hasn't told us a story yet. An old-time story."

"I don't know," Marna answered, turning to assess her father sitting beside her. He'd seemed subdued, kind of quiet and reflective all evening. "What do you think, Dad?"

"I don't know if I can remember any stories," Elijah said, rising, stepping over to the circle of boys. He picked up a small log and threw it onto the fire, sending a shower of sparks skyward.

"Come on. Sure you can. Jack says you're a great storyteller."

"Can't remember that I told him any stories," he said, smiling quizzically at Jackie. "I couldn't remember any."

"Come on, Elijah," Jackie said confidently. "Seems a shame to waste a good campfire." The three cousins looked at Jackie with envy.

"Well . . . just one . . . if I can think of one," Elijah said, lowering himself stiffly to sit beside them next to the fire.

"A good one," Jesse insisted.

"They're all good," Jake corrected his younger brother.

"A long one, then," Jesse said, cutting his older brother with a dagger stare.

"Okay, a good, long one. Let me think a minute," Elijah said, settling in, getting comfortable, staring into the flames. "Where to begin?"

"At the beginning," Elson offered.

Elijah laughed. "I supposed that's as good a place as any. At the beginning, then. And we'll just have to see where it carries us."

EPILOGUE

Bear in Search of His Shadow

"Just one more," the kids chanted. "One more . . . and then we'll go to bed."

Elson stood and stretched and gazed at the moon that had crested the summit of the ridge that rose above the U.S. Forest Service campground on the Feather River. The air was crisp, the campground quiet. It was the last weekend the campground was open, the weather turning sharply cooler already, here in the first part of October in the Sierras. Shafts of moonlight cut through the evergreens that spiked the ridge, spilling in pools of soft light around the fire where his two sons and their two cousins sat Indian-style on the ground. He lowered his head and gazed into the fire. He reached down and threw one more small stick of wood onto the fire.

"I'll tell you one more, and that's it. This is the first story my grandfather told me a long time ago. When I was about your age."

"Great-grandpa Elijah?" Ernie, his youngest son, asked eagerly.

"Of course, stupid," Joseph said, flicking his younger brother on the shoulder. "Just be quiet, okay. Let Dad tell the story."

Elson had planned the trip weeks before with his cousin Jesse. When Jesse had to be away unexpectedly on business, Elson insisted on bringing Jesse's two children with his own, as planned. Emma, eleven, Jesse's oldest, sat cross-legged in front of the fire, staring intently into the flames. Sam, her little brother, sat close at her side, his eyes shifting between his cousins, his uncle, and the darkness that encircled them. His small hand anxiously rested on his sister's knee, needing to maintain contact with another warm body to keep the night at bay.

312

Elson stood looking at the four children around the fire. It reminded him of the night that he and his two cousins and Jackie had similarly sat around a fire in the backyard at his aunt's house. And of other subsequent evenings together over the years when his grandfather shared old stories that had started coming back to him. Stories told to him when he was a boy. Stories shared around campfires of The People going back many, many generations. But the story of Ol' Bear and Little Rabbit had always been Elson's favorite.

"Long ago, before Kumash created The People . . ."

"Who's Kumash, Uncle Elson?"

"*Shh*. Quiet, Sam. Just listen to the story, will ya?" Ernie scolded his cousin, grateful for the opportunity to point out that he wasn't the only one disrupting the moment.

"It's okay," Elson interjected, reaching out and laying a hand on Sam's shoulder. "Kumash is He-Who-Created-All-Things."

"Like God?" Sam asked, curious.

"No. Not exactly. He is . . . he was . . . well . . . just . . . He-Who-Created-All-Things. God—as I know it—is different. Nobody ever prayed to Kumash."

"Uncle Elson, tell the story," Emma pleaded eagerly.

"All right then," Elson said, straightening, gathering his thoughts again. "Where was I?"

"At the beginning," Joseph said, irritated.

"At the beginning," Elson concurred. "Okay then. Before Kumash created The People, a long time ago, he created all the animals. He created Bear. And Deer. Rabbit and Fox. Hawk. Crow. Owl. Wolverine. All the animals. All the animals we know in the world today. And they could all talk then. To each other. They lived, in many ways, as we do now.

"High in the mountains to the north lived Ol' Bear. Ol' Bear had lived a very long time," Elson said, pausing, staring into the fire, recalling his grandfather telling the story. "He lived by himself. He hadn't always lived by himself, but for many years now, he had lived alone. And he was lonely. But it had been his own doing, for he'd always thought only of himself and his needs rather than the needs of others."

The fire crackled, and the circle of children settled collectively to listen to the story. Elson threw another small log onto the fire and they all watched, lifting their eyes toward the dark sky, following the shower of dazzling sparks that rose overhead.

"Ol' Bear had lived long and had seen much. But Bear's eyes—which had never been very good—were getting worse. He couldn't see clearly. Only he wouldn't admit it. He liked to think he knew everything there was to know about everything. And he knew that Hawk was a sharp fella, on account of his eyes. So Bear had to tell himself that his eyes were pretty good, too."

Elson slowly began to weave the spell of the tale of Ol' Bear. How one night, while he was sleeping in his den, Big Wind started blowing and blew all night long, causing the trees to moan mournful-like, disturbing Bear's sleep. Bear tossed and turned. He wasn't sure whether he was dreaming the wind or the wind was real. But come morning, Bear was tired and grumpy, and on top of that, he was hungry. He wanted to stay in bed all day, but he hadn't eaten in many days, and he knew that winter was coming and he needed to eat.

"He was just about to start out to look for breakfast when he saw something dark on the ground in front of him," Elson said. "In fact, what he saw was two dark things, kind of big and round, strutting around the way chickens do. And since his eyes weren't so good, he stared real hard to see what it was. And then he asked, 'Is that you, Crow?'"

"Now, Crow is a trickster. He's also what they call a shape-shifter. He can be one thing one moment, and then something else. He can be in two places at once. Crow can travel through a crack in time from one place or dimension to another. Crow loves to play tricks on people just because it mixes people up, and there's no telling what they'll think when it's over. So one Crow looked at the other and winked, and he answered, 'Yes. It's me.' And Bear asked who was that with him. And the one Crow looked at the other Crow and said, 'Nobody. It's just me here, Bear.' Crow knew that Bear's eyes weren't too good, and he decided he was going to play a trick on him.

"'Well, there is too somebody there,' Bear said, straining to see. And the one Crow said, 'Where?' And Bear said, 'Right there beside you.' And Crow smiled, and he said, 'Oh that. That's my shadow.'"

Elson explained how Bear had never heard of Shadow. He didn't know what Shadow was. But he knew he had been missing something. That he had a longing for it, though he didn't know what it was. Maybe this was it, but he didn't know quite how to ask Crow about it. So he decided he'd just pretend he knew.

"So he said, 'Good morning, Shadow. How you doing this morning?'

"Now, Crow thought this was hugely funny. And he teased Bear. 'Why you talking to Shadow? He can't talk.' And Bear said, 'Why not? He lose his voice?' And Crow laughed harder now, for it was obvious Bear didn't know what Shadow was."

Bear, Elson went on, could tell that Crow was mocking him, and after a night of not sleeping well because of Big Wind, he got cross with Crow.

"'I'm hungry now, Crow,' he said. 'And I've a mind to eat you and Shadow, too.' And Crow, playing along, apologized. And he began to strut around. And with every step one Crow took, the other Crow took a step in just the same way. So the two of them moved as if one was really nothing more than the shadow of the other. And Crow said, 'Bear, you can't eat me and Shadow, too, no matter how hungry you are. You can't eat Shadow. Why, what would happen if you ate your own shadow?'

"Because he'd never seen his own shadow, Bear had never thought of this. Being hard of seeing, and walking most of the time with his nose close to the ground, he'd never taken much notice of his shadow, and couldn't see much of one anyway. But this got him curious. He'd never heard of Shadow, and he knew that if he ran into somebody, and they started talking about Shadow, he'd better know what they were talking about. So he asked Crow, he said, 'What is Shadow? This is the one thing I don't know.'

"Crow, he knew he had Ol' Bear now. And he was just making this up as he went along, didn't know exactly how he wanted to mix Bear up, what lesson he wanted to teach him, so he just said what came to mind. He said, 'Why, Bear, I know you are the smartest creature in the woods, and it surprises me that you don't know what Shadow is. But I can see now that you don't have a shadow. You must have lost yours somewhere.' Bear immediately felt bad, although he was also excited, because maybe this was the thing that would fulfill his longing. And he forgot all about being hungry. He asked Crow how he could find it, the shadow that he'd lost. And Crow said, 'I guess the only way you can find it is to go look for it.' And Bear, he wanted to know where to start. And Crow knew he had Ol' Bear for real. He did a little dance, with the other Crow dancing right along with him because they were both so excited. And Crow said, 'You'll just have to follow your nose, see where it takes you. That's the only way I know how to find your shadow once you've lost track of it.'"

Elson stopped to take a sip of his coffee, which had cooled considerably since he'd begun the story. The faces of the four children stared at him, entranced, and Elson had to linger, keeping his cup to his lips so that they couldn't see the smile that pulled at the corners of his mouth. He threw another small stick onto the fire, but this time, the children paid no attention to the hail of sparks that rose from the flames. They waited eagerly for him to continue the story.

Elson went on at great length, embellishing the story as the urge and the opportunity presented itself. It was a story that he and his cousins had heard on several occasions after their grandfather Elijah had found a place to settle, finally, working at a stable in the foothills outside Sacramento that ran pack trips into the Sierras. Their grandfather had a gift for working with horses—had been a wrangler when he was a young man—but hadn't been around them much for many years. And then he decided it was time to give it a try again. His working in the foothills made it possible for Elson and his cousins to spend time with him, usually camping somewhere in the national forests. They'd camped together at this very campground. And Elson had heard the story of Ol' Bear around a campfire under the moon on several occasions, much as his children and Jesse's children were hearing it now.

Elson told about Bear forgetting all about being hungry and needing to prepare for winter, he was so curious to follow his nose and see where it led, in search of the shadow he feared he'd lost. He told how one day Bear ran across Little Rabbit, who had had a terrible run-in with Wolverine, who was stalking him now. Little Rabbit was frightened and wanted to go with Bear, but Bear said he was in a hurry, he had important things to do. And so Bear continued on, but Little Rabbit followed after him anyway.

The children listened raptly as Elson told of the adventures and the hardships and the trials Bear had looking for his shadow with Little Rabbit tagging along behind. Bear didn't really like Little Rabbit following along at first, as he was interested only in finding his shadow. But in time he came to feel for Little Rabbit, knowing Wolverine like he did. Bear and Wolverine were mortal enemies, and Bear knew Wolverine to be one of the slyest, fiercest creatures in the forest.

"It came one night, the night of a full moon, that Bear and Little Rabbit got separated," Elson said, his voice deepening, his tone more ominous. "Bear knew Little Rabbit was in trouble, he could just tell, the two of them had become such good friends. Because of their friendship, Bear no longer felt alone. They were like family, and Bear knew that he had to find Little Rabbit because he could sense that he was in danger.

"In a clearing in the woods, he came upon Wolverine, who had Little Rabbit in his clutches. Bear rose up on his hind legs, tall as he could stand,

and walked into the clearing where Wolverine could see him by the light of the moon, and he told Wolverine to let Rabbit go.

"Bear was much bigger, but Wolverine wasn't afraid of anybody. And bad as he wanted Little Rabbit, he wanted to teach Bear a lesson even more. But he hesitated. For if he let go of Little Rabbit, what was keeping Bear and Little Rabbit from running off again?

"Bear saw this. Saw it plain as the nose on his face—if his eyes were actually good enough to see it. And he heard the wind whisper to him, *In the turning, all things are possible.* So very slowly, Bear turned, twisting his big body awkwardly, raising his front paws over his head to help him keep his balance. Bear turned around, until his back was to Wolverine, as if he were saying, 'Here I am, come and get me.' And Wolverine couldn't help himself. He let Little Rabbit go. And he started slowly toward Bear, his razor claws glistening in the moonlight.

"And Bear stood there, feeling strange letting Wolverine have the jump on him like that. But he knew it was the right thing to do—to think of Little Rabbit before thinking what was best for him. And that was when he looked down. There in front of him on the ground, cast by the light of the moon, he saw his shadow. It had been with him all along, he realized. It was a part of him. They weren't two things, him and his shadow. They were one. Always had been. But in that instant, Bear knew also that his shadow wasn't truly what he'd been longing for.

"Now a really strange thing happened," Elson said, almost in a whisper. "Ol' Owl had been watching all this from high in a tall pine tree. Owl had been watching this adventure from the very beginning. You have to understand that Owl and Crow are like Bear and Wolverine. They don't much like each other. And Owl was annoyed by how Crow had tricked Bear. And he was impressed by how Little Rabbit had changed Ol' Bear. So Owl let loose. From high on his perch in the old tree, he swooped down soundlessly on silent feathers, down and down. And just as Wolverine flashed his claws to grab Bear, just as Bear was about to meet his end, Owl sank his talons deep into Wolverine—and *carried* him away!"

"What about Little Rabbit?" Sam demanded nervously, inching closer against his sister.

"Little Rabbit," Elson said, shaking his head, then pausing. He saw Sam's eyes widen with worry. Elson smiled slowly. "Well, Little Rabbit, he was safe."

"And Bear? What about Bear?" Emma wanted to know.

Elson let the question hang in the chill air. Every child's face was fixed on his.

"That's a good question, Emma," he said earnestly, pushing himself to standing, turning slowly, his back to the fire, warming his backside before needing to usher everybody to bed. "That's a *very* good question," he said empathetically, marveling at the sight of his own shadow cast by the moonlight. He thought of his grandfather, of his last years of life, living at Aunt Marna's, sleeping on the small cot in the sunroom much of the year.

"Bear learned he had to pay attention. That Crow sometimes can be very tricky."

A soft breeze blew through the canyon, intensifying the light of the fire, sending a shower of sparks heavenward. Elson turned to look up at the moon again, considering it. He sighed deeply.

"The most important thing that Bear learned, however, didn't have anything to do with his shadow. He learned that with some journeys, you don't necessarily end up finding what you went looking for, but instead, you find what is most important for you to find. He learned that even though he'd always lived alone, he could still change. He learned that being unafraid to be One Standing—one standing up for another, in his case, standing up for Little Rabbit—had truly made them family. And because of that," Elson said, eyeing each of the children around the fire, "Ol' Bear no longer needed to live in the world all alone. What he'd been missing—more than his shadow, what Ol' Bear had really been longing for was to find his way home again."

Author's Afterword

The *Dream Singer* story has been with me for many years. It evolved from a relatively simple idea sparked by two magazine stories I wrote about riding freight trains across the country and through the Pacific Northwest. Originally, it was a basic murder mystery, but morphed through numerous versions into the story of the life of Elijah McCloud, born of parents he never knew— a white father and a Modoc Indian mother, a member of a small, obscure tribe who once lived in the shadow of Mt. Shasta in northeastern California.

As the story evolved, I became increasingly cognizant that it ultimately might be very controversial. Not necessarily for the story, but because of the fact that I am white telling a story through the eyes of a Native American. Examples abound throughout American literature of authors crossing racial lines, igniting intense controversy—sometimes justified, sometimes not.

There are inherent risks in writers crossing such lines, most especially in this country when it involves a white author. Not only are there historic provocations for this, ranging from racial stereotyping to exploitation and worse, but also because of writers being susceptible to the cultural myopia of "white privilege"—despite the best of intentions.

I believe writers should have the liberty to write about whatever interests and engages them. The story of Elijah McCloud and his Modoc heritage grew to have immense fascination to me. The more I researched Modoc history, the more I felt that the frame of this story had never been adequately told. The challenge for me was to be as vigilant as possible in questioning my cultural assumptions, and in guarding against succumbing to racial stereotyping.

If *Dream Singer* sparks controversy, my hope is that it will also spur earnest discussion of issues around how Native Americans have been—and continue to be—treated and regarded in America. It is one of the most disturbing and tragic—and enduring—legacies in our history.

Acknowledgments

Great thanks to the many readers who have read various versions of this manuscript—some more than once—and who have provided sharp eyes and keen insights that have made this a better story.

First among first readers is my sister, Sandra Smith. Other first readers were Gary Eastham, Jim Braley, Meg Braley, Leigh St. Pierre, Dennis Milburn, Laurence Eubank, and the late Helen Johnson. I'm indebted to members of my book group, including Nick Burnett, Jean Maginnis, Jamie Moran, Marty Riehle, and Craig Tribuno for providing insightful feedback and encouragement.

Special thanks to a handful of editors over my career who have encouraged and championed me. Most especially Liza Nelson, Nancy F. Smith, and John Tarkov; as well as John English, Lee Walburn, and Jerry Lawson. Special thanks to my former agent Carolyn Krupp, who believed in the story and tirelessly advocated for it.

Very special gratitude to Terry Kay, a fine writer of the first order and a lifelong friend, who has provided me with unfailing encouragement over many years, reading—and rereading—this and other stories. I am also indebted to Pat Conroy, who inspired and encouraged me to follow my heart to become a writer—and who never held back, including giving me the desk he wrote his early books on. I also owe great thanks to Cliff Graubart, who allowed me to live under his antiquarian bookstore in Atlanta for a time when I couldn't afford to live elsewhere.

I'm indebted to Jay Harrington for years of friendship and support that helped illuminate my path. And to Dr. J. Herman Blake, my mentor and friend, who years ago influenced my worldview, which has so definitively shaped my sense of how to live in the world.

I owe a great debt that I can't repay to three people who created Artisan Island Press and saw to the publication of this book. This includes Jamie Moran, Leigh St. Pierre, and Jim Braley. You inspire me as a writer, a storyteller, and a human being.

Very special thanks to JURNE, internationally renowned graffiti artist who is now extending his talents to fine art, for the stellar book cover he created. Also to Sandra Anne Smith, quilt artist extraordinaire, for the author portrait. And to Anthony Arias for his great care and talent in designing the jacket and the interior of the book. Thanks to Laurel Robinson for the sharp eye and diligent care given to the copyediting of the manuscript.

I wish to express my heart's gratitude to Gaelen and Micah. They are the deep keel of my life. Thank you for reading and critiquing this and other stories, and lending your love and unique talents that flow through this book from cover to cover.

Dale Stephenson shares an orbit with no other in my world. She is the light that parted the darkness. Wife, best friend, and always my ultimate first reader, she has read almost every word I've ever written. My soul's debt to her will take many lifetimes to repay.

I am blessed with the grace of dear friends who buoy me, and an extended family that anchors me. To you all, great thanks.

Read an excerpt of *Déjà vu,*

a novel-in-progress by Frank O Smith

to be published in 2015.

Chapter One

I stood at the sink in running shorts staring out the window admiring the gorgeous play of light as it fell across the valley, grateful to be home again. It had been a long flight the night before from Chicago after a much-delayed departure, followed by an exhausting drive from San Francisco down the Salinas Valley to reach home. I had gotten only a few hours' sleep before I awoke to watch the dawn, as was my habit. I was looking forward to a quiet morning—a long run in the hills and then a trip up the draw to the little zendo where I meditate. Meditation had saved my life, providing me an unfailing anchor during my darkest hours in prison. The irony that meditation was a gift bestowed in prison never escaped me. Prison—and meditation—taught me the great value of staying in the moment.

A quicksilver flash of sunlight on a windshield caught my eye, a car turning off the highway over to the coast into my place. It was early for visitors, not yet eight, and I didn't recognize the dark sedan that clattered across the cattle guard and disappeared into the trees to climb the hill to the house.

I grabbed a T-shirt and pulled it on. Cup of coffee in hand, I went out on the porch and watched the Crown Victoria pull up in the circle drive. Doc, the big mixed-breed dog who shared my life, stood attentive off toward the barn, ears up like outfielders' mitts, nose sniffing the air to discern the truth of our guest.

I sighed wearily when Bobby Higgins stepped from the car. I could feel his stare even though I couldn't see his eyes through the dark aviator sunglasses he wore. Higgins and I had grown up together but had never been on the best of terms—even before I was sentenced to prison for murder. And my being exonerated and released certainly didn't win any sympathy from him. He had been the deputy sheriff who'd arrested me. The arrest had helped win him a fast track to detective with the Los Robles County Sheriff's Department. He chafed seeing me out of prison, my having a life he believed I didn't deserve.

"Morning," I called out as he crossed the dirt yard leading to the steep steps up to the porch. It didn't surprise me that he knew where I lived, even though he'd never been out to the house. I'd bought the remote piece of property and built the house myself with the money I was awarded from the civil suit against the county for the department's faulty handling of the case.

Higgins stopped at the bottom of the stairs and looked up at me, taking my measure.

"Want some coffee?"

"I want to know where you were three nights ago," he demanded. He started up the steps toward me.

"G'day to you, too," I replied. "Why are you so interested in my doings?"

"Just answer the question, Cain."

I settled instinctively into the gentle Tai Chi stance I often took when rip currents swirled around me. I drew a breath and exhaled, settling calmly, "rooting" myself, my bare feet absorbing the warmth of the early sun on the porch decking.

"You want to come in, Bobby?" I said.

I watched Higgins's face flush. When we were in school, everybody knew him as Bobby, but since he made detective he was insistent that people call him Robert. My reverting to his boyhood name was a kind of verbal Aikido move, using the force of one's opponent's attack to throw him off balance. I stood breathing easily.

"You have any idea why I'm here?"

"Should I?"

"Goddamn, man!" Higgins snorted. "Don't you follow the news?"

"Been out of town. Just got back a few hours ago."

"Where were you?"

"Away."

"Can you prove it?"

"You want the number for the Deputy Chief of the Chicago Police Department?"

Higgins made a disdainful face and half turned where he could look down the length of the porch toward the barn. Doc had settled with his nose down between his paws, keenly observing the stranger who'd come calling.

Higgins inhaled sharply, then sighed loudly. "You know anything about the death of Abby McCaskill?" he said, turning back to observe my reaction.

The news caused a hitch in my breathing. I steadied the rhythm. We stared at each other for a long moment.

"I'm really sorry to hear that," I said finally, my voice almost a whisper. "What happened?"

"Do you know anything or not? It looks like the kinda thing you'd know something about."

There were two ways one might interpret Higgins's comment: That I, Jake Cain, was in demand for my ability to provide assistance to law enforcement across the country in solving crimes and finding missing people. Or that I'd served four years of a life sentence for murder. For many people, it still didn't matter that I'd subsequently been fully exonerated. Despite my winning a suit against the county and being awarded a large judgment, there were those who thought I'd gotten away with murder. Most had forged hardened opinions about me long ago when I was young and out of control, always getting hauled in for something—drinking, smoking dope, joy riding, even burning down a neighbor's barn once. Higgins was a charter member of that group.

He and those of like mind thought my peculiar psychic talents were just another scam I was running. Precious few had any inkling that as a young boy, I hated being able to "know" and "see" things others could not. I felt demon possessed. It was only while I was in prison that I came to view it otherwise.

"I'm sorry. I don't know anything about Abby's death."

"Yeah, I'll bet you don't," Higgins seethed under his breath.

I inhaled long and slow and let the dig go. "What happened?"

He turned and looked out at the view from my porch. It was one of the things I loved about the place, but I imagined Higgins saw it only as testament to a grave injustice.

"Raped and murdered three nights ago," he said dispassionately. "Up in the Casa Grande Estates development."

I knew the place. Knew it well in fact. I used to hike up through there when I was a kid. A big developer from LA was putting in a high-end gated community—or at least trying to. But as if out of nowhere a group of Native Americans had coalesced to block it, claiming the site was sacred ground.

I sighed deeply, my eyes drifting out to gaze over the valley. One moment the world is steady—the next it's in chaos. Meditation and anchoring oneself in Taoist disciplines doesn't make you bulletproof to the world. The great lesson of the Tao was that everything was always in flux. Abby was here. Now she was gone.

Higgins shuffled his feet nervously. He slipped his aviator glasses back on. "I got my eye on you, Cain. I just wanted to drop by to put you on notice."

I slow-cycled another breath. "Thanks, Bobby," I said quietly.

"*Fuck you,*" he said as he spun and went down the steps toward his car. "Just remember," he called back as he opened the car door. "I got my eye on you."

I watched Bobby Higgins as he spun his tires in the dirt and headed back down the hill. This was not going to be the day I had imagined. Not by any stretch of the imagination. I had to get dressed and immediately go find my dear friend Maggie—Abby McCaskill's mother.